THE ETERNAL P

by the same author
Disappearer
Colin Cleveland and the End of the World
Girl's Rock
The Eternal Prisoner
Rogue Males

Mark Hunter series
Beautiful Chaos
Sixty-Six Curses
Trouble at School
Mysterious Girlfriend
The Beasts of Bellend
Countdown to Zero

The Eternal Prisoner

Chris Johnson

Samurai West

Published by Samurai West
disappearer007@gmail.com

Story and Art © Chris Johnson 2021
All rights reserved

This paperback edition published 2025
ISBN-13: 9798293273904

Part One
Arrival

Chapter One
How I Escaped from the Village

'The Village! Here we are—standing in the very midst of it at last! To our right, the Town Hall! Over yonder, Number Six's Residence! To our left the Chess Lawn; and rising above it, the Green Dome! And before us, as the ground slopes towards the sea-front, the Old People's Home and the Stone Boat! Magnificent! Everything just as it was in the television series!'

'It looks smaller than it does on TV.'

'Ah! An astute observation my diminutive friend. The Village does indeed appear to be somewhat smaller in real life than it appeared on television. But then, it has been said that the medium of television adds a few pounds to a person's weight—clearly the same must apply to the scenery! Yes, this must be the explanation. A sapient fact, and one which I must remember to add to my notes.'

I refer here to the research I am compiling in preparation for the writing of my book; a book which shall be the most scholarly, the most profound, the most exhaustively researched written examination of that profound and stimulating television classic, *The Prisoner*, in which Patrick MacGoohan, after resigning from his job as a British Secret Service agent, is abducted and awakens to find himself in a mysterious settlement known only as The Village: a carefully guarded dystopian community whose inhabitants all possess numbers instead of names. He himself has become Number Six, and in each episode he has to pit his wits against the Village chief Number Two (which, being a rotating position, made a convenient guest-star vehicle), who is determined to discover why he resigned, while our hero is equally determined to resist all efforts to break him and to escape from his apparently inescapable prison. The actual location for the Village, whose distinctive Italianesque architecture formed a key feature of the programme's visual appeal, is the village of Portmeirion; a private village situated on the northern coast of Wales, and designed by architect Sir Clough Williams-Ellis—and it is here that we now stand.

I will not go into any further detail regarding my proposed opus devoted to this timeless episodic television drama at this moment; let it suffice for now to say that it is partly my quest for on-the-spot research material that has brought me here on this pilgrimage to Portmeirion. I have condescended to allow my friend Darren to accompany me, he also being an aficionado of *The Prisoner*. Although needless to say, Darren's understanding of the series is considerably beneath my own. For him *The Prisoner* is merely a diversion, a source of entertainment. His poor brain simply cannot comprehend the show's subtle nuances, the allegorical intricacies, as one such as myself can. (Alas, Darren is not one of the most high-brow of individuals. He does his best of course, poor fellow, but his degree of acumen places him at the lower end of the medium-brow spectrum at best.)

Howsoever, even putting research requirements aside, it is generally considered mandatory that any *Prisoner* fan worth his or her salt should make a pilgrimage to Portmeirion at least once in his or her life; and myself having been a devotee of the series since the age of eighteen, and now having attained my thirty-second year, it was high time that I made the journey. And so, accompanied by my staunch friend, I have arrived at Portmeirion, and I now tread the sacred ground for the first time in my life, walking those very streets that have known the tread of Patrick McGoohan's canvas shoes. The weather has proved clement for our expedition, with there being only a slight overcast and no rain anticipated. Standing on the road adjacent to the Chess Lawn (minus the actual chessboard, which I understand is not a permanent feature), we have paused to admire the view.

Before us, the ground slopes down towards the beach (the tide is out), while all around us stand the villas, pavilions and colonnades of Portmeirion, embowered amongst landscaped gardens and abundant foliage.

A well-nigh mandatory requirement for a *Prisoner* aficionado's pilgrimage to the Village is that he should arrive suitably dressed for the occasion. Both myself and Darren have conformed to this regulation. I have attired myself as Number Six himself (although admittedly my somewhat generously-proportioned figure is more akin to that of Leo McKern's Number Two than the more athletic frame of Patrick McGoohan); the costume being a black blazer with white piping, a navy-blue sweater, beige trousers and the ubiquitous blue canvas shoes, worn by all the denizens of the village. (Although I should add, that for day-to-day usage, this type of footwear is neither the most practical nor economical: they tend to wear out very quickly.)

My friend Darren wished also to attire himself as Number Six for this occasion, but I was quick to place a firm veto on this proposal, pointing out that there could not be two Number Sixes walking the streets of the Village at the same time (apart from on in that one episode, anyway); and I have therefore had him kitted out in the garb of a generic Village citizen: to wit beige slacks and canvas shoes like my own, topped with a striped sweater in bumble-bee orange and black. Naturally, the fellow acceded to my injunction without protest, and is, I am sure, quite satisfied with the arrangement.

Darren is a fellow of my own age, diminutive of stature and possessing something of the rodent in the conformation of his facial features. His hair is thinning on top and his jaw is invariably prickly with stubble. (Whether this is because it grows back so rapidly when he shaves it, or if it is that he *never* shaves it and it just doesn't grow any more than it already has, I am unsure.)

'Still,' I say, 'apart from being smaller, it's remarkable how little the place has altered in over fifty years.'

'Yeah,' agrees Darren. 'You half expect to see a Rover come bouncing up the street towards us, don't you?'

I direct a sour look at my friend. '*A* Rover, did you say? *A* Rover? How many times do I have to tell you? It is just called *Rover*. Rover—singular and plural! Rover is the name of the Village's mobile, and perhaps semi-sentient, security system. The individual balloons are not called "Rovers"; they are all manifestations of "Rover." Understand?'

'Yeah, I know,' says Darren pathetically. 'But then sometimes I forget.'

'Then you need to train your memory; improve your recall,' I advise him. 'Yes, I shall be devoting a chapter of my opus to the subject of Rover. I am convinced of its semi-sentience. Of course, in his novel "Who is Number Two?" author David MacDaniel attempted to explain the system as a product of the science of "fluidics." Arrant nonsense. And why those novels had to rename Rover "Guardians" and to have them come in a range of different off-white shades as though they were birds' eggs, I cannot for the life of me comprehend. But then, those books were never a canonical extension of the television series, so anything established within them can be safely disregarded.'

'I never liked them books,' says Darren. 'I couldn't get into 'em.'

'Yes, but then you're not much of a reader, are you? Still, you haven't missed much. They were a negligible addendum to the television series. And did you know that one of those books actually had the effrontery to include a direct reference to Number Six's scrotum? I'm sure Patrick McGoohan could not have approved. After all, it was effectively *his* scrotum that was being placed on exhibition, wasn't it? I'm surprised he didn't insist on the offending paragraph being excised from the book.'

'Maybe he never read it.'

'Let us hope so, let us hope so.'

'I wonder how long they were here?' says Darren. 'Filming the series, I mean?'

'Dolt,' I say, giving him a thump on the lightly-thatched crown of his head. 'They weren't here the whole time the series was in production, you numbskull! The bulk of the filming was carried out at the Boreham Wood studios of MGM. Initially, they hired Portmeirion for a period of one month and executed the location filming for the first four episodes—this being the first four episodes in production order of course, which were actually episodes one, four, eight and nine in broadcast order. Then, when they returned to Boreham Wood to commence the studio filming, they simply recreated some of the Village exteriors in the studio for subsequent episodes, to save them having to go back and forth all the time. However, they did return to Portmeirion to film for location footage on some occasions, but, and again to save time, sending only a second unit, and utilising location doubles for cast members and employing a limited number of extras—which did lead to the Village appearing somewhat underpopulated in those later episodes. And then of course, there was the extensive Portmeirion location filming for episode seven, which was thirteenth in production order; but as this episode, 'Many Happy Returns,' featured the Prisoner in a suddenly and inexplicably deserted Village, no extras or location doubles were required at all: just McGoohan himself (who was also directing) and the film crew.'

I pause to draw breath.

Darren makes no reply; I surmise that perhaps I have overwhelmed the poor fellow with this example of my encyclopaedic knowledge of the production of *The Prisoner*, and that he now requires time to concentrate his limited mental energies in digesting the wealth of information with which I have favoured him.

Finally, he speaks.

'I wanna go back to the shop,' he says.

'What for?' I ask.

'I wanna get one of them mugs.'

'Then by all means, let us go back to the shop.'

We set off. 'The shop' in question here is the *Prisoner* merchandise emporium, which occupies the very bungalow which served as the location for Number Six's residence in the television series. Within its portals can be purchased all manner of merchandise including books, apparel, mugs, t-shirts, and even inflatable balloons. Facing the Chess Lawn as it does, the gift shop is only a few steps away from our present vantage point. Howsomever, these 'steps,' few though they might be, cause myself a sudden and alarming accession of physical discomfort in the area of the lower abdomen. It is my unfortunate lot to be afflicted with very irritable and unpredictable bowels, and the need to relieve myself in this area can often come upon me very suddenly and urgently. As I make my way with rapidly increasing and buttock-clenching discomfort, I am faced with the awful knowledge that *now* is one of those moments.

By the time we arrive at the threshold of the shop, where reposes a penny-farthing bicycle, it has become clear to me that delaying the inevitable is just not going to be a viable option—I must repair at once to the nearest toilet facilities. I know full well there will be none to be found in the shop. Its interior dimensions happen to be considerably more restricted than the studio sets for Number Six's residence would allow us to believe—in short, there is no *room* for any public conveniences. I shall have to look elsewhere.

I briefly explain the situation to Darren.

'I think I might try the Old People's Home down there,' I say, indicating the direction of the beach. 'In reality that location houses a restaurant, and as such ought to be equipped with toilet facilities for the use of its patrons.'

'Want me to go with you?'

'No, Darren. I am quite capable of going to the bathroom unassisted. You go into the shop and purchase whatever it is you wish to purchase; in fact, feel free to take your time; and I will meet you back here anon.'

'Alright.'

Darren disappears into the shop and I proceed down towards the waterfront, treading with dainty steps. Ahead I espy a couple of workmen by the roadside. As workmen often do, they have dug a hole in the ground, erected a temporary barrier around it, and are now standing in the hole. It occurs to me that these fine fellows might be able to direct to the nearest public conveniences, and so I bend my steps towards them.

Time for a code-change. As you will have already gathered, I am blessed with an extensive vocabulary and eloquent turn of phrase; the voice of an academic, one of the intelligentsia. Now if I were to address these honest workmen in my usual articulate and professorial manner, they would be unable to understand a single word of my discourse. And it is a lamentable fact that, with these labouring-class types, that which they do not understand they will inevitably laugh to scorn. So, having no desire to be the object of these fellows' mockery, I must modulate my speech to complement their own style discourse.

Stopping before their hole, I greet them with a hearty: 'Watchya, mates!'

The two hard-hatted ones look up at me. One is tall, the other small.

The latter speaks. 'Hullo there, boyo. Londoner, are you?'

Curses! Too late I realise my fatal error: In the urgency of the moment, I had temporarily forgotten I was no longer in the purlieus of the East London borough in which I find my home—and that instead of the utilising the broad Cockney of my native borough, I should have adopted a Celtic intonation!

Too late now. I must persevere.

'That's right, me old Chinas! I'm from the good ol' burra o' Morsham, sarf o' the river!'

'Is that right? On holiday, are you?' proceeds the same workman.

'Right again! An' bein' in the area, I thought I'd come and see this 'ere swanky village, even though you 'ave ter pay ter get in! But the thing is, I've been caught a bit short if, you know what I mean; an' I was wonderin' if you blokes could tell us where the nearest bogs is?'

'So, it's the toilets you're looking for, is it?' The workman scratches the side of his face, doubtless to stimulate his mental faculties. 'Now where are they…?'

'But 'ere, you ought ter know!' I say. 'I mean ter say, where d'you go when you want ter 'ave a slash?'

'Well, we've got our portaloo, haven't we?'

He gestures over his shoulder, indicating a bright blue cubicle standing by the roadside and previously unobserved by myself.

'Then can I jest nip in there, me old mate?'

'Well, I'd be more than happy to let you, boyo—but it's more than my job's worth, you see?' says the workman. 'Union rules, isn't it? See, if you were to go in there and have some kind of accident and injure yourself… Well, I'd be in big trouble, wouldn't I?'

'But 'ow I 'urt myself, jest goin' to the bog?'

'Well, it's not fixed to the ground, is it? It's free-standing, that's what it is. And if a sudden gust of wind were to come along and knock the whole thing over while you were in there doing your business… Well, you might hurt yourself real bad, mightn't you?'

He has a point. I have a delicate back which is a constant source of affliction for me; indeed, it is this that tragically disables me from seeking any gainful employment. Yes, if that wretched cabin were to be upset by a sudden squall rushing in from the Irish Sea, and I, seated on the toilet, were to land on my back… I shudder at the thought.

'Yeah, I wouldn't like ter risk that,' I say; and, pointing down the road: 'Tell yer what: that looks like a caff or somethink down there at the beach. D'yer reckon they got some bogs in that place?'

More face-scratching from the small workman. 'The restaurant…? No… I don't *think* they've got any toilets down there; have they, Russ?'

The tall workman shakes his head; his first contribution to the conversation.

'Oh, I know!' suddenly exclaims the small workman, clicking his fingers. 'I remember now! I remember where they told us the bogs were! They're in that place up the hill there.'

He points towards Portmeirion's most prominent landmark, an octagonal dome-roofed edifice, known, in the context of the television series as the Green Dome—otherwise Number Two's Residence.

'What, yer mean past that place wi' the green dome?' I ask.

'No; I mean it *is* that place with the green dome! That's where you'll find the toilets, boyo.'

I look at the man to see if he's pulling my leg. But no, he seems perfectly sincere. I am left with little choice than to assume he is telling me the truth.

'Well, ta for 'ead's up, me old china!' I say. 'I'll be gettin' along then! See yer, mates!'

I turn to retrace my steps.

'Hold up!' says the workman. 'What's your name, boyo? You haven't even introduced yourself, have you? I'm Ralph, and this is Russ.'

My name. Here's a dilemma. Don't misunderstand me: I do *have* a name, and a very good one. Randal C Fortescue is my appellation, and I think it suits me very well (although woe betide anyone who dares to address me the diminutive 'Randy'!); but it occurs to me that Randal C Fortescue is a title that ill-fits with the Cockney persona I have assumed for the purposes of my discourse with these two honest labourers. I must improvise a substitute.

'Fred's the name!' I say. 'Fred Blogs! Pleased ter meet yer!'

'Fred, is it?' says Ralph. 'Well, nice to meet you, Fred! You have a good one, okay?'

'An' the very same to you, me old mate!'

With this, and wondering if, by the 'good one' the fellow wishes me, he refers to my impending visit to the bathroom in particular, or to the rest of my day in general, I commence my ascent of the hill. Time is pressing; my bowels are becoming emphatic in their demands; I must proceed with as much celerity as my constricted muscles will allow.

I pass the shop. There is no sign of Darren outside; he is doubtless still within its precincts. What was it wished to purchase? Oh yes, a mug. As these mugs come in several different designs, Darren is going to be some time. The poor fellow's inability to make his own mind up about anything amounts to a clinical disability. Faced with making any choice, be it of little import or of large, his brain starts to reel, and he just cannot decide. On most occasions, Darren is fortunate enough to have myself on hand to make his mind up for him; however, on this occasion he will just have to make do as best he can by himself: I have much more pressing business to attend to.

I am now nearing the Green Dome. This distinctive feature of Portmeirion is built upon an eminence, and several flights of ornamental stairs have to be ascended in order to reach its portals. I am not looking forward to this; climbing stairs will require the use of muscles which are at the moment being utilised for the crucial task of keeping closed the floodgates.

I still find it hard to credit that they would have put the resort's public conveniences in this particular location. Aside from the building's importance to all aficionados of *The Prisoner*, it is not the most conveniently-placed of sites—*conveniences*, by the very definition of the word, ought to be *conveniently* located. The appalling idea suddenly assails me that this choice of location for the lavatories might even have been somebody's idea of a very crude jest. As I have said, in the context of *The Prisoner*, the Green Dome is the residence of the Villager's visible authority figure, designated Number Two; and it just so happens that 'Number Two' is also employed as a polite euphemism for effecting a bowel movement! Can someone have had such poor taste as to allow such a crude joke to be realised—if this is indeed what it is?

Outrageous!

It proves a slow and uncomfortable process, but I manage to climb the stairs without suffering a misadventure. As with everything else in Portmeirion, the Green Dome, as I look up at it, seems considerably smaller than it appears on television. I now step out onto the portico fronting the building. I am surprised to see that the door displays an engraved number '2'; surprised because I had always believed that numeral had only been affixed to the door for the purposes of the television series, and also because I would have thought a plaque bearing the legend 'toilets' would have been more in order. For the first time it occurs to me that—unwittingly, I trust—those two workmen may have misdirected me; and that the facilities I so urgently seek are not to be found within these portals.

The very idea is insupportable; too appalling to contemplate; there is absolutely no way I could make it back down those stairs without suffering a humiliating mishap—I hasten to enter the building and to discover my fate.

Conceive my surprise, dear reader, when, upon opening the door I find myself confronted with what appears to be an exact replica of the vestibule of Number Two's office, as seen on *The Prisoner*! Facing me are the panelled doors behind which, in the TV series at least, were a set of sturdy metal doors which would (or sometimes wouldn't) slide open to reveal Number Two's futuristic inner sanctum. And there is even a vase of flowers reposing on an ornate table before me. Now I had always understood this room to have been a studio set, as were all of the interiors of the Village; but here it is, exact in every detail...

But then, on my right and on my left, I espy two other doors; doors which were most definitely *not* in existence in the television series version of this room; the door on the right is emblazoned with the legend 'Ladies' and that on the left with the legend 'Gentlemen.'

O, rejoice, my heart! You have arrived at the correct location after all! I should never have doubted the veracity of those honest workmen.

I note with approval that the Albertus lettering font has been employed for the signs on the doors of these conveniences. This distinctive font is synonymous with *The Prisoner*, being used both for the series' logo and credits, as well as being the standard lettering font featured in the Village itself, appearing on all signposts, invitation cards, etc.

I enter the Gents room, which I discover to be spotlessly clean and scented with a fresh, antiseptic fragrance. Opposite the urinals stand a row of three toilet cubicles and—wonder of wonders!—each is adorned with the Village penny-farthing bicycle logo, and are numbered from '1' to '3'! Now this really is very tastefully executed work; indeed, a fitting tribute to the immortal television series which made this resort famous.

Observing that the cubicle number '2' is occupied, I step into cubicle '3,' and I can assure you that never have I felt so grateful as I do now for the opportunity to sit down.

Feeling blissfully relieved, I allow my thoughts to wander...

Number Three... Although I believe there was never actually a character with that designation in the actual television series, there was the case of Stanley Unwin, who played a Number Three in a production called *The Laughing Prisoner,* a pastiche of the original series produced by Channel 4 in 1987 to mark the show's twentieth anniversary, and which starred the musician and television presenter Jools Holland and the comedian Stephen Fry. I confess I have always harboured mixed feelings with regard to this particular production. Although both Jools Holland and Stephen Fry are both confirmed aficionados of the original series, one cannot help but think that their pastiche was perhaps somewhat lacking in reverence in the nature of some of the humour involved. Stanley Unwin however, speaking in his unique semi-comprehensible dialect known as 'gobbledygook' or 'Unwinese,' lent a degree of dignity to the proceedings with his performance as eccentric Village citizen Number Three.

'What are you doing here?'

This urgent query reaches me from the adjoining cubicle, interrupting my train of thought. My first thought is that my neighbour must be conversing by telephone, but I am swiftly compelled to dismiss this notion. These are the first words he has spoken, and it would seem to defy all logic to ring somebody up on your mobile device and to immediately challenge them with the words 'What are you doing here?'

And so, having dismissed the telephone theory, I am left with the conclusion that this fraught inquiry can only be directed at myself. His next words only serve to confirm this belief. He says:

'What are you doing here?'

You see? The original question repeated, and in an even more agitated tone. But who is he? And why is he asking me this question so urgently? His voice is not one that I recognise. Having no reason to answer the demands of an importunate stranger, I could have just replied with a lofty silence, but I elect to humour the fellow.

'If your question is directed at myself,' I say, assuming my most haughty tones; 'I am utilising these facilities for the purpose for which they were intended. That is why I am *here*. I hope this answer is satisfactory to you.'

'I don't mean why are you *here*?' responds the fellow, sounding irritable now. 'I mean, why are you *here*? Why did you come to the Village?'

From the use of the words 'the Village' I swiftly deduce that my interlocutor is a *Prisoner* aficionado. To anybody else, *here* would be Portmeirion.

'And why shouldn't I come here? This resort is open to any admission-paying visitor. I have as much right to be here as yourself or anyone else.'

'You shouldn't have come here!' insists my unseen neighbour, going back to sounding fraught. 'Don't you realise the danger you're in?'

'Danger? From whom?'

'From *them*! From the forces that run this place!'

I begin to see daylight. This fellow is clearly one of those *Prisoner* fans whose grasp upon reality is not of the most resilient. In short, he believes that *The Prisoner* is reality rather than fantasy. (I understand that many *Star Trek* fans suffer from the same lamentable condition.)

'I am sorry to disillusion you, my friend,' I say, 'but the only people who "run" this place is the charitable trust to whom the resort belongs.'

'You don't really believe all that, do you?' I now detect a sneer in the fellow's voice. 'That's just a cover. *They* are the ones who really run this place. *You* should know that more than anyone. They've been waiting for you, Fortescue! They've been waiting for you to set foot in this place! And you've done it! You've walked right into their trap! And now that they've got you here, they're not going to let you go!'

I begin to feel alarmed. How does this fellow know my name? As far as I know he is a stranger to me. Could there be some truth in his dire warning?

'B-but why would these people be interested in *me*?' I ask. 'I am of little significance; I'm not a spy or anything!'

'Of little significance? You *know* that that's not true! You're still a rebel, aren't you? A nonconformist? *That's* why they're interested in you! Don't you see? They know about people like you; they keep tabs on people like you; the people who are ideologically opposed to them. They know every potential troublemaker, everyone who could possibly be a threat to their organisation. And you're right at the top of the list, Fortescue! And now you've gone and walked right into the lion's den!'

'But I've never *done* anything!' I insist. 'I have always maintained a low profile…'

'It doesn't matter if you haven't done anything! It's what you're capable of doing! A mind like yours: intellectual, nonconformist, individualistic; you're a threat to them, I tell you!'

What he says sounds all too plausible. It would make sense that if such an organisation as the Village really existed, it would certainly be aware of, and be wary of, people such as myself… But I have always regarded *The Prisoner* as a work of fiction; a work of television art. Can it really be that…? And right here in Portmeirion…?

'B-but then, what should I do?' I ask, now seriously discomposed.

'Just get out of here, you fool!' hisses my interlocutor.

'But how? I mean, can you help me? And what about my friend Darren?'

'Never mind *him*! *He's* in no danger! Just get out of here while you still can!'

And before I have time to question the fellow further, I hear the flush of a cistern, the opening of a cubicle door. Rapid footsteps across the tiles and then the opening of the outer door.

My informant has departed (and without stopping to wash his hands.) My immediate instinct is to set off in pursuit of the fellow, but my present situation renders any immediate move impossible. However, I attend to my personal hygiene as rapidly as possible, and with hands still wet from washing, I hasten from the toilets, across the vestibule and out onto the portico. There is no sign of my interlocutor . I look down and see no-one descending the stairs; no-one in the street below.

The fresh sea air and quietude of the view begin to allay my fears. Could the fellow have merely been a kook after all? A practical joker? But then, how did he know my name…?

'Pssst!'

The sound comes from over my shoulder. I look around and descry a hand beckoning me from around the corner of the building.

'Pssst!' says the hand again, or rather the unseen person attached thereto.

My informant! So he did wait for me after all!

I bend my steps towards the beckoning hand. But then I remember that in *The Prisoner*, beckoning hands can sometimes come with fists attached to them; I proceed with more caution. Keeping clear of the wall, I turn the corner and I am taken aback to discover that the beckoning hand does not belong to my erstwhile interlocutor at all! This I can say with certainty, because although I may not actually have seen him, from his voice (not to mention his presence in the Gents) my interlocutor was unequivocally male—and the person now standing before me is a woman. From her complexion, I judge her to be of East Asian provenance, although she is by no means small in stature. She is, however, dressed in village garb: a red and white striped jumper, pale blue slacks, canvas shoes. Her hair is piled up under a peaked white hat of the 'mod' variety, and her eyes are concealed behind shades.

She leans against the wall. I sense that she is staring at me, yet she makes no effort to open the conversation.

I decide to take the initiative.

'And who—'

'Ssshhh!'

'But look—'

'Ssshhh!!'

I try several times to articulate a query and each time am interrupted in this summary (and increasingly annoying) manner. I submit with all the patience I can muster. I observe that the penny-farthing badge pinned to her jumper bears the number '16.'

She now lowers her glasses, studies me over them with her epicanthic optics.

'Were you followed here?' she asks.

'Followed where?' I demand. 'From the toilets? Across this clearly unoccupied portico?'

'It does not matter,' replies the woman, raising her glasses again. 'I must get you out of here. You are in imminent danger.'

My feelings of alarm surge back with a vengeance. 'You mean you're...? The man in the toilets...? Is he...? Are you...?'

She vehemently shushes me again.

'There is no time for talking,' says the woman. 'We must flee. I will do my best to escort you safely from this location.'

'But who are you?' I demand.

'You may call me Number Sixteen. And now, no more questions. We must make haste!'

She takes my hand—and then quickly releases it.

'Your hand is wet,' she says, her tone accusing.

'I didn't have time to dry them properly,' I say, nettled. The fact of my hands being wet is at least proof that I washed them. She ought to be more appreciative of this hygienic fact.

'Come.'

Indicating that I should follow, she sets off round the side of the building.

'Can't we go the other way?' I ask. 'I'm supposed to be meeting my friend outside the souvenir shop.'

'No; we cannot go that way. They are watching.'

Watching? I hadn't seen anyone watching.

From the rear portico we descend a flight of steps and enter a wooded garden.

'But, my friend—' I begin.

'Your friend will meet with no harm,' says the woman. 'You can rejoin him later, once you are safely outside the Village.'

There are statues here amongst the trees; white marble statues, some full figure, others just busts standing on columns. I had always believed the statues seen in *The Prisoner* to have been just props, added by the makers of the television series, and not part of the original architecture. And yet, here they are…

We come to the edge of the garden. A road is before us and on the other side stands a building I recognise as the Village cafeteria, as seen in the first episode. Beyond this building the ground rises sharply, thick with trees. We have reached the outer limits of Portmeirion.

Now I hear a vehicle approaching along the road. My companion pushes me—rather peremptorily, I might add—back into the trees.

'Stay out of sight!' she tells me.

Deeming this to be sound advice, I do as I am told. The vehicle draws closer and when it comes into view proves to be a Mini Moke, identical to those featured in the television series: white bodywork and adorned with a red and white striped canopy.

It pulls up beside Number Sixteen, who has made no effort to conceal herself.

'Any sign of the target?' asks the driver. He is a man of roughly my own years, thin-faced, clean-shaven and brown-complexioned. I would judge his ethnicity to be either Indian or Middle-Eastern.

And he addressed her by her number! So, they really do use numbers in this place!

'No, I have not seen him,' replies Number Sixteen.

'We've lost track of him. He must be found. Report in at once if you locate him.'

'I will do so, Number Twelve.'

Nodding curtly, the man drives off.

The target? Lost track of him? Must be found?

They mean me!

As soon as the Moke is out of sight, my conductress returns to me, grabbing me by the sleeve.

'Come! We must hurry! You have already been missed!'

We run across the road and, skirting the building, enter the woods.

'So, you—you're one of them?'

'Officially, yes,' replies Number Sixteen. 'But as you can see, I am nonetheless assisting you. If we were to be caught, my fate would be a worse one than yours.'

'But... but...' I puff. 'Is it all... real? All those... whew... underground control rooms...? Are they...?'

'Save your breath for climbing,' orders Number Sixteen.

I admit this is sound advice. I am unused to prolonged physical exertion, and this steep climb up the wooded slope is taxing my stamina. However, I struggle on.

It seems that the search is on! How many more of those golf-carts are rushing around looking for me? Is it...? Could it possibly be... an Orange Alert...?

Am I going to make it out of this dire predicament? Or will I have to resign myself to having Portmeirion as my new permanent place of residence?

We finally reach the top of the rise and the terrain, still heavily wooded, levels out. 'The man who spoke to me in the toilets,' I begin, having sufficiently recovered my breath. 'Is he a colleague of yours?'

'Yes.'

'And if you really work for the Village, why are you helping me?'

'Because I choose to. We do not all support the regime we are forced to serve.'

'Can we stop running now?'

'Not yet. We are still within the security perimeter.'

'Then, how much—?'

'Ssshhh!'

And before I even have time to inquire what she's 'ssshhhing' about this time, I find myself leapt upon and violently thrown to the ground amongst the underbrush, under the shadow of the trees. We lie belly to belly, Number Sixteen holding me firmly down. What is this in aid of...? Good lord! Suddenly I see it all: this has all been a deception! I have been lured into the woods under false pretences by a female sexual predator!

'Remove yourself from my person at once, madam!' I thunder. 'I will not submit to—'

'Sshhhh!'

'Don't you "shush" me, you nymphomaniac!'

'Not a sound!' she hisses, grasping me by the collar, her face close to mine. 'Keep perfectly still!'

And then I hear it. Quietly at first, but growing rapidly louder. Do my ears deceive me? Can I really be hearing what I am hearing?

I high-pitched oscillating electronic sound; and in tandem with it the disturbing and incongruous accompaniment of Gregorian chanting played backwards.

Now, there is only one thing on this planet produces this particular combination of sounds as it goes about its homicidal, air-passage-inhibiting business:

Rover!

Can it be? Can Rover, along with all the other paraphernalia of the Village, actually be real?

I feel myself trembling. The intertwined sounds grow louder in intensity. Rover is coming.

I squeeze my eyes tight shut.

Louder, ever louder, grows the sound; and now it is right on top of us. I see nothing—what with the intervening shrubbery and the fact of my eyes being clamped shut, I see nothing. But I *sense* it; I sense something passing by, just there, on the other side of the tree. It passes, and the sounds begin to diminish.

And then finally, blessed silence.

I release the pent-up breath I hadn't even realised I was holding. I open my eyes. I see my companion's face, close to my own. Was she as scared as I was? I am unable to tell. Her breathing is steady and her expression, what with the shades and her being an inscrutable Oriental woman, is unreadable.

Her words, however, are distinctly reassuring: 'We are safe. It did not detect us.'

She climbs to her feet and extends an arm to assist myself.

'Come,' she says. 'We are nearly through. Now is our best chance.'

We proceed. Beyond the bushes is a track, a deer-path or something; a wide avenue between the trees—certainly wide enough to have accommodated an ambulatory weather-balloon.

'Was that...? What just passed... Was it... Rover?' I gasp, as we cross the track and enter the trees.

'Ssshhh!' is all the answer I get.

'Don't just "ssshhh" me, woman! There are a lot of things I need to know here!'

'There is no time for talk. We must hurry. It is now or never.'

And hurry we do; until finally my companion slows to a walk. I gladly follow suit.

'We are outside the perimeter now,' she announces.

'And now what?'

'And now you must get far away from this place! You must return to your hotel in Bangor at once. And then tomorrow you must return to London!'

Now, as luck would have it, I was planning to do both of those things anyway. I inform my companion of this fact.

'That is good. Here we are.'

We emerge from the trees onto the road. Just ahead of us is a bus shelter. It is the very bus stop at which Darren and myself had alighted a few hours before; the bus that will take us back to the nearest town and thence onto the train to Bangor.

As we draw near to the shelter, I perceive there is a lone commuter seated within. And, much to my surprise, I recognise the owner of that bumble-bee striped sweater: it is Darren!

'You?' I exclaim. 'What are you doing here?'

'Waiting for you,' he replies, his features displaying no surprise at my advent. I turn to my rescuer.

'Did you know he was—?'

I break off. I am talking to thin air. Number Sixteen has gone! The road is deserted! There is no sign of her!

'Now where did she run off to?'

'Where did who run off?' inquires Darren.

'Number Sixteen, you numbskull!' I retort. 'The woman who was with me!'

The dolt looks at me like I've got two heads. 'What woman? You were on your own.'

'On my own?' My voice rises with my ire. 'There was another person with me: female, Oriental, dressed in a red and white striped jumper, wearing shades and a hat. Don't tell me you didn't see her!'

The rascal flagrantly disobeys me in this, insisting that he indeed did *not* see her.

'Then either you're going mad or I am,' I declare.

I seat myself as best I can on the bus shelter bench. These ridiculous contrivances are not really designed for ample proportions such as mine. I produce my handkerchief and mop my heated brow.

'So, what happened to you?' inquires Darren.

'What happened to *you*?' I retort. 'Didn't I say we were to meet outside the shop?'

'Yeah, but then this bloke came along and told me that you wouldn't be coming back to the shop, and that I should just wait for you out here, at the bus stop.'

'And who was this "bloke"?'

He describes a Caucasian male sporting a Village blazer, pink with black piping, and wearing a penny-farthing badge bearing the number one hundred. I surmise him to have been one of Number Sixteen's associates.

'As for my own adventures, I barely know where to begin,' I say. I look at him. 'By the by, which of the mugs did you elect to purchase? Where is it?'

The fellow grins sheepishly. 'Well, I couldn't decide which one…'

'…So you ended up not buying any of them. I might have guessed,' heaving a weary sigh.

'We could nip back—'

'"Nip" back! After I very nearly—! Dolt!' And I fetch him a thump upon the cranium. 'We are not *ever* going back, do you hear? Ever!'

Chapter Two
How a Conversation Turned from the General to the Specific

I awake to, or perhaps more accurately am awoken by, the smell of cigarette smoke permeating the air around me.

This can only mean one thing: I am not alone in my bedsitting room; that I have an uninvited guest. I know who this guest will be; there exists only one person who would just walk into my *sanctum sanctorum* as though she owns the place and blithely start polluting the air with the carcinogenic effusions of the noxious weed to which she is addicted—indeed, there is only one person who *could* just walk into my *sanctum sanctorum* as though she owns the place; this being due to the lamentable fact that the key to her own dwelling up on the second floor happens to also fit the lock of my own; a circumstance of which she is only too happy to take advantage whenever the fancy takes her.

Opening my eyes, I see the cloud of deadly vapor hanging almost motionless in the air, trapped in the haze of the morning sunlight which filters in through the curtained window. Turning my head to the left, I follow the cloud of fumes to its source: to wit, a cigarette held betwixt the index and middle fingers (nails painted black) of Gillian Draper, who sits upon my venerable upholstered armchair like a disreputable monarch on her throne.

'Wake up, sleepyhead,' says the intruder, regarding me with an insufferable smile fixed upon her countenance.

'A ludicrous request,' is my response; 'considering that I clearly *am* awake.'

'Well, if I said it while you were still asleep, you wouldn't hear it, would you?' says Gillian.

'Precisely,' I retort. 'Which is why I say it is a ludicrous request. To what do I owe the pleasure of this criminal invasion of my property and privacy?'

She shrugs two large shoulders. 'Nothing really. I was just bored.'

While I cordially invite her to go and be bored somewhere else, let me introduce you to my troublesome neighbour. Her name, as I have already stated, is Gillian Draper, and her age is the same as my own. (We first became acquainted while attending the same university.) The first thing that anyone observes upon seeing this female is that there is a lot of her. This is not to say that she is obese or rotund (words some people elect to employ to describe my own noble proportions); no, she retains, in their correct places, all of her feminine curves; but they are *large* curves. In fact, everything about Gillian, from her bone-structure outwards, is large. To call her figure an hourglass would be to understate the case; two or three hours at least can be encompassed within that framework.

Now, there are some of these more robustly-constructed women who can carry themselves with all the lightness and grace of their more slenderly-built compatriots: Gillian is not one of these fortunate ones. She clomps along in her size twelve boots with about as much feminine grace as I myself possess (which is to say, none.) She was, by her own admission, a tomboy as a child and she remains a tomboy today, having been unable or unwilling to evolve out of the tomboy phase; a tomboy even down to her carriage and deportment.

Her hair is black and wavy and in length lies somewhere between chin and shoulder length. She wears plastic-framed glasses and her facial features are, I will allow, although somewhat inclined to chubbiness, agreeable to look upon. From the neck down, it is her manner of dress that really sums her up; in addition to the aforementioned boots, she wears black denim trousers, a black and red check lumberjack shirt, unbuttoned of course and worn over a black t-shirt emblazoned with the name of some obscure and unlistenable rock band.

The vulgar term for people—usually males—who dress thusly and enjoy the same aimless lifestyle is 'slacker.' And Gillian freely acknowledges the aptness of this description when applied to herself; in fact she positively delights in it.

Aside from our long acquaintance, there is one other, and I believe *only* one other, factor which binds us (metaphorically) together: to wit, that she also is a fan of *The Prisoner*. Although in Gillian's case, I have to say that she is far too ready to criticize the series she allegedly adores. (This is also a very common complaint amongst *Doctor Who* fans, as has been well-documented.) To give you an example of Gillian's lack of reverence, I cite the occasion when, discussing the series, I remarked upon the perceptive satire regarding superficial electioneering tactics featured in the episode 'Free for All'—and she had the effrontery to suggest that this same subject had been dealt with just as effectively in an episode of *Batman*!

I ask you!

'Anyway,' says Gillian, after having declined to avail herself of my invitation to remove herself from my habitat. 'I haven't seen you since you got back. How was Portmeirion?'

I sit myself up in bed.

'Before I answer your query,' I say, 'will you kindly extinguish that tobacco product with which you are currently, and I might add, illegally, poisoning the air of my immediate environment and endangering my health and wellbeing?'

'It's not illegal for me to smoke in this place,' replies Gillian smoothly. 'Read the tenancy agreement: it says that smoking is allowed in the bedsitting rooms.'

'Yes, you are allowed to smoke in *your own* bedsitting room!' I retort. 'It doesn't mean you can just light up without so much as a by-your-leave in *other people's* rooms!'

Witness my facile grasp of these finer points of legislation. However, Gillian's only response to this is another one of those annoyingly insouciant shrugs of the shoulders.

'And I could also add that I have asked you on innumerable occasions to cease this taking advantage of the fact that your key can open my door and just walking into my room as though it were your own!'

Perhaps I should explain here that my place of abode is one of those former Victorian townhouses divided up into bedsitting apartments and let at exorbitant rates by unscrupulous landlords, that exist by the thousand in this great metropolis of ours. The apartment doors are of great antiquity, and although constructed of sturdy panelled wood, they are secured by the most primitive locking mechanisms turned by unwieldly passkeys. (Fortunately, this does not apply to the building's main front door, which is much more securely and comprehensively locked with devices of modern manufacture.) Because of the simplicity of these passkeys, it can be all too easy for locks to be turned by the incorrect key—and this is how it comes to pass that Gillian is able to gain access to my *sanctum sanctorum* using her own passkey. (Logically, you would have thought that this arrangement must work equally both ways, in that I ought to be able to gain access to Gillian's domicile with equal facility; you would have thought so, but inexplicably this is not the case. I can say this with authority because, on one occasion I tried to effect entry to Gillian's apartment, for no other reason than to teach her a condign lesson with regard to respecting people's privacy, and not only would my key not open the door but it became jammed in the mechanism! The result of this was that a locksmith had to be summoned to rectify the situation and I myself came perilously close to being evicted for attempted burglary!)

My room, as already stated, is a bedsit, although with the king-sized bedstead occupying most of the available space there is not so much room left for the 'sitting' part of the equation. There's the one armchair currently occupied by Gillian, and which she seems to consider hers by right whenever she is within these precincts, and over by the window a small dining table, which also serves as my 'desk,' and which is supplied with two chairs. My room is ground-floor front and would once have been a sizeable parlour, but the original room has been reduced in size by the introduction of a partition wall. Two doors in said wall give access to my bathroom and kitchenette, respectively.

'I didn't want to wake you up by knocking,' says Gillian, in reply to my comment about using her key to enter my domain.

'I would much rather have been roused from my slumber by the cacophony raised by your belabouring my door, than to be awoken by my internal self-defence mechanism alerting me that the air around me is being saturated with poisonous fumes,' I tell her.

'Would you stop complaining? Look, I've finished now, okay?' She holds up her ashtray the better for me to see her extinguishing her cigarette. (And that's another thing: she thinks it's perfectly acceptable for her to smoke in any given location, as long as she brings her own ashtray.)

'So, come on. How was Portmeirion? Smaller than it looks on the telly, isn't it?' (Gillian has already made her own pilgrimage to the North Wales village.)

'It is,' I say.

'What was the weather like? Did it rain while you were there?'

'No, the weather remained clement.'

'Well, come on, then! Did anything exciting happen?'

I smile. The very opening I have been waiting for. 'You could say that...' I say.

'Go on, then. What happened?'

I will forgo reporting here my verbal account of my adventures in Portmeirion. To reiterate the events of only the previous chapter would smack of being a gratuitous recapitulation perpetrated solely with the intent of boosting the word-count of this history. I'm sure you can remember my glowing description of those remarkable events; just imagine I have now related the same to Gillian and in more or less the same words. (Albeit on this occasion with numerous attempts on the part of my auditor to interrupt the flow of my narrative with idiot questions and expressions of disbelief.)

'You've been had,' are her first words after I have closed my report and given her leave to speak.

This is not the response I was anticipating.

'In what respect have I been "had"?' I inquire frostily.

'In "respect" of the whole fucking thing,' says Gillian.

I wince. This is another one of Gillian's more lamentable qualities: to wit, her readiness to voice obscenities.

'I always knew you were gullible,' she proceeds, 'but do you seriously believe that there's really some sinister organisation like the one in *The Prisoner*, and that it's actually based in Portmeirion?' She laughs. 'It's because they said they were after *you*, wasn't it? That's why you believed it. It made you feel all important, didn't it?'

More laughter. My ire raises.

'I have a right to believe the evidence of my own senses, do I not?' I retort. 'And if you mean to imply that I was the victim of a practical joke, then there are a few points of my narrative I would be very interested to hear you elaborate upon. First and foremost: How did they know my name? As I have stated, these people were all strangers to me.'

'Yeah, well obviously *they* knew you. They must have been some of your online friends you've never met in the real world—from one of those *Prisoner* forums you're on. I bet you told them that you were going to Portmeirion, didn't you? And I bet you told them the exact day…'

'I believe I may have mentioned it, yes…' I concede.

'There you are, then!' says Gillian, foolishly triumphant. 'It was some of your online friends pulling a prank on you!'

'With so many people involved?' I demand. 'There was a full-scale search on for me, remember?'

'No; they *told* you there was a full-scale search going on,' says Gillian. 'But think about it: you only actually saw or spoke to three people, didn't you?' She proceeds to count them off on her fingers. 'The guy in the bogs; the Asian woman; and the Indian guy in the golf cart. And that was all there was, I bet: just those three people.'

'You're forgetting the individual who told Darren that he was to meet me at the bus shelter,' I remind her.

'I haven't forgotten him. He was probably the same guy who talked to you in the bogs. So there you go! You were tricked by three *Prisoner* fans into thinking that Portmeirion was really the Village, and there was a full-scale manhunt on for you!'

She sits back, looking insufferably pleased with herself.

I play my trump card. 'And how do you explain the presence of *Rover*?' I demand, relishing the prospect of her discomfiture.

'Oh, *that*,' she says. 'That was just a sound recording, you wally. Don't you get it? That's why the woman jumped on top of you like that. She was making bloody sure you couldn't see the thing, cuz there was nothing there to see! It was just one of her friends hiding in the bushes with a tape deck. Christ, you really are gullible, aren't you?'

'When I related my adventures to Darren, I was not greeted with this scepticism. *He* believed me.'

'Yeah, that's cuz he's just as gullible as you. Nobody else would've believed it!'

'Wouldn't they, now?'

'No, they wouldn't!' She heaves an exasperated sigh—one that by all rights should have been mine. 'Okay. Let's say for a minute that's it all true. That there *is* some sinister conspiracy based in Portmeirion. First of all: are these people meant to have been there since *before* they made *The Prisoner*, or did they pop up there afterwards?'

'Neither of my interlocutors specified how long the organisation had been there,' I answer. 'My assumption is that it came into being subsequent to the television series, and in fact used the series as a template for its activities. Fact emulating fiction, as it were.'

'Okay. And what's this conspiracy about? I mean they can't really be keeping people prisoners in Portmeirion, can they? It's a bloody public tourist attraction!'

'I admit that nothing on the scale of the Village and its population as seen in *The Prisoner* would be possible in the real location; but perhaps something on a much smaller scale; a few inmates carefully guarded so as not to be able to interact with the sightseers. As for the purpose of the conspiracy: doubtless the suppression of individualists deemed to be a threat to themselves.'

'Good. That brings me nicely to my next question: Why the hell would they be interested in *you*?'

'What?' I cry, astonished at her lack of perception. 'Surely that must be obvious! In myself you see a prime example of an individualist and nonconformist! *Of course* they would be interested in me! It is only surprising they haven't attempted my incarceration before now!'

Gillian looks strangely unimpressed. 'Yeah, right,' she says. 'For "individualist" read "misfit." Hate to tell you this, Randal, but people like you are ten a penny. You don't fit into society because you fucking *can't*. But the Prisoner; he was a guy who *chose* to become a rebel; people like you don't have any choice about rebels; you were just born that way.'

'That sounds more like a slight on my character than a logical argument.'

'I'm just trying to point out that you're nobody special. I mean, Christ, Darren's just as much of misfit—sorry, "rebel"—as you are. Why didn't they go after him as well? Why did they just let him walk out of the place?'

'Do you really need to ask that?'

She annoyingly replies 'yes' to what was clearly intended to be a rhetorical question. I proceed:

'While Darren may be one of those societal "misfits" as you choose to call them, he is hardly a rebel of the same calibre as myself. His intellect is mediocre at best; his mind does not inhabit the same lofty intellectual level as one such as myself. *That* is what makes me a danger to them: a rebellious nature combined with a powerful intellect.'

I don't like the smile on Gillian's face. She says: 'Yeah? Well, if you've got such a "powerful intellect," then why is it that whenever anything goes wrong with your computer, you have to get "mediocre" Darren to come round and sort it out for you?'

I sigh wearily. 'That's not the same thing. I admit he is more adept than myself in the maintenance of computerised devices, but that, in the present day and age, is merely a technician's skill. It no more requires the mind of a great thinker than do the skills of plumber, electrician, etcetera, who one also calls to one's home when needed. No, the forces of oppression would not concern themselves with one such as Darren.'

'They were having you on, Randal,' insists Gillian. (Note how she avoids a direct reply to my last observation!) 'They must've worked out you'd be just the kind of gullible self-important idiot who'd be taken in by a trick like that. They were playing on your vanity! Can't you bloody see that?'

'I am not "vain,"' I tell her. 'I merely acknowledge my own abilities. That is not "vanity."'

'Yeah, well just go on your forums and see if anyone starts asking you pointed questions about what happened to you in Portmeirion.' She breaks off. 'Oh, yeah; *this* came for you.'

This is a letter in a windowed envelope which has been lying on the arm of Gillian's chair, hitherto unnoticed by myself. She tosses the letter over to me.

'And how did you get your hands on my private correspondence?' I thunder, picking up and examining the document. 'Don't tell me your mailbox key opens my mailbox as well! That would be the limit!'

'Of course it doesn't,' is the reassuring reply. 'The postman was in the hallway when I came down to see you; he had that letter for you and I said I'd take it in; that's all it was. No need to burst a blood vessel.'

'Well, the fellow shouldn't have handed it over to you just like that,' I reply. 'He should have placed it securely in my mail compartment. Private correspondence should not be handed over to anyone aside from the authorised recipient—at least not without leaving me a "something for you" card explaining fully to whom the letter had been entrusted. I could have the fellow's job for this.'

'He did leave a card,' says Gillian, holding up a 'something for you' card.

'And how did you get hold of that?' I ask, thundering again.

'He gave it to me with the letter.'

'And what in the name of goodness is the point of doing that?' I cry in my profound exasperation. 'You could have just purloined both letter and card and I would have been none the wiser! The fellow should have placed the card in my mailbox, or at the very least slipped it under my door.'

'He was going to slip it under the door, but as I was coming in here anyway, I said I'd just take it in along with the letter.'

I give up, unable to judge which of the two is more culpably irresponsible: the postal worker or Gillian.

'Aren't you going to open it?' asks Gillian.

'I *am* going to,' I say. 'In fact, I'm surprised you didn't open it yourself in order to save me the trouble.' I peruse the return address. 'The Unemployment Centre. Doubtless this is just the annual notification of the recalculation of my benefits.'

'Haven't you already had that this year?'

'Actually, I have… Then I wonder what it could be…?'

I tear open the envelope to discover. As I peruse the document before my eyes, I feel the colour drain from my face and the hand that holds the missive starts to tremble as though with the ague.

'…What…? How can this be…?' I gasp in a strangled voice.

'What's up?' inquires Gillian.

The unconcerned tone of the inquiry jars with me. '"What's up?" I'll tell you what's up! These pettifogging bureaucrats of the Unemployment Centre have deemed it right that I must attend a medical assessment with regards to my benefits claim! This is outrageous! Why do they need to conduct another medical examination? The results determined by my previous examination still stand, do they not? Nothing has changed regarding my condition; if there had been any such change, I would have advised them of the fact, as I am obliged to do! What is the point of going to all the trouble and expense of conducting another medical exam? Answer me that! Answer me that!'

'So, when was your last medical?' asks Gillian, still speaking in an insouciant tone which makes it clear that she fails to appreciate the awful gravity of the situation.

'Well, it was...' I ponder the question. 'Seven or eight years ago, I believe...'

Gillian—the wretch!—bursts out laughing again. 'Well what do you expect?' she chuckles inanely. 'That was *ages* ago!'

'"*Ages* ago",' I say, echoing with scorn the ludicrous terminology. 'It hardly matters how long has passed, does it? My spinal condition is chronic. It gets neither better nor worse. It rendered me unfit to seek gainful employment then, and so it still renders me now.'

'Then just go and tell them that, then,' says Gillian. 'One thing, though: I wouldn't mention your little trip to Portmeirion, if I were you. You weren't too "unfit" to make that one, were you?'

'I will have you know I experienced severe physical discomfort during the prolonged railway journey,' I tell her crisply. 'Howsomever, I endured it just as any devoted pilgrim of long ago would have endured the long, footsore trek of the journey to his particular holy land.'

'Yeah, very noble of you,' says Gillian, her tone strongly suggestive of irony. 'Even so, I still wouldn't mention it when you go to that medical assessment.'

'I had no intention of so doing,' is my haughty reply. 'What I choose to undertake in my spare time is no concern of theirs.'

'And when is this assessment happening?'

I consult the document again. 'Where is it…? Ah, yes; at least I have some respite: the examination is not scheduled until the 27th.'

'Of what?'

'May.'

'Yeah, that's today, you pillock.'

'What!' I roar. Panic seizes me with redoubled force. 'Today? How can they do this?'

'Here, what time's it for? If it's this morning you need to get your skates on.'

I hurriedly check the missive again. 'No… the appointment is not until this afternoon, thank goodness… But still; this is preposterous! This leaves me absolutely no window of time for preparation at all!'

'Maybe that was the idea,' says Gillian. 'Catch you with your trousers down.' A grin spreads across Gillian's face; one I like less and less the wider it grows. I sense instinctively that the thoughts which actuate it will not bode well for me. 'You know… It's funny this should happen the day after what happened in Portmeirion…'

'Two days after,' I correct her. 'Yesterday was our journey home.'

'Alright, two days, then,' says Gillian. 'But still, there might be a connection, mightn't there? I mean if those forces of the Village have got their beady eyes on you, maybe they're behind this surprise assessment? I mean, they're not going to just let you go just cuz you got past their security perimeter in Portmeirion, are they? They'll still be after you, and maybe this is their first move; maybe they want to make life difficult for you by getting you to lose some of your benefits. In fact, maybe…' She pauses for effect. '…They want to make you have to start looking for a *job*.'

Once again I feel the colour drain from my face. Could she actually be right?

Chapter Three
How I Endured a Harrowing Ordeal at the Hands of the Establishment

The borough of Morsham is situate in the Eastern regions of our great metropolis, and as such is fairly representative of its kind: here you will find a commendable level of ethnic diversity, drug and alcohol abuse, gang warfare, prostitution, unemployment, delinquency, drive-by stabbings, etcetera; in short, all the usual amenities.

However, in terms of reaching and being reached by the outside world, we are a bit 'off the beaten track' here in Morsham. No underground line ventures anywhere near us (although they keep talking about building one) and the one and only surface railway line which connects us with the other side of the river is situate right on the southern extremity of the borough, entailing either an additional bus journey or a very lengthy walk for any visitor who wishes to visit the bustling centre of Morsham. Not that there is much here to entice the tourist or sightseer. Aside from my good self, the only notable feature of the district is the famous Morsham Market, of which it is said that you can have your watch stolen at one end of the market, and a cheap Hong Kong replica of the same sold to you at the other. Aside from these two landmarks, there is little in Morsham to attract anyone other than the more intrepid of urban photographers.

For myself, I follow one very simple rule of life which enables me to survive with my skin intact in this microcosm of a self-destructing world: I never, ever, *ever* venture beyond the portals of my place of residence during the hours of darkness. A fairly obvious precaution, you would have thought, for any reasonable human being; yet you would be surprised how many people venture the experiment on a regular basis in spite of the glaring crime statistics. My own neighbour Gillian Draper, for example, often ventures forth in the chill of the night, usually to damage her ear-drums while watching some live rock music performance in a dank cellar reeking of spilt beer. I have warned her against this insanity of walking the streets after daylight has fled, but she merely laughs off my sage counsel. So be it. Just as long as she doesn't come crying to me when she finds herself sold into sexual slavery, or with her face burnt off with caustic solvents, her vital organs extracted for international retail, or her body a pincushion of knife handles.

Having said all this, Morsham can be a reasonably safe location during those hours when the sun shines down upon the streets, the criminal fraternity are tucked up in bed, and the ignorant masses (or, if you prefer, 'the decent, everyday folk') go about their lawful business.

My own place of residence is situated on Gissing Street, a relatively quiet residential street, and within reasonable walking distance of the administrative and commercial centre of Morsham, which is fortunate for myself as this afternoon I have to make my way to the Morsham Unemployment Centre to attend that ill-omened medical examination.

I don't know; but I am burdened with a deep sense of foreboding.

I get them sometimes, these feelings. I tell myself I must not pay too much heed to these things, these ethereal twinges. After all, I am no believer in the occult, and if I did possess any facility for anticipating personal danger, then those internal alarm bells ought to have been ringing for all they were worth the day before last, the very moment I set foot in Portmeirion.

Regardless, here I am, threading my solitary way through the crowded streets of my native borough. The shops are what you would expect; an endless succession of ethnic grocery stores, ethnic eateries; charity shops and thrift shops abound; small businesses of all descriptions; and of course betting shops: there is no shortage of those dens of iniquity.

All too soon I arrive at my destination: to wit, the Morsham Unemployment Centre. This bland three-storey structure is the busiest of all the town's civic buildings; unemployment being a key institution here in Morsham.

As I approach the steps, I espy the usual motley crew of unemployable ragamuffins loitering about the portals. These are the unfortunates, nearly all of them emaciated-looking men with beards, try how they might, just can never find themselves gainful long-term employment; lackadaisical by nature, slow at performing the most simple of tasks, bereft of both diligence and application, they are constantly in and out of temporary employment placements; placements which will be all the more 'temporary' for these unfortunates as they will invariably be dismissed for laziness or incompetence within a day or two of commencing work. Such people as this have existed since the dawn of humanity, their failings are endemic; these people ought to be pitied and yet they are despised. After all, consider how many other wastrels there are who, too lazy to perform honest work, turn instead to criminal enterprises to earn their livings! Now, by comparison, these hopeless unemployables haunting the Unemployment Centre ought to be praised for not having resorted to lives of crime, and instead electing to struggle on as best they can, claiming the weekly pittance that is Jobseekers' Allowance. But, alas no, far from being praised for their lofty principles, these unfortunates are despised even more than the homeless population by the narrow-minded and censorious ignorant masses.

It goes without saying that I do not regard myself as one of the above unemployables; were it not for my chronic back problems I would certainly have climbed high up the career ladder by this time. It is my curse to be denied this opportunity of proving my worth. All I have to do now is to make this sapient fact clear to whoever it was who decided on this completely unnecessary benefits assessment. Medical Examination indeed! Waste of everybody's time and money.

I enter the building. The reception slash waiting room is a spacious one as it needs to be; with its numerous rows of chairs facing a reception desk presently occupied by just one secretary. She looks somewhat dwarfed by her surroundings, there being room enough for at least half a dozen receptionists.

I march boldly up to this functionary, a blonde, bespectacled and insignificant-looking creature.

'I have arrived,' I announce, 'and under protest, for a completely pointless and unnecessary medical examination, and of which I might add, I was only given notification this very morning!'

I flourish the appointment letter to illustrate my point.

The receptionist says something. At least I think she does. I see her lips move.

'What?' I demand.

The lips move again.

'Speak up, woman! I cannot hear a single word you are enunciating!'

This time my ears definitely pick up some sounds; audible, yet too soft to be deciphered into recognisable words.

'Is that the best you can do?' I cry. 'Can you project your voice no more than that? You have the diction of a mouse, madam! A mouse, I say! Why on earth were you appointed to the position of receptionists when you cannot even make yourself heard to the clients you are receiving? This is ludicrous! Think how many unemployed people there must be who are possessed of clear, resonant voices, while you, with your inaudible articulation, sit here in clover! This is a prime example of one of the most glaring ills of society today! To wit, far too many people occupying posts for which they are completely unsuited!'

I turn to face the waiting room's seated occupants for signs of support and approval, and am disappointed to see none in those assembled faces; what I do see is a medley of angry and disapproving looks being directed at myself. Well, really! What is wrong with these people? Just who do they think is the victim here? Taking the side of bureaucracy instead of that of the downtrodden man! Have these people never heard of siding with the underdog?

I turn back to the receptionist. She appears to be upset about something. Problems at home, doubtless.

'Well?' I demand. 'Where do I need to go?'

The receptionist, applying a handkerchief to her eyes, points mutely to the waiting area. Apparently I am to wait here until I am summoned. Why couldn't she have just said that in the first place? I seat myself on a vacant chair. I shouldn't have to wait. The letter clearly states that the appointment time is 1:00 pm. I have arrived here promptly at that time. Wherefore must I wait? Are they merely tardy and inefficient in this establishment, or is it perhaps part of some deeper conspiracy? A deliberate plot to inflict tedious and unnecessary waiting upon the applicants? I wouldn't be surprised. After all, it goes without saying that in establishment such as this, it is a matter of strict policy for the administration to be hostile to the interests of their clients; it will be in their job-description that they must be as obstructive and as unhelpful as possible towards members of the public seeking to claim the financial assistance that is rightfully theirs.

A newcomer drops into the chair immediately adjacent to my own. It is on my lips to verbalise a protest as to this wholly unnecessary proximity and invasion of personal space, given the number of vacant seats available, but when I turn my head to do so, I find myself looking down upon the grinning visage of my compatriot Darren Nesbit.

We exchange greetings.

'Didn't expect to see you here!' remarks Darren.

'Would that I were not here,' I return. 'I have been summoned, and arbitrarily at that, to attend a medical examination.'

Darren whistles. It is a whistle not to my liking. It is a whistle that seems to say, in the whistler's vernacular: 'You're in for it!'

'You wanna be careful,' says Darren. 'It's the government: they're tightening up on all them disability benefits. When you go in there, you need to play it up as much as you can. Y'know, put on a really good show.'

He taps the side of his nose, winks at me.

I shoot him an annihilating look. '"Put on a good show"?' I echo, in suitably derisory tones. '"Play it up as much as you can"? You seem to be implying that my back problems are of an entirely fictitious nature. You of all people should know that this is not the case. You must have heard me on countless occasions giving voice to the physical discomfort inflicted upon me by my chronic condition.'

Darren hurries to rectify his mistake. 'Yeah, yeah, of course *I* know that! But *they* don't know that, do they? And it's them what you've got to convince!'

I perceive his point. I must go into this with eyes open and prepared for what will certainly be a hostile medical examination, with the hostility perhaps deceitfully concealed at the commencement, cloaked behind a façade of politeness, before the examiner slowly starts to reveal his true colours… Yes, I must not make of myself an unwitting Charlton Heston in the hands of a duplicitous Michael Moore…

'And what brings you here today?' I ask Darren.

A shrug. 'The usual. Signing on and finding out if there's any temping jobs going.'

Yes, this is Darren's life. Although somewhat bristly of chin, Darren is not like those poor wretches I described just now; for one thing, he lacks that hungry-eyed, emaciated look; and for another he seems to be perfectly happy performing all these temporary, minimum-wage jobs: going from one menial task to another… Yes, I can almost envy Darren; never expecting much from life, he is clearly contented with his lot…

Alas, it is the intellectuals like myself who are doomed to always feel restless and dissatisfied; it is a burden we have to bear…

And then it happens.

A jingle, brief but imperative, crashes over the air from hidden speakers—and then comes the voice.

'Can Mr Patwari please proceed to interview room five! We're waiting for you at interview room five, Mr Patwari!'

That voice! That fruity female voice with the audible smile! Fenella Fielding! And the jingle that preceded it…!

The Village announcement system from *The Prisoner*!

Flabbergasted, I turn to my friend, and my own dumbfoundedness is only increased by the fellow's look of asinine unconcern.

'What was that?' I say, my voice a strangled cry.

'What was what?' asks Darren, looking up at me.

'What? Didn't you hear it?' I demand.

'Hear what?'

'That announcement!'

'What announcement?'

'The one broadcast over the speakers just now, you oaf!'

'Oh, *that* announcement. Yeah, don't worry about it. It wasn't for either of us.'

'I know it wasn't for either of us! That's not what I mean! Didn't you hear? It sounded just like the one from *The Prisoner*!'

Darren thinks about this. (Why, for God's sake?) 'Yeah, I s'pose it did sound a bit like it…'

'A *bit*?' I echo, incredulous. 'It was identical! Are you trying to tell me they've always had an announcement system like that in this place?'

'No, it must be new,' says Darren, still infuriatingly blasé. 'They didn't have it last time I was here.'

'And don't you think it's at all strange?'

He shrugs, damn his eyes. 'Sometimes they put in new things, don't they?'

'Yes, but with that jingle? With that voice? It was Fenella Fielding!'

Darren looks interested at last. 'Was it?' he says.

'Yes, it was!'

'That's funny,' he says. 'Thought she was dead.'

My rejoinder dies on my lips. He's right. She *is* dead. Passed away a few years back, the obituaries paying more heed to her performance in *Carry On Screaming* than to her uncredited voice work for *The Prisoner*.

So, yes; he's right. It can't be her. But it was certainly someone who *sounded* like her.

And then it comes again. The merry jingle and then:

'Will Mr Fortescue report to Dr Wakabayashi in room six? Dr Wakabayashi is waiting for you in room six, Mr Fortescue!'

Darren taps my arm. 'That's you,' he says.

'I know it's me, you fool,' I reply through gritted teeth.

I rise to my feet. I notice the receptionist looking at me. (And I can certainly comprehend why *she's* not the one charged with making the announcements.) She mutely points with her biro to a door adjacent to the reception desk, a door that gives access to the inner precincts of this hive of bureaucracy.

Bidding adieu to Darren a set off across the room.

'Don't forget what I told you!'

Darren's words bring me to a halt. My back. Yes of course, my back. Was that a twinge I felt just this very moment? Yes, I do believe it was! A distinct twinge!

I rub the afflicted area.

'Your back giving you gyp again?' calls out Darren.

I turn to him, nodding an affirmative.

'Maybe you should ask 'em to get someone to help you? Y'know, help you walk to the examination room?' suggests Darren.

'No, I shall be able to make the journey unassisted,' I shout back to him.

'Okay then,' says Darren. 'I only asked. Cuz I know that back of yours does give you a lot of aggro.'

'Thank you for your kind concern,' I say, and turning, resume my walk.

'Yeah, poor old Randal,' proceeds Darren, as though addressing the room at large. 'Long as I've known 'im, he's always had troubles with his back!'

Yes, alright, Darren. Don't overdo it.

'...Chronic, it is, his lumbago. Why, sometimes it's as much as he can do to just walk down the street to the shops...'

Will you desist, you wretch! You're labouring the point to excess. People will start becoming suspicious!

'...And then sometimes it's been so bad, it has, that he hasn't even been able to get out of bed! Yeah, I've known him to spend entire days just lying in his bed, and all on account of that back of his! Shocking, it is...!'

I am going to wring your scrawny neck, Darren Nesbit! I am going to descend on you like the biblical whirlwind that levels entire cities! I am going to unleash the thunders of heaven and blast you out of existence! I am—

I reach the door, and as my hand reaches out to open it, the door opens of its own accord. Not so astounding in this day and age, you might think; an automatic door. Except that this one opens with the exact same mechanical sound produced by automatic doors in the Village!

I look back at Darren. Blessedly, he has now shut up. He gives me an encouraging wave. Has he not heard the sound the door has just made? But then, he's in and out of this place all the time; he must be accustomed to the sound; unless of course, the automatic doors, as with the announcement system, have only just been introduced…

I pass through the door into a corridor, a corridor positively clinical in its austerity. Numbered doors present themselves on either hand. Room number six, I want… And what was the examiner's name…? Wakabayashi… Yes, that was it. Wakabayashi; Chinese, unless I'm very much mistaken… I hope the fellow doesn't practice Chinese medicine! I am certainly not going to tolerate the fellow perforating my back with six-inch needles and forcing dried lizard's tails down my throat!

Just let him try!

I arrive at the door marked six. Six. Number Six. The Prisoner.

Is this a good or a bad omen?

I knock upon the door.

'Come in,' answers a voice. Female! I anticipated a male physician. Why would they give me, a man, a female examiner? I have no desire to disrobe in front of one of the fair sex. What should I do? Go back and demand a male physician?

But then, perhaps I will not have to disrobe. Yes, perhaps it is only a spoken examination that will be conducted…

I open the door and walk into the room.

Dr Wakabayashi is seated behind her desk; a young woman, severe-looking, her hair tied back in a bun, cat eye spectacles perched on her nose, a white lab coat worn over her clothing.

'Mr Fortescue? I am Dr Wakabayashi. Please take a seat.'

I drop into the chair facing her. I feel that there is something familiar about this female... Yes... She reminds me of Number Sixteen... The expression and the demeanour are different, the voice more crisp and authoritative... But still, in the arrangement of the features, the general height and build, there is an undeniable resemblance...

Wait a minute. They are supposed to all look the same, aren't they, these Orientals? (Not to each other of course, but to outsiders.) Yes, that will be all that it is! A mere trick of my unaccustomed Caucasian eyes!

'Now, Mr Fortescue,' says Dr Wakabayashi, picking up her clipboard. 'As you know, you have been called here to receive a medical examination in relation to your benefit claims.'

'Yes, I understand this,' I say. 'Although I would like to say before we commence, that this conference is entirely unnecessary; my condition has not changed an iota since the time of my last examination. So, if you just refer to my previous records, perhaps we can dispense with the—'

'We dispense with nothing,' she snaps, interrupting me. I don't care for the tone, nor the steely look in those eyes behind the cat eye spectacles. I sense this is going to be a hostile interview right from the outset.

'But even so,' I say. 'I trust you have familiarised yourself with my medical records, the finding of previous assessments—'

'Not necessary,' she cuts in once again. 'I will conduct my own assessment, Mr Fortescue. I do not wish to biased by opinions formed by previous assessments.'

'But you can't do that!' I protest, appalled. 'You have to take former findings into account! How can I possibly get a fair trial if you don't?'

'This is not a trial; it is a medical assessment. Just explain to me your condition in your own words, Mr Fortescue. I will ask questions and make notes; after that I will conduct a brief physical examination. This is all.'

'Very well,' I sigh. 'I will explain the nature of my condition; to put it succinctly I suffer from chronic lumbago—'

'Says who?'

'What do you mean "says who"? Says I! Says my general practitioner! You only have to consult him—'

'No consultations!' she snaps. 'So you say you have lumbago…'

'*Chronic* lumbago,' I emphasise. 'Not just some occasional twinges, you understand? I mean the kind of pain that affects me every day of my life, you understand? It affects my ability to perform everyday household tasks; it affects my mobility. Why, just making my way here today was an ordeal—'

'Yet you managed to go to Wales just a few days ago.'

I feel the blood drain from my face. How could she possibly—?

'H-how did you know that?' I stammer.

'Ah! So you admit it! You *did* go to Wales!'

Curses! Why didn't I fall back on a stringent denial while I had the chance? I've been ambushed! That's what it is: ambushed!

'Well, yes…' I admit. 'It's true I did undertake a necessary journey to Wales. But the journey was taken by train…'

'I didn't think you walked there, Mr Fortescue,' says Wakabayashi. She starts scribbling on a notepad. 'So, you are perfectly fine with taking a prolonged train journey…'

'No, I am not perfectly fine with a prolonged train journey!' I tell her hotly. 'Not fine at all. I… I experienced enormous discomfort. Why, I was bedridden until the next day after we got there.' We. That's a good point. 'And I couldn't have undertaken the journey at all had I been unattended! Yes! I needed support and supervision the entire time!'

'Who was your support unit?'

'Support unit? Well, his name is Darren. He performs many tasks for me. He's an invaluable assistant. Really, I couldn't function at all without him…'

'How much do you pay this support assistant?'

'Pay him? I don't pay him!'

'You don't pay your own support worker? Why not?'

'Well, I… You see, it's a rather informal arrangement… He doesn't do it by vocation as such… He's more a concerned friend, as it were…'

'He lives with you?'

'Of course not! I reside alone.'

'But he is always there if you need him?'

'Well… most of the time, I suppose… I mean, apart from when he's at work…'

'So, he has another job?'

'Nothing permanent. Short-term, minimum-wage work placements… In fact, he happens to be at this establishment today in search of employment—Yes! Why not have him brought here now? Yes, he can confirm my story, and how difficult it was—'

'No second opinions!' snaps my persecutrix. She closes her notepad. 'I have enough verbal information. Now we will proceed to the physical examination.'

'But I've hardly started yet!' I explode. 'I have considerably more information to impart regarding my maladies—'

'I have enough information, Mr Fortescue,' insists the harpy. 'Please disrobe.'

'But I demand a fair hearing!'

'Please disrobe.'

I look at her. She looks at me. I see no mercy in those bespectacled, Asiatic features; only cold, clinical determination.

I heave a sigh. 'Very well. Let us commence with the physical examination… But must I disrobe? Surely you can—'

'No. I must be able to view your spine without impediment in order to conduct a full assessment. Please disrobe, Mr Fortescue.'

'Very well,' I sigh. 'May at least disrobe behind the screen?'

'You may. Use the one behind you.'

The room is furnished with two of these curtained screens. The second screen I assume, conceals the examination table, as there is no sign of one elsewhere. I retire behind the screen indicated by the doctor, where I find a single chair. I remove my coat, jumper and vest and deposit them on the back of the chair.

I emerge to find that the doctor has risen from her desk. She stands waiting for me.

'No, Mr Randal' she says. 'When I asked you to disrobe, I meant that you should remove *all* of your clothes.'

'All of them!' I protest, incredulous. 'For a back examination? Surely, disrobing down to the waist is enough—'

My persecutrix is intractable. '*All* of them.'

I sense that further parley will be fruitless; this woman is inexorable. I retire once more behind the screen and, more and more dissatisfied with my treatment, remove my shoes, socks and unmentionables.

Now I happen to be very self-conscious with regards to my body, and as such am always careful to keep myself fully-covered at all times. As I have mentioned, I am somewhat inclined to corpulence, and consider my body not one suited to public display. Placed alongside one of those marble statues of Ancient Greece, I may be able to boast of having a similar complexion, but there the resemblance ends. And while I concur that disrobing for a member of the medical fraternity should be regarded as a process distinct from disrobing for anyone else, there is still cause for uncomfortable feelings when the physician in question happens to be a young, personable female.

As such, it is with some degree of embarrassment that I emerge from behind the screen dressed as Adam; a feeling which is in no way mitigated when Dr Wakabayashi proceeds to subject me to a silent and searching scrutiny, her eyes ranging up and down my exposed self.

'Let us proceed,' I say.

Instead of replying, she continues to study me intently, her attention clearly fixed upon my, ahem… middle regions; even adjusting the position of her glasses as though to see more clearly. Now, I did *not* disrobe for Dr Wakabayashi just so that she could stand here gawping at me! I am not some circus freakshow exhibit! The only thing that should be under her scrutiny is my afflicted back!

With this in mind, I march with forthright steps across the room and pull back the second folding screen with the intention of immediately arranging myself on the examination table and thus putting an end to this unwarranted peepshow.

However, my plans are thwarted when I discover to my confusion and consternation that behind the curtain screen there is no examination table at all, just another blasted chair!

I turn to face my antagonist. 'What's going on here?' I demand. 'How can you conduct an examination of my back without an examination table in the room? Were you planning to examine me standing up? If so, and I shouldn't have to tell you this, but a spinal examination can only be accurately conducted when the patient is in a recumbent position.'

'I know this,' is the reply. 'We will use the desk for the examination.'

'The desk! Are you out of your mind, woman? You cannot expect me to lie supine on a desk that size!'

'Do not worry yourself,' replies the sorceress. She raps the desk with her knuckles. 'The desk is very sturdy. It will support even your weight.'

'I wasn't referring to my weight!' I roar. 'I mean that the desk is too small. My head would be hanging off one end and my legs off the other!'

'This does not matter. Your torso will be fully supported. That is all that is necessary for conducting this examination.' She removes her clipboard from the desk. 'Now please, Mr Fortescue; arrange yourself on the desk.'

'I will do nothing of the kind!'

'If you do not cooperate in this assessment, your benefits will be automatically terminated.'

Damn her epicanthic eyes! My one weak spot! Whatever else I do, I cannot do anything to endanger my financial resources. However unwillingly, I am forced to submit to her demand.

'Very well; but I do this under protest!'

I climb onto the desk. It is cold. It is hard. As anticipated, I am forced to arrange myself with my head hanging over one end of the desk, and my legs—very painfully, just below the knee—projecting from the other.

'Good,' says my tormentor. 'Now I will proceed with the examination.'

'Proceed with haste!' I tell her. 'Lying like this is most uncomfortable, and furthermore, most undignified! A genuine medical examination couch should have been provided!'

The doctor proceeds to feel my spine, gently at first, pleasantly even, one might even say. My estimation of her medical capabilities begins to ascend. But then those probing fingers start to show an aggressive side, digging sharply into my vertebrae.

'Does this hurt?' (Jab!) 'And this?' (Poke!) 'Does it hurt here?' (Prod!) 'What about here?' (Thrust!) 'And here?' (Dig!) 'And here?' (Shove!)

'And what about this?' And she actually slaps my posteriors!

'How dare yo—!'

'And this?' She hits me again!

'And this? And this? And this?' She proceeds to shower blow after blow upon my hindquarters! I can hardly believe my senses!

'Desist this instant!' I thunder. 'Cease and desist! This is in no way orthodox medical procedure!'

'I will be the judge of that, Mr Fortescue!' says the harridan, thrashing my buttocks with increasing intensity.

'I demand that you cease this exhibition at once!' I roar.

She finally desists. But I am left with the feeling that she has desisted not in compliance with my protests, but simply because she has either exhausted herself, or else satisfied her sadistic urge. My posteriors are crying aloud at this ill-usage.

'The examination is over. You may get dressed now.'

I remove myself from the desk and hurry behind the screen before she can inflict further indignities upon me.

When I return, she is sitting calmly behind the desk, clipboard in hand.

'Please take a seat.'

I do so, uncomfortably.

'I have collated the results of my examination,' she says, scanning her notes. 'And I can find no sign of spinal weakness or abnormality.'

'What?' I cry. 'Are you suggesting I'm a hypochondriac?'

'No, Mr Fortescue' she says, looking at me squarely. 'Not a hypochondriac; just a malingerer.'

'What? How dare you! I demand a—'

'All of your disability benefits are cancelled, effective immediately,' she announces. 'You are hereby moved to Jobseekers Allowance track. Please report to the employment advisor.'

I feel the colour drain from my face. My bowels clench.

'You can't just arbitrarily reassign me like this!' I cry. 'It should take weeks to assess my claim—'

'You have the right to appeal,' she tells me.

'Very well. Appeal I shall! Please advise me of the procedure…'

'Here is the appeal form,' she says, pulling a document from her clipboard and placing it before me. 'Just sign and date it.'

'But don't I have to—'

'Just sign and date it.'

She proffers her biro and I duly sign and date the form.

She takes it back, studies it for about five seconds, and then proceeds to tear it into small pieces.

'Appeal rejected. Please report to the employment advisor.'

'You can't just do that!' I splutter. 'You haven't even heard my plea! This is—'

That wretched jingle slices through the air.

'Calling Mr Fortescue! Can Mr Fortescue please report to the employment advisor in room sixty-one? We're waiting for you in room sixty-one, Mr Fortescue!'

I look at Dr Wakabayashi. She studiously ignores me, studying her clipboard.

I rise from my chair.

The nightmare has begun.

Chapter Four
How I Became a Cog in the Machine

'Fred! Fred Blogs!'

The name, shouted out as I proceed along the street, halts me in my tracks. Although indisputably not my own name, it has a familiar ring to it; and not just the name, either; but also the voice of the one pronouncing it. A Welsh voice.

'Over 'ere!'

I turn my head in the direction indicated. I descry two workmen standing in a hole at the edge of the road. A tall workman and a small workman, the latter grinning and waving at me.

I am nonplussed. It is Ralph and Russ, the two workmen I encountered in Portmeirion, and who were good enough to direct me to the public conveniences. What on Earth are they doing in Morsham?

I walk over to them, slipping into my Fred Blogs persona.

'Watchyer mates!' I say. 'If it ain't old Ralph and Russ! I don't believe me pork pies! Watchyer doin' in this neck o' the woods?'

'It's the union, isn't it?' replies Ralph. 'Told us our next job was here in London, and here we are! Good to see you, Freddie! I was sayin' to Russ here, I says: "Why, Morsham's just where that feller Fred Blogs said he comes from! Maybe we'll even bump into 'im!" That's what I said, wasn't I, Russ? And here we are! Small world, isn't it?'

'Tha's just what I was thinkin', mate! "Small world, ain't it?" Them very same words!'

'And how's life treating you, Fred? You're lookin' all dapper there, aren't you? Almost didn't recognise you, I didn't, kitted out like that!'

Ah, yes. How to explain the suit. My current white-collar ensemble doesn't really fit with my assumed Fred Blogs persona. I feel that Fred would look more at home wearing a safety helmet and an orange work jacket and standing in a hole alongside these two worthies. Caught on one foot as it were, my powers of invention fail me—I am left with no choice other than to fall back on the truth.

'Yeah, I just got me a job at the local Unemployment Centre, y'see? An' in that place they expect yer to dress up all smart-like, y'see?'

'Oh, is that what it is, eh?' says Ralph. 'Administration job, is it?'

'That's right, me old china! That's just what it is: administration. Computers, filing; all that malarkey.'

'Rather you than me, boyo!' declares Ralph. 'Still, better than not havin' any job at all, isn't it?'

I could take issue with this glib statement, but the honest fellow doesn't mean anything by it, so I let it pass; and having exchanged with Ralph and Russ those tenuous and non-binding 'see you around, then!' valedictions, I proceed on my way.

I am immediately summoned to that cursed room sixty-one, when I arrive at the Unemployment Centre. It was to this very room that I was dragged after my health issues were so summarily dismissed at that mockery of a medical examination; a cubby-hole of an office where I found myself seated before an Indian gentleman, turbaned and full-bearded, who said he had heard (certainly not from me) that I was seeking employment, and that he was very happy to offer me a position here at the Unemployment Centre, as a data entry clerk in the administration office in which he himself served as section chief. I was just opening my mouth to decline the post when he went on to inform me that if I did not accept the position, I would be transferred from my former benefits onto that pittance known as Job-Seekers Allowance, and that even this would be denied me for a period of six weeks as punishment for refusing a perfectly good job.

I revised my response and accepted the position.

That was last week. I have now been employed in the administration office for three days... So why am I suddenly being summoned back to room sixty-one?

'You're fired.'

I look at the section chief's face; the twinkling black eyes and the brown beaky nose framed between the abundance of hair and turban.

'Fired?' I squawk.

'Most regrettably yes, Mr Fortescue.'

'And may I ask why?'

'You most certainly can ask, Mr Fortescue; and I will furnish you with an answer.'

Pause.

'Well?'

'Well what, Mr Fortescue?'

'What is the answer!'

'You have yet to ask me anything, Mr Fortescue. Please submit your question.'

'Why am I being fired? *That* is my question! What else would I be asking you?'

'In answer to your second question, I have no idea as to what other questions you might put to me, as alas, I am not gifted with the power to read other people's minds; in answer to your first question, you are being fired from your position in the administration office due to the unsatisfactory nature of your work.'

'In what way has my work been unsatisfactory?' I demand.

'Cast your mind back to yesterday afternoon, Mr Fortescue, when you caused the entire computerised database to crash. Had the files not been backed up, all of our data would have been irretrievably lost. As it was, our other administrators lost several hours' worth of data entry, all of which will have to be repeated. So, as you see, it was a most inconvenient state of affairs, Mr Fortescue, and most vexing to the other staff.'

'Well, yes, but what's that got to do with me?'

'I believe it has everything to do with you, Mr Fortescue. You were interfering with the data file system, and it was this interference which caused the system to crash.'

'I was not "interfering" as you call it: I was in the process of reorganising the files under a more logical system of my own invention. If the software could not cope with my system, then it is the software that is at fault, not myself. A good workman never blames his tools.'

I pause, with the vague sense that I may have just contradicted myself here.

'Nevertheless, Mr Fortescue, you were not asked to reorganise the filing system. In fact, the data entry work you were supposed to be performing has been piling up for three days, completely unattended to.'

'Yes, but—'

'Please, Mr Fortescue. The decision has been made. You have been relieved of your duties as a data administrator. This decision cannot be reversed, I regret to say.'

'So, what happens to me?' I inquire. 'Does this mean I have to start...' I gulp: 'signing on?'

'This brings me to the good news, Mr Fortescue. No, you will not have to sign on. Another position here at the Centre has become available, and I am very happy to be able to offer you the post, very happy indeed.'

'And what is the post?'

'Benefit assessment. You will be conducting verbal interviews with benefit claimants, reviewing their circumstances, etc. It does not involve any use of computers. We think this will be a most suitable position for you, Mr Fortescue. Your verbal skills are far superior to your technical skills.'

I sit back in my chair. Conducting interviews... Yes... I can see myself doing that... As he so sapiently observes, verbal communication is indeed my forte...

'Very well. I accept.'

'Excellent, Mr Fortescue, Excellent! You will commence your new duties tomorrow.'

We shake hands. I rise and turn to the door.

'One more thing, Mr Fortescue.'

I turn back. 'Yes?'

'Please go and have your hair attended to by a hairdresser. It looks like a very disorderly bird's nest.'

One area of *The Prisoner* in which I am at variance with my friend Gillian—aside from the *Batman* comparisons, whether the black cat in 'Many Happy Returns' was meant to be the same black cat featured in 'Dance of the Dead' (filmed prior to 'Returns' but aired immediately subsequent to it; and both episodes, I might add, penned by the same writer), and one or two other trifling issues—is the matter of Patrick McGoohan's hair. Gillian insists that it was fake; that the actor wore a toupee, a hair-piece, or as she crudely phrases it, 'a rug.' Myself, I see no reason to suspect anything of the kind; but Gillian is adamant. What's more, she even claims to have proof of her assertion. And what is this proof, you ask? Nothing more than the fact that, in the 1978 *Columbo* episode 'Identity Crisis,' McGoohan played a character who confessed in the story to wearing a hairpiece! Yes, that is the extent of her so-called proof! Well, as far as I am concerned, the only thing that *Columbo* episode proves is entirely the reverse of her claim! Think about it! If Patrick McGoohan had indeed been afflicted with premature baldness and was self-conscious enough about this deficit to cover up the fact by employing a hairpiece, would he then go and announce this fact to the whole world in an episode of *Columbo*?

I rest my case.

For myself, I am blessed with a full head of hair, and with as yet nary a grey strand to be found. It is, however, inclined to be 'unmanageable.' Freshly cropped, it is fine, but give it free rein to start growing, and it begins to veer off in all directions, while stolidly refusing to be brought into line by use of comb or brush. Yes, I know that there are 'products' available to combat this affliction—gels and sprays which will discipline the most recalcitrant of thatches, but I am wary of these cosmetics. To my mind, constantly assaulting the hair that nature gave you with all these artificial—not to mention often highly flammable—compounds, seems to me to be a good way of courting that very same premature hair-loss of which I have just been speaking.

Generally, not being vain of my appearance, I am unconcerned about the state of my hair; I will occasionally wash it, run a comb through it; but otherwise I leave it pretty much to its own devices. However, I have just been given a new job which will involve me dealing with members of the public, and this, presumably, is why I have been instructed to surrender my top covering to the ministrations of a barber. When I was ensconced behind the scenes at the Unemployment Centre, it was enough that I came to work wearing a suit, but now that I will be on full display to the general public, an even higher level of personal grooming is demanded of me.

I frequent a local barber's shop, whenever my unmanageable locks are in need of the attention of a pair of scissors; the unisex salons I eschew: these establishments insist upon washing your hair before cutting it, and then demand more than double the price in return for having done this. Well, I for one am quite capable of washing my own hair in my own bathroom, and if hair *does* need to be moistened in order to be trimmed – a fact of which I am far from convinced – then the simple application of water sprayed from a bottle should suffice (and *does* suffice at my own and most other barber's establishments.)

Another factor in favour of my local barber's is that one does not need to book an appointment in advance; one just presents oneself at the shop and you are either conducted immediately to one of the chairs, or if they are all taken, have to wait but a few minutes before being attended to. At these male-only establishments there are no lengthy appointments for perming, colouring, or afro-straightening; in fact, as many of the customers will only have hair remaining on the back and sides of their craniums, a quick application of a set of clippers and few snips to straighten the edges are all that is required. It doesn't take long.

I enter at the sign of the striped pole, and find that just one customer is present, being attended to but Luigi, proprietor of the establishment.

'Randal!' he greets me cheerfully. (The fellow is chronically cheerful; I have never seen him otherwise.) 'You're looking well, my friend; looking well! Take a seat, take a seat!' And then, throwing his voice into the back-regions of the establishment: 'Customer!'

I seat myself in the vacant barber's chair indicated, and then, through the large mirror facing me, I catch sight of an Oriental woman stepping through the inner doorway into the room. She approaches me, gown in hand, and I start at the sight of her, for her features suddenly remind me of Dr Wakabayashi, that sadistic medical practitioner who so barbarously assaulted my delicate back (not to mention other areas) and then cruelly deprived me of those benefits to which I am lawfully entitled by the Welfare State, and forcing me, in spite of my disability, to seek employment. (Clement Atlee must be spinning in his grave.) However, quickly remembering the similitude of these Eastern females, I compose myself. Besides, similar in cut though the features may be, the expression here couldn't be more different; this woman is all smiles, positively glowing with good cheer. Additionally, she wears no glasses and her hair is tied loosely back in a ponytail and not severely in a bun.

'Hello!' she greets me, deftly throwing the gown around me. 'I'm Takaco, and I'll be your hairdresser today!' Adding confidentially: 'That's Takaco with one K.'

'I see,' I say. 'Takaco… A Vietnamese name, isn't it?'

'Nope! It's Japanese!' she tells me. 'What's your name?'

'Randal Fortescue.'

'Ah! Landal! Nice to meet you!'

(Not wishing to be pedantic, I let the mispronunciation slide.)

'So! What would you like for your hair?' she inquires, ruffling the commodity in question.

'Oh, just a trim,' I answer. 'Something to neaten it up. I am about to commence a new job which involves dealing with the public, so my hair must not look wild or unkempt. Neatness always encourages a belief in efficiency.'

'No problem!' declares Takaco. 'I can make your hair look good. I have advanced diploma with honours!'

'In hairdressing?' I ask.

'Yes!'

She sets to work with her scissors.

'Aren't you a tad over-qualified to be employed in such a modest barber's emporium as this?' I venture.

'I guess I am,' she says. 'I'm just here temporarily. What I want to do is open my own salon.'

'Ah; your own hairdressing salon?'

'No, a beauty salon. I'm also a trained masseuse and beautician.'

'A masseuse as well? You have many skills. And you want to open your emporium here in this district?'

'Sure! I live here now—I just moved here! I just need to find a vacant shop, and then I have to take out a loan to get started up.'

'A loan? You don't have to buy the shop, you know; you can just rent the premises.'

'Sure, but I've got to buy all my equipment and fit the place up, right?'

'True. I hadn't considered those factors. But still: the idea of borrowing a large sum of money is not one that appeals to myself. You have to pay it back; that's the catch. In fact, you have to pay back considerably more than the amount you originally borrowed; they call it "interest".'

'Well, that's how these things work,' she replies, demonstrating her Eastern fatalism. (Wait a minute. Isn't it the *Middle*-Easterns who are supposed to be fatalistic? Perhaps she's just being philosophical. Yes; that would it! Philosophy kicked off in the Far East, didn't it?)

She proceeds with her appointed task, and we enjoy one of those 'companionable silences' for a while. And then:

'So, Landal Fortescue;' and, placing her mouth close to my ear: 'Is there a *Mrs* Fortescue?'

'Well, yes, there's my mother,' I say. 'She resides in Surrey.'

'I mean, do you have a wife?' she says, resuming her hairdressing.

'A wife? Good lord, no.'

'What about a girlfriend? Do you have a girlfriend?'

'No, I do not,' I say.

Why is she asking me these things? A wife? A girlfriend? What's she getting at? Is she trying to imply that I look like someone who would not be possessed of such a boon companion? That just because I happen to be somewhat generously proportioned and perhaps not classically handsome in the arrangement of my facial features, that I would be unable to find myself a companion in life; a significant other? Is that it? Is that what she's getting at? Impudent wench! Well, I most certainly hope she will have found her salon and cleared out of this place before the time of my next appointment comes around!

'Here we go! How about this?' she says.

Her words draw my attention to my reflection in the mirror. I am staggered. I blink my eyes to ascertain if they are deceiving me. They are not—Takaco with one K has styled my hair exactly like Patrick McGoohan's!

My first client proves to be Lucky Heather, no stranger to myself or anyone else who happens to reside in the borough of Morsham. She spends so much of her days wandering the streets, that many people believe that they are actually her place of residence; however, her being here at the Unemployment Centre proves that she must in fact be possessed of a fixed abode.

She sits across the desk from me, the cosmetics as badly-applied as always to her lined and faded features: cartoon circles of rouge adorning her cheeks, her thin lips a wobbly vermilion, her eyes shaded with flaky blue. She is known hereabouts as 'Lucky Heather' on account of her external resemblance to those gypsy crones famed for going about selling the stuff: dressed in scruffy black, with the regulation misshapen hat, woollen net shawl and fingerless gloves.

That the woman is soft in the head goes without saying, and her reason for being here today proves this fact beyond a shadow of a doubt.

'So,' I say, speaking in those calm, authoritative, measured tones designed to put our clients at their ease; 'you're here because you would like to be moved from the Support Group to the Work-Related Activity Group?'

'That's right, ducky,' she replies, studying her fingernails and sounding not more than half interested.

'May I inquire as to the reason for your putting forward this request?'

'Well, I thought I'd like to do a bit of work for a change,' is the answer. 'You know, try something new, like.'

'You do realise,' I say, 'that this move would entail a considerable reduction in your weekly unemployment benefits?'

'Well, it won't matter, will it?' replies the witless Lucky one. 'When I get a job, I'll get paid for it and that'll be added onto my benefits, won't it? Therapeutic Earnings; isn't that what they call it?'

'Well, yes they do, but what you have to understand,' I proceed, speaking slowly in the hope of facilitating that desired state of comprehension; 'what you have to understand is that, being in the Work-Related Activity Group does not automatically guarantee that you will actually find work. Work placements, you see, exist only in limited numbers at any given time; they cannot be manufactured out of thin air; and thus there is, as I say, no guarantee that you will immediately find the work that you so desire.'

'And why not?' is her mild challenge. 'If there's any jobs going, I can take one or other of them, can't I? I'm not fussy, you know; anything'll suit me. Just something to make a change, you know.'

'Yes, but,' I persevere; 'even if you apply indiscriminately for any opportunities that are available, there is no guarantee that you will be accepted. There will be numerous other applicants, and someone with your, er, disadvantages, will not always be first in the queue.'

'Ooh, hark at him,' says Lucky Heather, her voice taking on a scornful note. 'And what about you, then? Sitting behind that desk with your posh new suit and fancy hair-cut. If they'll give you a job, ducky, they'll give a job to anyone.'

I smile tightly. If they'll give me a job, they'll give a job to anyone… Well, if *that's* the way you feel…! 'You know what?—please disregard everything I just said. It was wrong of me to attempt to discourage you in your laudable aspirations. I see that now, and I heartily concur with and admire your sentiments, and I shall personally do my very best to see that your application for transfer to the Work-Related Activity Group is accepted. And now, I shall bid you a very good day!'

Requiring speech with the section chief I return to the open-plan administration office in which I was briefly situated before being transferred to my current location. The section chief has his desk at the room's furthest extremity; I wend my way thither.

'Hello there!' says Darren.
'Hello,' I reply, nodding briefly as I pass his desk.
And then I pull up in my tracks.
Darren? Here? Surely my senses deceive me!

I look back. My senses do *not* deceive me. Darren Nesbit, scruffy head emerging from a starched collar, ensconced at what was previously *my* work terminal!

I walk swiftly up to him. 'What are you doing here?' I demand.

'Working,' he replies. 'This is my new job! Just started today!'

'Did you, now,' I say. 'And pray how did you come to be selected for office work?'

'They wanted someone who knows something about computers, didn't they? They want me to sort out their filing system. Seems that some twat that was working here before nearly messed-up the whole shebang!'

I wince. Not merely on account of the vulgar expletive, but the fact the expletive in question happens to have been myself. Clearly Darren is unaware of this small detail; I elect not to enlighten him, and for this once, allow his uncouth language to pass without comment.

''Ere! You got yourself a Number Six!'

'I did what?'

'Your barnet! It's like the Prisoner's!'

'Oh yes,' I say, proudly stroking the coiffure in question. 'What do you think? It rather suits me, if I say so myself.'

'Yeah! Suits you right down to the ground! What made you think of having it done like that?'

'I didn't think of it,' I confess. 'My new hairdresser cut it for me like this without my even asking. Furthermore, she knew nothing of my fondness for *The Prisoner*. Quite a coincidence, isn't it?'

'Yeah... This hairdresser: was she a Japanese lady?'

'Yes,' I reply, frowning. 'How did you know that?'

He shrugs. 'Just guessing.'

Strangely accurate guess. Does Darren know something I do not? Was perhaps Patrick McGoohan's hair stylist a Japanese female? Hmm... I shall have to look into this.

Before me are the Brown family, parents and brood. A study in urban inbreeding, they are squat and flabby in build, and with facial features which seem to have receded from chin and forehead to take up their cramped residence in the centre of the facial plane. The mother looks shrewish, the father vacuous, the half-dozen bantlings vicious.

The shrewish-one is the tribe's spokesperson.

'One lamb doner, one lamb and special, one lamb and chicken doner, one chicken, one doner meat and chips, one lamb shish, two mixed and one special, no sauce.'

'Erm…' I say. 'I am here to discuss your benefits claim, Mrs Brown. I cannot provide you and your family with comestibles.'

The woman glares at me.

'One lamb doner, one lamb and special—'

'I want a lamb n' special, an' all!' cries out one of the bantlings.

'—*Two* lamb and special, one lamb and chicken doner, one chicken, one doner meat and chips, one lamb shish, two mixed, one special, no sauce!'

'You seem to misunderstand; I am not a kebab vendor; I—'

'*One* lamb doner, *two* lamb and special, one lamb and chicken doner—'

'I don't want salad on mine!' from another bantling.

'—One lamb and chicken doner, *no* salad, one doner meat and chips, one lamb shish, two mixed, one special, no sauce!'

'I say again—'

'*One* lamb doner, *two* lamb and special, *one* lamb and chicken doner, no salad, *one* doner meat and chips, *one* lamb shish, *two* mixed, *one* special, no sauce!'

'I see,' I say, picking up notebook and pen. 'And just to clarify, is that no sauce just on the special or no sauce on all of them…?'

And now I have to deal with a thug. Built like the proverbial outhouse; neck thicker than his head; Cro-Magnon brows; doubtless an enforcer for the local criminal fraternity.

'Yeah, I been feeling real depressed lately, y'know?' says the oaf, affecting—or attempting to affect—a doleful tone. 'Really down in the dumps. I got no energy; I can't concentrate on nothin'; I'm scared to go out of the 'ouse. I just feel really miserable all the time; an' I worry about things, y'know? I went to see me doctor about it, an 'e says it's depression an' anxiety. That's what it is…'

Depression, indeed. You need to have intelligence in order to experience depression; you need to have a fully functional cerebral cortex capable of reflecting as well as reacting; you need to have an IQ rating that is in more than two figures. Depression indeed. Listen to him. You can hear the quotation marks. He's just reeling off a speech that someone with slightly more acumen than himself has given him.

Depression and back problems. These, they say, are the two conditions most easy to counterfeit for those wishing to affect a disability, in order to avoid seeking employment. The criminal fraternity is well aware of this fact, so they drill their members into being able to verbally describe the symptoms of one or other of these ailments in order to obtain disability benefits. And they don't carry out this fraud merely for the sake of the money—being criminals they already have their own very lucrative sources of income: but they cannot just declare themselves self-employed and leave it at that; for then they would be liable for taxation. Nor would they care to be on the Job-Seekers' Allowance track, as this would entail upon them the inconvenience of appearing to be seeking work, of accepting temporary employment that was offered to them—therefore, the most convenient course open for these hoodlums is to get themselves put on the sick list.

And this is precisely what my client here is attempting to do. He's learned his lines well enough to fool his GP it seems; but in thinking he can pull the wool over the eyes of Randal C Fortescue, he has made a grave error. Why, it is on account of the actions of people like this that the benefits adjudicators are so suspicious of the validity of the claims they receive—and which in short has led directly to the termination of my own disability allowance.

As if I would allow this cretin, this small-time gangster, claim those very same disability benefits that have only recently been cruelly taken away from myself; when it is because of people like him that I am placed where I am right now, forced to sit for hours at a time in this chair at heaven knows what long-term cost to my bodily health…!

Well, you reap what you sow, as this fine fellow is about to learn to his cost!

'So, you have received a medical note from your general practitioner?' I inquire.

'You what?'

I sigh. 'Have you got a sick note from your doctor?'

'Yeah, I 'ave,' he says. 'I need time off work, I do. Lots of time. That's what 'e says, the doc. Says I should be on debility benefits, 'e does.'

'*Disa*bility benefits,' I say.

'Yeah, them. So that's what I'm 'ere for. I wanna be put on them debility benefits, so I don't 'ave to work or nothin'.'

'Yes, but you see, it isn't quite as simple as that,' I tell him, concealing an inward chuckle. 'You can't just come in here, request to paid certain benefits and then automatically be granted them; there is a protocol that has to be followed—'

The Cro-Magnon brows grow heavy. 'You what?'

'There is a procedure. Steps that have to be taken. Firstly, you will need to be assessed—'

'Tha's what you're doin' now, innit?' he demands. 'I've come to this appointment, and I'm tellin' you about me problems, ain't I?'

'Yes, but this is just the initial meeting. I am here to receive your claim and then you have to undergo an assessment—'

'Then bloody assess me, then!'

'—*conducted by a medical professional*,' I say. 'I am not a medical professional. You will need to be seen by a doctor—'

'I've already seen me fuckin' doctor, ain't I? It's 'im what sent me 'ere! Now just put me down for them debility benefits!'

'I cannot do that for you—'

He grabs me by the collar with a leg-of-mutton fist and rising from his seat, forces me likewise into the perpendicular.

'Now listen,' he says, his breeze-block face inches from mine. 'I got depression, right? I'm too poorly to work, right? Tha's what me doctor says, right? So just gimme those fuckin' benefits, an' stop messin' me around, right?'

He shakes me to emphasise his point.

'I shall endeavour to do what I can,' I gasp.

'You do that!' he says, and with a final shake for good measure, he takes his leave.

I am not long in following him from the room—I feel one of my sudden and imperative bowel movements coming on!

'Fucking piece of shit! Think you're so fucking clever, don't you? Think you're smarter than everyone else, you cunt? Wanker! Fucking piece of shit-fucking cunt-raping, shitting—'

This barrage of obscenity reaches my ears as I am about to knock on the door of my friend Darren's flat. The voice within is certainly that of Darren, but I almost don't recognise it; I do not recall that I have ever even heard Darren's voice raised in anger, and this is considerably more than anger: this is insensate, shrieking, delirious rage!

But who on earth is he shouting *at*? I can discern no other voice.

I decide to knock. Whatever the source, whoever the subject, I think it will be timely and prudent on my part to interrupt this altercation.

And interrupt it I do. The screeching ceases with my knocking. Silence follows. I can hear no sounds from within the apartment. Has Darren approached the door? If so then the spyhole should assure him that the caller is only myself, and not an irate neighbour.

Apparently this is so. The door opens slowly and Darren's face appears in the gap; a flushed, agitated face, with traces of spittle around the mouth.

'What do you want?' His voice is morose, subdued.

I assume a friendly smile to put the fellow at his ease. 'What do I want? Have you forgotten the day? The hour? It is time for our weekly luncheon with Gillian at the Chaplain of the Fleet! Happening to be making my way thence, I decided to take a slight detour in order to call for you, just in case you'd forgotten. And it seems I did well to make this detour! You'd forgotten, hadn't you?'

'Yeah, I… I can't make it today…' says Darren. 'I'm… I've… got something on… I'm… busy…'

I drop the unconcerned façade. 'Is something the matter, Darren?' I inquire with solicitude. 'Is there someone in there with you? When I arrived, I thought perhaps I detected the sounds of an altercation…?'

Darren's face starts to twitch. 'No-one's here,' he says. 'I mean… that is… I'm busy, okay? Maybe next time…'

'Look, Darren, if something is troubling you, perhaps I can be of some assistance? You know you only have to ask—?'

'Nothing's wrong. 'Bye.'

He closes the door in my face.

'Oh look! It's Fred Flintstone without Barney Rubble!'

These are the words with which Gillian greets me when I arrive at the Chaplain of the Fleet. Having arrived first, she has secured our 'usual table.' Also as usual, she has a pint of beer in front of her. Drinking at lunchtime! And she has to go back to work after this!

I sit down and take a refreshing sip of my glass of coke.

'If you are commenting upon the absence of Darren, he is unable to make it today,' I tell her.

'What's up?' inquires Gillian.

At first I hesitate, but I quickly decide to give her the pure unvarnished truth; the incident with Darren has left me strangely ill at ease; I feel the need of a confidant.

She looks suitably troubled by my account. 'And he was screaming and swearing at someone?' she summarises, brows knitted. 'And there wasn't anyone else in the flat with him?'

'Correction: I said I could not *hear* anyone else. However, Darren could have been untruthful when he declared that he was alone.'

'But who the fuck could it have *been*?' demands Gillian, lapsing into vulgarity in the heat of the moment, as she so often does. 'He doesn't even know many people, does he?'

'I believe his circle of acquaintance to be somewhat limited, yes,' I concur.

Gillian starts to gulp down her pint. (And if she hopes to facilitate her thought processes by imbibing that poison, she is sadly mistaken.)

'What about family?' she asks, having come back up for air. 'Has he got any family he doesn't get on with?'

'I'm not aware that he has much contact with members of his family. He rarely mentions them in conversation.'

'He's he got any pets?'

'Pets?' I explode. 'What in the name of sanity have *pets* got to do with anything? Pets don't *speak*—aside from parrots and other such birds, of course; but they are just mimicking sounds, so one cannot really consider speech with those avians to be conversation in any meaningful sense.'

'I know that, you wally. But, people like Darren, you know—misfits; sometimes when they get angry, they can start taking it out on their pets; I mean really going all out and swearing at them, just like you heard him doing.'

'I see your point, but unfortunately Darren does not possess any pet or pets, so we can dismiss that possibility.'

Gillian clicks her fingers. 'I know! He was on the internet! He was swearing at someone online!'

I rub my chin thoughtfully. 'Yes, that could be a possibility; but nevertheless, I would have thought the other person's responses would have been audible to myself.'

'No, I don't mean he was talking to someone on a webcam link or anything. He was probably just messaging—a type-written conversation; and the person he was chatting with wrote something he didn't like: and that's what set him off! Yeah, that's gotta be it!'

'A plausible deduction,' I concede, choosing to ignore her lapse in grammar. 'But then, why couldn't he have just told me about it? Why not just join us here for lunch as usual? You would have thought he would have appreciated the opportunity to get away from his internet correspondent and focus his mind on something else.'

'Yeah, but sometimes when you're worked up like that, you just don't feel like socialising. You want to shut yourself off from people.'

A plausible conjecture. However, at this juncture the comestibles we have ordered arrive, and we both turn from discussing Darren's behaviour to discussing our food. We have both opted for the traditional fish and chips, a dish at which this establishment excels.

'I'll tell you something funny,' says Gillian, presently.

'Please do,' I say.

'Right. Well, you know I'm reading that book by Andrew Pixley…'

'*What* book by Andrew Pixley?' I ask.

'His book about *The Prisoner*, you prawn.'

Andrew Pixley is a noted television historian. His book about *The Prisoner*, written to accompany the fortieth anniversary DVD boxset, is, while undeniably informative and scrupulously researched, a rather dry and colourless catalogue of information concerning the making of the series; not to be compared in any way with my own work-in-preparation, which will be an achievement of an entirely superior order.

'Oh, yes. What about it?'

'It was something he said about *A Day in the Life* that made me smile.'

A Day in the Life—one of the original trilogy of *Prisoner* novels; in fact the very one with that lamentable scrotum reference of which I have previously had occasion to mention.

'And what might that have been?' I inquire. 'Doubtless it referred to that dubious reference to the Prisoner's—'

'It was nothing to do with the scrotum reference!' snaps Gillian. 'Christ! You're *obsessed* with that; you never shut up about it!'

'I am *not* obsessed with it,' I retort. 'I merely find it to be a crude and unnecessary reference, upon which I *may* have happened to pass comment once or twice before in your presence—twice at the most. To suggest that I would be obsessed with one vulgar—'

'And would you stop talking with your mouth full!' interrupts Gillian, rather rudely. 'I'm getting sprayed with your secondary food here!'

A gross exaggeration on her part, needless to say.

'Look; just shut up and let me finish my story, okay?' she proceeds.

'Very well.'

'Ta. Well, you know that bit in the book where he has to kill those three people who collectively are supposed to be

Number One, yeah? And one of them's that Sir Charles whatsisname—'

'Sir Charles *Portland*,' I inform her. 'Father of—'

'Look, who's telling this fucking story?' she flares up again. (It doesn't take much to set her off.)

'I was merely—'

'Just let me *finish*,' she growls.

'Very well,' I sigh. 'Proceed.'

'Right. Well, get this: Pixley thought that the Sir Charles that the Prisoner shot was a *robot*.'

At this, she bursts into laughter.

'Just shows you, doesn't it?' she chuckles. 'He may be an expert at picking up facts and figures about archive television, but he's not so hot when it comes to interpreting experimental fiction, is he?'

Her mirth evaporates when she sees that I am not participating in it.

'Well, don't you think it's funny?' she says.

'I see nothing to be amused about,' I tell her, icily. 'The Sir Charles Portland that Number Six killed in that novel *was* a robot.'

'You what?'

'I suggest you peruse the text again. When you come to the chapter in question you will see that it clearly states that there was copper wiring visible inside the head that had been punctured by the bullet. Ergo, he was a robot.'

'No, you wally!' exclaims Gillian. 'What the author meant was that there was copper wiring inside his head *as well* as all the brains and stuff! It was like saying he was being controlled; that he had some kind of implant in there!'

'Nonsense,' I retort. 'The real Sir Charles Portland had been replaced with a robot duplicate in order to thwart the Prisoner's attempt to assassinate the three men who collectively comprised Number One. *That* was what the author was telling us.'

Gillian sits back in her chair, making some silly aggrieved noise. 'God! You're as bad as Pixley is! You just don't get it, do you?'

'On the contrary, it is *you* who fail to discern the woods on account of the intervening timber,' I tell her.

This argument serves to occupy us for the remainder of our luncheon—and Gillian remains obdurate; she just will not listen to reason; she insists on her fanciful notion that it was the real Sir Charles Portland whom the Prisoner assassinated and that the fellow had some kind of arrangement of copper wiring wrapped around his cerebral cortex.

When we step out of the pub onto the street, I immediately espy my hairdresser, Takaco with one K. She stands on the pavement a few yards off, arms akimbo, and glares at me wrathfully. The look of accusation in those epicanthic eyes puzzles me. What can I have possibly done to incur the woman's ire? Is it my hair? In combing it, have I somehow disarranged it from the style to which her deft scissors had moulded it five days before? Up until now I had believed I had diligently and faithfully retained the precise line and contour of the hairstyle with which I had emerged from the hair emporium—but perhaps not; perhaps I have erred in my personal grooming.

'Excuse me one moment,' I say to Gillian, and make my way to where my mute accuser stands, patting and adjusting my hair as I do so.

'Is something wrong with it?' I ask. 'If it is my hair, I've done my best to—'

'Who's she?' demands Takaco, thrusting out an accusing finger.

The accusing finger is directed at Gillian. Gillian's face wears that confused look of someone who can see that they are being pointed at, but is unable to determine why. Hers eyes turn to me for elucidation. I wish I could help her.

'"Who's she?"' I echo.

'Yeah: who's she?' repeats my accuser.

'Why, that's Gillian—'

'When I cut your hair, you told me you didn't have girlfriend! That's what you said to me, Landal Fortescue! No girlfriend! And now I see you with a girl! You lie to me!'

'I did not lie to you!' I protest helplessly. 'Gillian is just a good friend of mine. We have been acquainted for years. We live in the same apartment building—'

'Then why were you in the pub with her?'

'In the pub? Why, we always meet here for luncheon of a Saturday. It is a regular fixture. Usually there would be three of us, but today my friend Darren—'

'She not your girlfriend?'

'Certainly not!'

She appears only grudgingly mollified. 'You better not be lying to me…'

'I can assure I am not…'

'Hmph,' she says, and turns on her heel. Then, as if remembering something, she comes back, slaps a piece of pasteboard into my hand and then makes a second retreat, this time uninterrupted.

I look at the pasteboard. It is a business card:

SAKURA BEAUTY & MASSAGE PARLOUR
Proprietor – Takaco (with one K)
144 Blythe Street, Morsham

So, she has secured a location for emporium and the necessary funds to take out the lease already? That was quick work!

'What was all that about?' asks Gillian, who has joined me.

I show her the business card.

'Hm. Pretty aggressive way she's got of touting for customers,' she remarks. 'And what was she pointing at me for? Was she telling you I looked like someone who was overdue for a beauty treatment, or something? Cheeky cow!'

'It wasn't that,' I assure her. 'Although I'm certain you *could* benefit from availing yourself of a beauty treatment. No, Takaco was angry because she thought you were my girlfriend.'

'And what the hell's that got to do with her?'

'Well, nothing; except that when she cut my hair—'

'Oh! She was the girl who gave you your Patrick McGoohan cut!'

'Yes, and while performing that operation she happened to inquire of me whether or not I was in a relationship with a member of the opposite sex at the present time, to which I of course answered in the negative. Seeing me with you made her think I had uttered a falsehood on that score.'

'And *that's* what she was so worked up about?'

'For some reason, yes. Don't ask me why. There are aspects of the female psyche I have never been able to fathom.'

'You wally!' says Gillian, grinning all over. 'Don't you get it? She was *jealous*. She fancies you! *That's* why she asked you if you were seeing anyone! And that's why she so was pissed off when she saw you with me!'

'Fancies' me? Takaco with one K...? 'Fancies...?'As in has feelings for... as in, being in... love with...

In love with... me...

Preposterous!

Chapter Five
How I Became a Schizoid Man

'You see, the trouble is, Miss Hayes, you are simply not eligible for the benefits accruing to the terminally ill, as you are by all accounts in very good physical health, and no danger of imminent decease...'

In flagrant disregard of both professional etiquette and social distancing, Lucinda Hayes has planted her rump upon my desk, and brought the glossy brown expanse of her uppermost thigh into painfully close proximity to my seated self. In addition to this I can also smell her perfume—and while the scent is by no means an unpleasant one, the fact that she is close enough for me to be able to smell it so powerfully is an alarming one.

Lucinda Hayes is a black woman, and built on those very substantial lines not uncommon with females of her ethnicity: all legs, buttocks and breasts; everything aggressively curvaceous. She has straightened hair, long and plenty of it, adorned with a hat, and is dressed—barely—in boots, shorts and halter top.

'But I don't see why people who are gunna die anyway need all that money,' she proceeds, in her coaxing, seductive tones. 'It's just a waste of good money, isn't it? It'd be much better to give it to someone like me who knows how to spend it, right? Me, I know how to get the most out of life.'

'I'm sure you do, and very commendable of you,' I say, eager to placate the creature. 'But sadly, *joie de vivre* is not one of the criteria taken into consideration when allocating financial support…'

'Yeah, but you'll help me, won't you?' she coos. 'You're such a sweet guy, aren't you? I just love big, roly-poly teddy bears like you…'

She leans over the desk bringing her flagrant and alarming cleavage into close proximity to my eyes.

'You'll help me, won't you…?'

She tugs at the hem of her top, exposing still more of those voluminous breasts, where the smooth brown flesh gives way to the greater darkness of…

I spring from my seat with such alacrity that I send the thing spinning back against the wall.

'Well, I shall certainly take your request into consideration,' I say, as I edge rapidly around the desk and to the door of the office. 'I shall ensure that it is given the highest priority. And so, all you need to do now, Miss Hayes, is return home, and wait for a postal communication from the Department of Works and Pensions, which I hope will be a favourable one. But for now, I shall bid you good day.'

And with that I open the door and usher myself out of the room. Shutting the door firmly behind me, I now make a swift beeline to the staff toilet facilities. One of my sudden movements is coming on.

This is really intolerable! First, I have Gillian suggesting that my hairdresser harbours romantic feelings towards me, and now I have to endure this Hayes female utilising her feminine charms in order to cajole me into awarding her benefits intended only for the terminally ill! It's enough to irritate anybody's bowels.

I enter the Gents and gaining the sanctuary of an unoccupied toilet cubicle, I sit down to collect myself and relieve myself.

'Pssst!' comes a voice from the cubicle to my right. And then, in an urgent whisper: 'It's me!'

'Oh, is that you, Darren?' I reply. 'You don't have to whisper, you know. This isn't a public library.'

'It's not Darren, it's me!' replies the urgent whisper.

Me? Who's "me"? And then I realise; I recognise the voice: it is my unseen interlocutor from the toilets of Portmeirion!

'You again!'

'Yes; me!'

'Look, if this is going to be another one of your practical jokes—'

'This isn't a joke, you fool! I was deadly serious back then, and I'm deadly serious now!'

'You say that, but how do I know that wasn't some prank perpetrated by you and that Chinese female—'

'That was no prank! You were in deadly danger! You were lucky we managed to smuggle you out of the Village in time!'

'Well, as you say, I *did* get out; therefore I escaped whatever danger—'

'You're *still* in danger! Don't you see? They've followed you; they've taken over this place; and now they've got you working for them!'

His words send a chill down my spine.

'They're here? In the Unemployment Centre?'

'Yes! They've taken over—and they did it just so that they could get at you. They stopped your benefits, and made it so that you'd be forced to work for them right here! They're trying to break you down! That's how they deal with potential threats! They'll grind you down—and before you know it, you'll be turned into one of their drones! I know; believe me, I know! That's just what they did to me!'

'And just who are you?' I demand. 'What's your name?'

'My name? I haven't got a name anymore: I'm just a number. And by the time they've finished with you, you'll be just a number as well; you'll be the new Number Six!'

'Number Six!'

'Yes, Number Six! That's the number they've got reserved for you!'

This is appalling. I tremble on my seat. My escape from the Village: it was real after all. I had almost come to believe Gillian's story that the entire affair had been some elaborate practical joke perpetrated against myself—but it was real after all. Of course it was! No-one has come forward to admit responsibility; and what would be the point of successfully pulling the wool of someone's eyes if you never undeceived them? There would be no point to it at all, if you never let your victim know that he'd been duped! Yes, it had all been real: I *had* been in peril when I had been foolish enough to enter the precincts of Portmeirion; and I had been helped to escape from that peril…

But now my enemies have followed me back to London.

Yes, it all makes sense. That letter announcing my benefits reassessment arriving the very next day after my return; that flagrantly biased and inhumane medical examination to which I had been subjected, and which had resulted in the cessation of all my financial assistance; and then my promptly being compelled to accept employment here in the Unemployment Centre—Yes, it all makes sense! My enemies, by no means prepared to give up after my having successfully eluded their clutches on their home territory, have followed me back to mine! They are still determined to break me down, to crush my resistance and make me one of their mindless drones!

The very thing Gillian joked about—and it's actually true! The ramifications are staggering. I feel like I am sitting not upon a friendly toilet seat, but upon a fizzing bomb!

'B-but, w-what can I do?' I stammer.

'You've got to fight back,' says my interlocutor. 'I've warned you now, so you've got an edge over them. You're not oblivious anymore; you're onto them. You need to stay alert. Let them think you're conforming, while all the while you're watching, planning, looking for a way to turn the tables on them. Keep your eyes open.'

'But I'll need evidence...' I say.

'You trust the evidence of your own eyes, don't you?'

'Well, yes, of course...'

'Then you can get all the evidence you want, right where you are now!'

'What, in this toilet cubicle?'

'It's *not* a toilet cubicle, you fool!'

I look around me. It certainly *looks* like a toilet cubicle. And more to the point, I trust that it is because I've been using it as though it were one!

'Take hold of the handle on the cistern,' instructs my neighbour. 'Pull it up instead of down—*then* you'll get your proof! Go on: do it!'

Pull the handle upwards...? Reaching behind me, I grasp the handle and pull...

Suddenly I am sent spinning round and I find myself, although still firmly seated on the toilet, no longer in the toilet cubicle; before me stretches a corridor. And it is not one of the ubiquitous drab-painted functional corridors of the Unemployment Centre; this corridor looks like that of a stately home. The floor is richly carpeted. The walls are panelled and gilded, hung with framed oil paintings. Crystal chandeliers hang from the moulded ceiling.

And here am I, exposed, trousers round my ankles, sitting on a completely unconcealed toilet at the end of this corridor.

Fortunately for my dignity there is no-one around.

I confess that for a moment I sit mouth agape, unable to move or form any lucid plan of action. However, this moment quickly passes, and when it does my first thought is that I have seen enough for the time being and it would be wise to return to my previous location before anyone appears. With this in mind, I reach back and once more pull the flush mechanism upwards.

Nothing happens.

For a moment I am nonplussed, but then it occurs to me that perhaps in order to make the return journey to the toilet cubicle, the handle must need to be turned the other way.

With one such as myself, to think is to act and I depress the lever without hesitation.

The toilet flushes noisily.

A curse on that informant of mine! Instead of just *telling* me to pull the lever upwards, why couldn't he have verbally explained to me what would *happen* if I were to pull the lever upwards? Then I could have had time to prepare myself; time to make myself presentable and formulate a plan of campaign. Instead, here I am catapulted straight into this situation, with myself in a most undignified and vulnerable position and with my—ahem—smell—rapidly permeating the immediate area.

I rise to my feet and button and belt myself. Still nobody has appeared. Nor is there any sound to indicate the proximity of human beings.

Just where am I? Clearly some concealed portion of the Unemployment Centre; an area hidden from both the general public and lowly employees such as myself. The sumptuous décor reminds me of the corridors of the Town Hall in the *Prisoner* episode 'Dance of the Dead.' Number Six, when the Town Hall was opened on the night of the carnival, took the opportunity to explore the place, and discovered many rooms and passageways concealed from public view.

Has my informant sent me here expecting me to undertake some similar voyage of discovery? All very well. I asked for proof and here I have it with a vengeance. But what if I am caught in this place? My ability to resist the forces of the Village hinges on them not knowing that *I* know that they have established themselves here; if they catch me in these concealed regions, my cover will be blown. And then, who knows what measures they might resort to in order to ensure my silence and cooperation?

Yes. Clearly my priority must be, not to perform a thorough exploration, but to find a way out of here back to the more public areas of the building, before I am missed.

Yes. This is what I must do; and as quickly as possible.

After making another fruitless attempt with the flush mechanism to trigger the rotating wall, I set off along the corridor. My smell still hangs heavy in the air and I find myself wishing I had a can of air freshener about my person. I must remind myself to carry such an item at all times from henceforth; you never know when an emergency will arise which will require the use of air freshener.

One of the portraits on the wall attracts my attention: a military figure, circa nineteenth century. There is something about the cut of the uniform and the square-cut beard that suggests that this officer was not an Englishman; Prussian, perhaps. But the most jarringly incongruous element is the savage frown fixed upon the fellow's face; his eyes positively glare at you. Now why would anyone have had themselves painted with such a fierce expression fixed upon their countenance? It defies all common sense.

I move on. Still there is no sight or sound of human proximity, but perhaps this is not surprising; this concealed region would be unknown to the majority of the staff employed here—there will be only an elite few who have access to these corridors. All well and good. This increases my chances of being able to remove myself from the vicinity without being discovered.

At its terminus, the corridor itself branches off to the left and the right, while facing me are a pair of ornate doors. Even as I pause to decide which branch of the corridor it might be most judicious to follow, I am disturbed by the double doors opening of their own accord.

No-one emerges from within the portals; it seems that it is my own proximity which has caused them to open. The room beyond is in darkness, but as I take a step forward electric lighting flickers into life, revealing before me a rectangular chamber with the walls on either side lined with cabinets. The intervening area is occupied by a long table and a number of tall-backed chairs. I take another step into the room. The chairs and table both wear a venerable aspect. The filing cabinets lining the walls extend from floor to ceiling, and are composed of wood, the drawers very small in size. Drawers for index cards, perhaps. I attempt to open some of the drawers, but they all seem to be locked.

Thinking I have seen enough, I am about to exit the room when a concealed door in the rear wall opens before my eyes. I cross the intervening space to see what lies beyond this door, and I find myself looking into a cramped stairwell. Both stairs and stairwell are whitewashed. An ebony bust of some venerable sage reposes in a niche.

The Prisoner discovered a hidden stairwell such as this in 'Dance of the Dead.' The stairs before me descend. I am currently on the first floor of the Unemployment Centre; therefore, these stairs might lead me to a corresponding hidden exit emerging perhaps in a storeroom or cupboard; and from which I will be able to return to my office in safety, and with no-one the wiser of the journey I have taken into the hidden realms!

Yes. I will take the stairs. If I were to return to the corridor without, my chances of being discovered would be much greater.

I descend the narrow corkscrew staircase. It seems to take longer than I would expect, considering that the distance is only one floor; but perhaps this is due to the confined dimensions of the staircase and the small size of the steps. I at last reach the foot of the steps, whereupon another wall panel obligingly opens before me, and I step out into what is clearly not the storeroom or broom cupboard I had anticipated, but a bright and open corridor. This corridor, windowless, and the walls metal in construction, is very familiar to me. It is identical in its conformation to the futuristic corridors of the Town Hall depicted in the *Prisoner* episode 'The General.' This is not what I wanted. I am not back in the official regions of the Unemployment Centre at all; I am still most indubitably in the 'off-limits' area. And moreover, in corridors such as these one expects to see uniformed guards patrolling and guarding them; guards wearing grey overalls, tinted glasses and white helmets and boots—in short, the armed forces belonging to the Village!

I quickly decide that I was better off where I was back upstairs. I turn to renter the stairwell, but the cursed sliding door closes in my face! I vainly try to reopen the door by tapping the walls, swiping thin air in the hope of interrupting sensor beams; but all, alas, without avail. My retreat has been cut off.

I am standing roughly midway down this featureless corridor; at one end terminating with a pair of bright orange doors—and at the other joining an intersection of corridors.

Deciding that the orange doors are more suggestive of a swift exit from this place, I proceed towards them. The doors possess round, glazed windows, and when I peer through one of them I discover, not an exit from this place, but what appears to be some kind of operating theatre. A swathed figure lies supine on an operating table, surrounded by electronic consoles, all linked together by cables. The patient is alone; the room has no other occupants.

The intersection it is, then. I turn to retrace my steps, but am brought up in my tracks by the sound of approaching footsteps; swift, regular footsteps; military footsteps. Guards! Who else can it be? And they will soon be in sight! And when they come in sight of me, I, perforce, will be in sight of them!

This must be avoided at all costs. To enter the operating theatre and conceal myself behind one of the consoles is the work of a moment.

Over the pings and bleeps of the medical consoles I can no longer hear the footsteps without, so I wait with baited breath. Will the patrolling guards enter this room, or will they continue along the other arm of the corridor...?

A minute passes. A second one joins it. No one enters the room. The only sound is the electronic heartbeat of the medical consoles. I heave a sigh of relief. Clearly the guards did not intend to come this way.

I now stand up and the nearby bed and its occupant quite naturally command my attention. The head is completely concealed by bandages, and the body, which looks to be rather heavyset, is covered by a light sheet. For a horrible moment I wonder if I am sharing the room with a corpse, but then I detect a slight respiration. It appears that the patient is sleeping, most likely under heavy sedation. This would explain the lack of reaction to my advent. (Even ears muffled by bandages would surely have heard me enter the room.)

Who can it be...? The bandaged head and the plethora of electronic devices suggest intensive care... Perhaps the victim of some horrible accident...?

Too late I become aware of a presence behind me; I start to turn, my eyes catch a fleeting glimpse of a white-gloved hand, upraised, wielding a truncheon—and then an explosion of pain in my occiput and I start to fall...

'...And then, when I regained consciousness, I found myself lying in my own bed.'

Our Saturday luncheon meeting at the Chaplain of the Fleet. On this occasion Darren has condescended to grace us with his presence. I am relating my extraordinary adventures in the secret corridors of the Unemployment Centre—and find myself playing to a very sceptical audience.

'And there we have the explanation,' declares Gillian. 'It was a dream, you pillock. You just dreamt the whole bloody thing!'

'I did nothing of the kind,' I retort.

'Then how do you explain waking up in your bed?' she challenges.

'I would have thought that would have been obvious,' I say. 'After being incapacitated by the blow to the head, I was removed to my own apartment and placed in my own bed.'

'And why would they go to all that trouble?'

'Equally obvious, I would have thought: they wanted me to *believe* my experience had been but a dream. Clearly, they have fooled *you* into believing that, but they haven't fooled *me*.'

'But—'

'No, listen,' I insist. 'If it was a dream, then where does the dream begin? At what point? It is a fact that I was interviewing that nymphomaniac Hayes woman that afternoon; that will be on my work record. If you argue that my dream began subsequent to this, and with my conversation in the Gentlemens with my unseen correspondent from Portmeirion: then what has happened to my *real* memories of what occurred after I dismissed myself from Miss Hayes's presence? Hm? What happened to them? Can't answer that one, can you?'

'You probably just went to the crapper, came out again, and then finished up at work and went home; same as you do every other day. Nothing special happened to make it stand out, so you think you don't remember it at all. That's all it'll be.'

'Poppycock!' I reply. 'I tell you, it's the forces of the Village at work! They've taken over the Unemployment Centre and now they've got both Darren and my good self in their clutches!' I turn to Darren for confirmation. 'Isn't that right? We both know how things have changed in that place since our return from Portmeirion, don't we? Explain to this female!'

'Well, I...' begins Darren.

'Okay, Darren. Has anything weird happened to you since you've been working there?' Gillian asks him.

'Well, not really...' says Darren.

'I don't see why you have to be so disbelieving,' I tell Gillian. 'You yourself suggested the possibility that the forces of the Village had arranged my sudden medical assessment!'

'I suggested that as a *joke*!' insists Gillian. 'I didn't seriously believe it; and I still don't! And doesn't it seem strange that everything seems to happen to you and not to Darren? He's been right there with you both times: he was with you in Portmeirion, and he's with you at the Unemployment Centre... How come he doesn't see anything? How come everything only happens to you?'

'Because *I'm* the one they're interested in, of course!'

'Yeah... About that... Have you thought about...? I mean, maybe you should...?'

I see an uncharacteristic look of hesitancy upon her features.

'Maybe I should what?' I demand.

'You know... go and see your doctor...'

'WHAT?' I thunder. 'Are you suggesting that I have taken leave of my senses? That I am suffering from paranoid delusions, perhaps? That I am losing my grip on reality, and am becoming increasingly unable to determine that which is reality from that which is merely an illusion conjured up by a mind discomposed?'

'Well, yes I am' says Gillian. 'Maybe you've been working too hard. I mean, you're not used to it, are you? Working. It could be getting to you more than you think it is.'

'"Getting to me,"' I sneer. 'And what about my experiences in Portmeirion? Do you dismiss those too, as a delusion brought on by overwork? Because those events occurred before I commenced my current employment! Or had you forgotten?'

'Of course I hadn't forgotten,' says Gillian. 'Someone played a joke on you there; but you think it wasn't just a joke, so maybe that's what's triggered your delusions.'

'But I am *not* delusional! What about the announcement system they have installed at the Unemployment Centre; with the chimes and the voice that sound exactly like those of the Village announcement system in *the Prisoner*? That is there for all the world to see—or hear. You've been there, haven't you? You've heard it for yourself?'

Gillian declines to respond, and I see discomfiture is written on her features. Yes, she knows she cannot deny the fact of the announcement system!

Our food arrives.

'...Alexis Kanner clearly stated that they had proposed a sequel; that it would have involved himself as Number Forty-Eight, Leo Mckern's former Number Two and the diminutive butler Angelo Muscat. Patrick McGoohan would only have served behind the camera and the opening episode would have been set against the backdrop of the Tokyo Olympics.'

'Yeah, but you can't take everything Alexis Kanner said as gospel,' insists Gillian.

'And why not?' I retort. 'I have no reason to consider that worthy performer to have been an habitual liar.'

'I didn't say he was an *habitual* liar,' says Gillian (backing down, clearly!) 'But sometimes these celebrities, when they're reminiscing, they make stuff up; they like to embellish the past.'

'Embellish the past?' I echo disdainfully.

'Yeah! I mean, I once heard Kanner talking about doing the rollercoaster scene in 'The Girl who was Death,' and he talked about actually being on the rollercoaster with Patrick McGoohan; but it's pretty obvious when you watch it that McGoohan wasn't even there with them when they filmed at that fairground; he had a location double, and when the camera was actually on him, it was just back projection.'

'He may merely have misremembered the incident; after the lapse of so many years, it is surely understandable that he might be incorrect in his reminiscences as to minor details of that nature. But there is a great deal of difference between that and your accusation of him having manufactured the premise of a non-existent proposed sequel series entirely out of his imagination.'

Gillian sighs. 'Alright; forget it, then. You know, there *was* going to be a sequel. I don't mean the one Kanner talked about; this was a different one. This is one they were going to do in the eighties, and in it Patrick McGoohan would have been gassed in his apartment again, and this time he would've woken up to find himself locked up in an Australian women's prison—they were going to call it *The Prisoner – Cell Block H.*'

I frown. This is news to me. 'An Australian women's prison? But why would they do that? Was the proposed series going to be financed by one of the Australian television networks?'

Gillian grins broadly. I can see she is savouring having possession of this knowledge of which I myself knew nothing.

'Yeah, it was,' she says. 'Grundy were going to payroll it; and they were going to film it over there.'

'Hm…' I ponder this, wondering why Gillian has never thought to advise me of this information before. 'But why a *women's* penitentiary? How could McGoohan have been accepted as a legitimate inmate in such an institution?'

'Ah, well that would have been one of the mysteries running through the series.'

'I see…' This is fascinating information. I shall have to look into this further.

A spluttering noise draws my attention to Darren. He appears to be having a fit of some kind.

'And what's wrong with you?' I inquire, annoyed for some reason.

'Nothing, nothing,' he says, grinning stupidly. 'Just my hay fever.'

It comes time for us to leave the public house. Having risen from my chair, I stoop to pick up the carrier bag containing some items I had purchased from the shops before coming here—and the most indescribably excruciating pain suddenly lances up my back. Such is the agony that I utter a bellow of pain which disturbs the clientele of the house. All eyes are turned in my direction

'What's up with you?' inquires Gillian, with a frankly insulting air of unconcern. 'Your back playing up again?'

'"Playing up"?' I reply, gasping. '"Playing up?" It's agony! Sheer agony!'

I manage to straighten up and the pain begins to subside.

'But your back's always giving you agony,' says the callous one. 'You don't usually start bellowing like a cow in labour every time you get a twinge.'

A 'twinge' indeed!

Darren speaks up. 'Yeah, it's almost like his back's never really been hurting him at all until just now, ain't it?'

I glare at him. 'No-one asked you for your two penn'orth, Nesbit.' I try to move and the pain renews its assault. 'Ow, ow, ow!'

'Is it upper or lower back?' inquires Gillian.

'Lower,' I tell her.

'Then you probably just pulled a muscle when you were bending over. You're supposed to bend with your knees instead of with your back when you're picking something up; you ought to know things like that.'

'Yeah, it's almost like he's never really known about 'aving a bad back until now—'

'Will you shut up, Nesbit?' His impudence is really getting out of hand. 'Just call me an ambulance.'

'You don't need a fucking ambulance!' says pitiless Gillian, lapsing into vulgarity once again. 'Walking's the best thing you can do. Just keep your back straight and it shouldn't hurt too much.'

'Shouldn't hurt too much,' she says. Oh, yes. Overflowing with the milk of human kindness, this one. Shouldn't hurt too much. No-one could possibly understand the pain I am currently enduring, not unless they were to trade vertebrae with me. And there lies the whole lamentable problem: people only really understand their own pain; they have no sympathy at all for the suffering of others. My two so-called friends here are an excellent illustration of this precept. Here I am, suffering from pain indescribable, and yet witness how dismissive and off-hand they are about it, forcing me to walk with them through the streets, when by all rights I should be in an ambulance being rushed to the emergency ward. I'm convinced it must be a slipped disc at the very least. Each step is an ordeal. And the passersby—look at them! Just passing by. Not a glance of sympathy, even though one and all they must see the agony I am enduring; no, they just walk blithely past, only concerned about their own silly, trivial problems; not a thought for me and my suffering.

'Hey there! You come to see my shop?'

It's Takako, materialising out of the crowd in front of us, brightly-attired in pink jeans and a rather revealing top. She smiles at me, as heedless of my suffering as everyone else.

'Your shop? What shop?'

'You're standing right in front of it!'

She points to the sign over the nearest shopfront—

SAKURA BEAUTY & MASSAGE PARLOUR
Proprietor – Takaco (with one K)

'Oh, so this is your place,' says Gillian admiringly. 'Are you open yet?'

'Opened today,' is the reply. 'No customers yet.' To myself: 'You wanna look round, Randal?'

'That's very kind of you,' I say; 'but not today. I am currently experiencing a great deal of pain, and I just need to get back home and lie down—'

'You wally,' says Gillian (directed at me, of course.) 'You're standing in front of a massage parlour. She can probably do something for your back.'

'Oh! You've hurt your back?' inquires Takaco, looking from Gillian to me. 'I give you massage! Make you feel better! First customer—I give you free foot massage!'

'And how is massaging my feet going to make my back feel better?' I growl. The woman's mad! Either that or holistic.

'No, no!' says Takaco. She kicks off one of her sandals, and raises her foot for my inspection, pointing to it while hopping around on one leg to maintain her balance. 'I do rakkenho—massage using feet. See? I have very long toes—good for foot massage!'

'Yes, well that's very kind of you,' I say; 'but in my present condition, I really don't think I will accrue much positive benefit from your walking up and down my spinal column.'

'Randal!' erupts Gillian, for all the world like an enraged parent. 'She wants to help you, for Christ's sake! And she's a trained masseuse, so she knows what she's doing. Don't be so bloody ungrateful!'

'Yeah, I reckon you should go for it,' says Darren, once again proffering his unwanted two penn'orth.

'Yes, I be very gentle with you,' insists Takaco. 'Make you feel better.'

And so, I am escorted by Takaco into her emporium, whereupon she sets to work on me with her long-toed feet, and surprisingly I do feel the pain in my back much alleviated as a result of her ministrations—but what is even more surprisingly, is that on my preparing to depart, she invites me to join her for drinks at the Chaplain of the Fleet the following evening; and the most staggering surprise at all is that I find myself accepting this invitation.

Next morning, I awaken to find Gillian sitting in her usual chair, polluting the air of my bedsitting room with her tobacco smoke.

'Looking forward to tonight, then?' are her first words, accompanied with a wolfish grin and suggestive eyebrow movements.

'And what is occurring this evening that I should be so eagerly anticipating?' I ask. 'Is it the last episode of something?'

'No, it isn't the last episode of anything,' she snaps, the eyebrows now knitted in a frown. 'You're going out on a date, remember?'

'I have only just woken up,' I retort, testily. 'You could at least give me a chance to gather my thoughts.'

'Well, gather 'em then.'

'They are gathered. And what you are referring to as a "date" is simply my meeting an acquaintance for a quiet drink at the public house this evening.'

'You really are a fucking idiot, aren't you? She *likes* you, for Christ's sake; and when I say likes, I mean *fancies*. D'you think she'd give a free massage to just anyone? It was her first day and she hadn't had a single customer. She did it cuz she saw your back was giving you gyp and she cares about you. And if after she docs something like that, she goes and asks you out for drinks, it *is* a bloody date. And that's why I'm here; cuz I'm thinking you haven't been on many dates before, have you?'

'Oh, I see,' I say, a sneer in my voice. 'You've come to offer me sage advice, have you? You being an expert on "dating", of course.'

'Well, I know a bit more about it than you do, mate,' is the crass rejoinder. 'And I also know *you*—so I know in advance all the things you're likely to do wrong when you go on a date.'

'I say again, this "date" merely involves meeting at the public house for a few quiet drinks and light conversation. Well, I happen to be no novice in the art of maintaining a steady flow of agreeable conversation, and as I do not drink alcohol, I am in no danger of becoming inebriated and thus making a fool of myself. What more is there to say?'

'You don't have to be drunk to make a tit of yourself,' is the glib reply. (I would be willing to bet she came with that barbed rejoinder ready-prepared; I can tell by the smug grin decorating the lower half of her countenance.) 'For one thing: you're *not* good at conversation; you just think you are. You're good at talking, but you're not so hot when it comes to listening, are you? So, for a start, don't spend the whole evening crapping on about *The Prisoner*. When you're on a date, you're supposed to take an interest in the other person; so, let her talk about herself, and let her see that you're interested in what she's saying—and say as little about yourself as possible. Trust me, you're not good subject-matter for conversation.'

'Oh, really?' I say. 'And why, pray, am I such dreary subject-matter? Have you forgotten that I happen to be writing a book? Not everyone is capable of writing a book, you know?'

'I *do* know,' she says, pointedly. (Doubtless an acknowledgment of her own inability to perform that office.) 'And I also know there's nothing more annoying than listening to an author crapping on about the book they're writing. And anyway, you haven't actually *started* writing it, have you? You're still just *thinking* about writing it.'

'I happen to have been very busy lately,' I retort. 'I'm now forced to go to work every day, and when I return hither in the evening, I invariably feel too fatigued to apply myself to writing. And, I may add, preparation is everything, when it comes to writing a book such as mine. Which reminds me: you will have to tell me more about that proposed sequel series set in the antipodean women's penitentiary...'

'Yeah, forget about that,' groans Gillian, rolling her eyes for some reason. 'And just mention the book in passing, if you have to mention it at all—and then ask her what *she* does.'

'I know very well what she does; she's a—'

'I mean what she does in her *spare* time, you nimrod. Ask her what her hobbies are; take an interest in her interests, okay? And one other thing: on the subject of preparation, I bet you haven't thought about preparing for tonight, have you?'

Preparing? What's she talking about? 'You mean with regards to my person? Well, I shall perform my ablutions, of course. Perhaps a change of undergarments would be in order...'

'Yes, I think having a bath and putting on some clean clothes are both very good ideas—something you should do more often, by the way. But that's not what I'm talking about. Don't you think there's something you might need to bring with you when you meet up with Takaco tonight?'

She looks at me like I'm supposed to understand her. I endeavour to do so. 'Are you suggesting I should bring her a bouquet of flowers, perhaps? Or a selection of chocolates...?'

More eye-rolling. 'No. No, I don't think you need to bother with that. Knowing your luck, if you brought her flowers, she'd turn out to be allergic to them. No, what I mean is, don't you think there's something you might need to buy from the *chemist's shop* before you meet up with Takaco tonight? You know, in case she invites you back to her place afterwards?'

Her meaning is now plain. I favour her with my sternest frown of disapproval. 'And why do you assume that something of that nature is likely to transpire? Not all first dates have to terminate in sexual intercourse. I prefer to assume that nothing of the sort will transpire; and I feel that to arrive at our rendezvous with disposable contraceptives in my pocket would in itself be an unfair assumption that something of that nature was likely to occur—and indeed could be regarded as an insult to the lady I am meeting.'

I consider the above sentiments to be very worthy ones—Gillian, the degenerate, just laughs at them.

'Marvellous, isn't it?' she says, when she finds herself able to speak again. 'Most blokes have to be reminded that a first date *doesn't* automatically end in sex—but with you it's the other way round! And anyhow, I wasn't talking about condoms. Already got that one sorted.'

She reaches into the pocket of her lumberjack shirt and quite casually hurls a couple of blister-packed contraceptive sheaths at me. With great reluctance, I pick up the offensive articles with a thumb- and finger-tip.

'And pray, how do you happen to be in possession of these contraceptive devices? They are designed for *male* use.'

'Yeah, I know that. And I also know that when you go on a date the bloke will sometimes "forget" to bring any himself.'

'And pray when did *you* last go on a date?' I inquire scornfully. 'Did you examine the expiry date on these items before passing them onto me?'

'Cheeky sod!' exclaims Gillian. And then: 'Although... No; they should be alright.'

'Well, thank you very much for these,' I say, still handling them gingerly. 'But I very much doubt they shall be called into use this eventide. Nevertheless, I admit to being perplexed. If it was *not* for these items that you suggested I should call in at the chemist's shop, then what was it you had in mind?'

'I thought that'd be obvious: I meant the blue pill.'

'Blue pill?' I echo, completely at a loss. 'What blue pill?'

'Gor blimey! Viagra, you idiot; I'm talking about Viagra!'

'Viagra!' I thunder. 'The so-called impotence wonder-drug? Are you perchance suggesting I suffer from erectile dysfunction? Are you now my General Practitioner? Have you been perusing my medical records? No! Then how is it you have managed to ascertain this intimate knowledge regarding my physical health? Or do you profess to be able to detect such conditions merely by scrutinising the subject's facial features?'

Gillian sighs. 'Look, I'm not suggesting you're totally impotent, Randal. You may be able to get it up fine on your own—and I don't even really want to think about that one, anyway—'

'Then don't!' I roar.

'But, you know,' she proceeds, 'that doesn't always mean you can get it up when you're with another person. People can get nervous—especially people like you.'

'And what precisely is "people like me" supposed to mean?'

'Well, I mean you're a virgin, aren't you?'

I allow a pregnant silence to hang heavy on the air, following this bombshell. I want the full enormity of her words to sink deeply into Gillian's thick skull.

And then, in a voice pregnant with restrained wrath: 'I beg your pardon?'

'I said, "you're a virgin, aren't you?"'

'A virgin?'

'Yeah; a virgin.'

'A VIRGIN?' I thunder.

'YES!' retorts she.

I compose myself with an effort. 'Well, for your information, Gillian Draper,' I resume; 'the word 'virgin' happens to derive from the Greek *virgo intactus*, meaning 'hymen intact,' and as I do not happen to possess a hymen, how can I possibly be a virgin?' (terminating with a triumphant flourish in my voice.)

'Are you sure about that?' queries Gillian, looking perplexed. (As if *she* would know any better!) 'I'd always thought virgin originally meant just not being married... Anyway, that's splitting hairs—these days we always say virgin to mean someone who's never had sex: and that's you, right?'

'And is that any of your business?' in a voice of simmering menace.

Another sigh (as though *she's* the injured party.) 'Fine. You don't have to tell me. But whether you've done it before or you haven't, you can still get these first night jitters when it's with a new partner; so, all I'm saying is, just to be on the safe side, you need to get your fat arse down to Boots and pick up some Viagra before you meet up with Takaco tonight. Okay?'

And so, here I am on my way to the local branch of Boots pharmaceuticals to avail myself of a supply of that well-known erectile dysfunction corrective. And the *price* of it!

'About £30,' Gillian said—and just for a pack of four tablets! Does she think I'm made of money? That's what I asked her. Her answer was to point out that I was now a wage-earner. As if that makes any difference! Quite the opposite, in fact! The truth of the matter is, that now that I am employed, I have to pay both my rent and council tax; deduct those from my income, and I'm no better off than I was when I was receiving benefits!

But really, such an essential item as Viagra ought to be much more reasonably priced. (Gillian did say that I could probably find the thing more cheaply priced online; but alas there is no time for me to make any online purchases necessary for this evening.) Anyway, I really doubt I *shall* be needing the things. This is just Gillian's idea. Sex mad that woman is—never thinks about anything else. Well, I happen to be differently constituted; and so, I am sure, is Takaco.

I arrive at the shop and enter through the portals. I need to find the medicine section; the Viagra will be displayed under 'sexual health.' I locate the relevant aisle, and I peruse the shelves, feeling somewhat embarrassed at being here—and now it suddenly occurs to me that actually taking this product up to the cash register to purchase it is going to be an even more embarrassing business!

In fact, it will be downright humiliating!

Curse you, Gillian Draper! This was all your idea! Why couldn't you have offered to go out and make the purchase in my stead? It would have entailed no embarrassment for *you*...! I consider returning to the house and suggesting this very thing to her... But alas, I am unsure of her plans for today: what if I were to walk all the way back to Gissing Street, only to discover that she's gone out for the day? Then, I would be compelled to come back here and make the purchase myself anyway...

Wait a minute! I've just remembered something. This establishment boasts a number of those self-service checkouts! I have never availed myself of these devices before, as they have always looked to be rather complicated mechanisms to operate... Well, I will have to try. Yes, I will make use of the self-service checkouts, and thus circumvent the embarrassment of having to present my purchase of this erectile dysfunction drug to another—most likely female—human being!

Suitably pleased at this display of resourcefulness on my part, I make my way with my purchase to the self-service checkouts. And after all, they cannot be that difficult to operate; one sees people who are complete idiots making use of them every day—why, I believe even Darren is able to operate them! Ha! The final proof! Anything he can do...

I walk boldly up to an available machine. A touchscreen faces me, thanking me for my custom. This is somewhat precipitate; I haven't bought anything yet! What if I were to decide I didn't require this product after all, and were to go back and return it to its place on the shelf? Then I would have in fact done nothing to increase this establishment's daily takings, and the thanks they have so precipitately awarded me will have been entirely unearned...

I espy a scanning device on the flat surface beneath the touchscreen and, locating the barcode strip on the surface of the box, I swipe it across the scanner. Nothing happens. No bleep; nothing appears on the screen. The electronic eye has failed to read the barcode on the box. Well, it is a small barcode on a small box, I must have missed the target... I draw the box across the scanner more slowly this time. Again, there is no bleep of acknowledgement. I try it again. And again. Still nothing. Is the device malfunctioning? Perhaps I should move on to another machine... But then, if it's not the machine that is at fault, and it is myself who is doing something incorrectly, I'll be no better off than I am now... How infuriating!

I drag the thing back and forth across the scanner. *Still* nothing; still the blasted machine is just sitting there thanking me for the purchase I have yet to even transact!

'You have to reset it.'

The small, female voice at my elbow startles me. I look down. I see a small, female sales assistant. She offers me a timid smile.

'Pardon?' I say.

'You have to reset it.' She nods towards the touchscreen.

I suddenly remember what I'm holding in my hand. I quickly move it out of the assistant's view. Has she seen it? Has she seen what it is that I am attempting to purchase? I fix my eyes upon her in mute interrogation. Transfixed by my steely eye, she offers another weak smile. What does it mean? Is she embarrassed herself at the intimate nature of my purchase? Or perhaps it is a smile of meek apology for having seen that which I did not desire her to see…? It is difficult to tell; and the more I stare at her, the more flustered and discomposed she becomes… Well, regardless of whether she has seen anything or not, I shall retain my own composure.

'Please repeat what you just said,' I tell her. 'I didn't catch a word of it. Speak more clearly.'

'You have to reset it first,' she repeats, trembling and pointing weakly at the machine. 'On the screen.'

I turn to the screen. Reset it? Reset what? What is the woman talking about…? And then I see it, at the bottom of the screen—an icon marked 'reset.'

I stab the icon.

'Please scan your first item!' speaks the machine in a crisp and cheerful female voice.

At last!

'Thank you,' I say to the sales assistant. 'You may go.'

She departs. I breathe a sigh of relief. Now I can complete my purchase in comfort and privacy, and none of the staff and patrons any the wiser!

Serene and secure, I swipe the box across the scanner.

The machine beeps and then erupts into voice, announcing, loud enough for everybody in the immediate vicinity to hear:

'Please put your VIAGRA in the bagging area! I repeat: please put your VIAGRA in the bagging area!'

Wretched, backstabbing machine!

I lie on my bed in the darkness.

I should be heading out right now; I should be setting off for my meeting with Takaco with one K at the public house... But I can't move. I am nailed to the mattress. Oh, why did I ever agree to this rendezvous? It just slipped out. I answered 'yes' before I even realised what she had said to me. I *never* go out at night. It is one of my golden rules. The streets at night are far too dangerous. And if I *were* to go out, would she even be there? No; I'm sure she will have changed her mind by now; she will have had second thoughts... What does she want to meet me for, anyway? She doesn't know me. She's only even seen me on three occasions. She cut my hair... Yes, on that occasion she did ask me whether or not I was in a relationship. And yes, she did seem annoyed on that second occasion, when she thought I'd told her an untruth and that Gillian was my girlfriend... But she was probably only making polite conversation when she made the inquiry; and she was probably just annoyed on principle at the thought of having been lied to when she saw me with Gillian... Yes, I'm sure Takaco cannot harbour any strong feelings for me... That's just Gillian reading too much into things... I mean, after all, I am slightly overweight; women do not like that... And then there's mother—would she approve...? She's very fastidious, my mother... I remember... I remember it now... That one dreadful time... Caught red-handed in that tumbledown shed...

No, Mother! It wasn't me! It wasn't me! It was her! She started it! She did it! She started it...!

This time I am already awake when I hear a key rattle in the lock. I watch as the door opens and Gillian erupts into the room with her accustomed elephantine gracelessness.

'Oh, you're here,' she says.

'Were you expecting someone else?'

She drops into her usual chair with her usual disregard for the springs. 'I thought maybe you'd stayed out all night,' she says. 'I was up till about one and I didn't hear you come in.' She fixes me with a salacious grin. 'So how did it go? Pretty well, I'm guessing, since you were out so late.'

'I wasn't out late,' I tell her. 'I didn't go out at all…'

She frowns. 'Why not? Did she cancel on you at the last minute or something?'

'No, no; it was my decision.'

'Your decis—you tit! You complete and utter tit!' She looks furious. 'Do you think chances like this are going to come up for you every day? I keep telling you: that woman *likes* you. She *likes* you! And you had to go and bail on her… How did she take it? Was she upset?'

'How could I possibly know that?' I retort testily. 'I wasn't there, was I?'

'You weren't—' Gillian's face assumes a very serious look now. 'You mean you didn't call her or text her to tell her you wouldn't be going out?' she asks, her voice controlled, her eyes fixed on me like a judge's.

I admit it. I am feeling distinctly uncomfortable under that coldly accusing gaze. I'm actually squirming, pulling at the bedsheets. 'Well, I was *going* to…'

'Oh… you…' Her expression has veered from stern accusation to pure unbridled loathing. 'You… you… SOD! You little sod! You didn't even tell her! You made her get dressed up and go out to the pub, expecting to find you there, looking forward to spending the evening with you, and you…! You sod! That's not cancelling a date: that's standing someone up, you fucking little sod! I don't believe you! I fucking don't believe you!'

She removes her glasses and starts to rub her forehead. I really don't see that it's for her to be so vexed about all this; in fact, it's really none of her business at all. I've a good mind to tell her so—however, I don't.

Having completed the forehead rubbing, she looks up at me again, replacing her glasses in order to facilitate this.

'But she must have called you, she must have texted you, asking you where the hell you'd got to…? Didn't you even answer her messages…?' Now a disdainful look swings into play. 'No, I bet you didn't. I bet had your phone switched off, didn't you, you miserable coward? You had it switched off so you wouldn't be able to see her messages…' She looks around. 'Where is it? Where's your fucking phone?' She finds it, on the table beside herself. She picks it and throws it at me—yes, not *to* me, *at* me! 'Check it, you sod! Find out how many times she's called you and left messages!'

'I really don't see—'

'Do it!'

I switch on my phone—with some trepidation, I'll confess. However, my fears are soon allayed: no text messages, not a single missed call. I pass on this information to Gillian.

'I don't believe you,' is her response.

'I can assure it's true,' I say.

'Yeah, don't assure me: show me.'

I show her the screen of my device. She is compelled to accept the evidence of her own eyes, but for some reason she doesn't seem to share my sense of relief; her expression is distinctly downcast.

'You see?' I say. 'Not a single missed call or text message inquiry. Takaco probably wasn't even there; yes, I am sure she stood me up just as much as I stood her up. In short, we stood each other up.'

'No, she didn't,' says Gillian, her voice now quiet and weary. '*She* would have told you up front if she wasn't going to be able to make it. She was there alright.'

'How can you say that? You just said yourself, if she'd been sitting in the pub waiting for me, she would have sent me messages or tried to ring me—you said it yourself.'

'Yes… But I was forgetting she's Japanese, when I said that… Japanese people don't like making scenes; they don't like confrontations. Yeah… I can imagine her sitting there and waiting for you till closing time, but still not calling you… Especially if she was really upset…'

'Pure speculation,' I scoff. 'You don't know that she did that.'

She flares up again at this. 'Oh, you SOD. Don't you ever think about other people at all? If you've got one ounce of remorse for standing that woman up, you'll get your fat arse over to her shop the moment it opens today, and you'll get down on the floor and apologise to her. *That's* what you'll bloody do! Understood? Understood?'

'I… I can't…' I say.

'What do you mean "you can't"?'

'I can't… I can't face her… I couldn't face her last night; that's why I didn't go out. And now… you didn't ask me how I felt…'

She sighs. 'No, I didn't. I was too busy being pissed off with you… So, you're saying you were scared about seeing her? That that's why you didn't go out?'

'Yes…'

Another sigh. 'Randal… Why didn't you tell me you were nervous…? I know I was out most of the day, but you could've texted me; I'd've come back… It was about half seven I came in; I saw your light was out, so I just assumed you'd already gone out… But you were just sitting here in the dark, were you?'

'Lying here, yes.'

Gillian comes and sits next to me on the edge of the bed. She puts her arm around me. 'Look, maybe we can still save this situation. Go and see her; go and speak to her…'

'But what do I tell her?'

'The truth. Just tell her the truth. That you had a major case of the jitters. Just tell her that and apologise for not turning up. What were you so nervous about, anyway? I mean, it wasn't like it was a blind date; you've already met Takaco; you've already spoken to her… What was so different about meeting her last night?'

It's my turn to sigh now. 'Well… To tell you the truth, it was my mother.'

'Your mother?'

'Yes. Her spectre rose up before me… You see, she was always a rather… domineering woman, back when I was a lad… I couldn't do anything unless it was with her approval… I couldn't even be friends with anyone of whom she didn't approve…'

'Okay… I think I get the picture; and if you had a mother like that then it's a miracle you're not a serial killer—but what's that got to do with you being scared to go out last night?'

'There was an incident, you see… An incident buried deep in my past… A girl from school who came to see me… I really don't want to go into all the details, but needless to say, my mother did not approve of the girl; and she made this very clear to me. To the girl as well… It was a most distressing incident… I thought I'd forgotten all about it; locked it away; but last evening it rose up before me…'

Gillian strokes my hair. 'So that's what it is,' she sighs. 'Ghosts from the past; unresolved issues… But listen, Randal; look at me.' I do so, and see her sympathetic expression. 'Randal, your mother's dead and gone now; you've got to remember that; you can't let her keep controlling your life; you've got move on.'

'What are you talking about?' I demand, surprised. 'My mother is very much alive and well. She resides in Hampshire.'

Gillian's face now assumes the injured look of someone discovering they have been led up the garden path. 'She's alive? Then what was all that crap about her spectre rising up before you?'

'When I said that I was speaking metaphorically; I referred to the spirit of my mother from as she was back then, at the time of the incident I just alluded to; *that* was what rose up before me.'

Gillian now groans. 'Look, just go'n see Takaco and apologise to her. Either that or take the next train down to Hampshire and bludgeon your mother to death.'

Having settled on the first of the two courses of action suggested by Gillian, I make my way to Blythe Street, and to the Sakura Massage and Beauty Parlour. This diversion will result in my being somewhat late for work at the Unemployment Centre, but so be it. I arrive at the shop and peering cautiously through the plate-glass window, I immediately espy Takaco, sitting at her reception desk. (Needless to say, she acts as her own receptionist.) Catching sight of me, she smiles warmly and beckons me to enter. Ah! The omens are propitious! She appears to harbour no ill-feelings towards me for my nonappearance the evening before. Doubtless she has already intuited my reasons for failing to keep our appointment... Nevertheless, I must still do the decent thing and tender my apologies; and so, taking a deep breath, I enter the salon.

'Hi, Randal!' she greets me effusively.

Better and better. I clear my throat.

'Ah-hem. I feel I must apologise—'

'Oh, that's okay!' she interrupts me brightly. 'No need for apology. But you know, you didn't have to take off so early. If you waited, I could have made breakfast for you!'

'Early take-off? Make breakfast for me? What the blazes is she talking about?

'Ah-hem. No, I... I was referring to our meeting of last night; I—'

'I know! I had a great time, too!' And jumping from her stool, she throws herself into my arms, hugging me with great enthusiasm. 'Oh, Landal,' she says, positively purring like a cat. 'You make me so happy! Now we are lovers and we have many more nights like last night!'

I take her by the shoulders and pull her away from me. Not very gentlemanly I know; but either she's mad or I am!

'What are you talking about, woman?' I demand, scrutinising her face for some clue as to her behaviour. 'I didn't *see* you last night! I failed to present myself at the appointed time and place! In the vulgar parlance I "stood you up"! I came here to proffer my sincere apologies for having done this—and you start gabbling about us being lovers, and making breakfast! Are you delusional? Or have you merely confused me in your mind with someone else?'

Takaco looks hurt. 'What are you talking about, Randal? You didn't stand me up. We met at pub like we planned. Then we go back to my place and we make passionate love all through the night. Why do you pretend like it never happened?'

'Because it *didn't* happen!' I bellow. 'What is wrong with you, woman? I didn't set foot out of my apartment last evening! I dearly wanted to, but I couldn't! And as for making passionate love right through the night—preposterous!'

And now she starts to cry; as though *I'm* the one at fault. 'Why are you being so mean, Randal! Don't you like me anymore? Have you grown tired of me? Is our romance finished already?'

'Our romance hasn't even started!'

Wiping her eyes, she takes my hand, an imploring look on her face. 'No, Randal! No! Don't say this! I can still make you happy! My body belongs to you! Come; let us go into the back room right now and continue our lovemaking? I will rekindle the flames of your desire!'

And with this she starts to drag me across the room towards the inner regions of her emporium.

'Unhand me, woman!'

I snatch my hand from her grip. The woman's gone insane!

'Randal! Randal! Do not spurn my love!'

I retreat towards the door with precipitation.

'No, do not go! Come back to me, my love!'

I flee the premises.

Insane! The woman must be insane! Maybe she was mad all along, and I just didn't know her well enough to realise it! Either that, or she was so distraught at my non-arrival for our meeting last night that her fevered mind has manufactured this illusion of what she would have wished to have transpired, and now has managed to delude herself into believing it really *did* transpire…

So discomposed am I by this encounter, that I have arrived back at my apartment building before I've recollected that I should have bent my steps instead towards the Unemployment Centre. Oh, well. Perhaps this is for the best; after all, I couldn't possibly function at work today; I shall have to call in sick.

I enter the hallway, unlock the door of my bedsitting room and step inside—and I am discomposed anew at the sight of a stranger casually lying on my bed! Just lying there, casual as you please, legs crossed at the ankles, hands behind his head, smiling at me with this most insolent of smiles. The man is somewhat stoutly built, and is apparelled in 'Prisoner' clothes, identical to my own set; to wit, black jacket with piping, navy-blue sweater, beige slacks, blue canvas shoes. In addition to this, his hair is styled after Patrick McGoohan's…

The same set of Prisoner clothes that I possess; the same haircut that I am presently sporting… I look again at that insolently smiling face…

Good God! It *is* me! It's me!

Chapter Six
How I Became Embroiled in a Free for All

In an instant I am out of my room and precipitating myself up the stairs. I hammer on the door of Gillian's room, calling out her name in my anguish. Is she in? Is she in? Or has she gone out to work this morning?

The door opens. It's Gillian.

'Alright, I'm here!' she says. 'Is the building on fire or something?'

'I've got a double!'

'You what?'

'I said I've got a double! A duplicate! A doppelgänger! He slept with Takaco and now he's in my room!' I grab her arm. 'Come on! He's there now!'

'Let go!' She snatches her arm away. 'Now, just calm down and explain things slowly.'

'I haven't got time to explain things! Come on!'

I hurry back down the stairs; and much to my relief, Gillian follows me. I stop outside my door.

'He's in there!' I tell Gillian.

'Who's in there?'

'Haven't you been listening, woman? My double! My doppelgänger!'

Gillian looks at me. 'You've got a double?'

'Yes! As I've said about fifty times!'

'And he's in your room?'

'Yes!'

'And what's he doing?'

'He's just lying there on my bed. Open the door and see for yourself! Go on!'

Gillian opens the door. She looks inside. 'There's no-one here,' she says. She opens the door wide, and I see for myself that my bed is indeed now unoccupied.

'Well he was there a minute ago!' I tell her.

We walk into the room. I look around, but there's no sign of him. I turn on Gillian.

'You don't believe me, do you?' I accuse her.

'No, I don't,' she says, cruelly candid.

'But I tell you, he was right there!' I point at the bed.

'Was he asleep?'

'No, he was wide awake; just lying there like he owned the place.'

'And did you speak to him?'

'No, I didn't! As soon as I saw who it was, I just came rushing up the stairs to tell you!'

'And he looked exactly the same as you?'

'Yes! My spitting image! ...Although, not quite...'

'Not quite? How not quite?'

'Well, I mean physically he was identical to myself, but his body language was different; his expression also...'

'How were they different?'

'Well, he looked very relaxed, very sure of himself; arrogant, in fact. When he looked at me, he had the most insolent grin on his face. It was like he was challenging me to call him an imposter, and that he was all ready to hurl defiance in my face and say that it was *I* who was the imposter.'

The look of weary disbelief remains unchanged on Gillian's face. 'And what about his clothes? Was he dressed the same as you are?'

'No!' I say, suddenly recalling this fact. 'No, he was wearing my Prisoner clothes—Ah! That's a point: I wonder if they *were* mine?'

I rush to my wardrobe and throw open the doors. I do not possess a great many clothes, and at a glance I can perceive that my Prisoner apparel is not amongst them.

Ha!' I turn triumphantly to face Gillian. 'They're gone! My Prisoner clothes are gone! *He* must have stolen them! *He* must have—'

'Randal…'

'If you don't believe me, come and see for yourself! You know I keep them—'

'Randal!' insistently.

'What?'

'You're *wearing* your Prisoner clothes!'

I look down at myself. She's right: I *am* wearing them. I can scarcely believe it. I'm sure that when I dressed myself this morning, I attired myself in the suit of clothes I invariably wear to work. My Prisoner clothes I purchased for the occasion of my pilgrimage to Portmeirion, and have not worn since that time. What possessed me to dress myself in them today…?

'Well… that just means my double had his own set of Prisoner clothes…'

'Randal…'

Gillian takes my arm and guides me to the bed. We sit down on the edge, side by side, Gillian holding my hand.

'There was no-one in here, Randal,' she tells me, using her soothing voice. 'You're stressed out. You imagined it…'

'Oh, and I suppose Takaco imagined it, as well?'

'Takaco? What's she got to do with it?'

'As I informed you not more than two minutes ago, she spent the night with the wretch!' I tell her. She is about to interrupt, but I proceed, 'Listen: I made my way to her salon just now, all ready to offer her my apologies, as per your suggestion; and what does she do but turn round and tell me that we *did* meet up, and that I accompanied her back to her place of residence; and that we… ahem… became intimate… Repeatedly, it seems…'

'If she said that then she's yanking your chain, isn't she?' avers Gillian. 'If you'd gone home with her last night, then you would've still been there this morning.'

'Ah, well, but according to her I took my departure by dawn's early light, while she was still in slumber. She complained of this, maintaining I should've waited until she had arisen, and that then she would have prepared breakfast for me.'

'She said that, did she?' says Gillian. The look of weary disbelief has gone now; she looks genuinely puzzled.

'Yes, she did.'

'And that's when you first realised you had a double?'

'Of course it wasn't! I didn't think that then! I just thought the girl had gone mad; I didn't know I had a double until I returned here and was confronted with him lying on my bed! And then suddenly it all made sense! Don't you see? The man with the bandaged face in the operating theatre: that must have been me; or rather the man they were in the process of surgically adjusting to look like me—and now the work is complete, and I have a doppelgänger walking around! He's already made a cuckold of me, and goodness knows what villainy he's going to perpetrate next!'

I wait for Gillian's response. She doesn't make one; she just sits there looking thoughtful.

'Well?' I demand.

'Give me a chance,' she says. 'I'm trying to work things out…'

'What is there to work out? They've made a duplicate of me, I tell you! You either believe me or you don't!'

'No… There's got to be some other explanation…'

'Like what?' Another explanation indeed.

'Well, anything! Anything that's not about you starring in your own version of "The Schizoid Man."'

'The Schizoid Man': episode five of *The Prisoner*, seventh in production order. (The last episode to feature Rover before it was phased out; the creature being problematical to film as the balloons were constantly bursting.) The episode's story involves the Prisoner finding himself displaced by a doppelgänger; an imposter who has been physically altered to render him an exact physical counterpart of himself... Yes, the similarity with my own situation is undeniable—and if events unfold for me in the same manner in which they unfolded in the television episode, then my double is going to end up taking me place, taking over my life and my home, while I myself will be deemed by all to be the imposter!

The prospect fills me with dread.

'But that's precisely what *is* happening!' I cry. '"The Schizoid Man" is being replayed in reality, even as we speak! And if even you are not going to credit my story, then you are simply following the plot of the episode! You are allowing it to happen! Don't you see? And what about Takaco, eh? You're forgetting Takaco's testimony, aren't you? How could I have been with her last eventide when I was right here in my room? Answer me that one!'

'Well... Maybe you *weren't* here in your room; maybe you *did* go and meet her...'

I snatch my hand away from her. 'So you're calling me a liar now, are you? Well thank you very much!'

'No, I'm not saying you're a liar, Randal,' says Gillian, in a beseeching tone. 'I'm saying that maybe you *did* go out, but now you don't *remember* going out...'

I give her a sideways glance. She looks perfectly serious. 'Are you suggesting that I'm a somnambulist? That I somehow managed to sleepwalk through my entire date? Because in that case, I have to be the most versatile somnambulist the world has ever known, for not only was I sleep*walking*, but sleep*talking*, and sleep—many other things as well!'

'No, I don't mean you were sleepwalking, Randal. I mean you went out to the pub, wide awake and conscious of what you were doing; you met Takaco, you chatted with her, she invited you back to her place, and you went with her and you slept with her. And then you got up, at dawn, like you said, or maybe even earlier, and you came back home. And then when you got here, you climbed into bed, fell asleep, and then, when you woke up again, you'd forgotten all about your date with Takaco.'

I look at her. She maintains the air of someone speaking in all sincerity. 'I forgot about it, did I?' I say quietly. 'Given what apparently transpired between Takaco and myself, wouldn't you say it was a trifle odd that it should have slipped my mind?'

'It didn't just slip your mind, Randal. I mean that your mind has deliberately blotted the whole thing out.'

'And why would my mind do me that signal disservice?'

'Well... what were we talking about earlier? What was it you said, or *thought*, stopped you from going out on your date with Takaco? "The spectre of your mother," as you called it. I don't think she did stop you going out, but I think she made you feel very guilty about it afterwards. And that'll be why you snuck off from Takaco's place in the middle of the night, and why your mind has gone and blotted the whole thing out. It's that bloody mother of yours; she's the cause of it all.'

'Hm,' I say. 'Well, even if I were to accept your Freudian analysis of the situation, how do you explain the lookalike of myself I came face to face with in this very room just now? How do you explain the operating theatre? The secret corridors in the Unemployment Centre, eh? All of *that* occurred last week; long before my evening with Takaco had even been proposed! How do you explain that?'

'Randal...' She places a hand on my shoulder, so I know this is going to be patronising. 'Think about it: you've been working every day for the past two weeks—and you're not used to working, are you? It's been putting a lot of pressure on you, so it's not surprising if it's starting to get to you, that you're starting to... see things...'

'See things!' I roar, shrugging off the patronising hand. 'See things? So you think I'm cracking up? You think I'm starting to hallucinate? Apparently so! And why am I being reduced to this condition? Why am I coming apart at the seams? Just because, according to you, I cannot handle the pressure of performing a simple office job!' I rise to my feet. 'Get out of here, woman! I turn to you for sympathy and support, and this is what I get? You accuse me of possessing a feeble mind? Of being unfit to perform a simple job of work? Get out, I say! Remove yourself from my vicinity this instant!'

'Alright! I'm going!' she cries, getting up and acting for all the world as though she's the injured party. She makes for the door. 'Just lie down and rest, Randal. You need to calm down. I'll come back and check on you later.'

'Don't bother!' I tell her.

I must have dozed off.

Looking at my watch, I find that the day is now well advanced; it will soon be teatime. I'm lying on my bed, fully clothed. It's very quiet… How long have I been asleep…? I had that dispute with Gillian… That was a long time ago, before even lunchtime… Lunch… Did I even have any lunch, or did I just fall asleep? I can't say I feel especially hungry… I would have been just finishing up at work now, had I gone in today… Drat it. Unless my memory is at fault, I never called in to report myself unable to attend today… What will they do…? Dock my pay, I suppose…

An appalling thought strikes me. What if I *did* go into work today? Or rather, what if
my doppelgänger attended in my place? By my very act of staying at home, I have allowed him to do this! I have allowed him to make another move towards taking over my life!

Say he has been at the Unemployment Centre doing my job—what will he do next? What will he do now that it's clocking off time? Will he come back here? Try to turf me out of my own lodgings? Well, we'll see about that! I am firmly ensconced here, and I will not be shifted! Here I am, and here I stay! The drawbridge is raised; the portcullis is down; I am ready to repel all invaders who would try to storm the fortress!

But wait a minute. I have just remembered that, to milk the metaphor, I possess an undefended outpost: to wit, Takaco! What if the scoundrel decides to return home to *her* instead of to this place? What if he has already made arrangements with her to do this very thing? But wait another minute: Takaco and I exchanged phone numbers; for my doppelgänger to contact her by this means, he would need to possess a mobile telephone with the identical number to my own—is that even possible…? What am I saying? *Anything* is possible with these insidious conspirators. Then what should I do? What *is* there to do? I have already been shunted out, with regards to Takaco! It was *he* who fulfilled the appointment I myself failed to attend last night. It was *he* Takaco elected to take to her bed—ergo, it is *he* who is Takaco's lover, and not myself. What place have I to interfere…? No! No, no, no! It was supposed to have been me. *I* was the one whose back pains were relieved by Takaco's ministrations. *I* was the one she invited to meet her for drinks at the public house. It was *I* whom she desired to become her lover. This scoundrelous imposter wilfully took my place; wilfully deceived Takaco into believing that he was the genuine article; to wit, myself. Great God! This kind of imposture, taken to its carnal extreme, is nothing more than rape! Rape pure and simple! It is my duty to inform Takaco of the deception which has been imposed on her! She has to know that the man she took her bosom was not myself…! But then, what if she actually prefers my doppelgänger to myself…? That is to say, this morning she evinced extreme satisfaction with the performance of her partner of the night before… What if I…? That is, what if my own… ahem… performance… fails to measure up to that of my doppelgänger? And what if she, on discovering this fact, and being confronted with the truth of the situation, elects to retain my more virile counterpart as her lover, and not myself? Why, I saw the very same thing happen once, in a film with Roger Moore!

Oh, the humiliation!

My cogitations are interrupted by an imperative knocking at the door of my room. It must be him! My double has returned! He wants to take possession of my lodgings, my home, my life, my very identity! And from the urgency of his knocking, he is not going to give up his attempt easily! …But then, is it him? Would not he have his own duplicate key to the premises? He managed to affect entry whilst I was absent this morning—so why doesn't he just let himself in right now?

Yes… Perhaps my deductions are too precipitate; perhaps it is not my duplicate at all… Then it must be Gillian, here perhaps to apologise for her behaviour this morning… Wait; no. *She* would just let herself in as well… Then who can it be? They're not giving up; they're still knocking… But if it's not one of the other tenants—and I have very little contact with any of the tenants here save for Gillian—how did he even get into the hallway? No one without a front door key can gain entry to the premises…

I see no recourse other than to answer the door. Whoever they are, they seem to be convinced that I am within, and are not going to desist until their urgent summoning elicits a response…

I rise from my bed, and advance cautiously to the door. The knocking has abated. Have they gone? …No, there it goes again. Taking a deep breath, I turn the key in the lock, I take hold of the knob and I slowly open the door.

My caller is a complete stranger. A thin-faced, copper-skinned man and possessing a ludicrously large and bushy moustache of the type generally known as an "RAF moustache," or a "Jimmy Edwards moustache" after the entertainer and former airman who possessed such an adornment.

'Mr Fortescue!' says the fellow, speaking with a pronounced Indian accent. 'Please to come along at once! We are already very late! Very late indeed!'

'I do not have the pleasure of your acquaintance, sir,' is my lofty reply.

'And we do not have time to become acquainted, Mr Fortescue,' says the fellow. 'Not until we are in the vehicle. Come along, come along!'

And he grabs me by the arm and starts dragging me to the front door!

'What is the meaning of this outrage!' I demand.

'No outrage is intended, Mr Fortescue! But we must keep our appointments! Come along!'

He opens the front door. Parked in the street before us is a Mini Moke; a genuine *Prisoner* Mini Moke: white paintwork, striped awning—here, on a street in Morsham, East London.

My antagonist drags me down the steps, thrusts me into the passenger seat and runs round to take his place at the wheel. He turns the ignition key and we set off—and good God, he starts a hooter going; a hooter making exactly the same racket as a taxicab from the Village when it is demanding right of way!

I find my voice. 'Where are you taking me?'

'To the meeting, Mr Fortescue,' answers the man. 'Allow me to introduce myself: my name is Dhawan, and I am to be your campaign manager; and I am most honoured to be accepting of this position. Forgive me for not shaking hands with you, but my hands are presently occupied with the steering wheel of this motor-vehicle.'

We turn onto a major thoroughfare, hooter still blaring—and I am surprised to witness the traffic actually giving way to us! Cars slow, and pull into the kerb, making way for us, just as they would for a vehicle of the emergency services.

'You say you are my campaign manager?' I say to Dhawan.

'That is so,' is the response.

'And... what campaign would that be?'

'Your election campaign, Mr Fortescue. I am knowing of no other campaign in which you are currently involved.'

'Yes, of course...' I say. 'The election campaign... Just to jog my memory: what election are we talking about...?'

'The local parliamentary election, Mr Fortescue.'

'Ah, yes; that one... Excellent... Yes...'

This is my doppelgänger's work! I'm sure of it! I have no recollection of putting my name forward to represent this benighted borough in parliament—and that's not the kind of thing you just do and then just forget about. Yes, this clearly the work of my miscreant double!

'And... um... just to bring us up to date,' I continue; 'What, er... party am I representing?'

Apparently my question is an amusing one; Dhawan starts chuckling under that moustache of his. 'Oh, very good, Mr Fortescue; very good. "What party?" indeed. You are not representing *any* party, Mr Fortescue: you are an independent candidate—fiercely independent, I am thinking.'

Independent candidate, eh? I quite like the sound of that.

We pull before the façade of one of Morsham's more superior hotels; not a luxury hotel, of course; anything luxurious would be completely out of place in this borough; but still, a superior hotel—not just one of those overnight, bed and breakfast places.

'Here we are, Mr Fortescue. Please to hurry inside; everybody is waiting.'

'This hotel is the venue for the meeting we are attending?' I ask.

'This hotel is your campaign headquarters, Mr Fortescue. We have booked the hotel for the duration of the election campaign; it is entirely at your disposal.'

The entire hotel—mine? I admit to liking the sound of that, as well.

We ascend the steps and enter the building. Dhawan hurries me along a series of corridors.

'This meeting,' I say; 'what sort of meeting are we talking about, precisely? Like a board meeting?'

'Goodness gracious, nothing of the sort Mr Fortescue,' says Dhawan. 'This meeting is just to be presenting yourself to some of your supporters.'

Ah! That doesn't sound too daunting. An informal affair; drinks and a buffet, no doubt (I *am* starting to feel a tad peckish); and I just have to mingle, move from group to group, say as few words to my electors… Yes, I think I can manage that!

'Here we are, Mr Fortescue,' says Dhawan, opening a door. 'Please to be following me.'

I follow him, my mind full of canapes; we pass through a darkened outer room and step not into a function room, but onto a stage! A seated audience of alarming size faces the stage, and upon our advent, they erupt into applause!

I confess to being nonplussed. I wasn't expecting this at all. Public speaking has never been my forte… If I'd known it was going to be something like this, I would never have agreed to come along! But how can I retreat now, with any dignity? Everyone is looking at me, and Dhawan has already stepped up to the podium. My doppelgänger has really dropped me in it this time!

'Thank you very much for your patience,' begins Dhawan, his voice amplified by the plethora of microphones sprouting from the rostrum. 'I would now like to introduce to you a man who needs no introduction: our most illustrious independent candidate for the forthcoming local election, Mr

Randal Fortescue! Please to step forward and introduce yourself!'

More applause, and Dhawan beckons me to the podium. Left with no other recourse, I advance to the podium. Dhawan steps aside. 'Please to keep it short,' he mutters under his moustache. Ah! Just a brief introduction! I might be able to pull this off. Doubtless my double expects me to lose my nerve and humiliate myself—well, we shall see!

I take up position, gripping both sides of the podium. (I've seen statesmen do this, and I know it looks good; makes you look like you know what you're doing.)

'Thank you,' I say, 'for that warm introduction—or should I say, reception. You are doubtless all wondering why you are here today, and indeed, so am I. So let me first clarify my position with a few words of explanation. This borough, that is to say, the borough of Morsham, will very soon be going to the polls to choose its representative in both Houses of Parliament. As an independent candidate, I intend to stand so that I may sit in those illustrious Houses, as your elected representative. You people gathered here today, being, as it were, members of my constituency, each have your vote to cast—and I don't think I need to tell you what you can do with those votes. And so, to sum up, it is my very great pleasure for you to see me here today. Thank you.'

More applause. Many arms are thrust into the air.

'Yes, yes,' I say. 'If anyone needs to go to the bathroom, they may do so now.'

Dhawan is suddenly at my side, speaking *sotto voce*. 'No, Mr Fortescue, this is not a toilet break; this is the question-and-answer session. They are raising their hands because they are wishing to ask you questions.'

Questions and answers... This could be a bit tricky. However, I have advanced too far to even think of backing out now; I shall just have to improvise. Dhawan has vanished, so apparently it is being left to me to select my questioners. Fortunately, I know how this is done.

'Gentleman at the front with the loud bowtie,' I say, pointing.

'Why are you choosing to run as an independent instead of aligning yourself with any of the main political parties?'

'Good question,' I say. 'Good question. Yes... And the answer of course is that I am running as an independent candidate because I happen to be fiercely independent, and, I might say, completely misaligned. That is to say, as far as the main political parties are concerned... Next question! Erm... lady in the third row with the silly hat.'

'If you are elected to office, what will be your chief concern regarding the welfare of this borough? Which areas do you think are most in need of change?'

'I'm very glad you asked me that,' I say. 'The first thing I shall commit myself to addressing upon my accession to power will be the grossly unfair benefits assessment programme currently in force. I myself was—that is to say, I am myself acquainted with someone who was only recently subjected to a cruelly unfair and, I might add, downright outrageous and humiliating medical assessment conducted at our Unemployment Centre here in Morsham; an assessment which resulted in this man, although suffering from chronic back problems, being deemed fit for work! And this is happening all over the country! And why is this atrocity being perpetrated, you ask? I will tell you: it is for no other reason than to award the privileged classes of this country—who already have more money than they know what to do with—a reduction in their income tax rates! Well; this is an egregious state of affairs, and I can tell you all gathered here today, that when I ascend to power, I intend to put a stop to it!'

The audience erupt into cheers and applause of approbation. I've scored a bullseye here.

I find myself feted for the remainder of the evening. A formal dinner follows my speech, in which several speeches are made and champagne toasts proposed, in my honour. (Needless to say, I do not partake of the champagne myself; however, my needs have been anticipated, and I find myself well-supplied with a non-toxic substitute; to wit, sparkling apple juice.) Mr Dhawan, my campaign manager, can barely contain himself, praising me effusively for my opening speech and my inspired responses to the questions put to me. I have won them over one and all, and I now possess a substantial support base with which to push myself forward in the ensuing days of the election campaign.

Why I have never thought of running for office before this time frankly bewilders me—I am so eminently suited for the role! I have the charm and charisma necessary to reach out to my auditors, to touch that resonating chord of sympathy which beats within them; I have the command of language which allows me to deftly shape my thoughts into words and to present them succinctly and sincerely; and I possess the requisite knowledge and acumen to form humane and well-considered policies directed towards the prosperity and wellbeing of those it has become my destiny to represent… Yes, I have found my vocation at long last; I have found the career most suited to my unique and hitherto criminally undervalued abilities. Too long have I been forced to live in the shade, when it was always my destiny to bask in the sun! And now, and now my moment has arrived; I can see my glorious career unfolding before me: I shall sweep this borough from its feet; my electoral victory shall be a landslide; and then, I shall make a name for myself in the House of Commons; and subsequent to that—perhaps Downing Street!

Next morning, I awake to find myself recumbent on a well-sprung mattress and enveloped in crisp, fresh-scented bed linen. I have been allotted my own room at the hotel which is to be my campaign headquarters, the use of which room I am to enjoy for the duration of said campaign. I was first made aware of this fact last evening, upon requesting Mr Dhawan to drive me back to my lodgings. At first I had some reservations with regards to accepting this generous offer, for it occurred to me that by vacating my usual accommodation, I would be leaving it open to being taken possession of by my doppelgänger; but on reflection I realised I need have no such fear—my status has been elevated; I am now a public figure, surrounded by colleagues and involved in an election campaign: how can my double hope to assume control of my life while I am thus situated? Impossible! He hasn't got a chance! In short, my doppelgänger has outwitted himself! Doubtless he sought to crush me by imposing this election campaign upon me, but instead I have risen to the occasion, I have buckled my armour, girded my loins, and taken up my cudgels—and it is *he* who has been crushed!

The intercom phone at my bedside buzzes. I pick up the receiver.

'Yes?'

'Ah, Mr Fortescue! A very good morning to you! I am hoping you have slept well in your new quarters. I will see that your breakfast is being brought up to your room at once! Only the best for you, Mr Fortescue! And then, when you have sufficiently refreshed yourself, I will call upon you myself in order that we can be discussing your itinerary for today.'

I open my mouth to voice some specifications regarding the promised repast, but the fellow has already hung up. Doubtless he has already familiarised himself with all that pertains to my dietary requirements. Very efficient!

I rise from my couch. I have been allotted a crisp, well-laundered suit of pyjamas, which I hope I will be allowed to keep, as they are far superior to the suit I possess at home. I have just divested myself of these, and am standing in a state of nature, when, without warning of any kind, the door opens and in walks a woman, pushing my breakfast trolley! She is

Asian, and dressed in 'Village' attire: to wit, red and white striped jumper, pale blue cotton slacks, navy blue canvas shoes. In addition, a white mod cap sits on her head, and because of this attire I for a moment believe my caller to be Number Sixteen, the woman I encountered in Portmeirion—but I quickly perceive my error: Number Sixteen wore dark glasses; this woman does not. Furthermore, Number Sixteen never smiled; this woman is positively wreathed with smiles.

And it is a smile that I am familiar with—in short, my visitant is Takaco with one K!

'You could at least knock!' I protest, covering my modesty with my pyjama shirt, the situation uncomfortably reminiscent of my ordeal of being forced to strip naked by Dr Wakabayashi on the occasion of my medical examination.

'No need for embarrassment!' sings Takaco, still grinning from ear to ear. 'I've seen you naked before, remember?'

No, I don't remember, as it happens; because, as it happens, it wasn't actually me that you saw in all their glory that night.

Now, however, is not the time to be raising that subject.

'Are you now in the employ of this hotel?' I ask, with reference to the breakfast trolley.

'Oh, no!' is the reply. 'I just bring your breakfast up! I'm your assistant for the election campaign! I start this morning!' And so saying, she stands herself ramrod straight and favours me with a military salute.

'Well, er... that's very nice...' I say. 'But just how did you learn that I was a candidate? I only found out myself yesterday.'

'What do you mean how do I know? You told me all about it when we met on Sunday!'

A-ha! So it *was* my doppelgänger who set these wheels in motion! This is the final proof, if proof was needed.

'Oh yes, so I did... And once again thank you for your enthusiastic support—but would you be kind enough to just turn your back for a minute so that I may attire myself?'

'Why are you so bashful?' grins Takaco. 'You weren't like that on Sunday night!'

'Well, yes... but you know, that was at night, in a darkened room...'

Takaco looks confused. 'What? We had the lights on all the time! You say you like to always watch the tears falling from my eyes as we make love!'

Damn him, damn him, damn him!

'Nevertheless,' I say, controlling my temper with an effort; 'I always prefer to dress myself in privacy, so if you would be good enough to turn your back...?'

Takaco makes a 'humph' sound, and does as requested, albeit with the arms folded and nose in the air body language expressive of resentment.

As if *she* has cause for resentment, think I, as I hurriedly apparel myself. *I'm* the victim here! If Takaco is so much in love with me, how was it she never realised that it was an imposter whom she took to her bed that night? She ought to have *sensed*, or something, that it wasn't really me!

Having apparelled myself, I turn my attention to the breakfast tray; it is indeed a sumptuous spread. Eagerly, I wheel the trolley up to the bed and seat myself to inspect the covered dishes: eggs and bacon, delicately-sliced toast, a steaming bowl of porridge; pots of fruit preserves; and for liquid refreshment a pot of tea and a glass of freshly-squeezed orange juice. Excellent!

I am halfway through discussing my eggs and bacon before I perceive that Takaco is still standing with her back to me.

'Oh, you can turn round now,' I magnanimously inform her.

She does so. She is smiling again—it seems she's already got over that silly womanish pet of hers.

'You like your breakfast?'

'It is a veritable feast,' I say. 'My compliments to the chef.'

There comes a knock at the door, and Mr Dhawan walks into the room.

'Ah, Mr Fortescue! It is a pleasure to see that you have passed a comfortable night and are being in good health. I see you are enjoying your breakfast.'

'Yes, it's excellent,' I assure him.

'Good, good!' he says, coming to a stop beside Takaco. Like her, he also is dressed in Village raiment today: a blue blazer with black piping, a black rollneck sweater, green slacks and the ubiquitous canvas shoes.

'This,' I say, extending an arm towards Takaco; 'is Takaco. She has offered her services as my personal assistant—'

'There is no need for introductions, Mr Fortescue,' says Dhawan. 'I am being acquainted with Miss Takaco.'

'Oh! Well! Good!' I say. 'Then do you think that, as she intends to assist me throughout this campaign, that perhaps she could be like myself furnished with a room at this establishment? It would save her having to commute—'

I am interrupted by peals of laughter from both Dhawan and Takaco.

'Oh, very good, Mr Fortescue, very good!' chuckles the former. 'I am being most amused by your humorous jest! "Furnish her with a room," he says! Oh, Mr Fortescue; you a sly dog indeed; a sly dog!'

They both continue to laugh. For a moment I am nonplussed; but then I perceive a flicker of light—Takaco's own lodgings must be very close at hand, perhaps just around the corner from this establishment, thus rendering her having to take up residence here a needless expense. They believe I am just making a joke; but of course, as I was, and still am, in complete ignorance of the precise location of Takaco's place of residence, none was intended.

Howsomever, I consider it politic to allow them to continue thinking that I have made a deliberate jest.

'But we must turn to business, Mr Fortescue,' says Dhawan, after recovering his composure. He holds up a notebook. 'I am having here your itinerary for today.'

'Oh! And what am I to be doing today?'

'A great many things, Mr Fortescue. First you will be visiting one of our many care homes for the elderly. It is most important that these people should all have a say in the future they will not be around to enjoy. Then you are to take a tour of the North Morsham catmeat factory. That is for the making of meat *for* cats, not *out* of them, you understand? I think the main ingredient is horse. After that you will be conducting the opening of the new public lavatories on Cock-a-leekie Street. This will take us to lunchtime, when of course you will be dining with the mayor at the town hall. In the afternoon you will be giving an assembly to the students of East Morsham Comprehensive School. The voters of tomorrow, Mr Fortescue! It is most important to win them over. And then, our final visit will be to the offices of the Morsham Guild of Destitute Chimney-Sweeps. A dying art, Mr Fortescue; a dying art. Please show them your sympathy.'

'All that in one day...?' I say, hesitantly. 'Couldn't we perhaps hold one or two of those items back till tomorrow...?'

'Oh, Mr Fortescue! You do not know what you say! Your itinerary for tomorrow is also being very full. If we are to be always putting things back, we will never be completing all of your obligations before the day of the election vote! We must strike while the iron is hot, Mr Fortescue!'

So be it. It is a heavier workload than that to which I am accustomed, but one must make these sacrifices if one aspires to take public office. My time is no longer my own: it belongs to the people of whom I have taken it upon myself to represent! (Although it would be nice to have at least *some* time to myself; a man must have his leisure and repose... Perhaps I can have a glance through this itinerary and see if there are some visits that cannot be struck out. For a start, I fail to see the necessity of my tour of the catmeat factory; *cats* don't have the vote, do they...? Although of course there are a lot of strays inhabiting the borough... Perhaps it is time for them to be recognised as part of our homeless community...? Or, perhaps the homeless community should be encouraged to *eat* the stray cats...? No, no; that one would never float... Too many cat-lovers would oppose the move...)

'Time is pressing, Mr Fortescue,' announces Dhawan. 'Please let us be moving along!'

And so, having completed a hasty toilet, I join Takaco and Dhawan in the hotel foyer. Upon arrival, I am showered with greetings on all sides, from hotel staff and supporters.

'So... do we have any transport?' I inquire.

'Certainly we do, Mr Fortescue,' replies Dhawan. 'The vehicle in which I brought you here yesterday afternoon will be at your constant disposal. Miss Takaco will be your driver.' He pauses at the hotel's entrance doors. 'Come, Mr Fortescue; your public awaits.'

He opens the door for me, and stepping out, I see what he means. Crowds fill the pavement on both sides of the streets; Morsham residents, all gaily attired in striped sweaters, multicoloured capes, etc; and each and every pair of eyes directed at myself. On my appearance, an immense cheer erupts from them, banners are waved, coloured umbrellas are twirled; a brass band strikes up. And the placards—Good Lord; it's me! A monochrome image in portrait of myself! I have no conception of when the photograph could have been taken, but it is indisputably myself, and indisputably of recent origin—I am sporting my Patrick McGoohan haircut, and wearing the very blazer I stand in at this minute! And emblazoned on the placards in Albertus typeface the words

'Vote Fortescue'! And here they are: all over the place! Everywhere you look!

I stand dumbfounded, while the cheering and the music go on.

'Wave to them, Mr Fortescue,' comes Dhawan's voice at my shoulder. 'These are being your electors.'

Takaco, at my other shoulder, takes my arm and raises it. The cheers increase. I wave a friendly greeting with my free hand. Takaco, I notice, displays the V-sign with hers—doubtless with reference to Winston Churchill. (With her scanty knowledge of Great Britain, she probably believes that all British politicians employ this gesture.)

When we have waved to the crowd's satisfaction, we descend the steps to where the Mini Moke is parked on the roadside. Takaco takes the wheel, while Mr Dhawan ushers me into the back seat, seating himself beside me.

We set off through the streets, the Mini Moke's siren blaring its jingle. The cheering crowds salute us as we pass. The brass band follows in our wake.

I look sideways at Mr Dhawan. 'Erm... How did I become so popular so quickly?'

'Word has got around, Mr Fortescue. Your speech of last evening has been much reported by the news services.'

'Oh... So, people liked it, did they...?'

'They were liking it very much, Mr Fortescue, as you can see for yourself.'

Yes... Yes, there's no doubt about it—they like me, alright. All these people; the milling masses of the borough of Morsham, most of whom wouldn't have looked twice at me before now (unless it was to size me up to determine whether I was worth mugging); now they are cheering me and calling out my name. Calling out my name with 'Vote for' tagged in front of it! Suddenly I'm somebody to them! And they want me to be their representative in Parliament!

And well, why not?

'Oh, goodness gracious me, look at all these excavations everywhere,' comments Mr Dhawan, as Takaco has just been forced to stop at another set of temporary traffic lights. 'They are digging up the roads and pavements everywhere. Something else which you should take a firm stance against, I am thinking.'

'Yes, it does seem rather pointless, doesn't it?' I assent. 'They come along, they dig a great big hole in the ground; and then they just put a barrier around it, and leave it there, while they go off and dig another hole somewhere else. I suppose they do it just to keep the workmen employed. I shall certainly have to put a stop to this—oh, but wait a minute: it comes to mind that two of these excavators are personal acquaintances of mine, and very nice fellows too; I wouldn't want to deprive them of their livelihood…'

Dhawan shakes his head sadly. 'Ah, Mr Dhawan, already you are discovering the suffering felt by those who wield power. These painful decisions will have to be made, I am thinking. It is impossible to please everybody all the time—impossible! Why, not even you will be able to achieve this, Mr Fortescue!'

Really? I don't see why not!

It is evening, and I am enjoying my tea in the company of Takaco in the hotel's dining hall (the regular dining hall, not the banquet hall of the previous evening.) Mr Dhawan has disappeared, presumably having gone back home to his wife and octuplets. My day's round of visits has been tiring but very satisfactory; I have been received with enthusiasm wherever I have been. The Islamic schoolgirls at the comprehensive have been assured that I will support their right to wear their hijabs in the showers, and my speech at the opening of the public toilets is one that is sure to go down in the annals of history. Takaco has been of considerable service to me; she has driven me—displaying a commendable attention to road safety—to my various appointments, and when not at the wheel has stood at my side with her ready smile and her V for Victory hand sign. (I had considered it might have been more agreeable to have had Takaco sitting at my side in the back seat, while Mr Dhawan steered the vehicle; but I suppose a campaign manager out-ranks a mere assistant—and anyway, I'm not sure if would trust myself to Dhawan's driving. I'm sure I've heard somewhere that Indian men are very bad drivers.)

Having polished off my second slice of coffee- and walnut cake, I proceed to wash it down with another cup of Earl Grey.

'You've got this erection in the bag!' enthuses Takaco (meaning 'election.')

'You think so?' say I, modestly.

'Yes! Those Tory and Labour candidates: pah! They don't stand a chance!'

'Well, we mustn't count our chickens…' I caution. But then, when Takaco just looks confused and inquires 'What chickens?' I realise I need to cut down on the use of idiomatic allusions in her presence—she has a tendency to take everything you say literally.

'What did you think of my speech to the senior citizens?' I ask her.

'Oh, that was great!' is her ready reply.

'What about my speech to the chimney-sweeps?'

'That was great, too!'

'And my speech at the opening ceremony?'

'That also was great!'

'Really?' She has very good judgement, this female! A most excellent assistant! 'So… what would you say was my best one? Any of the above, or was it perhaps my speech to the schoolchildren, or my speech to the factory workers?'

'Oh, they're all so good, I just don't know which one to pick as best!' she replies.

Very complimentary, but I am however desirous of some more detailed feedback here. 'But surely you can put your finger on one particular speech that you think outshone the rest? For example—'

'Don't you think it's time for bed now, Randal?' she interrupts (rather abruptly, I feel.)

'Oh,' I say, somewhat deflated. 'You want to go home now, do you?'

A look of confusion again. 'Go home? What do you mean go home?'

'Well, you live just around the corner, don't you?'

'No… My apartment is on Maple Street, about five miles from here. You know that…'

I *don't*, but let it pass; instead, I inquire, 'Well if you don't live nearby, then what was all that laughing about this morning, when I made the very reasonable suggestion of your being given a room in the hotel?'

'Oh, *that*.' Takaco grins. 'You know why we laugh about *that*.' She playfully elbows me in the ribs.

'Do I?' I say. And then, 'Ah! I get it! You laughed because you already *have* a room here—so you have no need to secure another one!'

'That's right!' affirms Takaco. 'And I think we should be going up right now.'

'Well yes, it has been an exhausting day,' I concur. 'I suppose we should both be retiring to our rooms…'

'That's right!' she repeats, still grinning. I'm not sure why she finds the idea of retiring to rest in our respective quarters such an amusing one.

We exit the dining room and make our way to the lift. We step inside.

'Which floor do you require?' I ask. 'As you know, I'm on the third.'

'Me too!' says Takaco.

I depress the requisite button. The lift begins its ascent.

'A busy day tomorrow,' I remark, feeling it incumbent on myself to keep the conversation flowing.

'Yes!' agrees Takaco. She has a very enthusiastic, almost aggressive, way of pronouncing that monosyllable.

'Lots of places to visit.'

'Yes!'

'A lot more speeches I shall need to make.'

'Yes!'

'You know… with all these speeches I'm having to improvise, I hope I don't start to run out of material!'

'Oh, no! You won't run out!' Takaco assures me.

'Ah! So, you… think I have it in me, then?'

'Yes!' emphatically. 'You're full of it!'

Very perceptive woman, is Takaco.

The lift comes to a stop and doors slide open. Takaco follows me all the way to the door of my room.

'Well, these are my quarters,' I say. 'So I shall bid you a good night…'

I open the door. Takaco has made no move to depart.

'So, which is your room?' I ask, hoping she will take the hint.

'Room twenty-four!' she replies.

'Er, no,' I say, pointing to the number on the door. '*Mine* is room twenty-four; yours must be another one. Well, good night…'

I enter my room—and before I can shut the door on her, Takaco has slipped past me into the room!

'What are you doing?' I demand. 'I repeat: this is *my* room!'

'My room also!' says Takaco, grinning all over.

'You mean they've double-booked the room?'

'No double-book! We share because we are lovers!'

So *that's* it! *That's* what all that laughter was about! *Salacious* laughter, as I now realise. Well, we'll see about this! I did *not* agree to this!

'We will do nothing of the kind!' I tell her, employing my sternest tones. 'I require my own private quarters! You cannot stay here! You shall have to ask the staff to furnish you with alternative accommodation!'

Takaco's only response is to come up to me and fold her arms around my neck, squeezing her body against mine! My own arms remain resolutely at my sides.

'Don't be like that!' she purrs. 'You weren't like this night before last. You couldn't get enough of Takaco then!'

Curse my libidinous doppelgänger! Because of him, Takaco believes me to be some virile, insatiable, bedroom acrobat! And I haven't even got my Viagra with me! It's back at my apartment! (And what's more, if it hadn't been for Gillian and her 'advice,' it would never have occurred to me that I was even in need of having recourse to that particular drug—but look at me now: I haven't even used the stuff yet, and I'm already dependent on it!)

'That was then, and this is now!' I say, disengaging her arms from round me. 'I am much too tired this evening, for… that kind of thing… Please leave.'

I cross the room to the bed and sit myself down on it. Takaco makes no move to leave the room. I have to get rid of the woman! But how do I go about it? Send her out to get us some drinks, and then lock the door on her…? No, if I suggested drinks, she would just call room service…

Takaco crosses the room and now she stands before me, hands behind her back, looking coy. 'That's okay if you tired…' she says. 'You don't have to do anything… You can just leave it all to Takaco… Takaco have plenty energy!' She takes off her cap, and unclips her hair, shaking it loose so that it falls about her shoulders in its glossy raven plenitude.

'Well, that's very kind of you…' I begin. Now she's taking off her jumper! And she's wearing nothing more than a brassiere underneath it! 'You know… I've been thinking… In the event of my being elected to office… that perhaps you would like to become my fulltime salaried secretary… I'm sure it will be much more remunerative than your current work as a masseuse…' Good God! Now she's pulled off her shoes and she's taking off her trousers! And now; now she is naked but for her lacy undergarments! 'So… if you would like to go away and give the matter some thought… Perhaps you can get back to me with your decision in the morning…?'

She takes off her brassiere and throws it aside! She is topless! Her breasts in their alarming abundance seem like two offensive weapons, their brown muzzles aimed squarely at myself.

'…So… do, you have any thoughts…?'

'About what?'

She's doing it! Oh, dear lord, she's doing it! She's pulling off her briefs! She's… I can see her… private… hair in all its jet-black flagrancy.

'Abou…about what I was saying…'

She stands before me, the brazen exhibitionist, hands on hips, a smile on her lips and lust in her eyes. 'Sorry!' she sings. 'Takaco wasn't listening—when Takaco becomes sexually aroused all other thoughts go out of Takaco's head!'

'Well… that's very nice, but as I said… I am feeling rather tired—'

She pounces on me midsentence! I collapse under this assault, falling back upon the bed. And now she overwhelms me, squirming all over me! I fervently desire to dislodge her from my person, but that would involve touching her—and she's not wearing any clothes! I can't… I can't touch her unclothed body… I just can't…! Oh, who will save me from this predicament?

Now she straddles me and leaning in, she starts kissing me all over the face!

'Takaco is going to make you so happy, Randal. Takaco is going to take you to heaven! Takaco's body is full of love for you; so full of love!'

'Stop it!' I cry. (And why has she taken to talking about herself in the third person?) 'Stop it, I say! Desist at once!'

'Ohhh... You play hard to get? You pretend you not like Takaco? You not think she's cute? Naughty Randal!' She raises herself and she edges forward so that my line of sight is inevitably drawn to the hirsute junction of her parted legs...! 'Look, Landal... Look how cute is Takaco...' Her hands go down to her groin, and she starts... doing things to herself...! 'Look how cute...'

I look. I don't want to, but I am compelled to. Cute? Cute, she says? How could anyone think that *that* is cute? Teddy-bears are cute. Little bows and ribbons are cute. Cartoon hearts and flowers are cute. But this... this is hideous! Revolting! Obscene! It's like something out of HP Lovecraft's worst nightmares! And the stench emanating from it...!

And now... Good Lord, now she's stretching her legs even further apart...! She's starting to lower herself... lower that *thing* onto my face—

This is the last straw. A man can only take so much. Making a preternatural exertion of my limbs, I manage to remove myself from underneath my sex-crazed assailant. I tumble to the floor, a mischance that would certainly have incapacitated me in other circumstances, but in the present crisis, I am able to spring swiftly to my feet. Thereupon, I start to gather up Takaco's discarded clothing.

'Hey! What are you doing?'

'Get out!' I roar. 'Get out, foul degenerate woman! Leave my presence at once!' And having gathered up all of her garments (even the unmentionables) I move swiftly to the door.

Takaco jumps from the bed and pursues me. 'Hey! Where you taking my clothes!'

For answer, I open the door and throw her garments out into the corridor.

'What are you doing?' she demands angrily—and just as I had hoped she follows her garments into the corridor to retrieve them. The moment she is across the threshold, I slam the door shut, locking it and throwing all the bolts.

'Hey!' comes her outraged voice.

Switching off the light, I retreat to my bed, hurriedly disrobe, assume my pyjamas, and jump into bed, throwing the quilt over myself. The knocking and calling out persist. Wretched woman! She can't have even stopped to make herself decent! She's standing there stark naked, causing a scene, disturbing the entire hotel! Why can't she just desist and take herself back to her home?

Still the tormenting blows rain upon the door. And persistently shouting out my name, as well! She's making an exhibition of *me* as much as she is of herself, curse her!

Suddenly I recall having seen last evening a set of earplugs in the bedside cabinet. Switching on the headboard lamp, I open the drawer, find the earplugs and insert them into my aural orifices.

Blessed silence! I feel that a weight has been lifted from my shoulders!

I switch off the light, resume my supine posture, and am soon wrapped in the arms of Morpheus.

Chapter Seven
How I Was Unhappily Not Returned

And now I have my own office! A small office belonging to the hotel, and technically someone else's—but still, I have been given the use of it for the full period of the election campaign! This is the surprise that Mr Dhawan has ready for me when I arise the next morning.

I sit myself behind the desk. The chair is a tall-backed, leather-upholstered swivel chair. I experiment, executing a full 360° turn. Excellent! This is something! Not like that flimsy desk in that cubbyhole of an office I had back at the Unemployment Centre. This is the desk and chair of an executive, not of an employee; the desk of someone *important*.

'It is all to your liking, Mr Fortescue?' inquires Mr Dhawan, standing respectfully on the other side of the desk.

'Yes, it's most satisfactory,' I say; 'most satisfactory.'

'Good!' Dhawan looks at his wristwatch. 'Then, as you have breakfasted, it is now time for us to be moving along to the first of your appointments for today. Time is votes, Mr Fortescue!'

He starts moving towards the door, but I bring him to a halt with a clearing of the throat. Dhawan looks at me inquiringly. 'There is something you wish to be telling me, Mr Fortescue?' he asks.

'Yes, I... Miss Takaco will not be joining us today... We, erm... Well, the fact is she is no longer my assistant... I have dismissed her...'

Dhawan holds up his hands. 'Oh, Mr Fortescue; I am already knowing about this! It is a most regrettable incident; most regrettable!'

'How do you know about it?' I demand.

'From Miss Takaco herself. She was being most upset; most upset, Mr Fortescue! To throw her out of your room in a state of complete undress—! Oh dearie me! I would have thought better of you, Mr Fortescue! This is not being like a gentleman!' And he starts clicking his tongue and shaking his head sadly.

My ire is raised.

'How dare you?' I thunder. 'You are in no position to pass judgement upon me! You were not there! I was provoked! Provoked most outrageously! The woman's a card-carrying nymphomaniac! She actually tried to force herself on me! And she—she tried to smother my face with her... her genitalia—! It was... it was... *eugh!*' I shudder at the recollection.

'Most regrettable, most regrettable,' says Dhawan, still shaking his head.

'I know! You should have seen the thing! It was disgusting! Like... like raw mincemeat—*hairy* raw mincemeat!'

'Perfectly natural, Mr Fortescue; perfectly natural,' says Dhawan, now nodding his head.

'Precisely! Anyone would want to get away from such a repulsive sight!'

'No, Mr Fortescue: I am meaning that what you saw was perfectly natural, not your reaction to it. Your reaction to it was not natural at all.'

'How can you say that?' I demand. 'Do you expect me to believe that there are people who actually like...? Who like...?'

'Oh, Mr Fortescue! Although I would be very happy to spend the entire morning discussing with you the subject of the female genitalia, we have pressing business to attend to; pressing business! Now come! We must be getting moving!'

He's right, of course. I must endeavour to put Takaco and that whole distressing episode behind me. My election victory: *that's* what matters; *that's* the thing to be focussing on!

'...And I intend to take a very strong stance on gang warfare and the knife crime it inevitably leads to! I mean, what do these gangs even do? Nothing! Absolutely nothing! Most of them don't even retail cut-price counterfeit merchandise! In short, they contribute nothing to our community! All these gangs really do is *exist!* They exist; and for them, apparently, this is enough! They exist and they continually squabble over territory; "turf," as they call it! Turf? Turf? What turf? These people are not real-estate owners! All the buildings in this borough belong to their leaseholders; and as for everything else: the roads, the pavements, the parks... They all belong to the municipality! These people may like to hang around in parks and on street-corners, but they don't actually possess any legal ownership of those parks and street corners! In short, it's just children's games! They just pretend to own territory, or "turf"! What's the point of it, I ask you? There is no point! And quite clearly, the only rational way to deal with this problem is to give these young hoodlums something better to do! And what can that be, you ask? Well, I say that the answer is clear: conscription! Yes! Mandatory military service! Think about it! It's no secret that our armed forces are understaffed at the present time; recruitment levels are at an all-time low! What better solution than to conscript these young wastrels and put their aggressive tendencies to some practical use? These people would make excellent canon-fodder…!'

'…Reporting live from Morsham, one of the constituencies taking part in the upcoming bi-election. And I'm very pleased to have with me now Randal Fortescue, the independent candidate who is currently leading the polls, leaving the candidates for the three main parties way behind. Thank you for taking time out of your busy schedule to speak to us this lunchtime, Mr Fortescue.'

'Not at all, not at all. And please call me Randal.'

'The question everyone is asking, Mr Fortescue, is how have you done it? You are an independent candidate with no previous political experience, and yet you have taken your constituency by storm. So, what's your secret?'

'No secret, Naga. It is simply that the voters have become disillusioned with the representatives of the three main parties. I am a new voice in the borough; I speak from the heart and I reach out to the people, my words resonating inside them like a tinkling wind-chime. They know that I am a man to be trusted, a man who will keep his word, a man who can never be reasoned with, and who will never be dictated to by outside influences.'

'I see. And what do you say to those people who predict that, if you secure this borough and become a member of parliament, you will inevitably, sooner or later, surrender your independent status and align yourself with one of the main parties?'

'I say "poppycock." I would never betray my electors by taking such an action. I am a staunch individualist; the individual always comes first. I would never surrender my principles by becoming part of political gestalt and having to cast my vote as others tell me to cast it. I decide for myself, and once I have arrived at an opinion, I am stuck with it, and nothing and no-one can make me change it!'

'I see. Well, thank you for taking the time to speak to us today, Mr Fortescue. And now it's back to the studio...'

I am growing attached to this office—it has become like an extension of myself; a second home, as it were. This chair; it feels as though it could have been manufactured specifically to accommodate my frame, with such facile ease does it conform itself to my contours, cushioning and supporting my delicate back. But, alas—this room is only on loan to me; once I become an elected member of parliament, I must seek accommodation elsewhere. A pity, really. Having one's headquarters in an (or is it "a") hotel possesses many benefits; the dining facilities, the bedrooms and laundry service... Still, there is the inconvenience of the other guests coming and going... I had hoped that on entering parliament I would be furnished with an office actually in the House of Commons; but Dhawan has disabused me of that notion, explaining that there is not room enough in Westminster Palace to provide office-space for all six hundred and fifty members of parliament. Apparently, I will have to provide myself with my own administrative offices; which, when I am in receipt of my MP's wages, will be well within my budget. Yes, I'm looking forward to that generous pay-cheque... Of which I shall be earning every penny, of course; nobody works harder than a local MP... And I believe the expense account is well neigh limitless...

Still, it would be nice if I could be allowed to keep this chair, though. Perhaps its present owner can be convinced to sell it to me...? And of course, when elected, I will need to employ a fulltime personal secretary; you can't do anything without one of those... Takaco... Pity we had that falling out; I am she would have made an ideal secretary... Of course, her English isn't that good, and she probably can't write it any better than she can speak it... But then, she could have had a staff of under-secretaries on whom to delegate the merely clerical work... I've just remembered! That night, that very night of our misunderstanding—I had just offered the position to her; and I have yet to receive her reply! Yes! Yes, that would be a very reasonable reason for re-establishing communication with her! I could inquire whether she has come to a decision regarding my offer of permanent employment! She's had nearly a week to think it over now—! Oh no; wait a minute. I recall now that she said she hadn't been paying any attention to me when I made the proposal to her... Too busy taking her clothes off or something... Still, it wouldn't hurt to repeat the offer, would it? I could even pretend I'd forgotten that she hadn't heard it the first time; wouldn't be much of a fib, as I genuinely *had* forgotten until just now when I remembered it... And as for that business of me chucking her out of the room—well, surely she can forgive me for that little misunderstanding...? And it's not as if I actually chucked *her* out of the room; it was only her *clothes* I chucked out of the room; she followed them entirely of her own accord... And yes, I may have turned a deaf ear (two, in fact) to her pleas for readmittance... But she ought to be able to understand and forgive me. I mean, she forced herself on me, and that's not something you're supposed to do—and just because she's a woman doesn't make it alright! And I would have reasoned with her, I would have much preferred to have reasoned with her, but as she admitted herself: when she is sufficiently sexually aroused, she *cannot* be reasoned with; she is *beyond* being reasoned with! She admitted this much herself! So, I was left with no choice, was I? I was left with no choice than to take the measures I took to achieve her removal from my bedchamber... Yes; she is as much to blame as me, in spite of Mr Dhawan and all his head-shaking and tongue-clicking. She is as much to blame as me, and yes, I forgive her! I forgive her her out of control libido and that disgusting mess she keeps between her legs—and if I can forgive *her* errors, then she can surely forgive *mine* and she can accept the position as my personal secretary! Yes! An admirable plan! I shall have to explain it to Mr Dhawan at once.

Right on cue, there comes a familiar knock on the door. Wonderful fellow! Always there the moment you need him!

He enters my office.

'Please excuse me for disturbing you at this late hour, Mr Fortescue,' he says, polite as ever. 'But there is a lady who is wishing to see you, and she is being very insistent.'

A lady! Takaco! Yes, she's come back to me! Doubtless she has had time to realise her errors, and she has come to throw herself at my feet and proffer her abject, grovelling Japanese apologies! And I, yes I, in my infinite munificence, shall accept them, and offer her the very lucrative and rewarding position of private secretary to an up-and-coming member of parliament.

'Show her in, Mr Dhawan,' I say, joyfully; 'show her in at once!'

'Very good, Mr Fortescue.'

Dhawan bows himself out. I wait impatiently and then the door opens again and in walks—Gillian!

Something inside me deflates like a punctured inner tube; instead of the graceful and radiant Takaco, I behold Gillian in her ubiquitous boots, denims and lumberjack shirt, galumphing into the room like the bull when the doors of the china shop open for business.

'Oh, it's *you*,' I say. (Just establishing facts.)

'Yeah, it's nice to see *you*, as well,' is her sarcastic response, as she drops (uninvited I might add) into the chair facing me. 'Randal: what the fuck's going on?'

I wince. Ten seconds. She has been in my presence ten seconds at the most, and already she has dropped an F-bomb from her tobacco-scented lips.

'Please be more specific,' I request. 'With reference to what are you seeking clarification?'

'I mean you, you div. You disappear from Gissing Street, you're running as an election candidate, you ignore all my calls and text messages—'

I hold up a hand. 'With reference to the latter, I wasn't aware of having received any calls or text messages from you. In fact, now that I come to think about it, I believe my mobile telephone is still back in my Gissing Street lodgings. I haven't required the use of it recently; I have been far too taken up with my election campaigning.'

'Yeah, but why didn't you tell me you were planning on running for office? It's like it just happened overnight. It's like "Free for All," for God's sake!'

'Really? Are you sure you don't mean that *Batman* episode?' I sneer. However, she appears vexed and confused at my change of circumstances, so I endeavour to appease her curiosity on the subject. 'In a way it did happen overnight,' I tell her. 'It took me by surprise at first, I don't mind telling you. But as you will have seen, I have risen to the occasion and am fighting this election to the very best of my abilities. Have you heard any of my speeches, perchance? Which was your favourite?'

Gillian rubs her temples. Probably one of her headaches. 'Randal, this doesn't make sense. Last time I saw you, you looked like you were about to have a nervous breakdown; going on about having a double—'

'Ah, but that is perfectly true! I *do* have a double! And, I have him to thank for my current situation—but I have outwitted him, you see? I have been one too many for him!'

Gillian looks pained. (Headache getting worse, no doubt.) 'Randal, talk sense, *please*. What has your double got to do with you running for office?'

'Everything! Haven't I already explained? He was the one who put my name forward—put my name forward in my name, as it were. He obviously wanted to confound and humiliate me by thrusting this election on me, but instead I have risen to the occasion; I have—'

'Have you been seeing a lot of him lately?' cuts in Gillian.

'Seeing a lot of whom?'

'Your *double*.'

'No. I haven't seen him at all. Not since that first occasion in my lodgings. Why do you ask? Have you seen him?'

Gillian shakes her head. 'No… I saw someone, though. Some really sleazy guy…'

'Well, I don't really want to hear about your love life,' I say.

'I don't mean a boyfriend! It was some guy who called round the house; he was asking for you. I was just going out and here was there on the doorstep…'

'And did he look like me?'

'No; he didn't look like you. He might have been about the same size and shape as you, but he was older; in his forties or something. And he talked in this really plummy way: "Excuse me, but would this be the residence of Mr Randal Fortescue?" I told him yes, it was, but that you hadn't been around for the past couple of weeks. Then he said: "And you must be his friend, Miss Gillian Draper, I presume?" And then he looked me up and down in a really dirty way; this big, smarmy grin on his face.'

'Hm. That *is* unusual. Who would want to look at *you* like that?'

'Ha, bloody ha. So, I asked the guy how he knew who I was, and he just said: "Oh, I know all about Mr Fortescue and his circle of acquaintance. Good-day, Miss Draper; I'm sure we'll be meeting again." And then he just walked off. He seriously gave me the creeps, that guy. So, is he a friend of yours?'

'Why would do you assume a guy who "gave you the creeps" would be a friend of mine?'

She shrugs. 'I thought he might be one of your election cronies…'

'My only election "crony" is Mr Dhawan, my campaign manager; the gentleman who escorted you here. Who that other fellow was, I cannot imagine. He sounds like no-one I am acquainted with, and he certainly wasn't my double. My double, my doppelgänger, is so-called because he is *identical* to me—not just some vague, passing resemblance.'

Gillian is quiet for a moment. She looks at me. 'So, you're really running for office?'

'Obviously. This hotel is serving as my campaign headquarters, as you presumably know, considering you managed to find your way here. So, was it just to tell me about some chance caller who now that I think about it was probably just a door-to-door salesperson, that you have honoured me with your presence?'

Now she looks annoyed. 'No, it wasn't. I'm supposed to be your friend, remember? I've been *worried* about you!'

I cannot help but laugh at this. 'Why on Earth should you be worried? As you can see, I am *thriving* at the moment. I am riding on a tide of popularity. You have presumably been following the election campaign on television? My prospects couldn't be better. I see no cause for concern.'

'I do. This is wrong. This is all wrong. You—doing this. And what about Takaco? And Darren? Have you seen Darren recently?'

'Darren? No, I haven't seen him.'

'Then don't you think you're neglecting him?'

'If I am, he is equally neglecting me.'

'How do you know that? He might have been trying to call you.'

'I've been far too busy. You don't seem to realise: I'm being worked off my feet, here. My time is not my own—'

'And another thing! Just how are you paying for all this? Running an election campaign costs a hell of a lot of money—and you haven't got any! So who's footing the bill? Is it your double?'

'No, it is not my double,' I sigh. 'I have my financial backers…'

'Who? Who are they?'

'Well, it's Mr Dhawan, and…'

'Yes, this Mr Dhawan: how did he come into your life so suddenly? And why the hell would any reasonable person be financing someone like you as an election candidate?'

Now this is going a step too far. '"Someone like me"?' I echo, irefully. 'And what, pray, is that supposed to mean? Do you consider me unfit to take up office as a respectable member of parliament? Is that what you're so delicately implying?'

'No, Randal; I'm sure you're more than fit to take up office—any idiot can become a member of parliament, Christ knows! I mean look at the prime minister we've got at the moment! But it's suspicious, isn't it? It's suspicious.'

'What is suspicious?' I inquire.

Gillian spreads her arms wide, encompassing the expanse of my office with the gesture, or perhaps the entire hotel. 'All this! All this, coming out of the blue! Maybe you should—'

A discreet knock, and Mr Dhawan enters. 'Forgive the intrusion, Mr Fortescue, but I'm thinking that the evening is growing late, and that you have another busy day ahead of you tomorrow. Perhaps you should be considering retiring to rest now.'

'Yes... Yes, I probably should... I need my eight to ten hours...' I rise from my chair. 'Would you mind, Gillian, if we adjourn this conversation...?'

'Alright then,' she says (and I detect reluctance in her voice.) She stands up. 'I'll come and see you again, okay?'

'Of course,' I reply. 'Any time you like. My days are very full at present, but I'm usually to be found here in the evenings...'

'Alright then,' she says, in a more affable tone this time, and accompanied with a smile. 'Maybe I'll look in tomorrow evening. You take care of yourself.'

She moves towards the door.

'Yes,' I say. 'And you.'

'I will be showing the lady out,' offers Dhawan.

'Yes, thank you, Dhawan,' I say.

'I can find my own way out, thanks,' says Gillian. She walks straight past him.

Dhawan looks at me, then, with a brief nod, he follows her out through the door.

Sunday. My day of rest. Only a week till the polls. The political forecasters predict a landslide victory for myself. My place in parliament, this consummating recognition of my many talents, is well-nigh a certainty. Things couldn't be better. Gillian never came back, though... Strange... She usually keeps her word about this sort of thing... Still, I shouldn't let it bother me...

I lie, fully clad, upon my bed, conserving my energies. By my side lies a book on the subject of political economy, recommended to me by Mr Dhawan. I have been attempting to read it, but I undeniably find it rather heavy-going; so I have set it aside, allowing my subconscious time to digest the material and then present its findings to my conscious mind in concise detail. You can always rely on your subconscious for doing that sort of thing...

I am startled from my repose at the sudden advent of Mr Dhawan. He literally bursts into the room; and as this is something he does not usually do, I am immediately alarmed.

'What's wrong?'

'Oh, Mr Fortescue!' Both his voice and his expression (at least, what I can perceive of the latter behind that moustache of his) look woeful. 'A calamity! A calamity!'

'A calamity!' I echo. A thousand thoughts race through my head, none of them good ones. 'What sort of calamity? Can't you deal with it? It's your job to deal with calamities! Don't burst in here discomposing me with them!'

'Oh, I am sorry, Mr Fortescue, for my abrupt manner of breaking this news to you—But it's a calamity! A calamity!'

'*What* is a calamity?' I roar, infuriate. 'Don't just stand there wringing your hands and telling me it's a calamity! Explain the nature of this calamity!'

'At once! At once, Mr Fortescue! A calamity, a calamity!'

'Look: I am going to strangle you if you don't tell me right now, as soon as I finish uttering this sentence, the exact, precise nature of this—calamity!' I came close to saying 'bloody' just then. That's how worked up I am.

'It's another candidate, Mr Fortescue!' declaims Dhawan. 'Another candidate has put his name forward and entered the race!'

'Another candidate?' Relief floods over me—relief and perplexity. 'Is that all? What are you getting so worked up about? So what if there's another candidate? It's less than a week to the polls; he hasn't got a chance of stealing my majority in that time! Be reasonable, man!'

'Oh, Mr Fortescue! You are not understanding the full story!' (Yes; because you haven't told me!) 'This new candidate: he is basing his platform on attacking *you!* He is saying many bad things about you! Many bad things! And people are listening to him! They are listening! Look, I will show you!'

He goes to the room's plasma-screen television and picks up the remote.

'You mean he's been on TV?' I demand.

'He's *everywhere*, Mr Fortescue! The media are having a field-day!'

Dhawan has switched on the set and called up one of the news channels.

'Ah! You see! Here he is! This is from the rally he held yesterday!'

I see a huge crowd of people and a man on a stage angrily holding forth. The shot switches to a close-up of the speaker—It's Darren! Darren Nesbit! My so-called best friend! My senses reel, my fingers become nerveless. It's him! It's really him! Scruffy and unshaven as usual, dressed in his ridiculous bumble-bee Village apparel... What's he saying...?

'...And then he says he'll put your interests before his own: Don't believe him! This man has never put anyone else's interests before his own in his entire life! Not once! He's a pompous, self-serving, egotistical, delusional megalomaniac! He is the kind of person who, once given a taste of power, will never let go! He will become a dictator! Don't trust him! He promises you everything, but if you allow him to be elected into office, it will mean the end of democracy in this nation! This man is so intolerant of opposition, that he will *ban* all opposition! He will silence all of his critics! He will seize the reins of absolute power and will never let go of them! This is what will happen if you vote for Randal Fortescue! Down with him! Down with him, I say! If you value your freedom, do not vote for this man! You will be voting for your own abject slavery! Vote for me, Darren Nesbit, your candidate for the Little People's Party! The Little People's party is here to champion the neglected, the downtrodden! We're here to protect you from the clutches of vain megalomaniacs who seek to bully and trick you out of your votes with their empty promises and platitudes! It's time for the Little People to rise up and have their say!'

I can take it no longer! 'WRETCH!' I thunder at the television screen. 'Ingrate! False friend! Viper at my bosom!'

I start to pace the floor in my righteous indignation.

'Please to be calming yourself down, Mr Fortescue!' implores Dhawan. 'Am I to understand that you are knowing this man?'

'Know him? *Know* him? He is—or *was*—my best friend! The man I've given my time to; who I have distinguished with the honour of my enduring friendship and patronage! And now he... he... Wretch!'

'I'm taking it you have had a falling out with this man?'

'Not at all!' I retort. 'Admittedly I haven't seen him for a couple of weeks, but the last time we did meet, we parted company on good terms; as far as I can recall. And now he does this! Setting himself up in opposition to me! Vilifying my good name! "Little People's Party" indeed! What does he think this is: *Land of the Giants*? The vile, backstabbing traitor! Wait till I get my hands on him! I'll pound him into the dust! I'll throttle the life out of him! I'll—I'll—!'

'Calm yourself down for pity's sake, Mr Fortescue!' begs Dhawan. 'An act of violence against your rival would be the final nail in your coffin! We must compose ourselves, and think about this rationally...!'

'How can I compose myself! You heard what he said about me! And in front of the whole world, as well! It's treachery! It's slander! It's—Yes: slander! I'll sue the wretch for slander! Ha! He won't be able to win the election if he's languishing in a prison cell! Call the police at once!'

'Mr Fortescue; please! The wheels of justice do not turn that quickly. The election is on Thursday—There is no way Mr Nesbit can be tried by a court of law before that time! All that you could hope to do would be to file a formal charge against him.'

'Well that's enough, isn't it? I shall file the charges! He can't fight the election if he's in prison!'

'No, Mr Fortescue; people charged with slander are not remanded in custody. He will still be at liberty to pursue his election campaign.'

'Drat it! There must be some way we can silence him! There has to be! I can't have him going around besmirching my good name like that! My reputation will be in ruins! You heard what he said: "Pompous megalomaniac!" "Delusional!" "Bully!" How dare he—! Why, he couldn't even have *written* that speech! It would be completely beyond his abilities to do such a thing! Someone's put him up to this! He just couldn't do it by himself, the semi-literate aitch-dropper—!'

'I did not hear him dropping his aitches, Mr Fortescue...'

'That's precisely what I mean! Someone has been coaching him! Writing his speeches! Giving him elocution lessons! But *who?* Who the devil could it be?'

'Perhaps it—My goodness! Isn't that Miss Takaco?'

Dhawan's eyes on the television screen. I follow his gaze. Darren is still on the stage, smiling and waving to his blind, idiotic audience—and yes: standing at his side is Takaco! Smiling at Darren's cheering admirers; just as she used to smile at my cheering admirers! Dispensing victory signs left, right and centre; just as she used to do for *me!*

Vile harpy! Turncoat! Treachery, thy name is Woman!

'There's your answer!' I roar, pointing at the screen. 'She's the one! She—No, wait a minute: Takaco can barely speak English herself! *She* can't be writing his speeches and giving him elocution lessons! But then who—?'

I turn to Dhawan. 'What are you standing there for? Why haven't you done anything? This man needs to be stopped! He'll ruin my election chances! You're my campaign manager: *do* something!'

Dhawan holds out his hands helplessly. 'What do you suggest I do, Mr Fortescue—?'

'I do not suggest! I expect you to come up with suggestions! Now, go and see to it! There's not a moment to lose! Get out and start doing something! Remedy this situation! Now! At once!'

'Mr Fortescue—!'

'AT ONCE!'

Dhawan bows and makes a hasty exit.

Alone, the first thing I do is to turn the television off, silencing the praise being heaped on my treacherous quondam friend. I pace the room up and down, striving to collect my thoughts... Who's pulling the strings? Who's the power behind the throne? Darren is clearly being manipulated by someone who is dedicated to achieving my downfall... Not Takaco... Yes, she's clearly gone over to the other side, but she cannot be the driving force... Good lord! I know who it is! My double! My doppelgänger! It's him! Yes, it can only be him!

After our little misunderstanding that night, Takaco must have gone back to her home, and I bet he was there waiting for her! He knows where to find the place, after all! Yes, he's got her in his clutches! Probably convinced her that *he's* the genuine Randal Fortescue and that *I'm* the imposter! And being the sex-maniac she is, she'd be only too ready to believe the word of that libidinous interloper! Yes; that's why she's there with Nesbit...

I see it all! My double first sought to humiliate me by putting my name forward as an election candidate; but when he saw that I, instead of collapsing under the burden, have risen to the challenge, he had to formulate an alternative plan for effecting my downfall! And this he has done by setting up a rival candidate! Yes! Yes, it all makes sense! *He* is the author of those slanderous speeches; *he* is the one who has been coaching Darren in his speechifying... But wait a minute! How could he do this without revealing himself to Darren? Revealing himself as my doppelgänger? Takaco might be fooled into thinking the imposter is the real me... But Darren... No... Dunce that he is, he has known me too long. He would be able to tell that this smug, smarmy imposter was not the man he's always known... Ah! My doppelgänger probably just wears a disguise in Darren's presence! Yes, a false beard, a pair of smoked spectacles... It wouldn't take much to pull the wool over Darren's eyes; he never was the sharpest knife in the drawer...

But, what to do...? I must get in touch with Darren! I must warn him that he has become the tool of a vile conspiracy, and convince him that he has to stand down as a candidate...! Yes; I should have realised—Darren would never have turned on me like this; not of his own volition! He has been duped; tricked into believing scandalous lies regarding my impeccable character; and tricked too, into believing that he will make a suitable election candidate! Poor deluded fool! I must endeavour to undeceive him and bring him to his senses with all possible dispatch!

Dhawan! Where's Dhawan? The fellow's never around when you want him!

I have to get out. Even this hotel, my very campaign headquarters, has become a hostile environment. I see them looking at me, the hotel staff, looking at me with mingled anger and disapproval. Like everyone else, they believe the lies that have been put into circulation—the lies that I am a ruthless, bullying, self-serving egomaniac with a Napoleon complex. They all feel like they have been deceived by me; that's what it is; they feel that I entered their establishment flying under false colours. And I never even chose their blasted hotel in the first place—that was Dhawan's doing!

I have to get out.

I exit the hotel, wearing a beret and dark glasses. I know it's not much of a disguise, but it makes me feel slightly better. The glasses are something to hide behind. It's the day before polling day, a sunny afternoon. I need a walk. Perhaps

I should just walk back to my old place and resume my former life. It's hopeless now. I know that much. I'll be lucky if I get a single vote. The Little People's Party reigns supreme.

My efforts to seek an audience with Darren have proved unavailing. He has been surrounded with an impenetrable barrier—at least as far as I am concerned. The official response is that Darren declines to see me face-to-face on account of his fearing physical violence at my hands. That's what they're saying. Of course, they are words that have been put into his mouth by his controllers. As if I am the type who would resort to physical violence! The old Darren would have known that...

Passing some hoardings, I see one of my election posters from the commencement of the campaign. My likeness has been defaced by the addition of a Hitler moustache and above my shoulder a swastika emblem. Further along the hoarding a second poster, this time with my upper lip adorned with what is apparently a Stalin moustache, judging from the hammer and sickle emblem accompanying it... After this, a third poster; this one sees me wearing a Napoleon Bonaparte bicorn hat, and at my shoulder the London Transport sign for Waterloo Station... Objectively, I have to admit that, considering the locale, the satire evinced in this last one actually verges on actually being clever—I would have more expected Morsham graffiti artists to have simply executed a crudely-drawn set of male genitalia issuing from my forehead...

I now come to a fourth poster—it features a crudely-drawn set of male genitalia issuing from my forehead...

Oh, what's the use? I proceed along the street, observing the people as they pass me—the same people who, only a week ago, were cheering me everywhere I went... And now look at them. Nothing. I think some of them may have penetrated my disguise, because I receive some distinctly dirty looks from one or two of them. Oh, fickle fortune...

No, make that fickle public opinion; swaying hither and thither, depending on which way the wind blows... And to think that I have been running myself ragged these past weeks and all for their benefit. Ungrateful swine... Most ignorant of masses...

I hear the sound of a brass band somewhere ahead; a familiar tune; until a few days ago it used to follow me around wherever I went. A crowd has gathered at a crossroads ahead. The music grows louder... And then the procession heaves into view, and the crowd starts to cheer. A slow-moving vehicle appears; its sides adorned with huge versions of the by now all-too-familiar placard of my successful rival's features and adorned with that ridiculous slogan that everyone's shouting: 'Vote Big – Vote Little!' Now, an open-topped Mini Moke appears—and Darren Nesbit stands in the back of the vehicle, grinning inanely and waving his hat; by his side is Takaco, taller than him, and saluting one and all with the victory sign. Takaco, the mistress and dupe of my doppelgänger, my nemesis.

I turn away and walk back down the street.

It's all over now. The votes have been counted. Darren Nesbit of the newly-formed Little People's Party has been elected MP for the borough of Morsham, ousting the previous Labour Party representative. And I... I did not receive a single vote. Not one. Never in the history of British democracy has a candidate been so signally crushed.

Chapter Eight
How I Spent What Would be the Last Evening I Ever Saw Gillian Alive

I have decided to hand in my resignation.

Having spent the greater part of the day reposing in my bedsitting room at Gissing Street, immersed in deep meditation, recovering my energies from the gruelling ordeal of my ill-starred election campaign, I have reached this decision: I shall return to my former place of employ, to wit, the Unemployment Centre just this one last time, and I shall do so for the sole purpose of tendering my resignation.

It is around teatime that I arrive at the portals of this administrative facility—my course of meditation has been a protracted one—and entering, I march straight up to the reception desk with a forthright step.

'I wish to see the section chief,' I announce.

The receptionist (fortunately, not the one whose diction is off the audible scale) looks up at me. 'Oh, Mr Fortescue! It was terrible about your election defeat—'

'Yes, never mind that,' I interrupt her. 'I require an immediate audience with the section chief.'

'The section chief? I don't think he can see you right now, Mr Fortescue. Can you come back—'

'No, I *cannot* come back. Just call the section chief and tell him that Randal Fortescue wishes to see him on a matter of the utmost urgency.'

'Well, if you insist...'

'I *do* insist.'

She picks up her phone and dials up the section chief's extension. She states my request, receives a response, replaces the handset.

'He'll see you right away. If you'll just—'

'I know the way, thank you.'

And without further ado, I cross the room, enter my number in the keypad, and pass through into the corridors of the administrative section. I make my way to the section chief's office, knock peremptorily upon the door, and without waiting for a response, enter.

The section chief, bearded and turbaned, sits at his desk.

'Ah, Mr Fortescue! Let me offer my condolences on your—'

'Yes, never mind that,' I say, standing before him. 'I have only one thing to say to you—'

'Please, take a seat, Mr Fortescue.'

'I prefer to remain standing. I have come today for one purpose only, and that is to give you this.'

I reach into my jacket pocket, withdraw a plain white envelope and throw it on the desk before the section chief.

'What is this, Mr Fortescue?' he inquires, looking at the document, but making no attempt to pick it up. 'You do not owe me an apology letter. Your recent absence from the office has been recorded as official leave—'

'It is not an apology letter,' I snap. 'It is my letter of resignation.'

This makes him look up. I see surprise, well-simulated no doubt, in his eyes.

'Why do you wish to resign, Mr Fortescue?'

'As if you didn't know. I *know* what's really going on in this place. Some of it, anyway. And what's more, I know that you know that I know. Or did you really think I would believe it was all just a dream?'

More well-simulated confusion occupying the exposed area between beard and turban. 'Believe that *what* was all just a dream?'

'Oh, come on. It's a bit late for the innocent act. The staff gentlemen's toilets; third cubicle from the left. The entrance to the secret regions of this establishment. The hidden files and the operating theatre. One of your guards incapacitated me with a blow to the cranium—and then, while unconscious, you had me placed in my own bed, hoping that when I regained consciousness, I would dismiss the whole thing as a dream. Ha! You underestimated your man there. I know it wasn't a dream, and I know who was lying on that operating table under all those bandages: it was my double!'

'Your double?'

'Yes, my double! You created him here, didn't you? Doubtless this was the whole reason you forced me into employment here in the first place: you were using the opportunity to collect visual data, in order to perfect an identical duplicate of myself. Well, from now on, you'll just have to employ *him* here instead; because I'm resigning! And what's more, I'm going to do what I should have done in the first place: I'm going to appeal against the decision reached by the conductress of that egregious travesty of a medical examination—or rather I'm going to appeal against the decision not to allow me the right to appeal against the decision! Yes, I shall be making immediate contact with the Citizens Advice Bureau! I intend to know my full rights! Rights that you seem to think you can ride over roughshod! Well, we shall see about that! We shall see!'

And with that, I bring my fist smartly down on the desk, turn on my heel, and exit the room.

Ow-ow-ow-ow! My hand!

'Oi you! Yeah, you: Mr La-di-da!'

I look round and perceive my old acquaintances Ralph and Russ, performing their usual office of standing in a hole they have excavated by the side of the road. Judging from their expressions, or rather from Ralph's expression, the other not possessing any to speak of, they seem to be aggrieved at me for some reason or other. I approach them, still nursing my injured hand. (I'm sure it's starting to swell up. I've undoubtedly torn some ligaments.)

'Can I help you gentlemen?' I ask.

'Yeah, you can,' replies Ralph, glaring daggers at me. 'Mind telling us what all that "Fred Blogs" guff was about? Eh, Mr Randal Fortescue?'

Curses! My code change; my Fred Blogs persona: I'd forgotten all about it! I now perceive the source of their ire: with my having been in the limelight during this accursed election campaign, they will now know full well that my name is not really Fred Blogs, and that moreover I do not even *talk* like Fred Blogs!

'Bloody patronising us, wasn't you, boyo?' proceeds Ralph, before I even have time to form my response. 'Just cuz we're working fellers, him an' me, you reckon we're too stupid to understand your la-di-da talk, so you put on that cockney accent, didn't you?'

'I can assure you I never sought to patronise you gentlemen,' I explain. 'It was merely that I thought we could better understand one another—'

'Yeah; you were bloody patronising us, boyo!'

'No, no, I assure you! It was simply a code change—'

'Yeah, well you know what you can do with "code changes," don't you? And I'll tell you something else: me an' him, *we* didn't vote for you! Not that we had a vote anyhow, cuz we don't live here—but even if we *did* have a vote, we wouldn't have voted for you, boyo! So you can just clear off can't you, Mr Bloody Patronising La-di-da Randal Fortescue! Too good for the likes of us, aren't you?'

'But you were the one who called me over here!' I protest.

'Yeah? Well, now I'm telling you to clear off, isn't it? So, clear off!'

Off I clear. My hand is killing me and I really have neither the time nor the inclination to fully explain myself. I procced along Blythe Street, trying to remember why I ever even told them my name was Fred Blogs. I think back to the day I first crossed paths with those two gentlemen; that day in Portmeirion... I can recall why I deemed the code change prudent, but why on Earth did I feel the need to conceal my real name…?

I'm approaching the Sakura Beauty & Massage Parlour. I see that the shutter is down. Closed for the day. Good. I have no wish to encounter Takaco at this juncture… No, wait a minute! Not closed—closed *down*! The signboard is gone, a 'retail unit to let' sign fixed to the shutter… I stop and stare. Closed down already? But she can't have been in business for more than a month! That's not even enough time to go bankrupt…!

And then the answer occurs to me: she will have found better-paid work for herself elsewhere, won't she? She joined Darren Nesbit's election campaign, and now that he has been successfully returned to office, he has doubtless awarded Takaco a salaried position as his private secretary—the very thing I had once planned to do had I been elected…! I really ought to pay Darren a visit sometime, to congratulate him on his victory, and to demonstrate that I am not a sore loser and that I bear him no malice… I believe the Little People's Party has set up its offices on Thurston Street. I shall have to call in sometime… But not now… Not right now…

Yes, it wasn't Darren's fault, poor fellow; that bitter election platform of his; all those slanderous accusations he made about myself… It was my double; he was the one who put Darren up to it… And Takaco… Is she also my doppelgänger's dupe? Has he succeeded in deceiving her into believing that he is the genuine Randal Fortescue and that I myself am the imposter…?

And what is he going to try next? Will he be satisfied with my election humiliation, or is he planning further devilry?

Not even a week has passed since the election, and not a single word about the event in the *Morsham Gazette*. While the campaign was running, they couldn't talk about anything else, but now that's over, they couldn't care less about which individual is the borough's elected representative in parliament. And it won't just be the local media; their lack of interest is simply a reflection of that of the general public—once the race has been run, everybody soon forgets about the winner.

Contrary to my established policy, I have been passing the evening here in the Chaplain of the Fleet, perusing the national and local newspapers. I am seated in my usual place at the table I have always shared with Gillian and Darren for our Saturday luncheon meetings. Several weeks have elapsed now since our last luncheon meeting, and I wonder if they will ever resume again… If they do recommence, I suspect they will be minus Darren.

I become aware of an altercation at the bar. Some inebriate, female by the sounds of things, is imperatively demanding to be supplied with alcohol, while the bar staff are—quite rightly—refusing to do this on the grounds that she has already ingested more than enough of that intoxicant. As is invariably the case in these situations, the inebriate is firmly denying her state of inebriation and is becoming increasingly aggressive in her demands. There's something about her voice… Slurred as it is from the effects of excessive alcohol-intake, I nonetheless feel it to be a voice I have heard somewhere before…

Putting aside the newspaper, I peer round the partition of the booth towards the bar, where a tall woman in a lumberjack shirt stands with her fists on the counter, leaning forwards the better to shout her demands at the resolute bar-steward.

'Look, jus' gimme a fuckin' drink! D'you know who I am? Do you? I'm a regular here! Come in here all the time! Wasn' for me, this place'd've closed down ages ago! Pay your fuckin' bills, I do!'

It's Gillian!

I quickly rise from my seat and make my way to the bar.

'I don't care how many times you've been 'ere!' the bartender is saying. 'You're too drunk, you're causing a scene and I'm telling you to leave.'

'Now, look—'

'Gillian!' I place a restraining hand on her shoulder. 'Cease and desist!'

So violently does she swing round, I take a step backwards, expecting a blow from her fist. She eyes me blearily at first; but then recognition seems to penetrate her befuddled brain, and her features relax into a smile (and a rather asinine one at that.)

'Oh look!' she says. 'Iss Mr No-Votes! Whaddayou doin' here? Drownin' your sorrows, are ya?'

'No, I am perfectly sober thank you,' I say. 'And regardless of that, as you seem to have drunk enough for both of us, why don't you desist from harassing the bar-staff and just come and join me at my table where we can converse congenially and quietly?'

'Conver… conver-what?'

'Where we can have a chat!' I turn to the bartender. 'If you will allow me, I will take charge of this person, and I undertake to ensure that she behaves herself. If you could just bring a glass of tap-water to our table…?'

The bartender accedes to my terms and I take Gillian by the arm and escort her back to the booth. She appears to have difficulties performing basic ambulation, and leans on me heavily.

'Mr No-Votes…' she chuckles.

'Oh, shut up,' I say. 'You could have at least cast your own vote in my favour, couldn't you? At least then, I would have had one vote to my credit.'

'Didn't feel like voting…' she says.

'Oh, didn't you?' I manage to deposit Gillian in her usual chair. 'Might I remind you that people got trampled to death by horses just so that you could exercise your right to vote.

You might try and show a bit more gratitude for the sacrifices they made.'

'Whatever…' is her insouciant response.

I resume my own seat, and the bartender deposits a pint glass of water in front of Gillian.

'Whass this?'

'It's called water,' I tell her, 'I suggest you drink it; if not for your own sake, then for your liver's.'

The blowing of a raspberry is all Gillian's response to my sage advice.

'And just how long have you been poisoning yourself with alcohol anyway?' I pursue. 'I haven't seen you all weekend—Good Lord, you haven't been at it since Friday, have you? You haven't been on one of those monopoly board pub crawls, have you?'

'No!' retorts Gillian, swaying in her seat. 'Iwenoamfuduweekend.'

'I comprehended not a single word of that!' I tell her. 'Please enunciate clearly and lucidly.'

Gillian growls. 'I said: I WENT HOME FOR THE WEEKEND!'

'Oh, I see. You went to visit your family. I trust you had a pleasant time?'

'No, we just argued a lot,' says Gillian, suddenly maudlin. Her gaze wanders, and then suddenly returning to myself, she stares at me as though she's only just realised I'm here. 'So you're back at Gissing Street?'

'Of course. The hotel was only my residence during the period of the election campaign.'

'And where's that Paki bastard?'

'If you are referring to my campaign manager Mr Dhawan, we have parted ways. And I must say that I am both shocked and surprised to hear such discriminatory language issuing from your lips.'

'I'll fuckin' call the bastard what I fuckin' like—he fuckin' threatened to kill me, the Paki bastard!'

'Don't be ridiculous, woman! Threaten to kill you? You're drivelling! Mr Dhawan would never do that!'

'Oh yeah? Why'dya think I didn't come back, eh? Why'dya think I didn't come to see you again?'

'Yes, why *didn't* you come back?' I demand. 'You distinctly promised that you would.'

'I just told you why!' snaps Gillian. 'Cuz that bastard threatened to kill me!'

'Preposterous!'

'He fuckin' *did!* After I'd spoke to you, he followed me out o' the hotel, an' he said, he said he'd kill me if I came back and tried to speak to you again! He did! And he meant it! The way he was lookin' at me—it was like he was suddenly diff'rent; an' he talked diff'rent, no Paki accent, and his face was all… threatening and serious and… threatening…'

'How can you expect me to believe something like that? He was my campaign manager, my invaluable assistant during the election period—'

'Yeah? Then why dinnee vote for you?'

'Vote for me?' This brings me up. I hadn't considered that. 'Well… I… I imagine that as my campaign manager he wasn't entitled to vote for his own candidate—'

'Bullshit. 'Course he could've voted for you! *You* could've voted for you! So why dint he?'

'Well, I… Perhaps he… He was…'

'He set you up! That's why he didn't vote for you! He set you up! It was him!'

'It wasn't him, Gillian. As I advised you previously, it was my double who orchestrated the whole election fiasco—'

'Would you shuddup about your fuckin' double? You haven't got a fuckin' double. It was that Paki bastard. And just what the fuck did you do to piss off Darren Nesbit so much?'

This takes me by surprise. '*Now* what are you talking about, woman? I have never done anything to incur the poor fellow's wrath. If you are referring to the fact of his running in direct opposition to myself in the election, the poor fellow was simply duped and coerced into doing what he did; in short, he was the puppet of my doppelgänger.'

'Puppet, my arse. Y'know, I went to see 'im today, I did. Wannid to know what he was playin' at.'

'You went to see him? Where?'

'At his Little Party People's People headquarters. That guy's got serious fuckin' issues, he has. You must've really pissed him off about somethin'. We had an alterca... alterc... we had a row. Turfed me out of the building, they did.'

'You mean you caused a scene at Darren's party headquarters? I take it you were already inebriated when you paid this visit, yes?'

'No. Started drinkin' afters... afterwards...'

She picks up the glass of water and drains it.

'Yeeurck!' she says, slamming the glass down on the table, an expression of profound distaste written across her visage. I suspect she had forgotten the glass contained only tap-water and had been anticipating a pint of gin, or some similar poison. 'What the fuck was it?'

'It's called water,' I inform her. 'I can understand you're not being accustomed to the taste of it.'

Her stomach visibly heaves. She clamps a hand to her mouth. 'Gunna be sick...'

'Then repair to the ladies' room, woman!' I exclaim. 'With haste!'

She rises with alacrity and, with incredible speed considering her bulk and present physical condition, makes a beeline, not for the conveniences, but for the exit. I follow her footsteps and emerge onto the lamplit street in time to witness Gillian loudly vomiting the contents of her stomach against the wall of the pub—in full view of the bouncer at the door as well as several passers-by.

Having finally completed this nauseating exercise, she stands upright, wiping her mouth with her sleeve.

'That's better…' she says, smiling stupidly at me.

'A disgusting exhibition,' I tell her, wrinkling my nose. 'Why couldn't you have repaired to the ladies' room, as I suggested?'

'Didn't think I'd make it…'

'Didn't think you'd make it?' I echo with some heat. 'The distance to the ladies' room from our table was no greater than the distance to the exit! Less, if anything! Well, now that we are outside anyway, shall we commence our journey homewards? It is getting rather late.'

'No, I'm feelin' better now,' says Gillian, still grinning inanely. 'Got room for another drink or two now,' patting her stomach.

She makes for the entrance, but the security officer firmly interposes himself between her and the door.

'You're not going back in there,' he tells her.

'But iss alright now,' says Gillian, giggling. 'I threw it all up. You saw me. So I'm sober now.'

'Actually, Gillian, it doesn't quite work like that,' I inform her. 'The alcohol you have imbibed will still be circulating in your bloodstream; that which was stagnating in, and which you ejected from, your stomach, was merely the detritus.'

A spluttering laugh from Gillian. 'Listen to 'im,' she says to the doorman confidentially, nodding her head towards me. 'Thinks he knows it all, doesn't he?'

The bouncer is unimpressed with this familiarity. 'You're not going back in,' he says.

'Why not?' demands Gillian, swaying back and forth.

'Because you're banned from this pub, that's why,' says the bouncer. 'Now fuck off.'

'You can't ban me!' protests Gillian. 'This is my local! I come in here all the time!'

'I don't care,' is the response. 'People who throw up all over the place like you just did get banned.'

'You can't do this!' rages Gillian. 'I've given this pub the best years of my wife! Life!'

'I don't care. Fuck off.'

Gillian is now staggering all over the place in her drunken impotent wrath. I take hold of her arm. 'Come along, Gillian. Let us return home. You've drunk more than enough for one evening.'

Thankfully, she allows herself to be led away, although she still turns back to shake a fist at the doorman. 'You haven't heard the last of this! I'm gunna speak to my lawyers!'

'Come along, Gillian,' I say, giving her a tug. 'We can resolve this situation on a future occasion. I will personally speak to the landlord in your favour; but for the nonce, please just endeavour to focus your attention on walking in a straight line.'

'This is all your fault,' declares Gillian. 'Getting me banned from my own pub.'

'How on Earth is it my fault?' I retort. '*I* didn't tell you to get so ludicrously inebriated, did I?'

'Yeah, but you told me to drink that pint of water!'

'But never did I tell to you to pour it down your throat in one gulp!'

As we proceed through the streets, I cannot but reflect upon how the mighty have fallen. Only a week or two prior to this, I seemed destined to take my place in the Houses of Parliament; my victory seemed assured; my mind had formed so many future plans… And now here I am, staggering home with a noisy, unwieldly female inebriate through the perilous nocturnal streets.

'So where's 'e gone, then?' asks Gillian.

'Where has whom gone?'

'Wassisname, your bastard champagne manager bastard.'

'My *campaign* manager's name was Mr Dhawan, and as I already said, we have parted ways.'

'Yeah? An' whaddid 'e say to ya?'

'What did he say to me about what?'

'The erection. After you lost it.' She splutters with laughter. 'You lost your erection! Should've had some of that Viagra! Then you would've *come* first!'

This apparently is very funny. Gillian is now convulsed with laughter, nearly sending us both down onto the pavement.

'Control yourself, please; or you'll do us both an injury! And to answer your question, Mr Dhawan did not say anything to me upon the event of the election being lost. To be honest, I departed from the hotel without bidding him a formal farewell; I was not in the most sociable of moods at the time.'

'Huh. Bastard set you up.'

'I still find that hard to believe. He seemed so genuine.'

'That was a fuckin' *act*. The real Darwin was the one who said he was gunna kill me—*that* was the real fuckin' Darwin!'

'Dha*wan*.'

'Whatever. An' I'll tell you somethin' else: that Japanese bitch was in on it an' all.'

'Not with any personal malice, I'm sure,' I reply. 'I believe she was manipulated into cooperating by my doppelgänger.'

'Oh, fer Christ's sake!' groans Gillian. 'You haven't got a fuckin' doopledangger... doople-double. That Texaco bitch was in it up to her slanty eyebrows! Her shop's closed, y'know? Did ya know that? Closed right down, it has.'

'I *know*,' I reply. 'We happen to be walking past the premises this very moment—something you would have noticed if you'd had your wits about you.'

'Oh yeah,' says Gillian, stopping abruptly to look at the vacant premises. 'Well, there you go! That shows you! She's cleared off like your champagne manager.'

'I don't think she has. I suspect that she has merely found employment with the Little People's Party. I'm sure Darren will have given her some administrative position at their headquarters.'

'Says who? I was there today, an' I didn't see her.'

'That doesn't prove anything.'

'Proves that… proves that…' she pauses. '…I dunno whaddit proves, but it proves it!'

'Very eloquent.'

'Well, at leas' you don' hafta feel bad about it!' she says, throwing her arm around my shoulder, and squeezing me clumsily.

'Do you mind? Remember my delicate back! And what don't I have to feel bad about?'

'Loosin' the erection! You were meant to lose it! Planned from the start! So, you don't hafta feel bad cuz it wasn't you that made you lose; it was them! Right?'

'Well, yes… I suppose that is one way to look at it…'

'Right!' Another bearlike squeeze. 'So, chin up! Back straight, pecker out and march onwards to victory! Hup-two, hup-two!'

And with this she starts marching me down the street! Propelled by her motion I am left with no choice but to fall into step with her—to stop would be to fall, and to fall would be to be dragged along.

'Hup-two, hup-two!'

Fortunately, this burst of energy on Gillian's part soon exhausts itself, and I am back to supporting her, guiding her, preventing her from taking wrong turnings, until we are finally back at Gissing Street. Reaching our apartment house, we mount the steps to the front door.

Gillian removes her arm from around my neck and starts rooting around in the pockets of her jeans for her front door key.

'Stand aside,' I say. 'It will be much simpler if I were to unlock the door.'

'No, no; I got this,' insists Gillian, with a display of alcoholic stubbornness.

'Look; if you will just let me—'

Gillian shakes her head resolutely. 'No, no, no. I got this, I got this—ah!'

She has found her keys and displays them proudly. 'See! I told you I got this.' She commences shuffling through the keys on the ring. 'Which one... which one...?'

'Oh, for goodness—'

'No, no; I got this, I got this... Ah! Yeah, this is the one!'

She now turns to the door and endeavours to insert the key into the lock. It soon becomes apparent that, with her present lack of physical coordination, this simple act is more than she is capable of performing.

'I got this, I got this...'

This is more than my patience can withstand. 'Really, Gillian, I must insist that you stand aside! *I* will open the door, or we shall be here all night. I'm not even convinced you're using the correct key; if you get it jammed in the lock...'

'No, no; I got it, I got it...'

'Stand aside, woman!' And without waiting for her to comply, I push her firmly to one side, and producing my own set of keys, unlock and open the front door. I am about to step over the threshold when I observe that Gillian's attention has been caught by something on the far side of the street. She is staring intently, and a frown has knitted her brows.

I follow her gaze and see a figure standing motionless on the pavement directly across the street from us. His general form is picked out by the nearest streetlight, but no details are visible. All I can perceive is that he is a tall man of stocky build, and he appears to be looking directly at Gillian and myself.

A chill hand seizes my heart.

'What are you gawping at?' Gillian shouts across the street.

The watching figure neither replies nor moves.

'Never mind, Gillian; let us go inside,' I say, taking hold of her arm. 'Quickly, now!'

She complies and follows me into the hallway, whereupon, and with last anxious glance at the figure across the street, I immediately shut the door.

I turn to Gillian. 'You realise who that was, don't you? That was clearly my doppelgänger! You see! I am not suffering from delusions—there he is! You saw him yourself!'

'Would you shaddup about your stupid doople-gangle,' says Gillian. 'Wasn't him. I know who that was...'

'Whoever you think it might be, you are wrong!' I insist. 'That man across the road is my double! My doppelgänger!'

All Gillian's response is to blow another one of those disparaging raspberries.

I now proceed to escort Gillian upstairs to her room. When we get to her door, we are on the brink of suffering a repeat of the farce of the front-door key—until I snatch the keyring from Gillian's fumbling hands and open her door myself.

Inside her room, Gillian heaves a sigh of relief and immediately collapses onto her bed.

'You could at least take your boots off first,' I say. 'Well, I shall now bid you goodnight. I'm sure you will have little trouble getting to sleep—although I believe "passing out" will be a more accurate description.'

I turn to the door, but Gillian calls me back.

'What is it?'

'C'mere, c'mere...'

She is speaking quietly now, so I crouch down beside her bed and lean towards her, the better to hear her words.

'Thanks for tonight, Randal,' she says, looking at me with bleary eyes.

'Yes, we must do this more often,' is my dry rejoinder. 'Let me remove these for you…'

I take off her glasses and deposit them on the bedside cabinet.

'Thanks, Randal…' she repeats. Her voice grows quieter; she is dropping off to sleep. 'Thanks for everything…'

She sounds sincere. I find myself strangely touched.

Something suddenly occurs to me. 'Perhaps tomorrow, when you have recovered from your inevitable hangover… If you could…? For the book I am researching…?'

'What about your book…?'

'Well, if I could furnish me with some more details regarding that proposed *Prisoner* sequel…? You know, the one in the Australian women's prison…'

For some reason, Gillian seems to find this amusing. She starts to chuckle quietly to herself. But before I can inquire as to the source of her mirth, her eyes have closed and the chuckling has become the deep ventilation of a heavy slumber.

I exit the room.

Upon gaining my own quarters, I immediately go to the window and peer cautiously through the curtains into the street. The figure standing across the street has gone.

Next morning I arise early; having nothing else to do, I decide to venture upstairs and check upon Gillian. The house is silent as I mount the stairs, none of the other tenants having surfaced as yet. As I ascend, I become increasingly conscious of a sharp metallic odour pervading the air. I am reminded of my metalwork classroom at school. Has someone here been performing some DIY metalwork?

The odour is much stronger when I attain the landing; and I also see that Gillian's door is ajar... Now, I distinctly remember closing that door when I left her room the previous evening... Has Gillian already arisen...? But then, where would she have gone, and why would she have left her door open...?

I walk up to her door. That smell; it's even stronger now; it is definitely issuing from within her room... What on Earth is it...?

I tentatively push open the door...

The sight that greets my eyes will haunt me forever. Blood. Blood everywhere. The bed is saturated with it. And Gillian lies stretched out on the bed. Gillian, mutilated, desecrated, her unclothed body slick with blood...

I stagger back from the door. The landing spins around me; and then all recedes into darkness and I am falling, falling, into a yawning abyss...

Part Two
Hammer into Anvil

Chapter Nine
How I Experienced a Change of Place

A face fills my field of vision, hazy at first, but then slowly swimming into clear focus. The face of a young Asian woman; she is wearing glasses and smiling at me. She has a white cap perched on her head.

'Takaco...?' I say. My voice is cracked and husky.

'Welcome back, Randal.'

No, it is not Takaco. Takaco doesn't wear glasses.

'Who are you...?'

I'm a nurse,' says the woman; 'and my name is Stella. See?'

She points to a badge pinned to the apron of her uniform: a white disc emblazoned with the name 'stella' (no uppercase first letter) in black lettering. The Albertus font...

'Am in hospital...?' I inquire.

'That's right,' replies Stella brightly. 'You're quite safe.'

And indeed, as I start to take in my surroundings, I perceive that I'm lying in a bed not my own, wearing a suit of pyjamas not my own, in a room not my own. Daylight enters through a window behind me. The room has more the appearance of a modest hotel apartment than a hospital room. The room is carpeted, tastefully furnished, supplied with a television... A private hospital...?

'What happened...?' I ask.

'You've been asleep, Randal,' replies Nurse Stella. 'You've been in a deep sleep for the past three days; completely comatose.'

'Why—?' I begin. Then it comes back to me. Gillian. Gillian lying on a blood-soaked bed. Did that really happen...?

'My friend Gillian: is she really dead? Or did I dream—?'

'I'm afraid she is dead, Randal,' says Stella. 'Discovering your friend was the event that triggered your collapse. The shock was too much for you. Your mind just refused to accept it and shut down.'

'And so I'm in hospital…? Which one?'

'You are in Morsham Psychiatric Hospital, Randal. We'll take good care of you here.'

'Psychiatric hospital? Why am I in the psychiatric hospital? Shouldn't I be in—'

'Your illness is a mental one, Randal. We're the best people to help you.'

The door, which my bed is facing, opens and a second nurse enters, pushing a trolley. She is a black woman, and I see from her badge that her name is Patricia. She wheels the trolley up to the bed.

'Sit up and have some breakfast, Randal,' says Stella. 'You need to get your strength back.'

With Stella's assistance, I sit up in bed. An overbed table is pushed into position and Patricia takes the breakfast tray from the trolley and places it before me.

'Why do your badges only have your first names?' I ask.

'It's because we like to be informal here, Randal,' answers Stella. 'We all have them: staff and patients. See? You're wearing one yourself.'

I look down and there is indeed a badge bearing the legend 'randal' pinned to the shirt of my pyjamas.

The lid is lifted from the breakfast tray, revealing a small pot of tea, hot toast, and a jar of preserves.

'Just a light breakfast,' says Stella. 'You haven't eaten for days, so too much food will only make you sick. Just take your time and eat slowly, Randal. And then I'll take you to see our director, Dr Tombs. He's very anxious to meet you.'

'Dr Tombs? And what's his first name?'

'Dr Tombs is Dr Tombs,' replies Stella.

Patricia, pushing her trolley, exits the room, and I turn my attention to my repast—and I do indeed find that my appetite has diminished. One would have thought that, after three days' abstinence, the reverse would have been the case. Three days. It hardly seems possible. It seems like only an hour ago that I was confronted with the horrific sight of Gillian; her room blood-soaked like a slaughterhouse, reeking of the stuff...

And I can remember passing out, overcome by the horror of it... I felt like I was falling into a bottomless abyss; and after an interval of a second, or of an eternity, my eyes opened again, and before me was the face of Nurse Stella...

I have eaten all I can and refreshed myself with two cups of tea when Nurse Patricia returns, this time pushing a wheelchair.

'Right on time!' says Stella. 'Now we can take you to see Dr Tombs.'

'A wheelchair?' I exclaim. 'Do you mean to say I am paralysed? Have just three days of disuse caused my lower limbs to atrophy—? Wait a minute; no: no, I can feel my legs; I'm not paralysed at all!'

'Yes, your legs are fine, Randal,' says Stella. 'But after three days of inertia, your constitution will be weak, and it is quite a distance from this room to Dr Tombs' office; we don't want you to over-exert yourself.'

'Ah! I see.'

Stella places a pair of slippers beside the bed. She then pulls back the covers, and I swing my legs out of the bed, placing my feet in the slippers. Assisted by Stella, I then rise hesitantly to the perpendicular.

'Are you okay, Randal?' asks Stella.

'Yes, although I do feel rather weak.'

'That's only to be expected.'

Patricia comes forward with a dressing gown, and helps me into it. I tie the cord around my waist and then the two nurses assist me into the bathchair. (Which, by the way, I have always considered a very strange and misleading name for a wheelchair; it seems to imply a bathtub and a conveyance all in one, which it manifestly isn't.)

Stella takes command of the wheelchair, and we leave the room and pass along a number of corridors; and again the décor looks more like that of a respectable hotel than of a mental institution.

We enter a lift, Stella reversing me in so that I am facing the doors. On the keypad are a vertical row of buttons marked B, G, 1, 2, 3 and T—and it is the latter button which Stella depresses.

The lift begins to ascend.

'What does "T" stand for?' I inquire. '"Top Floor"?'

'No; "t" is for "tower",' replies Stella. 'Dr Tombs' office is up in the tower.'

'A tower? What sort of building is this? Are we in a castle, or something?'

'No, it's a mansion house. I think it's Victorian.'

'I see.'

The lift comes to a halt. The doors slide apart and my conveyance is wheeled into an immense circular chamber—no, perhaps not actually immense, but it gives you the impression of so being from its being completely unfurnished save for a substantial wooden desk, curved in shape, and placed in the very centre of the room. The floor is carpeted, a pale green in colour, and the walls, white in hue, are adorned with framed works of art of all shapes and sizes. I confess to being no expert on the subject of painting, but the canvases I see around me now, which I believe to be of the impressionist and surrealist schools, look to me to be frankly tasteless and grotesque. However, I am scarcely giving them my full critical attention at the present juncture, being far more interested in the occupant of the desk. Upon our arrival the chair was turned away, but now, as we advance across the room, the chair revolves with a smoothness which suggests automation, and its occupant is revealed to me.

'My dear chap, I'm so delighted to finally meet you! Come in, come in!'

So this is Dr Tombs. He is a man of indeterminate middle-age, tall and rather stocky in build, clean-shaven, his dark hair streaked with grey. Rising from his chair, he comes round the desk to meet me, his face, which is smooth and heavily-jowled, wreathed with smiles. He is clad in a white high-collared laboratory coat, buttoned up to the neck; below its skirts can be seen the legs of beige trousers and a pair of canvas shoes.

Stella brings my chair to a halt before the desk, and Dr Tombs eagerly takes my hand.

'Pleasure to meet you! Pleasure to meet you!' he enthuses, vigorously pumping my hand. 'Our sleeping beauty awakes at last! Ha-ha-ha!' He turns his attention to Stella. 'And how is our patient today, nurse?'

'Very well, Doctor,' is the reply. 'He has just eaten a small breakfast, and seems to be recovering his strength.'

'Excellent, excellent! And what about his memory? Any signs of amnesia?'

'None at all, Doctor. He seems to have full recall of all events leading up to his collapse.'

'Good, good! Capital!' Tombs pats my shoulder. 'We'll soon have you back in tip-top condition, eh, my boy?' To Stella: 'You may leave us for now. I want to have a little chat with our patient.'

Stella departs and Dr Tombs resumes his seat behind the desk, and, placing his elbows on the surface, looks across at me with that broad smile fixed to his face. I do not like that smile, I have to admit. There is something about it, an air of self-satisfied superciliousness—and I also feel like I have seen that smile somewhere before; only I cannot for the life of me think where…

'So, Randal; what do you think of my little collection?'

'Your what?'

'My paintings, my paintings!' He waves his arms to indicate the daubs adorning the walls.

In deference to my host, I make a second cursory survey of the paintings, and I cannot say they improve upon renewed acquaintance.

'Yes, very impressive,' I allow. 'Although, not being an expert, I am unable to place the artists… That large canvas there,' pointing, 'is perhaps a Dali…'

This provokes a belly-laugh from my host. 'My dear fellow, none of these paintings are from renowned artists; they are strictly amateur efforts, each and every one of them. In fact, they are the products of art therapy sessions. Psychiatry is my field, and I find these paintings of the mentally ill to be an endless source of fascination.'

Art therapy. The mentally ill. I begin to understand why these daubs all look so grotesque.

Dr Tombs is facing me again. 'And there is one other significant factor these paintings all have in common; can you guess what it is?'

'No,' I say, not being in the mood for guessing games after my Salvador Dali blunder.

'I'll tell you,' says Tombs impressively. 'The thing they have in common is that each and every one of the artists whose work you see before you, subsequently took his or her own life! Yes; suicides, each and every one of them. What do you think about that, eh?'

I re-examine the paintings, this time with a modicum of curiosity. 'Well, I… It's certainly fascinating… But, well… I am compelled to say it doesn't really say much in favour of the track record of this institution.'

This provokes another belly laugh. It seems I've dropped another clanger.

'My dear chap, these painting aren't the work of patients of mine! They've been gathered from mental institutions all around the world! Ha-ha-ha! But yes, you're right: it wouldn't have said much for my track record as a mental health practitioner if they *had* all been from my patients! Ha-ha-ha! Mind you, I cannot say I've *never* lost any of my patients that way—no institution can boast that. With the worst cases, it becomes a battle of wits, you see. They are determined to destroy themselves, these suicides; while we, on our side, are equal in our determination to prevent them from destroying themselves. But alas, every now and then, one of them gets the better of us. You see, it's not just despair that motivates these people; in fact they may not even feel despair at all—it's simply that their minds are telling them that they *have* to destroy themselves; that it's the only logical and reasonable thing they can possibly do. It's becomes an imperative with these people; an overwhelming urge.'

Dr Tombs' eyes are fixed on me as he speaks; his brown eyes twinkling with amusement. It's all wrong. No-one's eyes should be twinkling like this when talking about such a dreadful subject. It's all wrong. I confess I do not like this man.

His voice becomes quieter. 'Have you ever felt that way, Randal?' he inquires. 'Have you ever felt that to destroy yourself is the only solution? The only way out?'

'No; never,' I answer, truthfully.

'Well, I'm very glad to hear that!' he exclaims, ebullient once more. 'And now that you're back amongst the living, how do you feel you are coping? Has your mind now accepted the fact of the rape and murder of your friend Gillian Draper?'

'Rape?' I squeak, aghast. 'She was raped as well?'

'Oh yes, repeatedly, my dear fellow; repeatedly. The coroner's report makes grim reading. Her ordeal was a protracted one; her death was not a quick and painless one—quite the reverse in fact; quite the reverse.'

Once again, the eyes and the voice clash with the nature of the words being spoken.

'Still! At least you're off the hook now! The police know that *you* didn't do the deed.'

'You mean I was a suspect?' I exclaim.

'My dear chap, of course you were! You were found unconscious at the scene of the crime!'

'And how does that make me a suspect?' I demand.

'Well, you see the police had the idea you might have committed the crime while in a frenzy of rage and lust, and that then, having done the deed, you returned to your senses, and were so appalled at the sight of what you had just done, that you collapsed on the spot! I believe your landlord was also suspicious of you; something about you once having tried to break into Miss Draper's room…?'

'Ah, now, I can explain that—'

'My dear fellow, it doesn't matter now! As I said, you're off the hook. While you were locked in the arms of Morpheus, the police helped themselves to a sample of your DNA. They compared it with the killer's DNA, and—no match. And anyway, since then they've made an arrest—although last I heard they've still yet to charge the fellow.'

'They've arrested someone? Who?'

'Another friend of yours, as it happens. Or perhaps he's more of a quondam friend since he successfully ran against you in that bi-election.'

'You mean Darren Nesbit?' I exclaim. 'They've arrested him?'

'Yes. Seems that on the day of the murder, he'd had a furious row with Miss Draper. She barged into his office or something, and whatever it was they were arguing about, he did not have the best of it. So there's your motive. On top of that, the fellow has no alibi for the time of the murder. There's your opportunity.'

'But this is ridiculous!' I say. 'I've known Darren for years! He's incapable of committing such an horrendous crime!'

'My dear chap, if there's one thing I've learned in all my years as a psychiatrist, it's that almost anyone is capable of *anything*, given the right, or perhaps I should say the *wrong*, set of circumstances.'

'But even if he had the intent, he couldn't have done it! He would have been physically incapable of doing it! You must have seen the fellow on TV! He's five foot two and weighs about seven stone. Gillian was five foot eleven and must have weighed at least twelve!'

'Yes, but the coroner's report says there was a very large quantity of alcohol in Gillian Draper's bloodstream. This would have seriously inhibited her ability to defend herself; especially if she was taken by surprise while she was asleep—which is precisely what they believe to have been the case.'

'Well, yes; Gillian was very drunk that evening,' I allow. 'But even so, I know that Darren didn't murder Gillian, because I know who did!'

This gets his attention. He clearly wasn't expecting this.

'You do?' he asks eagerly. 'And whom do you suspect?'

'My double,' I reply, folding my arms with satisfaction.

He looks at me blankly. 'Your double? I'm sorry old chap, but you've lost me there.'

'I have a double. A doppelgänger. He's a relentless fellow and capable of anything. And what's more, I saw him loitering across the road from our apartment house on the very night of the murder!'

'I see…' says Dr Tombs (quite clearly *not* seeing!) 'But this double of yours… if he was your twin so to speak, wouldn't his DNA pattern be identical to yours…?'

'I didn't say he was my clone! He is an individual whose features have been surgically altered to be identical to my own.'

'And his voice as well? Did they alter that?'

'Well, I've never actually heard him speak, but yes, presumably. In fact, yes, he must sound identical to me, because he's fooled other people into thinking he's me.'

Tombs rubs his (upper) chin thoughtfully. 'And erm… how long have you been afflicted with this malicious counterpart? Has he always been around, or is he—?'

'No, he hasn't always been around. He was only created recently.'

'And who created him? Do you know?'

'Yes, I do. It was the people at the Unemployment Centre who created him.'

Dr Tombs pauses to reflect on this one. 'I see… The Unemployment Centre… But, according to my records those people are your current employers, aren't they?'

'They *were* my employers, yes,' I confess. 'But as it happens, I handed in my resignation the very day that… Gillian… died…'

'So, the people at the Unemployment Centre created this duplicate of you… And why did they do that, Randal?'

'To cause me mischief, that's why!' is my vehement response. 'First he seduced the woman I was supposed to be meeting up with; and then he put my name forward as an election candidate!'

'You didn't put your own name forward as a candidate? Then why on Earth didn't you withdraw when you found out what the other fellow had done? You didn't have to go through with it just because you'd been nominated!'

'I know that! But I had hoped to outwit the man! My double, I mean. He wanted me to fail, so I decided to accept the challenge, and win the election. And I would have won it, as well! I was way ahead of the other candidates! But then the rascal coerced Darren into running against me, and wrote those speeches of his, those scandalous defamatory speeches! And thus, defeat was snatched from the jaws of victory, and my double triumphed after all.'

'Well, this is most interesting,' says Dr Tombs. 'Absolutely fascinating, in fact! Tell me: how many times have you actually met your doppelgänger? You say you've never heard his voice, so you haven't spoken to the fellow; but how many times have you actually seen him?'

'Only on three occasions, to tell the truth,' I reply. 'The first time was in the operating theatre at the Unemployment Centre—'

'The operating theatre at the Unemployment Centre? I didn't realise that place was equipped with medical facilities…'

'Yes, they are. But they're hidden away. You have to go into a toilet cubicle and push the flush handle upwards to get there. Anyway, that was the first time, although at the time I didn't realise he was my double; his face was swathed in bandages, you see.'

'I see. And when was your second meeting with your double?'

'That was when I returned to my room one morning, and I found the fellow lying stretched out on my bed.'

'I see. He was asleep on your bed, was he?'

'No! He was wide awake! And he was looking at me with this smug, supercilious smile on his face—like he was daring me to challenge his right to be there.'

'Then why didn't you challenge him? Why didn't you exchange words with the fellow?'

'Well, I… because I was so surprised! Anyone would have been! My first thought was to run upstairs to Gillian's room and tell her about it. But alas, by the time I returned downstairs with her, my double had fled the scene.'

'He had, had he? And what about Gillian? Did she still believe your story, in spite of the lack of physical evidence?'

'Well, no, she didn't; and I was very annoyed with her at the time, but in hindsight I realise she only reacted the way anyone else would have.'

'And you say the third time you saw your duplicate was on the night of Miss Draper's murder?'

'Yes. I was returning home from the public house with Gillian, and I saw him standing across the street. We both saw him!'

'Ah, so Miss Draper did see the fellow on this occasion?'

'Well, yes, but it was dark you see; so she couldn't actually *see* that it was my double—but *I* could tell it was him! You couldn't see his features admittedly, but I could tell it was him by the general outline of the figure.'

'That general outline being your general outline?'

'Yes! And what happened to Gillian proves that it was him! He must have broken into the building when everyone was asleep, and, and…'

'…And carried out that frenzied and fatal assault upon your friend. I see, I see… But why would he do that? What grievance could he have had with Miss Draper?'

'None! He killed Gillian to get at me, of course! Just to get at me! He'd already turned Darren against me; and next he wanted to part me from the only true friend I had left! Don't you see? This is all about *me!* It has been from the start!'

'I *do* see, Randal,' says Dr Tombs. 'All is very clear to me now; very clear. I can't tell you how glad I am that we have had this little chat. It has been most illuminating; most illuminating. Let us adjourn for now, and we can have our next little talk, say… this time tomorrow morning. How does that sound?'

'Yes, that's fine with me,' I say. 'Tomorrow morning. That will be when you'll be discharging me, then?'

'Good heavens, no!' exclaims Dr Tombs. 'Discharge you tomorrow? No, no; that would be the height of irresponsibility! I have no intention of discharging until you have been completely cured.'

I frown at this. 'Cured? But I *am* cured. I have emerged from my prolonged state of slumber. True, I'm still feeling a little weak, but that will soon pass—so I really don't see what else there is that needs to be cured…'

'That's because you can't see the wood for the trees, old chap. I'm talking about your persecution mania! Your delusional belief that a conspiracy has been hatched against you; a conspiracy that has become symbolised by this imaginary double you believe yourself to be afflicted with!'

I am aghast. I thought Dr Tombs actually understood me! I didn't particularly care for the fellow, but I assumed he knew his own job!

'But I do have a double!' I protest. 'He's out there right now, plotting who knows what mischief!'

'No, Randal; he's not out there—he's in *here*!' Dr Tombs taps the side of his head. 'That's where he is. He's lodged inside that noggin of yours, and it's going to be my job to winkle him out!'

This morning I have been wheeled out onto the terrace to partake of some fresh air. As I had been informed by Nurse Stella, the hospital is a mansion house of considerable size. The walls of the house, with their white paintwork, bask in the light of a bright sun in a cloudless firmament. The terrace looks out upon the extensive back gardens, which are planted with coniferous trees and shrubberies, and intersected with meandering footpaths upon which some of the patients are stretching their legs. Marble statues stand at intervals along the paths. Other patients are seated here upon the terrace, which is supplied with tables and chairs; some of them just sitting, others engaged in activities such as sketching, knitting, jigsaw puzzles… My chair has been wheeled right up to the marble balustrade. I have by my side a book, borrowed from the hospital's well-stocked library, but at present I am just reposing myself, enjoying the warmth and fresh air. It is so quiet and peaceful—hard to believe we are in the middle of teaming London. From the absence of traffic noise, we are clearly far from any main road.

I have already enjoyed—although I can't really say I 'enjoyed' it—my second interview with Dr Tombs. He insists that my doppelgänger is a figment of my imagination, a symptom of a mental malaise. It is common for people with certain types of mental disorder to believe themselves afflicted with a double, he says, citing works of fiction by Dostoevsky, Poe and Vladimir Nabokov as illustrations of this fact. All very well, and far be it for me to dispute the findings of those eminent writers; however, in *my* particular case, the duplicate is a reality, a fact—the cause of, and not a symptom of, my mind's excited state. And while Dr Tombs may be determined to convince me that my double is a fantasy, I am equally determined to convince him of the contrary. And we will see who will emerge triumphant from this contest!

I discover that I have become the object of scrutiny from one of my fellow patients. He (I think it's a he) sits some distance along the terrace from me. His head is shaved completely bald, his age indeterminate, and he stares at me with eyes bulging and with a ludicrously inane smile stretched across his face. He seems to be taxing his facial muscles to their utmost to produce the widest smile he can without actually parting his lips. I suspect it is this very exertion which is causing his eyes to bulge to such an extent.

I don't know why he's doing it, and bearing in mind where we are, probably neither does he—but nevertheless, I do not like it. I do not care to be stared at in this ridiculous manner.

'Can I help you?' I inquire, in my frostiest tones.

The fellow offers no reply. He continues to stare at me, the smile unwavering.

'If you have anything to say to me, then kindly just say it,' I proceed. 'It is very rude to stare at people like that.'

He still offers no reply, and still he smiles at me.

'Look, my good man: I repeat, if you have anything to say—'

'My dear chap! He's not going to *speak* to you!'

I look up. Dr Tombs has appeared on the terrace, jovial as usual, hands thrust in the pockets of his laboratory jacket.

'Why not?' I ask.

'Because he *can't* speak!' answers Tombs. 'Acute mutism. That's why he's here—he hasn't uttered a single word for five years; not a syllable.'

I look at the man (still smiling at me), then back at Dr Tombs. To not utter a single word for the extent of five years; the prospect makes me shudder. 'Hasn't spoken for five years?'

'Not a murmur.'

'Brought on by trauma, I suppose?'

Dr Tombs shakes his head. 'No. No trauma.'

'Then… was he always a quiet one?'

Another headshake. 'Used to talk the hind legs off a donkey.'

'Then is he doing it for a bet?'

'Of course not. If he was doing it for a bet then the person he was betting against would have to be keeping a close watch on him all the time, wouldn't they?'

'Yes, I suppose they would…'

'Well, enough of that,' says Dr Tombs, leaning himself against the balustrade. 'I've got some news that will interest you.'

'Really?'

'Yes. Your friend, or former friend, Darren Nesbit: the police have released him without charge. Cleared of any involvement by a DNA comparison.'

'Just as I told you!' I say triumphantly. 'I knew it wasn't Darren. The very idea was preposterous! So, what do you say now, eh? Still think my doppelgänger is a figment of my imagination?'

'My dear fellow, of course I do!' declares Tombs, grinning insufferably. 'Young Nesbit being cleared doesn't prove the existence of your double.'

'But of course it does! Who else could have murdered Gillian? There isn't a single other suspect!'

'There is, you know: there are the other tenants in the boarding house—that's who the police are turning their attention to now. Three of them are men, aren't they? And then there's the landlord himself; the very man who pointed the finger of suspicion at you. That's who the police are looking at now: all of the people who have keys to the premises.'

'A list which includes my double!' I insist. 'I know he has a set of keys because he got into my room on one occasion! Add to that the fact that I saw him standing across the road on the night of the murder! And Gillian saw him too!'

'You saw a *figure* standing across the street,' counters Dr Tombs. 'It was dark and it could have been anyone.' I am about to protest further, but Tombs holds up a restraining hand. 'Now, now, my dear chap. I didn't come out here to take up our previous argument; that can wait until our next session. I just wanted to let you know the news about your friend, and having done this, I will leave you to enjoy the sun and fresh air.'

And, patting me on the shoulder, he takes his leave.

That confounded mutist fellow is still smiling at me.

I keep dreaming about Gillian.

It's the same dream every time. It's the morning after the murder, and I am walking up the stairs to Gillian's room, just as I did in actuality—except that in my dream I already know what I'm going to find. I'm not smelling the blood—does one ever experience odours in dreams? I don't think I ever have—but still I know what I'm going to see when I open the door. And I open the door, and there she is, stretched out upon her bed, weltering in her own blood. (In reality she was lying there naked, but in my dreams my subconscious has chastely supplied her with clothing.) And then she sits up in bed. She's dead, but somehow she sits up, and she turns her blood-splattered visage and she looks at me; she looks at me with an imploring look in her eyes, as though she is mutely asking me why I allowed this to happen to her...

At that juncture I always wake up. As I say, I have experienced this identical dream every night since emerging from my coma. And there is some bitter irony attached to all of this, because I remember once having had a conversation with Gillian on the very subject of recurring dreams, in which she had declared that recurring dreams never actually occurred in the real world; that they were merely a useful device employed by writers of fiction. (Split-personalities, she claimed, were another example of this.) And so, here am I, experiencing a recurring dream myself, and a dream that involves the very person who once claimed that recurring dreams never really happened!

I think she would have been amused if she could have heard about this.

Today I have been pronounced fit enough to walk by myself unattended, and I plan to take my first stroll in the gardens I have previously only observed from the terrace. The weather has remained clement, and I have now resumed my everyday apparel, to wit, my black blazer with white piping, navy-blue jumper, beige trousers and canvas shoes. My name badge is now pinned to the breast of the blazer.

According to Stella, one of the main functions of these name badges is to facilitate easy communication between the patients in the hospital. With our names clearly emblazoned on our chests, we are all, in a manner of speaking, immediately on first-name terms, obviating the need for formal introductions. And similarly, with the staff also displaying these name badges, the patients should similarly feel able to communicate with them in a relaxed and informal manner. (Dr Tombs being the single exception to this rule first-name, for some reason.)

Traversing the main hallway leading to the back doors, I find myself suddenly face to face with one of the uniformed orderlies, a thin-faced Indian-looking man, who appears without warning through the open doorway of one of the common rooms.

'My apologies,' he says, favouring me with a brief smile. 'Wasn't looking where I was going.'

I feel I have seen this fellow before; not here. But somewhere else. I see from his badge that his name is Malcolm.

'Have we met before…?' I inquire.

'We haven't spoken before,' says Malcolm; 'but I work here, so I know who you are, of course.'

'I meant… have we met before on the outside?'

Malcolm shakes his head. 'No, I do not believe we have met before on the outside, Randal.'

And with this he takes his leave. I proceed on my way, still possessed of the nagging feeling that I have seen that man before, but in a completely different context.

Outside, I descend the terrace steps and set off on my stroll, following the footpaths which wind amongst the trees and shrubberies of the garden. I have proceeded for some distance without encountering a soul, when a fellow wearing an incongruous top hat appears on the path ahead of me. I've seen him around before: a young man in his earliest twenties, one of those pretty-boy types, and who looks like a nuisance. Catching sight of me, he doffs his headgear and strolls up to me. I see from his badge that his name is Spike.

'All's well that ends well, eh?' he says, grinning at me.

'What's all well?' I inquire, modulating my tone to make it clear to the fellow that I'm not particularly interested.

He taps the side of his nose. 'So… You been having sex with your wife again? Have you? Now, what have I told you about having sex with your wife?'

'Having sex with my wife?'

'Ah-ha! So, you have, have you? But did you have sex with her by accident, or did you have sex with her deliberately, and with malice aforethought?'

'With malice a— Look, I don't even *have* a wife, you cretin!'

'Then whose wife was she? Eh? Eh?' He sidles up to me, nudges me in the ribs. 'You ever been knifed at rapepoint?'

'Knifed at rapepoint?' I echo, incredulously. 'What's that supposed to mean?'

'Knifed at rapepoint. That's when your nefarious assailant threatens to rape you unless you let him stab you to death with a knife. So, Randal, have you ever undergone that particular ordeal? Have you? Have you?'

'No I have not! And if I had, I wouldn't be around to tell you about it, would I? Ipso facto.'

'Hm…' The fellow ruminates on this one. My logic is infallible of course; but whether this fellow has any grasp of logic is another matter. 'You ever been to the shops and found out they were closed?'

'I suppose so… I can't bring to mind any particular occurrence, but I suppose it must have happened at one time or another…'

'So you admit it!' he crows. 'You admit that the shops were closed! And you only found out they were closed after you got inside, and you realised you'd just walked through a steel security door and a plate-glass window and you're standing there in the shop and the alarms are going off! You admit it!'

'I admit nothing of the sort, you imbecile!' I retort. 'Do you think I could be so unaware of my surroundings as not to notice that the shutter was down? And even if I didn't, how could I possibly walk straight through it? I'm not a Cyberman!' He opens his mouth to speak but I stop him with an imperative gesture. 'Look, sir, I came out here to take a constitutional, not to stand around talking utter nonsense with the likes of you. Now will you please let me pursue my way? And *don't* follow me!'

Spike doffs his hat. 'Pleasure talking to you, sir. I look forward to enjoying future conversation with you. Enjoy your walk!'

I proceed upon my way without reciprocating the sentiments. I shall endeavour to avoid that man's company as much as I can—his nonsensical blathering is enough to drive anyone up the wall!

But then of course, if the fellow was perfectly sane, then he wouldn't be here, would he? At least they are not harbouring any dangerous lunatics in this facility: Nurse Stella assured me of this when I expressed my concerns on the subject.

And then I see it. Through a gap in the foliage of the trees, standing against the clear blue sky—

A green dome.

The Green Dome.

I freeze in my tracks, staring open-mouthed at the awful sight. The Green Dome. It's right there in front of me. I've been tricked, duped, deceived! I'm not Morsham at all—I'm back in Portmeirion!

But it *can't* be…

I leave the path, and pass between the trees, keeping the dome in sight. Unless I have completely lost my bearings, the dome is situated exactly where the building in which I have been staying stands, and which I have been led to believe is the Morsham Psychiatric Hospital. Could it really be…?

I step into a clearing and the building comes into full view. Yes, it *is* the hospital. And the green dome rises from the very centre of the building… Blessed relief floods over me. It's not the Green Dome at all; not the Portmeirion Green Dome. I see now that it is smaller in dimensions than the Green Dome of the Village, which anyway stands adjacent to a building, and does not form the centrepiece of one, as this one does. But yet, as far as memory serves, the architecture is indeed identical…

Good lord! Have I fallen once again into the clutches of the Village? True, the actual Village hospital featured in *The Prisoner* was a castle; it stood just outside the Village itself and its architecture was of a completely different nature… But the television series was produced over fifty years ago; perhaps since that time the original hospital has been demolished and replaced with the building I see before me now?

Yes… Why didn't I realise before? This can't be Morsham! The clean air; the absence of sound…!

I start running. I run and I burst onto a pathway. My eye is caught by the sight of a bench with a single occupant; a small, skinny man slouched in a dejected posture.

It's Darren! Darren Nesbit! Thank goodness!

I call out his name and rush towards him. He looks up at me; his features do not reflect my own feelings of joy; but then, Darren's not the most demonstrative of fellows. I sit myself down beside him and clap a friendly arm around his shoulders.

'Darren, my friend! I can't tell you how glad I am to see you! I was starting to have the most dreadful suspicions that I had been abducted and taken back to the Village! Can you believe it? And just because the green dome on the top of the tower yonder happens to resemble the Green Dome in the Village! But I suppose it must just be a coincidence of appearances, after all! Or else, this hospital was designed by the same architect, Sir Clough Williams-Ellis. This *is* Morsham Psychiatric Hospital, I take it?'

''Course it is,' says Darren.

'Yes, of course! I mean, if we weren't, you wouldn't have been able to come here to pay me this visit! And I must say, I am exceedingly glad—'

'I *didn't* come here to visit you,' interjects Darren sullenly.

I remove my arm from his shoulders. 'You didn't? Then there's someone else here you came to see…?'

'I'm a patient,' says Darren. 'Same as you.'

'A patient?' I gasp. 'Since when?'

'Since today.'

I look at him, and for the first time I discern that he is indeed wearing a name badge upon his striped jumper. 'So you're a patient… But what, er, what happened to you…?'

'I had a kind of breakdown…' says Darren.

'A breakdown, eh? Oh! On account of being arrested and suspected of Gillian's murder? You shouldn't let that get to you! Why, I knew all along that you were innocent; and now you've been *proved* innocent—by that DNA test! The whole world knows you're innocent!'

'It's not just that,' says Darren, still staring at the ground.

'Oh… Did something else happen, then…?'

'Yeah. I got chucked out by my party.'

'Your party…? Oh! The Little People's Party! Chucked you out? But how could they do that? I thought you were in charge of that party! I believed you to be its originator! And *why* would they dismiss you?'

'It was after I got arrested. The papers started writing things about me; about how I'd been friends with you for a long time, and that I only run against you in the election cuz I'd fallen out with you and had a grudge against you…'

'But that's ridiculous!' I exclaim. 'They said that on account of those speeches you made? Those speeches that assaulted my good character? But you didn't even write those speeches yourself! Didn't your party colleagues know that?'

Darren looks at me at last. He looks puzzled. 'How did you know I didn't write them speeches?'

'How did I know? Because I know you of course!' giving him a hearty squeeze of the shoulders. 'Those speeches were far too polished and articulate for them to have possibly been the offspring of *your* brain! It was as clear as day they were way beyond your meagre capabilities! You could have written nothing more than the most inept and clodhopping of speeches even if your life depended on it! So, worry not, my friend! Worry not! I knew from the start that you were nothing more than a figurehead; a patsy, a stooge. As if you could even launch, let alone successfully prosecute, a political campaign by your unaided self! The very idea is ludicrous! So, worry not! I knew well that those slanderous remarks you were making, those defamations of my good character, were not of your invention! I knew that you were no more than a puppet, with others behind you pulling the strings! And I bear you no malice for those scandalous words that you were compelled to pour forth from your lips—Good lord!'

I have only just noticed Darren's face. He is staring at me wide-eyed, and the entire righthand side of his face is twitching epileptically: the eye, the cheek, the corner of the mouth—he seems to be on the verge of some kind of fit.

'My good man!' I cry sympathetically. 'What have they done to you? You may not be aware of it, but your face is involuntarily twitching—this is a sure sign of suppressed anxiety! How are you feeling? Shall I get you a glass of water?'

He seems unable to form an articulate reply. His lips are twitching violently, vague, unintelligible sounds issue forth. Now his entire body is starting to shake as with an ague, while all the time his bulging eyes remain fixed upon myself. If I read them aright, he is silently pleading with me for comfort in his distress. Now he raises his hands, they are shaking, his fingers curled like claws, reaching towards me—reaching out like a drowning man reaching out for that one piece of driftwood which will save his life…

Suddenly Nurse Stella appears, as if out of nowhere, and assists Darren to his feet. 'Come along, Darren,' she says. 'We need to get you back inside. Time for your medication.'

She assists Darren into a wheelchair, held by Nurse Patricia.

'Please take good care of him,' I command, having risen to my feet also. 'He is a good friend of mine, and he has been through some trying times. I would suggest that a period of bedrest might be in order.'

'We'll take good care of him,' answers Stella. 'Don't you worry about that, Randal.'

The two nurses wheel Darren off back towards the hospital building. 'I will come and look in on you later!' I call out after him.

Darren, although still shaking alarmingly, manages to voice a reply, although I am unable to discern it—doubtless an expression of his gratitude for my concern.

In actuality, several days elapse before I am able to see Darren again. His fit proves to be a severe and protracted one, and no-one aside from the medical staff who are treating him has been permitted to see him.

On one occasion, upon ascending to pay him a visit (Darren's room is situate on the floor above my own), I have the door rudely closed in my face by Nurse Stella, and from within I hear the sounds of my unfortunate friend spitting obscenities, accusing the world of ill-treating and conspiring against him; it is distressing to hear, and reminds me of an occasion, several months ago now, when, calling upon Darren at his apartment, I heard similar sounds issuing from within. I realise now that he was experiencing a fit on that occasion, demonstrating that his breakdown has in fact been a long time in the making, and is not simply a result of his recent ordeals and setbacks.

But that being the case, what could have been the primary cause of poor Darren starting to come apart at the seams? I cannot fathom it. Until our recent dissension, I had been Darren's constant companion, and I know of no circumstances in his life that could have been provoking such internal turmoil in the poor fellow—I really am at a complete loss to determine the cause of his mental disintegration.

However, Darren is in good hands and has been responding favourably to treatment (so I have been informed); and now on the fourth day since the seizure, I have been granted permission to pay a brief visit to Darren in his room.

I find him sitting up in bed and apparently in good spirits. There is a smile on his face; indeed it seems to be fixed there. In addition, his head is swaying somewhat from side to side. If I didn't know better, I'd say the fellow was drunk; has he managed to smuggle some alcohol into his room? Or perhaps bribed one of the orderlies? (I've always heard that orderlies in mental institutions are amenable to this type of bribery.)

'Hello there,' he greets me. 'Take a pew.'

I seat myself upon the chair at his bedside. His room, in its essentials, is identical to my own; and indeed, as I have perceived from open doors I have passed, all the patients' rooms in this facility follow the same pattern.

'And how are you this fine day?' I inquire.

'Oh, I'm peachy,' replies Darren, still smiling. 'Just peachy.'

'Excellent!' I say, discreetly sniffing the air he has just exhaled. No... No, I cannot discern any whiff of alcohol fumes. 'Well, you're certainly looking better! Positively jolly, in fact!'

Darren giggles. 'Yeah, I'm jolly,' he agrees.

'Yes, you are,' I say. 'Very jolly indeed.'

Another giggle from Darren.

'It's the medication they've got me on,' he supplies. Ah, of course! Medication. I should have thought of that.

'Well, let's just hope it sets you up and you can get of here,' I say. 'Have they... have they given you any prognosis as to how long you are likely to remain here?'

Darren shakes his swaying head. 'Nope,' he says.

'They haven't, eh? The same is true in my own case. You er… you know why it is that I have been admitted to this institution…?'

'Cuz of what happened to Gillian,' replies Darren, the smile fading now. 'Horrible, that was. Horrible.'

'It was,' I concur. 'It was indeed… But you see, that's not entirely why I have been compelled to remain here. You see, Dr Tombs—have you met Dr Tombs?'

'Yeah, I've met him.'

'Well, Dr Tombs, you see, erroneously believes that I am suffering from a delusion. It's my double, you see: he just doesn't believe in the existence of my double!'

'Your double,' says Darren, smiling once more.

'Yes: my double! So, I thought if you were to confirm my testimony, if you were to assure the good doctor of your own personal knowledge of my double…'

Darren giggles. 'Personal knowledge of your double…?'

'Yes! He was writing your speeches, wasn't he? In the election campaign! He was the one writing your speeches!'

'Your double was writing my speeches?' echoes Darren, still giggling. 'First I heard about it.'

'Don't give me that, you little wretch!' I say with some ire. 'You're not going to tell me you were writing them yourself, are you?'

'Well, no…' he admits.

'Then, it was my double, wasn't it?' I thunder. 'My double!'

'Look, I dunno *who* was writing 'em,' says Darren. 'And I never saw no double of you. I got them speeches from Takaco. That's all I know.'

'Well, that proves it, doesn't it?' I declare. 'Takaco was the go-between. She's working for my double; probably his mistress, in fact!'

'Takaco's your double's mistress?' giggles Darren.

'Yes! You don't think she was following you around during the election because she was enamoured of you, do you? She wasn't sleeping with *you*, was she?'

'Well, no, she weren't,' admits Darren, and I am pleased to see that making this confession nettles him somewhat. 'She was just helping me out; giving me my speeches…'

'Yes, but she wasn't *writing* them, was she? She couldn't even *speak* fluent English, so she wouldn't have been able to *write* it!'

'Yeah? She can talk it well enough when she wants to. Mind you, there *was* someone else: but I never saw 'im. And Takaco, she never said who he was. The only ones I saw was her and Dhawan.'

'*Dhawan!*' I thunder. 'My campaign manager? *That* Dhawan?'

'Yeah,' chuckles Darren (for which I feel the urge to slap him.) 'He was in on it an' all!'

'*Dhawan…?*' I am thunderstruck. 'Gillian—she insisted that he had to have been involved in the plot… But I didn't believe her… But, how *could* he have been plotting with you behind my back? During the election, he was with me practically every minute of the day…'

'Not *all* the time, he wasn't,' chuckles Darren.

'And you can stop that laughing,' I tell him. 'I may have been set-up, but so were you, don't forget. Where's Takaco, eh? I bet she vanished the moment you won the election—I noticed her beauty parlour has closed its doors. It was my double, you see. He was the one behind it all: first he entered me into the election; and then he arranged for you to enter the race for the sole purpose of knocking me down. That was what it was about! And the moment you'd won, they didn't need you anymore—and so they dropped you like a hot potato! Didn't they?'

'Yeah, they did…' admits Darren, crestfallen. This I consider to be the appropriate frame of mind; but suddenly he perks up and is chuckling again, the wretch! 'Yeah, I wonder what happened to Takaco? Where's she got to, eh?'

'I fail to see what you find so amusing,' I say, drily. 'She deceived you every bit as much as she deceived me; more so, in fact.'

The door opens and in walks Nurse Stella.

'Well, look 'oo it is!' exclaims Darren, launching into renewed floods of mirth. I fail to see what he finds so amusing about the advent of Nurse Stella.

'That will be enough for today, Randal,' Stella tells me. 'Darren here needs his rest.'

'Of course,' I reply, rising from my chair. 'I am most pleased to see how well you're recuperating, Darren. I shall speak to you again anon.'

Darren chuckles a response. As I pass Stella, I say, *sotto voce*, 'You might want to reduce the dosage of his medication a touch…'

'Post-Traumatic Stress Disorder,' pronounces Dr Tombs.

I am back in Dr Tombs' office for another therapy session.

'Post-Traumatic Stress Disorder?' I echo.

'Indeed. This is the underlying cause of this recurring dream of yours. Your mind is struggling to process the fact of Gillian Draper's violent demise. Perfectly natural, of course. With these sudden bereavements, the reaction can often be a delayed one. And in your own particular case, I suspect that your suppressed grief is aggravated by an equally suppressed feeling of guilt.'

I look at him. 'Guilt? What do you mean guilt?'

'I mean,' says Tombs, his eyes boring into me; 'that nagging feeling in the back of your mind, that *you* are responsible for Miss Draper being murdered.'

'Me? What are you talking about? I didn't kill her! I've been cleared! The DNA test—'

'My dear chap, I don't mean that you actually did the deed. Not at all. I am referring to your guilty feelings of having opened the door for her killer—almost literally opened the door, in fact.'

'Opened the door? What are you talking about? Please speak plainly.'

'I will, I will. Cast your mind back. When you returned to the apartment house with Gillian that night, you helped her up to her room, didn't you?'

'Yes...'

'And you put her to bed, didn't you?'

'Well, in a manner of speaking... Really, she just threw herself down on the bed, and almost immediately went to sleep.'

'Quite so. And then what did you do?'

'What did I do? Well, nothing. I departed. I went down to my own quarters.'

'Did you leave her door open?'

'Of course not! I closed the door as I left.'

'And did you *lock* the door?'

'Well, no... How could I? I couldn't have locked the door without locking her in, could I? I would had to have taken her key away with me. Our room doors don't have letter boxes, so I couldn't have slipped it through the door...'

The office seems to be growing darker, as though the lights are being gradually dimmed.

'Yes, but you could have slipped the key *under* the door,' continues Dr Tombs.

'I... I don't think there would have been room for that...'

'You don't *think* there was. But you didn't check, did you...?'

A spotlight comes on, fixing me with its interrogating glare. I look up at it and it dazzles me, forcing me to return my attention to my interlocutor.

'No...' I say. 'I... It didn't... at the time, it didn't seem important...'

'Well, of course it didn't, my dear chap! You're not psychic, are you? How could you possibly have foreseen what fate had in store for your friend...? But, nonetheless, you *did* leave her door unlocked, didn't you? And that's what's been bothering you, isn't it? It's been there, at the back of your mind, nagging away at you, hasn't it? "If only." That's the thought you've been trying to push away, isn't it? "If only I'd locked her door..."'

Dr Tombs has become imbrued in a green light. All other colours have been washed away from his face; his smooth, flabby features have become positively demonic; a chiaroscuro of green light and black shadow. His eyes, with their heavy underlids, glare at me with an unflinching intensity. I want to look away from them, but I cannot; I have become trapped by them.

The white light shines on myself, the green light on Dr Tombs; and around us lies an ocean of inky darkness. I try to voice my denial of his accusation, but the words stick in my throat. I can no more speak than I can turn away from that satanic visage.

'Yes... "If only I'd locked the door..." Perhaps it was one of the male lodgers... Overcome by an insensate desire, he left his room and crept up to Miss Draper's door... How did he hope to gain entrance? Perhaps, if she was still awake, he had hopes of simply talking her into opening the door for him...? Or perhaps he intended, as you once did, to discover if he could open her door with his own pass-key... But in the event, he finds he doesn't have to hazard either of these experiments: he turns the handle and he discovers that *the door is not locked*... And so, he carefully opens the door and he looks into the room, and he sees the dark form of the occupant lying stretched out upon her bed... and he hears the laboured breathing of the inebriate passed out from excessive drinking... Lying there oblivious, helpless, completely at his mercy. The very thing he has been seeking; a warm, female body with which to satisfy his lusts...'

I want to stop him; I want to refute his claims; to tell him that the murder was one of premeditation, not of opportunism; that the culprit was my double, who having gained entry to the lodging house, would have doubtless come provided with the means of effecting entry into Gillian's room, perhaps even possessing a duplicate key... This is what I want to tell him; but still I am powerless, still I can neither speak nor look away.

'...Do you know what the intruder did to prevent Miss Draper from crying out and raising the alarm...? No...? It's all in the police report... First, he manually dislocated her jaw; then he used a filleting knife to cut out her tongue; and finally, he forced the knife-blade deep into her oesophagus in order to paralyse the vocal cords; and he taped the knife into place, thus preventing the victim from being able to even eject the obstruction by using her throat muscles... It's all in the police report, Randal...'

He's smiling; smiling as he tells me of these horrors; smiling, his face, bathed in that green glow, like the jade statue of some sadistic Eastern deity. I can feel my body shaking, tears are pouring from my eyes, sweat is oozing from every pore of my skin. And still I can't look away...

'Yes, poor Gillian's last moments would have been agonisingly painful, and her ordeal was a protracted one... Repeatedly raped, systematically tortured... And finally, but by no means rapidly, expiring from blood-loss engendered by the countless wounds to her body... It's appalling to contemplate... And you, you having to carry around with you that awful knowledge that you were the one who left Gillian's apartment door unlocked, that you enabled the assailant to gain entry... Small wonder that in your nightmares Gillian looks at you with those reproachful eyes, those eyes that are a reflection of your own intolerable feelings of guilt...'

With an inarticulate cry, I tear myself from my chair.

Dr Tombs' demoniac laughter pursues me as I flee across the darkened room. I run into the wall, and my groping hands find, instead of the expected metal surface of the lift doors, a picture frame upon the wall; one of those daubs of the mentally ill. The picture suddenly lights up, backlit as though the image were painted on glass—and the immense round eyes of a hideous grey-visaged caricature glare at me; the eyes of a maniac, burning with intense light. I jump back from the thing with a scream, as renewed laughter echoes around the room.

The doors; I know they must be nearby. I grope along the wall—and another canvas erupts into light, a tortured landscape from a tortured mind; an awful wilderness of rocks twisted into impossible shapes. I stumble onwards. A third picture blazes into light; an obscene chaos slabs of human flesh piled together in no recognisably human form, glistening tumours and strange orifices; and then a fourth, assailing me with a vivid crimson slaughterhouse nightmare of blood, bone fragments and internal organs.

I lurch onwards and now, at least, my hands encounter a surface of polished metal. Mercifully, the lift doors slide open, and I tumble into the car. The protracted mocking laughter of Dr Tombs is finally extinguished when the doors close on the now pitch-black room.

The lift ascends and I burst into the corridor and into the light of day. With relief, comes reaction, and I feel my bowels urgently demanding to be relieved of their burden. I traverse the corridors with as much speed as still my weakened limbs will allow, and gain the haven of the nearest set of Gentlemen's toilets.

No sooner have I seated myself in a cubicle than the sluice gates open. I heave a sigh. My body has been eased of its burden, even if my mind has not.

Dr Tombs is a monster! I will not suffer another day under his so-called ministrations! I have to get out of here!

'You've got to get out of here,' comes a voice from the adjacent cubicle.

'You again!' I exclaim, recognising the voice. 'Why do you only ever speak to me when we're in the toilets like this?'

'Because it's the only place that's safe! Even now I can't talk for long, so listen: They've got you this time; they've got you good. You're a prisoner!'

'I'm not a prisoner! This is just a mental hospital! I can leave whenever I want!'

'This *isn't* just a mental hospital! This is the Village! You've seen the Green Dome, haven't you?'

'Well, yes, I don't deny the architectural similitude to the dome in Portmeirion, and I admit that for a brief time I did entertain some suspicions—but now Darren is here! He wasn't brought here in a state of unconsciousness as I was; and he has confirmed that we are in Morsham Psychiatric Hospital!'

'If he says that, then they must have tricked him. This *isn't* Morsham Psychiatric Hospital! Morsham doesn't even *have* a mental hospital! You ought to know that!'

'Well, I'll admit I'd never heard of such a place until I found myself here, but... Are you trying to tell me we're back in Wales?'

'England, Wales; it doesn't matter! The Village can be anywhere! *This* is the Village! And who do you think Dr Tombs is?'

'He's a monster; that's who he is!' I declare with some feeling.

'More than that: he's Number Two! And you're a number as well! Look at your badge!'

'My badge merely states my name: Randal.'

'*Look* at it! Take it off and look at it.'

'If you insist.' I unclip the badge from my jacket. 'I'm looking at my badge. It still says "Randal."'

'Feel around the edge. There's a second layer underneath. You can peel it away.'

I feel around the edge of the badge—and yes; my fingertip does encounter a slight ridge. I push it upwards and I am able to peel away the top surface of the badge.

My heart takes a leap. Revealed now is the second, true surface of the badge: displayed on a white background is a penny-farthing device, and within the large front wheel, emblazoned in red font, a single numeral:

6

Chapter Ten
How I Became Six of One and Half a Dozen of the Other

At this critical moment I hear the outer door open and someone enter the room.

'Anyone in here?' inquires a voice, and from the tone of authority I take it to be that of a staff member.

'Yes, I'm in here,' answers my interlocutor in the neighbouring cubicle. 'Nearly done. I'll be with you in a sec.'

I hear the toilet flush and the cubicle door open.

'Get a move on, then,' speaks the newcomer. 'We're needed in physio.'

Footsteps cross the tiled floor. The outer door opens and closes.

I know not for how long I just sit there, staring at the penny-farthing badge, the words of my unseen informant reverberating around my head. Time becomes a meaningless concept. I am not a patient, I'm a prisoner. I am not in Morhsam, I'm in the Village.

And I am Number Six.

And that monster Dr Tombs is Number Two.

I had my suspicions, but then Darren arrived and my suspicions were put at rest because he confirmed we were in Morsham Psychiatric Hospital, and he was not brought here in a state of unconsciousness like myself—but now my informant, my inside man, tells me Darren was tricked somehow, that there is no Morsham Psychiatric Hospital, and that we are somewhere else entirely.

Try walking out of here if you don't believe me.

I reach a decision.

Having cleansed my fundament and washed my hands, I emerge from the toilets, and instead of returning to my quarters, I bend my steps towards the main staircase. The main staircase descends to the main hallway; the main hallway serves as the hospital's reception area and waiting room for arriving patients and visitors; facing the foot of the stairs are the main entrance doors; through these, and one steps down onto the main forecourt and thence to the main drive leading directly to the main gates. This is the route I shall follow. I have to know. I have to know for sure whether I am indeed a prisoner in these precincts.

I eye with suspicion everyone whom I pass in the hallways, patients and staff alike. Until now I believed these patients to be mentally unsound members of my own local community. Now I know that they are not—but whether they are dupes, prisoners like myself, or if they are all imposters, just another facet of the deception being imposed upon me, I do not know. And as for the staff; while I know that one of them is secretly my ally, the balance of them, if my informant's account is a veracious one, are my enemies, my gaolers.

Just as I am thinking this, Nurse Stella suddenly appears in my path at the top of the staircase.

'Where are you going, Randal?' she asks. 'Shouldn't you be in therapy right now?'

'No, I shouldn't!' I retort. 'I have had more than enough of your "therapy!" I am leaving this place—discharging myself!'

She looks surprised. 'You're going? But you haven't even packed your belongings!'

'You know, you're right! It completely slipped my mind! Would you be so good as to pop back to my room and do that for me now? Just throw everything in a suitcase. Much obliged! I will meet you down in the foyer!'

And, without affording her time to articulate a response, I step round her, and rapidly descend the two flights of stairs to the reception area—where much to my confusion, I find Nurse Stella awaiting me, hands on hips, blocking my path.

'Really, Randal! What's come over you? You can't just walk out like this without a word to anyone!'

'On the contrary: I *can* just walk out of here!' I retort loftily. 'I know my rights. You have no authority to keep a patient in a mental institution from leaving if he so wishes, unless that patient has been sectioned—and *I* have not been sectioned! Therefore, I bid you good-day!'

'But there is still a protocol that needs to be followed,' insists Stella. 'You haven't filled out your discharge papers!'

'Send them to me in the post!' And with that, I adroitly navigate past her and I cross the hallway with a firm step, making straight for the entrance doors. Stella does not call out to me, nor do I hear her dogging my steps.

Good! She has given up at last!

I reach the entrance doors unmolested, and open them—and there is Stella, standing under the shady portico.

'I really can't let you go like this, Randal,' says the infuriating woman. 'Let's just go back to your room and then we can calmly talk this through with Dr Tombs.'

'I have no desire to engage in any conversation with Dr Tombs!' I thunder. 'I wish never to set eyes on him again! The man is a fiend! Now, I insist that you let me pass!'

'Now, Randal; I cannot, in good conscience—'

'I have no interest in the workings of your conscience, madam, be it good, or otherwise! I will leave you to wrestle with it at your leisure!'

And skirting round this starched obstacle once again, I descend the steps to the gravel forecourt and make a beeline for the treelined avenue leading to the front gates. I have observed these gates from a distance during my rambles of the past few days, and they are of solid metal construction; not the grilled gates one would normally expect to see at the entrance to a mansion house such as this one. Previously, I had surmised that grilled gates had been eschewed as being too easy for absconding patients to scale and effect an escape, but now I wonder if the solid gates are not in fact there to prevent people from being able to see what lies beyond them.

These gates now come into view—and Nurse Stella, damn her epicanthic eyes, is standing there before them! And what's more she is not alone: two burly-looking male orderlies stand at her shoulders, and all three of them have their arms folded over chests in a resolute manner.

'Open those gates!' I shout, as I cross the intervening space. 'You have no authority to keep me here!'

'I'm afraid I cannot do that, Randal,' is Stella's calm reply. 'I have spoken with Dr Tombs, and he is insistent that you should not leave us in this hasty and ill-considered manner.'

'And I am equally insistent that I *shall* leave you in this hasty and ill-considered manner!' is my crushing rejoinder. 'Open those gates at once!'

I now stand before her, and refusing to be intimidated by the presence of her muscular attendants, I glare upon her the full force of my unassailable resolve.

'No,' she replies, calm as anything. 'I will not open the gates.'

'Not open them?' I echo. 'What do you mean, not open them? You have no authority to forcibly restrain a patient, unless that patient—'

'—Has been sectioned. Yes, I know, Randal. And if you persist in this violent and irrational behaviour of yours, sectioned is just what you will be.'

Sectioned! A shudder runs through me, as though in anticipation of the deluge of cold water with which they treat such unfortunates. Nurse Stella looks at me with a calm, yet determined mien. That look—not to mention the presence of the two burly orderlies—informs me that her threat is no idle one.

I pause to consider my options.

'If you were to open those gates…'

'I'm not going to open them.'

'Yes, but if you *were* to open them,' I pursue; 'what would I see…?'

'You would see a road, Randal; and on the other side of the road you would see Morsham Common. That is where this hospital is located.'

'Yes, yes, Morsham Common… But perhaps, if you were just to open the gates for a second—just for a second, mind!—so that I could just take one brief refreshing look at Morsham Common…? It has always been my favourite nature spot, you see; and to glimpse just for a second that mighty vista of the lush greensward unfolding itself towards the gauzy horizon, the landscape embellished with those noble stands of venerable trees, whose leafy crowns extend towards the azure heavens as if in homage to the majesty—'

'No, I cannot open the gates for you, Randal,' interrupts Stella.

'Why not? I assure you I have no intention of making a break for it, if that's what you're thinking! And even if I had, I am sure you and your two associates here would be more than enough to thwart any such attempt on my part. So, just a quick peek…?'

'No.'

'Why not?'

'Because there is no need. If you are in need of nature therapy, there is more than enough verdure within these grounds to satisfy your requirements.'

'Yes, but for nostalgia's sake—?'

'No.'

'And that's your final word on the subject?'

'It is.'

'Very well.' I glance from her to her two attendants. Their heavy features are impassive, and have remained so throughout the forgoing duologue. 'Then I have no choice but to adduce from your stubborn refusal, that you are deceiving me; that it is *not* Morsham Common that lies beyond these portals, but some other location entirely! Yes! You think you have successfully deceived me! But you are wrong! Oh, so very wrong! Well, you haven't heard the last of this! I withdraw for now, but my spirit remains unbroken! I will be freed from the shackles you have been tightening around me!'

And with this, I turn upon my heel, and march back up the driveway. I have impressed even myself with my impassioned speech of defiance—all that lies before me now is to work out how the devil I'm going to make good on it.

I arrive at the haven of my room and am more vexed than surprised to find that Nurse Stella has arrived there before me, and is calmly awaiting my return. I really wish she would leave me alone.

'You seem suddenly very suspicious of us, Randal,' are her first words. 'And I also notice that you are not wearing your badge. Is there any reason for this?'

'Yes!' I tell her. 'A very good reason.' Making a sudden decision, I reach into my breast pocket, produce the badge—

still denuded of its adhesive upper surface—and I thrust it before Stella's eyes. 'You see? I've found you out! I have peeled back the adhesive layer of deception and uncovered the truth! What about your badge, "Stella"? What does yours say underneath?'

'Shh!' is the unexpected response, accompanied with an index-finger-over-mouth gesture. 'Quiet, you fool!'

I am nonplussed. Stella seems suddenly changed. Gone is the cool, professional demeanour; she seems tense, wary. And strangely familiar as well…

'Why are you shushing me? Don't think you can—'

'Shhh, you idiot!' she hisses urgently. 'Look. Don't say anything; just look.'

And with this, Stella peels back the surface of the name badge pinned to her nurse's uniform. Underneath it is the Village penny-farthing motif, and emblazoned on it in red, the number sixteen!

From being nonplussed I am now completely flabbergasted. While I return her silent gaze, I examine her features closely; I picture shades instead of transparent lenses; I picture the hair tied up under a jaunty mod cap; I replace the nurse's dress with blue trousers and a red and white striped blazer…

Yes, it's her! The woman from Portmeirion! Number Sixteen!

'It's you!'

'Shhhh!'

Yes, it's her alright.

Resuming her Nurse Stella persona, Sixteen escorts me down to the rear gardens. We set off along one of the pathways, and then, attaining a particular spot deep within the trees, Number Sixteen, after looking to ensure that we are unobserved, guides me off the path and into the trees, and we emerge in a small clearing, completely concealed by the surrounding foliage.

'We can talk here,' she says, heaving an audible sigh of relief. 'This is a blind-spot; we're out of the range of all surveillance, visual or audio.'

'So this place is the Village!' I exclaim. 'And I'm a prisoner!'

'I'm afraid so,' answers Number Sixteen. 'Unfortunately, there was nothing we could do to prevent your being brought here; but now that you *are* here, I will endeavour to help you in every way I can. You've got to get out of here! You must escape at all costs! That is imperative!'

'But you only just *stopped* me from leaving here five minutes ago!' I retort, in my wrath perhaps somewhat shortening the intervening passage of time. 'Why couldn't you have just opened the gates for me?'

She starts 'shushing' me again. Just like old times. 'Keep your voice down, you idiot! If you bellow like that, every microphone within a fifty-metre radius will be able to pick you up!'

I drop my voice to an urgent whisper and repeat my question. 'Why didn't you open the gates?'

'Because, although I am on your side, those other two men weren't! They would have stopped me! And even if I had opened the gates, you wouldn't have got far! The alarm would have been raised immediately and you would have been brought straight back! You can't escape from here by just brazenly walking out in broad daylight—and I would have been signing my own death warrant if I had openly assisted you in any way.'

'So, what do we do?' I demand. 'I have to get away from that monster Dr Tombs! Or Number Two, I should say. The man's a fiend: he's worse than John Sharp and Patrick Cargill put together!'

'I know he's a fiend,' replies Number Sixteen. 'I am as well acquainted with that fact as you are, believe me.' Her face assumes an expression of bitterness which informs me that she and Number Two have some previous history—the details of which I strongly suspect I would not want to hear. She seems to shake off her unpleasant memories and returns her attention to myself. 'Yes, he is a fiend, and he's determined to break you down, and so the first thing you need to do if you want to get out of here is to pull yourself together! You're not going to get anywhere by behaving like you were behaving just now!'

'Oh, really? And just how am I supposed to behave?' I demand.

'Shhhh!' hisses Number Sixteen. 'And you have just illustrated my point. It is all that bombast and bluster you must get rid of first! Think about it: you are the new Number Six; try living up to your number. That is what you need to do!'

Her words strike home, quashing the ireful retort that was rising to my lips. Yes. Yes, she's right. If I want to survive this ordeal, if I want to escape, I first have to adapt myself to my new environment. My new environment is effectively the Village, and it was only a personality like that of Patrick McGoohan, the original Number Six, that could defy all attempts to break him down, thwart his opponents, be resolute in his determination to escape from his prison... Yes; I must effect another code change; now that I wear his badge, I must endeavour to become like the original Number Six! As to the outer man, I already possess his general appearance: I have his hair, I have his clothes, (admittedly I also have a few additional pounds in weight, but that is a minor issue); all I have to do now is to cultivate the mindset; I must learn to think like my illustrious predecessor.

Think like him, and *talk* like him.

'Need to talk to you. Privately.'

Darren, seated at a table on the terrace, dressed in his bumble-bee sweater and beige slacks, looks up at me.

'Uh?'

'Need to talk to you. Privately.'

'Alright then,' he says. 'I'm listening.'

'Not here,' I say. 'Somewhere more private. Come on.'

I descend the terrace steps into the grounds, Darren following. I take the path that will lead us to that surveillance blind-spot to which Number Sixteen took me yesterday.

'So, what d'you want to talk about?' asks Darren, falling into step at my side.

'Not now. Walls have ears. So do statues.' I incline my head towards the example of statuary we are passing at that moment.

Darren looks at it. 'Yeah, it does have ears,' he says. 'He'd look silly without 'em.'

'Ears in *both* senses of the word.'

Darren transfers his gaze to me. 'Why are you talking like that?'

'Don't know what you mean. Talking like what?'

'Talking like that. Your voice is different, and you're not using all those big words like you usually do.'

'People change. Sometimes they have to.'

'You weren't like this yesterday.'

'Lot of things have happened since yesterday. That's what I want to talk to you about.'

We reach the clearing.

'We can talk now,' I tell Darren. 'They can't hear us here.'

Darren looks around. 'What are you on about? Who can't hear us?'

'Them! This place, this so-called hospital, is covered by blanket surveillance, sound and vision. But there are a few blind-spots for those who know about them; this is one of them. You see, Darren, you are not where you think you are; you are not where you have been led to believe that you are. We're not in Morsham, and this place is actually part of the Village!'

'Come off it,' snorts Darren. 'That's just you thinking things.'

'No, it is not just me "thinking things"; and if you want some solid proof, I'll be happy to oblige.'

So saying, I peel back the upper surface of my name badge, revealing the penny-farthing badge underneath.

'You see? Under the façade of our names, we're all just numbers—and I'm Number Six!'

Darren looks at it. The sight has clearly sobered him up. He looks at the badge, and then he looks up at me.

'You did that...' he says. 'You made that thing yourself...'

'I did nothing of the kind!' I grate, emulating my predecessor's best angry voice. 'Your badge is just the same! Everyone's is! Go on! Peel back the lying façade of your badge; find out what number you are!'

With seemingly great reluctance, Darren examines the badge pinned to his jumper.

'No... It can't be...'

'Go on! Feel around the edge with your finger nail!'

He does so, and he discovers the division between the two layers. He looks at me, alarmed, and then he peels back the upper surface. The penny-farthing logo is revealed, and his number is Forty-Two. Darren twists the badge around to examine it himself.

He raises inquiring, almost imploring, eyes to myself. 'What does it mean?'

'Means you're a number,' I tell him tersely. 'Means you're a prisoner like me.'

Darren starts to shake his head. 'No... no, that isn't right; that can't be right... We're in Morsham Psychiatric Hospital... This is just a hospital...'

'This is *not* just a hospital, and we are *not* in Morsham! This is the Village! And the man in charge, the man who calls himself Dr Tombs—he is Number Two!'

'Then what am *I* doing here?' wails Darren. 'I didn't do anything! It's you they want; not me!'

'Get a hold of yourself, man!' I snap. I'm surprised. Darren seems to be on the verge of a full-blown panic attack. I didn't foresee he would take it this badly. 'I'm not sure why they brought you here; and yes, you're right: it's me they're primarily concerned with. Perhaps their object was in the way they brought you here. They tricked you into believing you were still in Morsham; maybe they did that just so you would allay my own suspicions as to where we really were.'

'But we *are* in Morsham!' insists Darren, still in that pitiful wailing tone. 'I was took here in an ambulance! I was wide awake the whole time—it couldn't have been more than twenty minutes!'

'They tricked you, Darren. You were in the back of the ambulance, yes? Couldn't really see where you were being taken? Who was in there with you? You weren't on your own, were you?'

'No; there was a couple of medics…'

'Right. Well, they drugged you, or used hypnosis, perhaps. Either way, you were made to lose consciousness, and then they brought you round in such a way that you were completely unaware that you'd ever been unconscious, or that any time had passed. That's how they did it.'

Darren looks flabbergasted. 'Then… we could be anywhere…?'

'Yes. I have no idea of our true location. I'll have to ask Number Sixteen. She's on our side and she should know.'

'Who's Number Sixteen?'

'You already know her: she's Nurse Stella. She's supposed to be working for them, but really she's on our side. She's the woman I met that day in Portmeirion, remember? The day this whole business started. She's going to help us; help us make our escape.'

'Oh, *her*. Is she the one what told you about all this?'

'Yes. Her and my other informant; the one who only speaks to me unseen; he's here as well.'

For some reason this amuses Darren. He starts to giggle.

'Stella? She's Number Sixteen, is she? Ha-ha-ha! Worked out she was the same person, did you? Ha-ha-ha! Nothing gets past you, eh? So we're all prisoners? Ha-ha-ha! Can't rely on anyone these days, can you? Yeah, we need to get out of here, don't we? Ha-ha-ha! Run while we can! Run while we can! Ha-ha-ha!'

And then the silly fool does just that: he starts running!

'Come back you imbecile!' I roar, dropping out of character in the urgency of the moment.

I set off in pursuit, but he's too fast for me, nimble little rodent that he is, and he soon leaves me far behind. (I learn later from Number Sixteen that he has experienced another relapse and has been confined to his room. Clearly my revelations have been all too much for him—and after I had anticipated that my greatest difficulty would have been in convincing the poor fellow to believe me at all!)

Now that I have adopted the original Prisoner's mindset, I must formulate a plan of escape. The Prisoner was a driven man, and his mind was perpetually focused upon effecting a method of escape from his place of confinement—therefore I must be just as single-minded in my endeavours. Thoughts of escape must be with me always, plans must be continually evolving and refining themselves in my fertile and active brain.

Let me consider some of the methods of escape employed by the Prisoner during the course of the television series… First, there was escape by sea; that happened in two episodes. In 'The Chimes of Big Ben' the Prisoner built a boat; in 'Many Happy Returns' he built a raft. In this second attempt he was actually successful—although his escape proved to be only temporary. Actually, that episode is somewhat problematical, as it seemed to state definitively that the location of the Village was a Mediterranean island; yet in the final episode the Prisoner and his companions were able to drive from the Village back to London in a truck.

True, they did first pass through a tunnel of indeterminate length, so perhaps this tunnel did indeed extend from the Mediterranean to the Southern Coast of Great Britain. Another explanation is that the Village in *The Prisoner* was in fact in the same location in which it exists in reality: to wit, North Wales. This apparent contradiction of physical location was giving me many a headache in the notes I was compiling for my book. Regardless of this, the immediate barrier between myself and freedom is not the ocean but a twelve-foot-high brick wall—this being the case, the building of a boat or raft must be ruled out as a viable method of escape.

Secondly, we have escape by helicopter. In the television series people were brought to, and taken from, the Village by this method. Again, this avenue of escape was attempted twice. On the first occasion the Prisoner attempted to fly himself to safety, but his attempt had been anticipated and control of the machine was wrested from him and he was flown back to his starting point. On the second occasion, he attempted to leave as a passenger in the helicopter, pretending to be his own double—and he almost succeeded, had not his imposture been detected at the last minute by Number Two. The first of these methods is out of the question for myself: I am not a qualified helicopter pilot. The second method can only be employed if my own double were to show his face here, which so far he has not. In addition to this, there is also the obstacle of there being no helicopter serving this installation. I have yet to see or hear of one, at any rate. Therefore, for the time being at least, helicopter must be ruled out as a means of surmounting the walls of my prison.

In conclusion: with sea and air travel being eliminated as options, the only way to surmount the obstacle of the twenty-foot walls which encompass my prison will be to climb them on my own two feet!

I must formulate a plan wherewith to effect this.

I encounter Number Sixteen as she is emerging from Darren's quarters. Upon seeing me, she firmly closes the door and places herself in front of it to bar my entrance.

'Darren is still not well enough to be seen, Randal,' she tells me. 'If you were to come back this evening...'

'But I must speak to him,' I say. 'I need to discuss my escape plans—'

'Shh!' hisses Number Sixteen. 'Not in here!' And then, in a louder voice. 'I'm sorry, but Darren is not well enough to converse with you right now. As I say, if you were to come back this evening...'

'Then what about you?' I demand. 'Are you "well enough to converse with"? I haven't had a proper talk with you since—'

This sets her off again. 'Shhh! My opportunities for meeting you outside are extremely limited,' she tells me in an urgent whisper. 'If we are seen together too often it will raise suspicions. Even now someone might be watching us and wondering what we are whispering about!'

'Ah, my dear fellow; there you are!'

It's Dr Tombs—or Number Two as I now know him to be. He strolls up to us, smiling that insincere smile of his. I assume the indomitable frown and tight-lipped determined demeanour of the original Number Six. I am not going to be cowed by this man. I will not be bullied or harassed, or coerced by him in any way.

It was bad enough when I believed to be a genuine psychiatrist who honestly believed my doppelgänger to be a figment of my imagination—but now that I know he is Number Two, I know that he has been aware of the reality of my double all along; and what's more he knows that my double was Gillian's murderer, and that the crime was a premeditated one, and not an opportunistic assault contingent upon my having left the door of Gillian's apartment unlocked. The monster knew this, and yet he still did his utmost to inflict upon me the burden of guilt for Gillian's death!

'I haven't seen you for days!' he says, addressing me. 'You know, if I didn't know better, I'd think you'd been deliberately avoiding me!' chuckling, as if at some witty remark.

'Sorry to burst your bubble, but you *don't* know any better,' I tell him, indomitable frown in place; 'because I *have* been deliberately avoiding you!'

'Well, it pains me to hear you say that,' says Number Two, evincing a hurt look that is no more convincing than his smile. 'And when we were making such excellent progress with our one-to-one sessions! Our last session—'

'*Was* our last session,' I interrupt him. 'There will be no more. As therapist and patient, we are completely incompatible.'

'I think that is more something for me to decide,' argues the scoundrel. 'And really, I can't have you shirking your treatment programme. As long as you are a patient at this facility, it is my responsibility—'

'Forget it!' I snap. 'I don't mean to crow; but what do you do in your spare time?'

'Excuse me, Dr Tombs,' interjects Number Sixteen; 'but I was thinking that perhaps it might be time to move Randal on from individual to group therapy. In fact, he could join my own group. I have been observing Randal, and so far he has made very little effort to integrate with the other patients here. He is being very unmutual.'

'Unmutual, eh?' says Number Two. 'Well, we can't have that, can we?' Turning to me: 'That's the trouble with you individualists: always wrapped up in yourselves, aren't you? No community spirit.' To Stella: 'But even so, I would prefer to continue my own one-to-one sessions with Randal for the time being. At present he might be too much of a disruptive element for group therapy.'

'Very well, Doctor,' accedes Number Sixteen.

'Yes, my dear fellow,' says Number Two to me. 'We must resume our sessions forthwith!'

'Certainly we must,' I say. 'By mail!'

I have formulated a plan.

Accepting that my only viable method of escape is that of physically scaling the perimeter walls, then the main obstacle to overcome is surveillance: if I am seen climbing the walls, I will be stopped and brought back. The solution: I must *not* be seen climbing the walls! The means of achieving this: firstly, to locate and take advantage of an area of the perimeter wall that is not covered by surveillance cameras—in other words another blind-spot, like the clearing Number Sixteen introduced me to; and secondly, to effect my escape under cover of darkness, thus minimising the risk of being observed by passersby.

For this plan I will require a detailed map of the hospital's rear gardens, one delineating the exact position of every surveillance camera. Armed with this information, I will then be able to plot a path through the trees which will take me to the desired area of the perimeter wall without being observed by any of the cameras. As I cannot rely on Number Sixteen being able to furnish me with such a map, I must produce this map myself—and having acquired a sketchpad and pencils from the art therapy studio, I take to the grounds in order to draw my map. Of course I shall be in full view of the surveillance cameras in the statues, but to any observers it will appear that I am merely drawing sketches of the statues themselves; a harmless pastime.

A rather clever little deception, if I do say so myself. One worthy, I am inclined to think, of my illustrious predecessor!

When the time arrives for my next private conference with Number Sixteen, I am sure she is going to be suitably impressed.

'This plan is terrible.'

We are standing in the blind-spot clearing. Number Sixteen looks at me over the top of her glasses. I recall her doing this on the occasion of our first meeting in Portmeirion; on that occasion she had been wearing shades, so the gesture seemed to have some meaning to it then.

'What do you mean terrible?' I retort. This unexpected reaction feels rather like a stab in the back. 'What's so terrible about it?'

'I hardly know where to begin,' is her answer. She holds up the sketchpad she has just been perusing. 'For a start, this map you have drawn is completely wrong.'

Another knife-thrust. Until just now I had been highly pleased with the results of my cartography. 'How can it be wrong? Do you know how long it took me to draw it?'

'It is the results that must be judged; not the amount of effort put into the achievement of them,' is the merciless reply. 'You ask me what's wrong with the map? Everything. The scale; the position of the footpaths—everything. For practical purposes it is completely useless. And even if it wasn't, I can see at a glance that the path you have calculated for getting from the terrace to the wall is in full view of several surveillance cameras.' She turns the sketchpad to face me and points. 'See? Here, here, and here.'

'Ah, yes, but if you look again, you will see that my proposed route is on the blind side of those surveillance cameras; they're facing the other way.'

'Randal, the surveillance cameras are not always looking in the same direction.'

'But they're statues—!'

'Nevertheless, they are not always looking in the same direction.'

'Oh,' I say, somewhat crestfallen. 'Ah, but don't forget: this escape will take place at night. If we were to keep low, crawling through the underbrush, I'm sure we'd still be hidden from view...!'

'Perhaps so. But there is another major obstacle which will make your plan completely impossible: at night, after curfew, the guard dog is released into the grounds.'

'The guard dog?'

'Yes. A very fierce guard dog. It is called Rover.'

'Rover?' I hear the capital 'R' and I feel a thrill of terror. 'You mean—?'

'Yes. The very same guard dog that nearly caught us that day in Portmeirion. It patrols these grounds all night every night. It is impossible to avoid detection.'

'Well, that's that, then,' I say, completely deflated. 'I wished you'd told me about Rover earlier…'

'I wish you had told me about your escape plan earlier; I could perhaps have prevented you from wasting your time drawing this map.' She sighs. 'But really, Randal. Even if you had managed to make it to the perimeter wall unmolested, how did you plan to scale the wall? It is twenty feet in height; you would require equipment.'

'Ah, now that I *had* anticipated,' I say, perking up again. 'I discovered a gardener's shed—it's clearly marked on the map, see?—and I was going to borrow an axe or a hatchet, and I would have chopped down one of the trees nearest to the wall, and chopped it so that it would have fallen diagonally against the wall; thus becoming a convenient ladder, you see.'

Number Sixteen frowns. 'But then how did you propose to get down the other side? You couldn't have jumped from that height without injuring yourself.'

'Well, no… but we would have just pulled the tree up, and then tipped it over the other side of the wall… Again, like a ladder, you see…'

'Yes, but a tree is considerably heavier than a ladder; it would have been humanly impossible for you to just "pull it up."'

'Yes, but there would have been two of us, don't forget… Darren would have been with me…'

'Even for two it would have been an impossible task,' insists Number Sixteen. 'And you have no idea what the terrain is like on the other side of the wall. For all you know there might be a moat at the foot of the wall; or a pit filled with spikes.'

'Well, why don't *you* tell *me* what's out there?' I retort. I'm finding myself somewhat chagrined at this unending stream of criticism. 'You're supposed to be helping me with this, aren't you?'

'I have no more idea than yourself what lies beyond that wall,' says Number Sixteen.

I look at her. She looks completely serious. (But then she always does. I'm not sure if I've ever seen her smile. I try to picture her smiling and I just see Takaco, for some reason.) 'Are you seriously telling me that you, a member of the staff, were brought here in a state of unconsciousness, the same way I was?'

'No, I am not saying that.'

'Or in a closed ambulance, like Darren was?'

'Nor that, either. I arrived by train, Randal. All of the staff stationed here come and go by train.'

'Well, then! You must have seen *some* of the scenery out there! How far is this place from the train station? You must have seen *something*.'

'I saw nothing of the scenery outside, Randal. The train station is here inside the grounds.'

'It is not!' I exclaim. I snatch back my sketchpad, rapidly running my eyes over my plan of the grounds. 'No…! There's no train station! I would have included it on my map! It's not like I could have missed something that big…!'

'You didn't see the station because it is not *in* the grounds, it is *under* them. It is an *underground* railway by which we are all brought here; a secret underground railway belonging to the forces of the Village.'

I stare at Number Sixteen, flabbergasted. A secret underground railway! Now I'm completely out of my depth; nothing like this ever happened in the television series.

Chapter Eleven
How I Found Myself Checkmated

It is night. I pull the cord to open the curtains and look out of my window upon the verdurous gardens of the sanatorium (or whatever this place really is.) In the hours of darkness those groups of trees merge together and the garden appears to be one vast tract of woodland. My eyes range over the shadowy landscape, seeking any sign of movement. According to Number Sixteen, Rover patrols those paths and groves; an untiring guardian, ready to pounce on and smother any who would be foolish enough to defy the curfew.

Rover. I encountered it in Portmeirion, on that fateful day, the day that my life changed. I didn't actually see it on that occasion; I was too afraid to even look—but it passed very close to me, and I heard it, heard that strange medley of sounds it produces: reversed Gregorian chanting played over the emanations of a flying saucer…

Just what is Rover? This was one of the many enigmas left unresolved by the television series. Whenever it was spoken of, it was spoken of as being some kind of device; a security system that could be activated or deactivated at the flick of a switch… But in its actual presence it seemed to be more some kind of impossible creature; an amorphous white sphere that could move independently and that roared like a monster when it pounced upon its victims…

Of course, in the reality of the production of the series, Rover was simply a prop, a weather balloon pulled along on a string or propelled by a wind machine; and the balloons were fragile and burst very easily. (In the first of the *Prisoner* novels, Number Six actually discovers the skin of a deflated Rover—called Guardians in those novels—and utilises it to construct a hot-air balloon in an escape attempt.)

And now, looking out into the darkness, I see something. Yes! There is a distinct light moving amongst the trees over yonder; a strong, steady white light. The movement is fluid, and seems not like that of a person on foot carrying a torch… Does Rover glow in the dark? In the television series, what with its reliance on day-for-night filming, it was hard to tell… I recall one brief moment in 'Free for All' in which the Prisoner suddenly found himself inside a cave, and there were a number of people sitting in chairs around a stationary Rover—that one I am sure had been glowing with an internal light! (And what were those men doing sitting there staring at the thing like that? It seemed almost like some species of religious ceremony.)

The light appears to be moving in this direction, moving towards the hospital building… Good Lord! Has it seen me? Can it sense when it is being observed by human eyes? Perhaps it is a crime to even look at it!

I hastily withdraw from the window and pull the curtains shut.

'…The station is directly beneath the hospital building; very deep, of course; too far down for any sound of it to reach the surface.'

'And how does one get down to this subterranean train station?'

'There is a secret lift, known only to staff members. Its entrance is located in the main hallway on the ground floor; the doors are concealed to resemble the wooden panelling of the walls.'

'And how does one access this lift?'

'From a control panel, also concealed in the wall.'

'Then this is just what we wanted, isn't it? Couldn't I escape from here on board this train?'

'It is a possibility, yes. But there are many difficulties...'

I can't sleep now. I've started thinking about lava lamps.

Lava lamps were ubiquitous in the Prisoner; there seemed to be one in every room of Number Six's house, and presumably in everyone else's houses as well. It's the same here. There's one sharing my room with me right now, just as there is one in every patient's room. It's sitting there now, atop the chest of drawers to the left of my bed. I can't see it, because the light dims itself at night—but I know that it's there, and it's making me feel like I'm sharing my room with a ticking timebomb. I've already had to accustom myself to the idea that I have no real privacy in my quarters; that I will be under constant observation—but now, now that I know that Rover is here, I am faced with the hideous possibility of its being able to suddenly materialise itself right here in the room.

I have no wish to speak ill of the dead, but this is all Gillian's fault. She put the idea in my head. It was in one of our conversations about *The Prisoner*: Gillian was talking about the lava lamps, and she suggested a reason for their presence—that perhaps the lava lamps were actually receptacles for Rover! She pointed out how the creatures were always small when they first formed and that they always emerged from water (usually the ocean, but once from a fountain); and therefore, she maintained, those globular forms inside the lava lamps were actually embryonic Rover units; and that if required, they could suddenly burst out of their receptacles and appear full-sized in anyone's living room. She cited as further evidence the fact that the large screens on the walls of Number Two's office sometimes displayed lava lamp images, and sometimes images of Rover itself. At the time I had conceded that there might be something in Gillian's theory—but now, I wish I'd categorically denied it, because now I am a prisoner myself, and I'm sharing a room with one of those cursed lava lamps!

What I'd really like to do is pitch the thing out through the window; but I daren't. What if in picking up the lava lamp I disturb the thing inside it, and it breaks out of the lamp before I've had a chance to get rid of it?

I'm not going to be able to sleep a wink now; I know I'm not.

'…We were flown by helicopter to an abandoned factory building in the middle of the countryside. We were escorted into the building and into an elevator; this took us down to the subterranean train platform. A train arrived and we boarded it; it took us to this location. There were no intermediate stops. The journey took forty minutes.'

'Yes, but what about the helicopter flight? How long did that take? Do you think you were still in England when you landed at that factory?'

'I believe so, yes.'

'So where we are now must be in England as well, yes?'

'Not necessarily. We could have crossed into continental Europe during the train journey…'

According to Number Sixteen, neither the station beneath us here or the one beneath the factory are terminuses (termini?) She has no idea of the extent of this secret railway system employed by the forces of the Village. No other staff members she has spoken to on the subject has any idea either. Number Two will know, of course, but he's not saying anything…

Does this system extend across the entire UK mainland? Across all of Europe? The entire world? I recall once being bored out of my skull by a fellow university student who insisted on my watching with him this interminable foreign film of which he was enamoured; sitting through this opus was truly an exercise in endurance and fortitude on my part.

There was, however, one interesting element in the film: to wit, the existence of a secret trans-Continental subterranean highway employed by the military wing of the United Nations (and for nefarious purposes, apparently.) If the vehicles using this system employed fossil-fuel-burning internal combustion engines, one wonders what they did to evacuate the fumes…? If they didn't have some kind of ventilation system in place, the air down there would soon have become unbreathable…

Yes, when you think about it, electric trains would be a much more sensible option for the purposes of a subterranean transport system…

Why didn't they have a train episode in *The Prisoner*? In the last episode they had a lorry and an underground tunnel—so, perhaps there *was* an underground railway system, and the truck drove along the railway line to make its escape…? But wait—could the lorry have driven along the tracks like that? And the tracks of an underground railway would be electrified, wouldn't they? Wouldn't the lorry—and its passengers—have been electrocuted? But then, the tires would be rubber, wouldn't they? Ergo, they would have been insulated!

Yes… Perhaps there was a railway system after all…

Darren is up and about today, having recovered from his latest relapse, and I waste no time in taking him to the 'blindspot' glade in order to bring him up to speed with events. Darren's latest cure seems to have been effected by the simple expedient of considerably increasing the dose of his medication; he walks with a vacant, blissful smile fixed upon his face, and frequently chuckles to himself for no discernible reason. I'm going to have to do something about this. If we are going to make a successful escape together, I will need him to be more focused than this. We arrive at the clearing, and I impart to him the news concerning the underground railway station beneath the hospital.

'There's a tube stop down there?' he says. 'So we *are* still in London! Told you were we! Ha-ha-ha!'

'No, you dolt,' I snap. (Perhaps a touch out of character: I'm not sure McGoohan's Number Six would have used a word like 'dolt.') 'I said *an* underground railway, not *the* Underground. And in case it had slipped your mind, Morsham isn't even connected to the London Underground system. Or did you think that they'd built that extension of the Bakerloo line during the week or so that we've been away?'

'So, what's this railway for, then?' asks Darren.

'It's for conveying the staff here to and from the facility.'

'Oh yeah? *I* didn't come 'ere by train.'

'That's because you're not staff, you oaf! And therein lies the main obstacle to our employing this railway as a means of escape: it is only accessible to staff members. According to Number Sixteen, when leaving the facility, all passengers have to surrender their number badges to a ticket machine when they arrive at their destination; if the badge is not slotted into the machine, the doors will not open to allow them egress.'

'Yeah, but we've got number badges, an' all; why can't we just use ours?'

'Because they won't work. The staff member's badges are different; they contain a microchip, or have been treated with a special chemical compound or something of the kind—Number Sixteen isn't entirely sure which it is—but whatever the reason, patients' badges would not be accepted by the ticket machine as valid tickets. Number Sixteen is endeavouring to procure us staff member's badges so that we can make our escape.'

'Should be easy enough,' says Darren. 'When'll we be getting these badges, then?'

'It's *not* that easy. Number Sixteen has to be extremely circumspect; understandably she wishes to facilitate our escape without incriminating herself. If she was discovered to have aided and abetted our escape, the consequences for her would be dire.'

For some reason Darren finds this funny. 'Yeah? I reckon she'd get over it.'

My scowl deepens. 'Listen, you insensitive clod: Number Sixteen is putting her life on the line in order to aid our escape, you could at least demonstrate some compassion for her! She has not furnished me with the details, but I believe that that fiend Number Two has some sort of hold over her. She hides it, but I'm sure she's terrified of him.' I pause. 'Well, let us adjourn this conversation for now. I just wanted to apprise you of the situation. When Number Sixteen does procure for us the means of safely using the underground railway, will we probably have to move quickly; so be ready to leave at a moment's notice. You won't need to bring anything with you.'

Perhaps it is a case familiarity breeding contempt, but I have gotten so accustomed to having these conferences in the glade with either Darren or Number Sixteen, and with no-one being around whenever we leave or return to the footpath, that I realise too late that I haven't been taking adequate precautions, because on this occasion when we step out of the greenery and onto the path, we walk straight into Number Two!

At first he seems as surprised as us at the sudden rencounter, but his face quickly resumes its customary unctuous smile.

'Well, well, well, Randal and Darren!' he says. 'Straying from the beaten path, are we?'

'I wasn't aware it was against the rules to leave the footpaths when taking a morning constitutional,' I reply, having quickly gathered my scattered wits.

'Well, *technically* it isn't,' he replies. 'But, nevertheless, we do encourage our patients not to stray from the clearly defined pathways; we don't want people to start losing themselves.'

'Perhaps I prefer to choose my own pathway,' I say.

'Yes, but if you do that, you never really know where you're going to end up, do you? You might find yourself somewhere you didn't want to be, and then you'd be wishing you'd stuck to the straight and narrow path.' He claps his hands. 'However, be that as it may, I am very glad to have run into you, dear fellow, because I do so want once again to strongly urge you to resume our counselling sessions. We really were making excellent progress, and I would simply hate to see all that effort on your part go to waste.'

'I never waste my efforts.'

'Capital! Then shall we say tomorrow afternoon at three? My office as usual.'

It is on the tip of the tongue to voice a vehement negative, but then a second thought strikes me: it was as Randal Fortescue that I fled from our last therapeutic session—but if I were now to lock horns with Number Two aka Dr Tombs as Number Six, he might not have the best of it; he might find he has bitten off more than he can chew!

'Alright then,' I acquiesce. 'Tomorrow afternoon at three.'

'Excellent! I'm so glad you've come around at last! I really shall be counting the hours to when next we meet!'

'Pssst!'

I am woken from deep slumber. The room is in darkness and someone is shaking me by the shoulder.

'Pssst!'

'Who is thi—?'

'Shhhh!'

I need to voice no further inquiries as to the identity of my nocturnal visitor. I would recognise that peremptory 'shhhh!' anywhere. My eyes adjust to the gloom and I see that it is indeed Number Sixteen who kneels at my bedside.

'What's wrong?' I ask, dropping my voice to a whisper.

'We need to swap badges,' replies Number Sixteen.

'Swap badges?'

'Yes. I have been unable to procure you a staff-member's badge; you will have to take mine.'

'Take yours? What; now? Is the escape happening now—?'

I start to sit up in bed, but Number Sixteen pushes me back down.

'Calm yourself,' she says. 'The escape is not now. There will be no train stopping here at this hour. I came to you now as the best time for us to exchange badges.' So saying, she unclips her badge from the breast of her uniform. 'Where is yours?'

'My jacket,' I say, indicating that article of clothing, slung over the back of the chair adjacent to my bed. Number Sixteen takes the jacket and unpins the badge from the lapel. She then proceeds to remove the adhesive upper surfaces from each badge and exchanges them, placing that which bears her name on my badge and that which bears my name on her own. She then clips the former to her uniform and the latter to my jacket.

'Now you have your ticket out of here,' says Number Sixteen.

'Yes, but what about Darren?' I ask. 'What's he going to do?'

'I told you, I cannot procure any other badge… You could just escape by yourself…'

'Never!'

'Shhhh!'

'Never,' I repeat, whispering this time.

I hear a sigh. 'I can assure you that Darren is in considerably less danger than yourself.'

'Nevertheless, we make our escape together. The matter is not open for discussion.'

'Very well. The only thing to do then is for both of you to escape using my badge. But in doing this you must be extremely careful. When the machine accepts your badge and allows you to disembark from the train, you must both step out at exactly the same moment. The train will know if two people attempt to leave the train at once—you must deceive it into thinking only one person is leaving; you must walk out precisely in step with each other.'

'Like a three-legged race, you mean? Moving in tandem?'

'Yes.'

'And have you worked out when this escape should be attempted?'

'Yes; it will be tonight. There will be a train stopping here at eleven o'clock this evening, which I happen to know nobody will be boarding. This will be your best opportunity.'

'I see. So the train always stops here, even if nobody's getting on or off?'

'Yes. It operates as would a regular train service.'

'But what about you? If our escape is successful, it won't take them long to work out we went via the train; and then they'll discover it was your badge we used! Won't that get you into a lot of trouble? Why don't you escape with us? Yes! Get out of that monster's clutches once and for all!'

'No, Randal. That I cannot do. I cannot enter into details, but other people would be placed in danger if I were to run away. There are others like me, remember? For instance, the man who has spoken to you on several occasions…'

'Yes; who is that fellow? Is he that orderly named Malcolm? You know, the Indian-looking fellow. I'm sure I have that fellow somewhere before; I mean, before I came here.'

'You have seen that man before, Randal, and he is no-one you can trust. Malcolm is really Number Twelve.'

'Number Twelve? I don't recall—'

'Think back to our first meeting, Randal. The man driving the Mini Moke to whom I briefly spoke. *He* is Number Twelve; and he is one of them.'

Oh yes! *Now* I remember him!

'Then, the fellow who speaks to me in the toilets: who—?'

'Now is not the time to discuss this, Randal,' cuts in Sixteen. 'Just be ready to make your move this evening. Tell your friend, as well.'

'Yes, but what about you? I really don't see how you can escape having suspicion falling on your head…'

'I have considered that. That is why I have come to your room like this, in the small hours of the morning.'

'What do you mean?'

'I will not have been unobserved by the surveillance cameras. When questioned, I will say that I came to your room for… romantic reasons. My story will then be that you must have effected the substitution of our badges while I was in a post-coital slumber…'

'Post-coital slumber?' I cry, pulling the duvet defensively up to my neck.

'Shhh!'

'You mean we—you want us to—I mean, do we have to—?'

'No, we do not, Randal. It is dark, so the cameras will not be able to discern what we do or do not do together. However, you must allow me to remain here for a further hour or so, in order to cement my alibi.'

'And what are you going to do?' I inquire suspiciously.

'I will simply lie down here beside you, if you will permit me.'

'Under or over the covers?'

'Over, if you prefer.'

'Very well, then,' I accede.

I shuffle over to the further extremity of the bed, and Number Sixteen, after pulling off her shoes, arranges herself fully clothed by my side. She says nothing and neither do I. I start to find the silence uncomfortable.

'May I ask you a question…?' I say quietly.

'Of course,' replies Sixteen.

'It's about the lava lamps…'

'What about them, Randal?'

'Well, I was wondering... do they contain... do they have... Rover inside them...?'

'No, Randal. The lava lamps do not have Rover inside them. They are merely decorations.'

I heave a sigh of relief. I am glad to know that my fears on that score have been groundless.

I don't actually know how long Number Sixteen remains beside me on the bed, because, very soon after this exchange—and much to my surprise given the extreme discomfort of the situation—I fall back to sleep.

It's time for my appointment with Number Two, aka Dr Tombs; my very last appointment, although the fellow doesn't know it. Tonight, I will be taking a permanent leave of this facility. I have already informed Darren of our escape plan, and advised him to be dressed and ready to move after the ten o'clock curfew. Buoyed up by this knowledge, I am more than ready for my passage of arms with Number Two; indeed, I am looking forward to it with great relish. Doubtless he expects me to be his helpless victim, ready to be further crushed under the weight of spurious guilt he will attempt to heap upon me like hot coals.

Well, he is in for a surprise. Because this time I am ready for him; this time I am prepared to withstand his assault, and indeed to pay him back in his own coin.

I step into the lift that will take me up to his office in the tower (otherwise the Green Dome.) I smile a grim, tight-lipped smile, very much as my predecessor would have done had he been in my position. Number Two doesn't know it, but I have beaten him before the contest has even begun. Tonight I will be leaving this place, slipping from between his very fingers, and he is blissfully unaware of the fact—the balance of power has shifted in my favour, and he knows it not; he is expecting a lamb, and he is about to discover that he has a tiger by the tail!

The doors slide open and I step out into Dr Tombs' office. He is seated at his desk as usual, and greets me with his unctuous smile.

'Come in, dear fellow, come in,' he says. 'I'm so glad that we can finally resume our sessions.'

'Missed me, have you?' I say, dropping into my chair.

'Well, of course I have!' replies Two. 'I have missed you a great deal. Why, I can honestly say that you're the most fascinating patient I have under my care. This postponement of our sessions has been a great personal loss to me, as well as retarding your own journey along the road to recovery.'

'Maybe I've been walking along that road under my own steam,' I tell him. (Rather good, that one, I think!)

'Yes, but without myself to guide you, you might find yourself heading off in the wrong direction.'

'Straying from the beaten path?'

'Precisely!'

'Well, maybe the path I choose for myself is the better one.'

'My dear fellow, you really ought to let me be the judge of that. I'm the doctor and you're the patient, remember?' He claps his hands. 'But enough of this: shall we pick up where we left off last time?'

'With pleasure,' I tell him. 'I *know* who murdered Gillian, and that the crime was a premediated one. It was *not* in any way a result of my having left Gillian's door unlocked that night; I know that for a fact, and that is a fact you are not going to shake me on!'

Much to my annoyance, Number Two merely waves a dismissive hand. 'My dear fellow, I know that. I never thought any differently; I merely wanted you to confront and overcome those needless feelings of guilt you were suppressing and that were manifesting themselves in that recurring nightmare you were having. That's done. We can put that one away. Now, however, I would like us to move onto the matter of your inability to perform sexually.'

'WHAT?' I bellow, dropping out of character in my enraged surprise. The fellow continues to look at me with that infuriating smile spread all over his face, which does nothing to diminish my ire. 'Who says I suffer from any form of sexual dysfunction? *I* certainly didn't. And anyway, what possible connection can this have with what we were discussing in our last session? Nothing! It has nothing to do with it, I say!'

'My dear fellow, it has *everything* to do with it,' replies the exasperating fellow. 'I'm referring to your recurring dream, and the fact that by your own admission your subconscious mind has in that dream clothed the body of your friend, who in reality was quite naked when you discovered her! A clear sign of sexual repression!'

'And you are founding your diagnosis of sexual dysfunction entirely upon *that?* Preposterous!'

'Well, not just that. There's also the incident with that masseuse woman; the one who was with you during the early part of your ill-fated election campaign—what was her name…? Takaco! Yes, Takaco!'

'With one K,' I involuntarily add. 'To what "incident" might you be referring?'

'What else but that night she wanted to sleep with you, and how you responded by forcibly ejecting her from your hotel suite.'

I feel my face burning. 'How… how could you possibly know about that…?'

'Why, it's in your file, dear fellow,' replies Two, tapping a folder on his desk. 'It's all in there; everything I need to know about you.'

Then there's way too much in that file—but I let the matter drop, remembering that the original Number Six had to endure the same thing; *his* file was also comprehensive. Instead, I say: 'I ejected Takaco from my room on that occasion because her advances towards me were entirely too aggressive and quite inappropriate. That was all. I do not care for anyone, regardless of how physically personable they may be, attempting to force themselves upon me.'

Fiddlesticks!' retorts my tormentor. 'You rejected her advances entirely because you knew you would be unable to respond to them, to "rise to the occasion" as it were! You knew that the sight of her naked beauty ought to have triggered a corresponding physical arousal in yourself, and you were ashamed at yourself because that hadn't happened, had it? That's what it was, old chap!'

'It was nothing of the kind! In fact I found the sight of her genitalia—which she forced into far too close a proximity to my eyes—to be extremely repulsive.'

'Yes, but my dear fellow, in these intimate situations there is a very fine line between repulsion and its opposite number, attraction. You may have thought you were repulsed by the sight of her reproductive organs, but in fact you were actually attracted! Yes, there was a sensual attraction, but alas no corresponding physical arousal. You were ashamed of your sexual impotence, and your mind sought to deny these feelings by turning the feeling of shame into indignation at the forward behaviour of the young lady; and *that's* why you turfed her out of the room!'

'Oh, did I, now?' I snap. 'You're very good at telling people what they're thinking, aren't you?' (Sounding more like Number Six again here!)

'My dear fellow, I'm a psychiatrist! It's my *job* to tell people what they're thinking! Ipso facto. And I can assure that you are a textbook case: sexual dysfunction owing to deep-routed and longstanding issues that need urgently to be addressed. As things stand, you'll just keep on throwing up barriers every time you find yourself faced with the need to perform sexually. You will either fiercely reject your potential partner and remove either her or yourself from the situation, or you will just shut down, avoiding the sexual encounter by falling into a heavy slumber. I assure you it's all textbook stuff.'

Falling into a heavy slumber. I am forcibly reminded of the events of the small hours, when Number Sixteen joined me in my bed—but no! Sex wasn't even an issue on that occasion; it had not been on the agenda. I had been abruptly woken up by her in the small hours of the morning, so I simply went back to sleep because I was still tired! Yes, I was merely resuming my interrupted slumber, that was all! I wasn't *avoiding* anything!

'And another thing,' proceeds my remorseless adversary; 'don't think I haven't noticed this playact you've been performing over the past few days. And I should warn you: no good can come from it! Trying to be someone you're not can be disastrous for your mental health.'

'I don't know what you're talking about,' I snap, turning my head one-quarter profile.

'Oh, yes you do! I'm talking about that frowning brow, that tight smile, those clipped sentences.' The wretch chuckles. 'Trying to act like a certain celluloid spy, eh? And *which* spy, eh? Not James Bond, is it? Not, the virile, sexually promiscuous 007! No! You take on as your role model Danger Man, the celibate secret agent!' More chuckling. 'That really says it all, doesn't it? And you're not even very good at keeping *that* up, are you? You keep slipping out of character, you know; the true Randal Fortescue keeps poking his head out!'

Lost for a comeback, I fall back on endeavouring to stare down my nemesis, brows knitted to the fullest, sardonically smiling lips at their tautest. Infuriatingly, the fellow just bursts into renewed laughter.

'Oh, yes; very good! Better watch out, old chap. If the wind changes direction, you'll be stuck like that!'

I would dearly like to tell the fellow how wrong he is; that my character interpretation is *not* that of John Drake, aka Danger Man; but is in fact that of the nameless Number Six, who although admittedly was portrayed by the same actor and possessed an identical personality, was *not*—for official purposes at least, as this would have engendered paying royalties to *Danger Man*'s creator Ralph Smart—was *not*, I repeat, the same character at all! Yes, I would dearly love to say this, to put the wretch in his place, but alas, I cannot. To make any reference to *The Prisoner* would be to tip my hand, to alert Dr Tombs, aka Number Two, that I know more of the truth in relation to my current situation than he is aware of—and arouse his suspicions I must not; not when on the very brink of making my escape from his clutches.

'Why this fear of sex?' pursues Number Two. 'This crippling apprehension of intimacy with a woman? Why do you think you are afflicted with this fear, Randal?'

'Why don't *you* tell *me*?' is my caustic response.

'I will, and with pleasure: It's your mother, isn't it? Your mother. She's the cause of all these inhibitions; she's the spectre looming over your entire existence, isn't she? Come now, you're an intelligent chap; deep down you know this as well as I do!'

Damn the fellow! Damn him, damn him, damn him! Why does he have to bring my mother into this? Why now, of all times? This situation is getting entirely out of hand; I had carefully planned how this session would unfold, I had all my cutting responses ready to hand—but this wretched man's not sticking to the dialogue I had marked out for him! And now he's bringing my mother into the conversation!

'So you see, that's what we need to talk about here. That's what we need to get out in the open. We need to confront that mother of yours. Or rather, *you* need to confront her. And I shall be the one to help you with this.'

By now I am literally squirming in my chair. This is not good; this is not good. 'My mother is none of your business!' I snap.

'I'm your psychiatrist, Number Six! Everything about you is my business. So come now, let's not be silly about this. I see from your file that you haven't had any contact with her for several years now, correct? Now, you may think that avoiding her is solving the problem, but I can assure you it's not; avoiding your mother is nothing more or less than avoiding the problem. And however far away she may be from you in geographical distance, you're still shackled to her as much as you ever were! She is still the dominant factor in your life, influencing everything you say and do, every thought that you think!'

I rise to my feet. 'Poppycock!' I declare. 'I did not come here to have some Freudian debate on the subject of my parents! What about that double of mine, eh? The one you were apparently so convinced was a figment of my imagination? I notice you haven't had much to say about him, have you?'

'My dear fellow, I haven't forgotten about your double at all!' replies Two. 'In fact, I was just about to raise the subject as further proof of your inherent sexual repressions.'

'And what's my double got to do with *that?*'

'Why, *everything*, my dear fellow! This double you've created for yourself is your precise opposite in every respect; and most significantly of all, he is sexually potent while you—alas!—are not! By your own admission, you believe your doppelgänger to be Takaco's successful lover, while you yourself had signally failed to become her lover. Yes, you may revile him, deeming him to be your persecutor, but at the same time you're envious of his sexual prowess, aren't you, eh? *He's* not tied to your mother's apron-strings, is he? Only *you* are!'

'Poppycock! Arrant nonsense! My double is real! He is not some manifestation of these repressions you choose to assign to me—he's real! I know it, and what's more I know that you know it! This meeting is over!'

And without waiting for his reply, I turn and walk briskly to the lift doors. They slide open, and I step inside, turning to face my adversary. He has risen to his feet and, hands in the pockets of his laboratory jacket, smiles at me as the lift doors close.

'Be seeing you!' he says.

No, I think, as the lift begins its descent; *I'll* be seeing *you*.

No, wait a minute; that's not right. I mean, I *won't* be seeing you. Yes, that's it. I won't be seeing you—not after tonight.

It is after curfew; patients and staff have retired to rest. I make my way along darkened hallways up to Darren Nesbit's room. Reaching it, I knock discreetly on the door.

The door opens.

'Is that you?' I whisper.

'Yeah, it's me,' comes the reply.

'Good! Come along then.'

Darren joins me, and we now make our way to the main staircase, encountering no one. My senses are all atingle with anticipation and—I cannot deny—trepidation. This is it. We are about to make our escape from this so-called mental hospital. All we have to do is descend to the ground floor hallway; there we will gain access to the concealed lift (Number Sixteen has described to me where to find it and how to operate it); we then descend to the subterranean railway station; we board the train that will arrive there at 2300 hours precisely; and after a forty-minute journey we will reach the next stop, and there ascend to freedom.

I pray that nothing goes amiss; that we will not be intercepted ere we reach the lift; or that there will not be any unexpected commuter waiting at the platform…

As we near the main staircase there seems to be a diminution of the darkness, and reaching the head of the stairs, there is indeed light filtering up the stairwell from the ground floor.

'Curses!' I hiss. 'Someone's still down there!'

Darren, however, does not share my misgivings. 'Might not be,' he cheerfully dissents. 'They prob'ly always leave the lights on down there. Some people do that.'

'What? Are you perchance suggesting they leave the hallway light on to deter burglars?' is my acid rejoinder. 'In case it has slipped your mind, we're not in the middle of an urban housing estate: this is a house in the middle of extensive grounds, encompassed by a twenty-foot wall and equipped with a lethal defence system!'

'Oh, stop moaning,' is Darren's airy—and rather insolent—reply. 'Bet you there's no-one down there.'

And with that, he actually starts descending the staircase! Look at him! Thinks he's running the show now! I too take to the stairs and quickly overtake him.

'Now listen here,' I say, interposing myself between Darren and any further downward progress. 'May I remind you who's in charge around here?'

'Who's that, then?' says Darren, grinning idiotically.

'Dolt,' I say, bringing my fist down on his sparsely-furnished crown. '*I'm* in charge. This is *my* escape bid. Kindly remember that. And I could have just escaped by myself, you realise? Number Sixteen even suggested as much! Yes; so think yourself lucky that I even brought you along! Now, come along. *I* shall lead the way.'

And suiting the action to the word, I set forth down the stairs. I hear Darren mutter something.

'What was that?' I demand, stopping to look back at him.

'Nothing,' grins Darren. 'Just talking to meself.'

'Well, *don't* "just talk to yourself",' I retort. 'We are supposed to be proceeding with stealth. And that means quietly!'

'Aye, aye, captain,' says Darren, saluting me—and neither the words nor the gesture have the ring of sincerity.

I look at him narrowly. 'Have they increased your medication again?'

'Nope. Still the same as before.'

We continue our descent. As we come to the final flight of stairs, I proceed with more caution. I can see the tiled floor of the hallway now, or at least a section of it. There is no-one in sight, nor do I hear any sounds to suggest the presence of people. We descend further and now we are below the level of the ceiling. No, there's nobody here. The coast is clear. I had thought perhaps there might have been someone occupying the reception window adjacent to the main doors, but no, the little office is in darkness.

Moving as silently as possible, we cross the tiled floor to the further end of the room where the walls are panelled with oak.

'Now…' I say; 'according to Number Sixteen, the button that summons the lift is concealed within an embossed floral escutcheon in the panelling…'

'You mean in the wainscot,' says Darren. 'It's called a wainscot.'

I look at him. His face displays the self-satisfied demeanour of someone who believes he possesses superior wisdom. I lose no time in disabusing him of this notion. 'It is *not* called a wainscot. It is only called a wainscot if the panelling covers just the lower portion of the wall. If, as in this case, the panelling covers the entirety of the wall from floor to ceiling, then it is simply called "panelling." Do you comprehend?'

'No.'

'You don't comprehend?'

'No, I mean I don't think you're right,' persists the presumptuous fellow. 'It's called a wainscot.'

'It's called panelling!'

'I say it's called a wainscot.'

'You will say nothing of the kind! It's called panelling, I tell you! Panelling!'

'Wainscot.'

I control myself with an effort. 'Look, I do not have time to debate this with you right now. We're going to miss our train at this rate. Now where's that embossed panel…?'

'Here,' says Darren; and without so much as a by-your-leave he reaches out and depresses the central disc of the carved flower with his stubby index finger. There is an audible click and now an entire section of the wall panelling slides aside, revealing a pair of metal doors. With an electronic hum (the familiar one) these doors part and reveal the illuminated interior of a lift car.

'Who said you could do that?' I demand angrily. 'This is *my* escape bid; ergo it was *my* job to press that button, not yours!'

'Yeah, but you were taking all day,' is the insolent reply. 'Let's just get in the lift before the doors shut again.'

And once again the wretch ignores all protocol and steps blithely into the lift car. I am about to follow him and voice my opinion as to his insubordinate behaviour when a hand drops heavily upon my shoulder.

'You're fuckin' nicked, me old beauty!'

So sudden is the shock that my delicate bowels very nearly betray me—with a superhuman effort I keep them from venting themselves. Caught! On the very brink of freedom, and caught! ...But who could be the owner of that gruff voice? It is unfamiliar to me...

I turn to face my assailant—and my fear turns to relief and annoyance; it is only that top-hatted imbecile, Spike, clearly also a curfew-breaker like ourselves. His features are presently contorted into a ludicrous imitation of pugnaciousness.

'Get your trousers on, you're nicked!' he growls.

'"Get my trousers on"?' I say, shaking off his restraining hand. 'As can be plainly seen, I am already wearing those particular articles of clothing.'

'Now listen, you slag,' continues the numbskull, pointing a finger at me. 'I've 'ad about enough of you!'

'And I have likewise had more than enough of you,' I tell him. 'So, why don't we just each do ourselves a favour and part company?'

His expression changing to one of portentousness, he leans in close to me. 'I wouldna give saxpunce if ye were to goo oot onter the moors ternicht! Take heed o' my words, laddie!'

What is he blathering on about now? Time is pressing, and I need to quickly rid myself of this numbskull. What would my illustrious predecessor have done in a situation of this urgency…? How would Number Six have dealt with this importunate fool? The solution flashes before my eyes. To think is to act. My fist lashes out and, connecting with Spike's jaw, the fellow is sent flying backwards across the room. I am surprised myself at the success of my punch.

Feeling rather pleased with myself, I quickly join Darren in the lift. The doors close and we begin our descent.

'Blimey!' ejaculates Darren, eyeing me with unmistakable admiration. 'That was some right 'ook you got there. Didn't know you had it in you!'

'Well, one doesn't like to resort to violence,' I reply, with becoming modesty; 'but needs must when the devil drives; desperate circumstances necessitate desperate remedies.' I glance at my wristwatch. 'Excellent. We haven't lost much time. We should still make it to the train platform with time to spare.'

'Lift's taking it's time,' remarks Darren.

'Well, obviously we're going very deep underground,' I say. 'It is a secret railway, is it not? They would not want the trains to be audible to the patients up above.'

The lift finally comes to a halt. The doors open and we step out into what looks very much like the corridor of a London Underground station: to wit, tubular walls composed of white-enamelled brickwork. The corridor stretches off in both directions, but we are left in no doubt as to which direction to take: a sign, facing the lift doors displays an arrow pointing to the right, and above it the legend:

This Way

'I s'pose we go that way, then,' says Darren.

'I suppose we do,' I concur.

We set off. In spite of the similarity in décor, we are patently not in a London Underground station: for one thing there is a complete absence of commuters aside from ourselves, and in addition to this, the posters adorning the walls at frequent intervals are not the usual media and product advertisements; instead they all bear slogans printed in white in the Albertus type-font against a variety of different-coloured backgrounds:

Your Village is Watching You

Surveillance is Peace of Mind

Privacy Makes for Mistrust

Acceptance in Happiness

Dissension is Despair

Heroes Don't Sweat

to quote but a few. Interspersed with these messages are frequent arrow signs, guiding us on our way, and bearing legends such as:

Keep Going

This Way

Follow the Signs!

etc, etc. There appears to be a considerable maze of these corridors, as we encounter crossroads and junctions frequently. With there being apparently just the one train platform down here, I cannot help but wonder what this proliferation of tunnels is in aid of and to where the other branches might lead…? Perhaps they lead nowhere; perhaps they are simply a maze for those who choose not to follow the signs to lose themselves in…

Finally, however, we find ourselves stepping out onto the platform. Here the resemblance to a London Underground station persists, albeit minus any signs announcing the name of the station. Nor is there any electronic timetable informing commuters of the arrival time of the next train. There are just more of those propaganda posters, including a giant one, adorning the wall facing us, across the train tracks, and featuring a monochrome image of Dr Tombs, here wearing his full Number Two garb, including the ubiquitous vertically-striped college scarf. Pictured from the waist up, he stands with his hands clutching the lapels of his blazer, smiling what is supposed to be a benevolent smile, and beside him the words:

Ask Not What You Can Do for Your Village, But What Your Village Can Do for You

'You see?' I say to Darren, pointing to the poster. 'There's your final proof that Tombs is really Number Two!'

'I didn't say he wasn't, did I?' retorts Darren. 'But that don't prove we're not really in London, does it?'

'You still think that, do you? You still think we're in London? And I suppose you think this railway is just going to link up with the regular service, and that we'll find ourselves getting off at Tottenham Court Road station?'

'No, I don't reckon we'll be getting off at Tottenham Court Road...' And he starts to giggle inanely.

I give him another one of those narrow looks. 'Is something amusing you?'

'No, I'm just... y'know...'

'Yes...' I say. 'That's another good reason for my bringing you along: by getting you out of here I will be getting you away from whatever medication it is they're dosing you up with—which can only be a good thing.'

At this juncture we hear, emanating from the tunnel to our right, the familiar sounds that announce an approaching train. I look at my watch.

'Precisely on time,' I observe. 'Just as Number Sixteen said it would be.'

A light appears in the tunnel, and then the train emerges. The train's carriages are completely white in colour, and the windows of the driver's cabin appear to be tinted; I am unable to discern who is inside. The forward carriages slide past us as the train rapidly slows; they are all brightly lit within, and appear to be devoid of passengers. Good. All according to plan.

The train stops, and a quick survey is enough to determine that the carriage now facing us is likewise innocent of passengers. The doors slide smoothly open, and we step inside. The interior of the carriage also corresponds with that of a London Underground train, with the seating facing the aisle. Everything looks very clean and new, and there is an absence of route maps displayed above the windows. Darren and I seat ourselves on the chair immediately adjacent to the doors.

'Please stand away from the doors,' comes a crisp, male voice from a speaker unit affixed to the wall beside the doors. 'This train is about to depart. Please be ready to surrender your tickets when you reach your destination.'

'That speaker box must be the receptacle in which we have to deposit our badge,' I say to Darren, as the doors close and train sets off. 'Did you recognise the voice? It was just like the voice of the machine in "The General"; you know, when they had to slot in those security discs to get into the secret parts of the Town Hall… I wonder if this machine will have a little plastic hand that pops out and takes the ticket like the one in that episode…? Pity we've only got the one ticket for both of us; but never fear, I have taken steps to ensure that we will both be able to disembark safely.'

'Oh yeah?' says Darren. 'What "steps" have you taken?'

'Ah,' I say, ignoring the tone of scepticism. 'According to Number Sixteen, we just have to step off the train at the very same moment, as though we were participants in a three-legged race; that was how she described it: like a three-legged race.' I reach into the pocket of my jacket. 'And in that regard—*voila!*'

I proudly display the cord from my dressing gown. 'With this I shall tie our legs together when we reach our destination, and then there will be no mistake: we will be able to exit the train *exactly* like the participants of a three-legged race! Except of course, that we will be walking, not running.'

Darren's face does not display the admiration at my ingenuity and foresight that I was (quite reasonably) expecting; instead, he continues to look sceptical.

'Don't you reckon that's overdoing it a bit?' he says.

'No; I don't "reckon that's overdoing it a bit"!' is my cutting rejoinder. 'We will only have one shot at this, so we have to get it right! That box over there will know if two people step off the train at once, and so we have to make it believe that only *one* person is leaving! I thought I had already made this clear to you.'

'Yeah, but what if we do just walk off the train like two people?' pursues Darren, stubbornly adhering to his contrary argument. 'What can they do about it, anyway? You said there won't even be any people at the next station; you said it's just an abandoned warehouse…'

'Factory, not warehouse,' I correct him. 'And yes, but while there may not be any people, they will certainly have security measures in place with which to apprehend fare dodgers. I confess that Number Sixteen neglected to enter into details, but perhaps the lifts will be disabled, preventing us from leaving; or—oh, dear. They might even have…'

'Have what?' demands Darren.

'*Rover*,' I reply, dropping my voice to a portentous whisper.

Darren emits a raspberry-blowing sound. 'Rover,' sneers the wretch. 'You still going on about that?'

I knit my brows. 'Spare me your cynicism, Darren Nesbit. I've already told you that I clearly saw Rover patrolling the grounds of the hospital on the night preceding the last—why you refuse to believe this established fact is beyond me.'

'All you saw was a light through the trees,' replies Darren. 'It was prob'ly just a guard with a torch.'

'It was *not* just a guard with a torch, you nincompoop! Aside from any other consideration, Number Sixteen has verbally confirmed the existence of Rover herself; and might I remind you of what an appalling risk she has taken in order to allow us to escape? You might show a modicum of gratitude instead of branding her a liar.'

'Yeah, yeah, yeah,' says Darren.

'Look, you want to get out of this, don't you? You want to escape? Yes? Well, just do as I instruct you and we will succeed. We've already cleared the first hurdle. All we have to do now is to pull the wool over the eyes of that automated ticket collector when we arrive at the next station, and we're home free.'

'We'll be home free, will we?'

'Certainly. Well, admittedly, we don't know the location of the disused factory we will be arriving at; but it seems more than likely it is on the UK mainland, so all we have to do is find a road and keep walking, and we will soon get our bearings. You cannot walk far on this small isle of ours without encountering some signs of civilisation.'

The underground train continues on its journey; outside the windows all is darkness. Once or twice I press my face to glass, endeavouring to catch sight of something, even if only the brickwork of the tunnel wall; but I can perceive nothing. I also, compelled by curiosity, walk to first one extremity of the carriage and then the other, in order to look into the adjoining cars. Windowed doors allow me to see into the interiors, and both of the neighbouring carriages are completely empty. The communicating doors, however, seem to be locked; apparently direct communication between carriages is not permitted on this service.

When the allotted forty minutes of the journey come close to expiring, I produce my dressing gown cord and proceed to bind my lower right leg to Darren's lower left. I ignore Darren's tiresome complaints of this being an unnecessary precaution, making sure to tie the knot securely, so as to obviate the possibility of the binding coming undone at a critical moment. This done, we rise to our feet, and upon my command commence walking up and down the aisle of the carriage, in order to accustom ourselves to ambulating in this manner—there is a degree of awkwardness in our movements, attributable to the marked discrepancy in height between Darren and myself, but we soon get the hang of things.

'Excellent! We're all set to go!' I glance again at my watch. 'And we should be arriving at the station any moment now.'

Darren, however, stubbornly refuses to dismount his hobby horse. 'But I don't see the point of it. We could just walk off the train standing next to each other like this, *without* having our legs tied together.'

'Yes, but for the five hundredth time,' (a slight exaggeration, I confess), 'with our legs bound together we move as one person!'

'Yeah: one person with three legs,' mutters Darren.

'It doesn't *matter* how many legs we have!' I tell the fellow, a weary sigh manifest in my tones. 'It's a matter of synchronisation! If we move as one then that wretched machine will think we are one! It's as simple as that—ah! The train's slowing down; we must be here.'

We move to the doors. The train slows to a stop. The platform now before us is a far cry from the one from which we departed: the lighting is dim, the walls composed of rusting metal panels and girders. It all looks as dank and dingy as Number Sixteen described the factory above us as being.

'Please surrender your tickets and exit the train one at a time,' comes the commanding voice of the box on the wall. Simultaneously the doors slide open.

'See?' cries Darren. 'They've opened the bleedin' doors anyway! We don't have to mess around with tickets; we can just get out!'

And the fool commences forward, forcing me to fall into pace with him as the only alternative to falling over.

'Wait, you buffoon! There's probably a—'

And then it happens: the sudden feeling of being punched by a fist the size of my whole body, and Darren and I are both knocked flat on our backs on the floor.

'Do not attempt to leave the train without surrendering your ticket,' comes the commanding voice. 'The second attempt will be fatal.'

'You fool!' I yell at Darren, as we endeavour to climb to our feet. (No easy matter; we hadn't practiced this.) 'I told you this was like "The General"! Couldn't you have surmised there would be a forcefield guarding the door?'

We finally attain the perpendicular, and advancing to the box on the wall, I remove my badge. I perceive a slot at the top of the machine, and place the badge in it. A hatch adjacent to the slot pops open and a tiny plastic hand extends itself and takes possession of the badge. Both hand and badge disappear into the metal box, and the hatch snaps shut.

'Ticket accepted,' comes the voice of the machine. 'You may now exit the train.'

'This is it,' I say. 'The vital moment. Just do as I do. Best foot forward!'

'What's our best foot?' inquires Darren.

'The two that are tied together,' I tell him. 'My right and your left.'

I give Darren's shoulder an encouraging squeeze—which he fails to reciprocate by squeezing my back in return, but then Darren never was very demonstrative, so I endeavour not to take it personally. We extend our bound legs and place our feet on the platform. So far so good. 'When I say "now", move your other foot,' I tell him. '…Now!'

And then we are out of the train with both feet on the platform. No alarms ring. No terse words of protest from the ticket machine. Success! We've done it!

'We're home free!' I say, patting Darren on the shoulder. 'Come along; that passage yonder must take us to where the lifts are.'

We set off along the platform. No-one else—thank goodness—has emerged from the train. As we attain the entrance to the passageway, the carriage doors behind us slide shut and the train starts into motion; and soon it has gone and the sounds of its progress fade into silence.

We proceed along the passageway. It is cold down here; the walls of the passage are sheets of rusting rivetted metal; our path is illumined by murky orange lights set at intervals along the walls. There are no posters with slogans here, nor are there any direction signs.

'Hang on a minute,' says Darren, stopping in his tracks, forcing me to do the same.

'What's the matter now?' I ask.

'Why are we still walking with our legs tied together?'

He makes a good point. I'd grown so accustomed to our walking together like this, that it completely slipped my mind that it was no longer necessary. We squat down and I endeavour to loosen the knot fastening the cord; but I soon discover the knot has become so taut that it is impossible to loosen it.

'I can't undo it,' I tell Darren. 'The knot has been pulled too tightly. This is your fault, you know. It will be from when you made us walk into that forcefield that knocked us off our feet; the jolt must have strained the cord and caused the knot to tighten.'

'Well, that's great,' grumbles Darren. 'Can't we just pull the whole thing off? Pull it down like a sock or something…?'

'I don't know… The whole thing feels extremely tight… Look, let's not mess around down here. We'll leave it till we get up to the surface; we might find something in the factory building that we can use to sever the cord; a shard of glass from a broken window-pane or something of that nature…'

'So we gotta walk all the way to the lift like this?' complains Darren, as we rise to our feet again.

'Well, nobody's going to see us, are they?' I point out irritably. 'And who knows, the distance from the platform to the lift might be much smaller here than it was back at the hospital…'

In the event, it does turn out to be a fair old trek to the lift. But on the plus side, although there is many a twist and turn in the passageway, we never encounter any multiple branches, so we are in no danger of taking a wrong turning. Finally, we turn into a corridor which terminates in what are clearly a pair of lift doors, their smooth and polished surface in contrast with the surrounding rust and grime.

Recalling my own suggestion that the lift might be immobilised as a security measure to prevent the escape of intruders, I feel a tense moment when I depress the lift button—but a moment is all it is: the doors slide open almost immediately. We step inside and, turning to face the doors, discover that performing a simple 160° turn is not such a simple operation when you are tied at the leg to another person (especially when the two people at first try to turn in contrary directions.)

The doors close and we begin to ascend. It is very dark in this lift; a pale green light on the control panel being the only source of illumination; and it is still rather chilly. However, my mood is one of elation.

'We've made it!' I chuckle. 'This lift was the final obstacle. Once we're up on the surface we'll be out of their clutches for good…!'

'Don't count your chickens…' says Darren.

'Oh, don't be such a pessimist!' I admonish him. 'You should be pleased with yourself! And indeed, you should be pleased with me. You certainly wouldn't have made it this far without myself to guide and sustain you!'

'Yeah, ta for that,' is his response. And then he starts to chuckle. Standing shoulder-to-shoulder (in a manner of speaking, of course; my shoulder being much higher up than his) as we are, I can feel it as much as hear it.

'Now what's amusing you?' I demand.

'Just me medication,' he says, airily.

'Yes. Well, you've seen the last of that, thank goodness.'

The lift comes to a halt and the doors open. All without is in inky darkness. We step out of the lift and I immediately sense that something is amiss. The air is suddenly much warmer, and there hangs in it a familiar antiseptic scent… A very familiar scent…

'I fear you were right after all about counting those chickens,' I tell Darren. 'I believe we have been vilely deceived.'

'Well, one of you has,' comes a plummy voice from the darkness.

And then the lights come on and my fears are confirmed. We are back in the main hallway of the hospital; the lift we have just emerged from is the very same one we descended in an hour before. Standing before us is Dr Tombs, now dressed in full Number Two attire, leaning on the handle of his shooting stick umbrella. Flanking him are four uniformed guards—Village guards in grey overalls, white boots and helmets and dark glasses (one of the people I believe to have been responsible for that blow to the head I received while exploring the hidden regions of the Unemployment Centre.)

Number Two chuckles at the discomfiture he doubtless sees written on my countenance.

'Welcome back, Number Six,' he says. 'I trust you enjoyed your little round trip...?'

Chapter Twelve
How I Was Condemned to be Forsaken

At a signal from Number Two, one of the guards steps forward and, unsheathing the commando knife strapped to his belt, squats down and cuts the cord binding my leg to Darren's.

'How did you do it?' I demand. 'Is there more than one platform down there? Or did you change everything while we were on the train?'

'That would be telling,' answers Number Two.

'I suppose it was Spike who gave us away...?'

'Who? Oh, Number Forty-Eight! Goodness me, no. We knew all about your planned escape bid long before you gave that young man a demonstration of your pugilistic skills. You see, you made the mistake of confiding your plans to the wrong person.'

'What are you talking about?' I say, frankly perplexed. 'I didn't confide my escape plan to anyone! I only told Darren...'

'Precisely!' says Number Two, his face wreathed with smiles. 'That was your mistake. He is the one who informed on you.'

'Poppycock!' I retort. 'How can you expect me to believe that? Darren wouldn't—' I break off. Turning my head, I see that Darren has moved a few paces away from me, and he stands there grinning and glaring at me with the most diabolical expression of malignant triumph fixed upon his rodent visage. So unexpected, so unprecedented, is this look, that I can scarcely credit it. It is as though he has suddenly become another person.

'That's right: it was me!' he pronounces, his voice trembling with emotion. 'I did it cuz I wanted to see you fail; cuz I hate your fucking guts you fat bastard! And you know what? I've always hated you! Ever since I've known you all you've ever done is boss me around like I'm your slave or something; lording it over me, hitting me, calling me names, looking down at me all the time just cuz you're taller than me! I fucking hate you so much I can't stand it! I feel like my head's going to explode! Just the sound of your stupid poncy voice drives me up the wall! Talking like you think you know it all, using all them big words just to confuse me and make me look stupid! I fucking hate you, you big, fat, lard-arsed piece of shit on a stick! Acting like you were doing me a big favour by hanging around with me; taking me for granted! That time we went to Portmeirion—I couldn't even go dressed up like the Prisoner cuz *you* said so! I was just as much a fan of it as you were, but no, only *you* could dress up like the Prisoner, so *I* couldn't be dressed like him as well, could I? No; I had to dress up like one of the Villagers, one of the fucking extras! And just because you fucking said so! But then I got my chance to get even with you, that day at Portmeirion; cuz when you went off to find a crapper, *they* come up to me, and they made me a deal: they said if I worked for them that they'd help me; they'd help me get my revenge; they'd help me destroy you, humiliate you, grind you into the dust! And that's what I did at that election! I stole it all away from you; I let the whole world know what you're really like! *I* won and *you* lost! But then it didn't work out like it was supposed to cuz you wouldn't even believe that it was really me that did it! Even after all that you still couldn't see that I hated your fucking guts! You just kept saying I was a puppet; that it was other people what put me up to it! Kept going on about that fucking double of yours! I fucking smashed you in that election, but you just acted like I was the poor innocent victim in someone else's plans! How am I supposed to get my revenge on you, when you don't even act like I've done anything to you? You do my fucking head, you do! You just do my fucking head in! Every minute of every day, you do my fucking head in!'

He breaks off, panting for breath, his face red, eyes bulging, literally foaming at the mouth. I turn from him and fix Number Two with an accusing glare.

'You unspeakable fiend! Look what you've done to my friend here! Corrupting his mind, distorting his personality! Brainwashing him into hating me—*me*, his staunchest friend—just to further your evil schemes!' I turn back to Darren. 'Don't worry, my friend; I will protect you from these monsters!'

Darren screams, clutching his head, as though in pain. 'What is fucking wrong with you? You're still doing it! You're *still* fucking doing it! How many times do I have to fucking tell you? It's not them: It's me! It's me! It's *me!* They didn't make me hate you cuz I've *always* fucking hated you! Why can't you get that through your thick, stupid head? *They* haven't messed with my head cuz the only fucking one who's ever messed with my head is *you!* You-you-you, you fat fucking bastard! Why don't you fucking get it? Arrggghh!'

He continues to scream, clutching his head as though in pain. And then, abruptly, the screams cease, and Darren collapses to the ground, and lies there motionless.

Silence. I am paralysed.

'Good lord,' says Number Two, breaking the silence. 'I do believe you've killed the poor fellow.' He crouches down beside Darren, takes hold of his limp wrist. 'No, no; there's still a pulse. Stretcher!'

Upon this command, a stretcher on wheels (I believe it's called a gurney) propels itself across the hall, slowing to a halt beside the supine Darren.

'Take him to the infirmary,' orders Number Two.

Two of the guards take up Darren's limp body, place it upon the stretcher, and depart with it, disappearing through a pair of doors across the hall. I move to follow them but Number Two blocks my path.

'I must go with him!' I cry.

'No, no; not right now,' demurs Number Two. 'I think that Darren's best chances for survival lie within you and he exercising a degree of social distancing for the time being. Yes, I think it will be much better if I were to have my other two men here escort you back to your room. The hour is late, and we can take up this discussion in the morning.'

The two guards step forward and I am compelled to acquiesce. Truth to tell, I am rather tired after all the drama and exertion of the evening, and once back in my apartment, stopping only to remove my jacket and shoes, I lie down on my bed and quickly fall asleep.

I am awakened by the familiar odour of cigarette smoke assailing my nostrils. I immediately think of Gillian and my heart leaps. Could it be…?

No. I open my eyes and the face that swims into focus is an unfamiliar one. Although female, the features are harsh and unfriendly. A half-smoked cigarette depends from the corner of her mouth.

'Strewth!' comes a voice with an accent distinctly antipodean. 'It *is* a feller!'

I take stock of my surroundings. I am lying on a pallet bed in a room with three walls composed of naked brick walls and the fourth of iron bars. A number of women are gathered around the bed, regarding me with expressions of marked interest. The women are dressed in identical blue denim dresses worn over khaki or yellow shirts. They are a motley collection, none of them what you would call visions of pulchritude, and all of them possessing stern features and feral eyes.

'What's a feller doing in this place?' says one of the women.

'Beats me,' replies her with the cigarette. 'Must've sent him to the wrong prison.'

'Prison,' I say, vainly trying to gather my senses. 'Wh-where am I?'

'You're in Wentworth Prison, cobber. Cell-Block H.'

Cell-Block H…? Cell-Block H…? Of course! The proposed Australian sequel! Yes; they must have finally made it! *That's* why I'm here!

'So, whadda we do with him?' asks one of the women. 'Do we tell old Vinegar Tits?'

''Course we don't, ya silly cow,' is the reply. 'You don't look a gift-horse in the gnashers, do ya? I haven't had a bloke for ten years—I say let's put him to good use while we've got him!'

'Too right! I could do with a shag an' all!'

'Me too!'

'I want him first!'

'Join the blooming queue, ya dirty slag!'

'Now, please ladies…' I begin, attempting to rise from the bed. 'Let's be civilised, I beg you…!'

'He's tryin' ta get away! Hold him down!'

'Yeah! Someone get his strides off!'

'Too right!'

They pounce on me. I struggle madly, exerting all my strength, but I find I am as weak as a kitten; I can barely move. There are too many of them—their hands are all over me, pulling at my clothes.

'Wake up!'

The voice is male peremptory. I am being shaken roughly by the shoulder. I see a white helmet with a chinstrap; between the two a pair of shades, a nose and a mouth. A guard. A second guard stands behind him. I am in my hospital bedroom, lying fully dressed on my bed and on top of the bedclothes.

'What... what is it...?' I mutter, still struggling with the last vestiges of my dream.

'Number Two wants to see you,' is the gruff reply. 'Get up.'

I do not like the tone, but am compelled to obey. I swing my legs over the side of the bed and put on my canvas shoes. It seems that, after my escapade of last night, I am to be given the strongarm treatment; no more of the gentle touch from smiling female nurses... Having tied the laces of my shoes, I reach for my jacket and I immediately see that my Number Six badge—minus the adhesive surface bearing my name—has been restored to its place. Number Sixteen last had possession of this badge—I hope that no suspicion has fallen upon her. Her cover story was to be that it was solely myself who was responsible for the transposition of the badges; I trust that her story has been believed.

As we make our way along the hallways, I observe that everyone, staff and patients alike, are now displaying penny-farthing number badges in place of the previous name badges; what's more, the presence of these uniformed guards, unseen in this facility prior to last evening, causes no looks or comments of surprise. In fact people, patients in particular, deliberately avert their eyes as we pass them, and I cannot help but suspect that this is more on account of myself than of my military escort—I have the distinct impression that I have become *persona non grata* in the wake of my escape attempt.

When we reach the lift that ascends to Number Two's office, I am somewhat surprised that my two conductors join me, having thought it most likely that they would leave me to ascend alone. Have they been issued with orders not to let me out of their sight for a second...? It all seems rather excessive.

When the lift doors open, I receive yet another surprise—although perhaps I should not have been surprised at all. Number Two's office has now really become Number Two's office; that is to say, the one from the television series. A circular chamber, metallic, futuristic. The segmented walls are of a purple hue, and appear to be lit from within. To the immediate right and left of the entrance the walls are fitted with cinema-sized screens, both of them mutely displaying a psychedelic lightshow; multicoloured threads of light swirling and intertwining with one another... From the threshold of the lift, a shallow metal ramp descends to the circular floorspace, at the centre of which stands a globe chair, adjacent to which is a control desk, supplied with a number of cordless telephone handsets. Behind the chair, at the further end of the room stands a penny-farthing bicycle, the real-life counterpart of the Village logo. And there is Number Two, sitting crosslegged in the globe chair, attired as he was last night, embracing his shooting stick umbrella.

'Good morning, Number Six,' he greets me, smiling unctuously. 'Come in, come in.'

I descend the ramp. The guards, I observe, take up positions either side of the lift doors.

'Take a seat,' invites Number Two, whereupon a chair rises up out of the floor. Seeing nothing to gain by remaining standing, I avail myself of it.

'And how are we this morning?' inquires Number Two. 'Sleep well?'

'Yes; although I had rather a rude awakening courtesy of your uniformed thugs,' I reply. 'How is Darren?'

'Darren? Oh, he's as well as can be expected,' says Number Two.

'Is that all you can tell me?' I demand.

'It's all I'm *going* to tell you,' is the reply.

'But I demand to know—'

'My dear Number Six, you're not in a position to "demand" anything,' interjects Number Two. He smiles, shaking his head. 'Really, Number Six, what are we going to do with you? Fancy trying to run away like that... What on earth did you hope to achieve by doing that?'

'I was trying to escape.'

'Escape? Escape from what? The things you so desperately want to run away from you're carrying around in your own head! Haven't I already made this fact clear to you? So, no matter how far you run, they're still going to be there with you: all the delusions, the repressions, the unresolved issues you've got spinning around in that noddle of yours. You can't run away from *them*. They have to be confronted; beaten on their own ground. That's the only way you're going to get rid of them, my dear chap.'

'Look, if you've just brought me here to continue your therapeutic counselling sessions—'

'No, I didn't bring you here for that,' says Number Two, his expression hardening. 'I brought you here to discuss the matter of your punishment.'

'P-punishment?' I say. This is not something I had anticipated. I begin to experience a creeping feeling of alarm.

'Well, don't look so surprised! You have committed a succession of breaches of the rules; this is a very serious matter. So yes, of course you're going to be punished! Did you seriously think you could just go back to how things were as though nothing had happened? Doesn't work that way, old chap, doesn't work that way. The rules are made for the good of the community, and they must be obeyed for the good of the community. The establishment is the benevolent parent that watches over the community; it guides, it protects, it provides for its needs. That is how a civilised society sustains and perpetuates itself. Imagine if a parent were to raise a child without imposing any rules or restraints upon it—a child raised in that way would grow up into a savage, a barbarian; a self-serving, undisciplined wretch, obeying all its worst impulses, never sparing a thought for those around it. It would only take a few such people to undermine the whole infrastructure of society— and that is why these rogue elements have to be suppressed, and at the first sign of their emergence, severely punished. Let us examine your list of violations of the rules: breaking curfew, entering areas of this facility off-limits to all patients, unauthorised use of staff transport, appropriation and misuse of a staff member's identity badge, physically assaulting a fellow patient. I could add to that list the driving of another fellow patient to a complete mental and physical breakdown, but I'm willing to concede that that one at least you did not do on purpose. But even so, this is a serious catalogue of crimes, Number Six. Your behaviour has been unmutual to the highest degree; and you have proven yourself to be a danger both to yourself and to the community as a whole. And as such, I think a period of solitary confinement is in order, to give you time to reflect upon your misdeeds, to atone for your unmutual behaviour. This will be your punishment, Number Six.'

I perk up at this. 'Oh! Well, if that's the case then, I willingly accept the punishment. So I'll just get back to my room and—'

'My dear chap, you won't be confined to your own room!' says Two, bringing me up in my tracks. 'Where would be the punishment in that? You're far too comfortable there! No, we have a special room that we reserve for cases like you: the solitary room. Very dark, very isolated; where you won't be disturbed by the outside world, by the passing of linear time… That is where you will be spending the next thirty days.'

'Thirty days?' I exclaim, now seriously alarmed.

'Certainly. Although of course as you will have no way of marking the passage of time, the precise duration of your solitary confinement will I am sure seem a great deal longer than thirty days to you.'

'B-but what about food?' I exclaim. 'I will be fed, won't I? You're not going to starve me?'

'Oh no, you will be fed,' says Number Two.

'Ah, good! So I will receive regular meals?'

'Meals, yes; but they won't be regular. We can't have you being able to set your clock by them. In our solitary room, you will experience almost complete sensory deprivation, and you will find that this will completely throw off your body clock, your internal alarm clock. You see, a person's biological clock is influenced almost entirely by external sensory data, and in the solitary room, you will be severed from that source of information.'

'But that will be torture!' I protest. 'Sheer torture! You can't do this to me!'

'Well, it isn't supposed to be pleasant, is it? Otherwise, it wouldn't be punishment, would it? You've brought it on yourself, Number Six. You need to be cured of your selfish disregard for others. Once you've experienced a period of real isolation, you might start to appreciate the value of being Mutual, of being a member of a community, and not just a selfish individualist.'

'But thirty days—! I'll go insane! Couldn't we just—?'

'This conversation is over,' says Number Two, crisply. To the guards: 'Take him away.'

The two guards march purposefully down the ramp, placing themselves either side of my chair.

'Goodbye, Number Six. See you in thirty days.'

And with that, Number Two swivels his chair around, presenting the sleek black surface of its back to me. I have been dismissed.

Chapter Thirteen
How I Experienced a Day in the Life

I have been thrown into my cell, the so-called solitary room, and the door closed and locked behind me. Darkness now surrounds me. I stand where I am while waiting for my eyes to adjust to the gloom. I have no idea of the exact dimensions of the room I have been consigned to, but one expects a solitary cell to be on the small side. However, I can discern nothing; the darkness remains absolute.

I now walk cautiously forward, arms extended, expecting at any moment to make contact with one of the apartment's furnishings, or with a wall; expecting to bark my shins against some obstruction or other... Nothing; I take step upon step, and I make contact with nothing. But there must be *something*—I had anticipated spartan conditions, but there has to be *something*: a pallet bed, a lavatory, a hand basin... Surely they haven't consigned me to a room with absolutely nothing in it; a Black Hole of Calcutta...?

The chamber must be larger than I anticipated... But just how much larger? By the very definition of the word, a cell should be a small chamber, not an extensive one. I advance more rapidly, arms exploring—but still there is nothing. This is madness...!

No. Wait a minute. What if I'm not in a cell, but in a corridor? Yes, it could be I have actually been introduced into a connecting corridor, and that my actual place of incarceration lies at the far end of it... Then, if I have been advancing along a corridor, if I make a ninety degree turn, I should soon encounter one of its walls... I perform this manoeuvre and advance slowly; one step, two steps, three steps... Ten steps, and still I have not encountered the wall! What is this...?

I now make a one hundred and eighty degree turn and retrace my steps. After ten steps, I begin counting again from one... Ten more steps and *still* no wall! I am most indubitably *not* in a corridor!

I now turn ninety degrees to my right and turn my steps back towards the door by which I was introduced to this place. There at least I can get my bearings, and, by following the course of the wall, I will be able to ascertain the dimensions of this chamber, as well discover the location of its fixtures and fittings...

Buoyed up now that I have a definite plan and purpose, I retrace my steps, hands held out before me, braced to encounter the surface of the door or the wall. How far did I walk from my starting point before I branched off to explore the left and the right...? At least forty paces, I would think... No, call it fifty...

Deducing that I must now be nearing the wall, I reduce my pace. Any minute now... Any minute...

What's this? Still nothing! Impossible! I am certain, quite certain that I did not advance further than fifty paces forward from the door—I have carefully retraced my steps: I should be back at my starting point...!

I take a few more paces. Still no wall! Impossible! Unless... unless I have completely lost my sense of direction, and I am not back at my starting point at all...

Baffled and alarmed I start flailing around with my arms, striking off first in one direction and then another...

'WHERE IS THE WRETCHED DOOR?' I yell in my rage.

'Where is the wretched door...?'
'...wretched door...?'
'...wretched door...?'
'...door...?'
'...door...?'
'...door...?'

My heart freezes over. Echoes! Echoes of my voice! And reverberating from a great distance! A *very* great distance! I'm not in a cell at all—I am in a cavern; a vast subterranean chamber! *This* then is my punishment; *this* is the solitary room!

With this awful realisation, my feelings of claustrophobia suddenly switch to its opposite number, agoraphobia. I am exposed, adrift; I am out in the open but am helpless, involved in inky blackness; I have no way of knowing what may be in this place with me; enemies could be lurking anywhere in this vastness!

A dread panic overwhelms me. Compelled by the instinct of flight, I start running. I run and I run, yelling incoherently, my head forward, shielded by my arms, simultaneously fearing and desiring collision with an obstruction; something—anything! I run and I run, my footsteps reverberating around me, until I am forced to sink to the ground from sheer exhaustion.

I sit there panting, struggling to catch my breath, while the last echoes of my screams fade in the distance. And then silence falls, a silence as thick and heavy as the darkness itself. Although unable to perceive it with my eyes, I am painfully conscious of the emptiness around me. I am sitting here completely lost in a vast subterranean wilderness. In my mad dash I must have distanced myself even further from the entrance to this place, my one point of reference, and am now even more adrift than when I first came to realise I had missed my way. I know I am underground—on leaving Number Two's office, we descended in the lift to the basement floor... And I shouldn't be surprised that a place such as this exists here. In the television series, there were caves and corridors and all manner of strange places beneath the Village; and the hospital above my head is patently some sort of annexe or extension of the Village...

As I recover my breath, my fears begin to give way to feelings of profound indignation, as the truth sets in that I have been vilely tricked by Number Two. This is not the kind of solitary confinement he had led me to believe I would have to experience—this is no ordinary method of solitary confinement: it is more like a sadistic joke played on the part of my captors to consign me to a place such as this.

I break into voice.

'Can you hear me? Yes, you! I'm talking to you, Number Two! Are you listening…? Yes; of course you are! You can probably even see me as well, can't you? You will have night vision cameras trained on me, won't you? You wouldn't want to miss witnessing the results of your sadistic joke, would you? No. Where would be the enjoyment then? Solitary confinement, you said! That's what you said! But this isn't a cell you've put me in; it's a maze. Admittedly, it's not the kind with hedges, but it's still a maze, isn't it? A vast maze without a map in which I am expected to find my way… Well, where are my basic amenities? I'm entitled to those, aren't I? I need a bed to sleep on, a toilet to use… It could take me days to even find them! Assuming they're even here! You claim to know everything about me: well, in that case, you must know about my very unpredictable bowels! I could be caught short at any moment! What am I supposed to do if I can't find where the blessed toilet is? This is in contravention of my basic human rights! Every man is entitled to a toilet! And a bed, as well! How am I supposed to sleep, if I can't even find where my bed is? I can't sleep on this hard floor, can I? No-one could! This is not a legitimate form of punishment! And even if it was—what were my crimes? That so-called list of offences: they were all things you allowed me to do! You knew about the escape plot in advance—you could have stopped it from happening! You could have nipped it in the bud! You could have confronted me with your knowledge—taken away the badge I'd appropriated! But no: you allowed it all to happen, just to play a trick on me! You allowed me to get into that lift! You allowed me to get onto that train! And even if my striking Spike wasn't part of your plan, that unfortunate act of violence on my part would never have occurred if you had prevented the escape attempt in advance! The only thing I would have been guilty of then would have been the swapping of badges with Number Sixteen! And that crime on its own would not have merited thirty days of this! This is rank injustice! It's not fair, do you hear me! It's not FAIR!'

'It's not FAIR…!'

'…not fair…!'

'…not fair…!'

'…fair…'

'…fair…'

'…fair…'

The echoes, of course, are my only reply. I know he's listening; he *must* be listening… Unless he's *not* listening… Unless I really have been abandoned… No! No, he just wants me to *think* that; yes, that's what it is. Yes, he won't reply, because he doesn't want me to know that he is listening and watching; he wants me to feel my isolation to the full. Curse the fellow. Why is he doing this to me? Why has he singled me out for this treatment? I didn't even know him; hadn't even met the fellow until I was brought here to this hospital… But now he's become my nemesis, the bane of my life, just as my doppelgänger was the bane of my life back in the outside world… My doppelgänger… What's happened to him? It's like he's slipped completely off the radar since my being brought to this place; it's like he's faded out of existence, and left Number Two to take up the task of persecuting me… But of course, being in charge, Number Two would have been the one behind my doppelgänger and his activities all along; he would have been there in the background watching over me the entire time; long before we ever actually met face to face… So, why hasn't my double shown himself here in the hospital…? Obviously, he could not appear as Number Two; Dr Tombs is Number Two… In the television series, the Prisoner's double was Number Twelve, twelve being the 'double' of six... But that Indian man is Number Twelve, so my double cannot assume that number either, so who would he...? Oh my goodness. Could it be...? Why did I never think of this before? Could it be that... that my double is actually Number *One*...? No. No, that can't be right... Can it? Can it? The TV series, the final episode: that nail-biting moment in which the Prisoner finally confronts Number One... But, no. This is ridiculous. To say that Number One was the Prisoner's evil twin would be to interpret the scene in a childishly literal sense. Symbolism was the intention there; the prisoner being also his own jailer was the message we were supposed to deduce... No, my double is no symbolic figure like Number One; my double is flesh and blood, a made to order duplicate of myself as was the Prisoner's double in 'The Schizoid Man.' I know that; I saw my double in that operating theatre while they were still in the process of creating him... So, where is he now? *Has* he disappeared for good, after all? Has he been discarded, having served his purpose...? Or, could he be still out there in the real world? Perhaps he has taken full possession of my existence? Perhaps he's out there now, living my life, so that nobody is even aware that the real me has been spirited away...? But, if that was the case, wouldn't Number Two have apprised me of this? Knowing how unwelcome the news would be to me, wouldn't he have taken great pleasure in informing me that my existence in the outside world had been usurped? Homer Simpson was replaced with a double when he was brought to the Village— No, wait a minute; that one wasn't canonical... It's funny, when I first got here, believing I was still in Morsham, Number Two would still bring me news of the outside world, at least so far as the progress of the police investigation into Gillian's murder was concerned... But then that tailed off... The last I heard was that the police were turning their attention to the landlord and male tenants of the apartment house, and that news must have been about a week ago now… Since then, nothing; I have heard no reports at all… It seems that now that I have been isolated from the outside world, I have ceased to be permitted to hear any news of that world…

And now… and now what? Where is this all going to end? Even if I escape from this present nightmare; where is it all going to end…?

A light.

A light has appeared! Directly in my line of sight, a single white point of artificial light… It's small and my eyes tell me that it is far away… Is it moving…? I focus on it, searching for the slightest change, the slightest movement or enlargement… No; no, the light, whatever it is, is completely stationary, neither moving towards me or in any other direction… And *what* is it, this light? Why did it suddenly appear? Perhaps it is a signpost; a signpost directing me to those much-needed amenities I require for my survival in this place…?

I have little choice. I have to go to this light and find out. I climb to my feet and commence walking towards it.

This could be another trick from that fiend Number Two; a trick designed to raise my hopes only to dash them to the ground. His scheme might be to exhaust me; to entice me to drain my energies walking towards this glimmer of hope, and then to only discover, after having covered goodness knows how much ground, that the hope is a delusive one. Perhaps the light will disappear as suddenly as it appeared; perhaps it will move with me, always remaining a tiny speck in the far distance.

I keep my eyes fixed firmly upon the light as I progress towards it. *Is* it getting any larger? Yes—yes, unless my eyes deceive me it *is* slowly growing in size… The light is directly in my line of vision as I walk, but with no other objects, nay, not even a horizon line to judge by, I cannot tell whether or not this light is level with the ground or suspended in the air… Not at ceiling height, of course; I have no idea of the precise elevation of the ceiling of this chamber, but to judge from the echoes, I am sure it must be very far above me. Therefore, this light, if it be not sitting on the floor, must be affixed to a wall, and as such, when I reach the light, I will have reached one of the boundaries of this chamber—and this in itself will be a major victory; I will not feel so horribly cast adrift.

Yes, the light is most definitely growing larger... I can discern its shape now: it is round; a sphere of intense white light, surrounded by a diminishing, hazy aureole... If it is an illumination, a light bulb affixed to a wall, I must be drawing close to it now—and yet I can discern no surrounding objects; the light still appears to be completely isolated; the radiance it sheds does not bring into relief any other objects...

No... Something is wrong... The light is still growing in size as I advance, thus it cannot be a mere light bulb at all... But then, what the devil *can* it be...? A doorway...? An open doorway with exterior light shining through it...? But the shape of the light is most definitely circular, and doorways tend to be rectangular in configuration... A round window...?

A hideous thought stops me in my tracks.

Rover.

Is the light I see before me Rover...? Could that creature be down here as my gaoler...? Number Two said that I would be deprived of human contact—it occurs to me now that he said nothing about *in*human contact.

I remember looking out of my bedroom window into the night; and seeing that bright light moving amongst the trees—from this I know that Rover *does* radiate a light when involved in darkness... Could this light I see before me be...?

With racing heart and senses alert, I strain my optic nerves to their utmost, scrutinising the light before me... Movement... Is there any movement...? My experience of the television series informs me that Rover is rarely completely inert, completely stationary... Even when not in locomotion, it wobbles, it trembles, it quivers with life; even that time it was occupying Number Two's chair... Is the light before me trembling? Is it quivering with life...? At first I think it is not; that the light is completely motionless... But the more I look, the more I think I can detect a slight motion, a subtle shimmering around the edges of the corona of light...

I screw my eyes shut, rub them with my fingers. My eyes are starting to hurt from the effort. How many muscles is it they say that a person has in their eyes? I know it is a large number; I must be exerting all of them to the limit...

Can I perceive movement, or are my eyes playing tricks on me?

Wait a minute. I can't hear anything. Rover emits sounds; a medley of strange sounds; even when stationary it always emits sounds—at least I think it does... I can hear nothing. Could it be that I am just too far away from the thing...? I listen intently; but still I can hear nothing... Perhaps I am alarming myself without reason; perhaps the light ahead is *not* Rover...

Summoning all my courage, I resume my progress towards the light—but now walking more slowly, with more caution... The circle of light grows ever larger, but still it seems to my eyes no more than an intangible source of light, and not a discernible physical object... And I do not believe it *is* moving after all; the quivering I thought I perceived must have been a trick of my eyes, a result of staring for too long and with too much intensity into the light; I strained my eyes so much searching for movement, that I started to perceive movement when really there was none!

With renewed confidence, I increase my pace. My mind reverts to its original supposition: that the light ahead indicates some kind of relief from this monotony: food, amenities, somewhere for me to lie down and rest myself...

Howsomever, I have not progressed much further when I am brought up in my tracks once more; because now I *can* hear a sound! A sound coming from the direction of the light ahead. It is very faint; a kind of electronic buzzing sound, it seems to be; like interference on a low-band radio frequency... It is not one of the sound-effects one usually associates with Rover... But what can it be...?

The sound is constant, uninterrupted; I resume walking, trying to identify it... The clearer the sound grows, the more it sounds like... birdsong! Yes: birdsong! The chattering of a large number of birds of different varieties...

It is! There's no doubt of it now: the sound I am hearing is indubitably birdsong!

This can only mean one thing: the light I see ahead of me is an exit from this place; a portal leading to the open air—and that light, that light that has been drawing me towards it, is nothing less than the light of day shining into this inky sepulchre!

Yes! All becomes clear to me now: I have eluded my captors! Clearly, when I succumbed to panic and fled precipitately, I must have run much further into this chamber than my captors ever supposed I would dare to venture! In short, I have exceeded the perimeters of their surveillance devices! And ahead of me, unguarded and forgotten (perhaps even unknown) is an outlet from this vast underground chamber—an outlet into the open air and, considering the sheer distance I must have travelled, an outlet which surely must be beyond the perimeter walls of this so-called mental institution!

Ha! And to think: when I was venting my rage at Number Two back there, I must have been talking to myself! *That* is why I received no reply! I had already taken myself beyond the range of their listening devices! Ha-ha-ha!

Tingling with anticipation, I increase my pace once more. The chatter of my feathered friends grows ever louder and clearer... and yes, now I do believe I can feel a suggestion of warm summer air… and a scent, yes, an aroma of the outdoors, of fruit and flowers and verdure…!

The circle of light grows ever larger in intensity and in dimensions… Way too large to be Rover… Still, strange that I cannot descry anything within that light; no suggestion of blue sky, of trees or other verdure… Yet the sounds and the smells are unquestionably real… I have been too long wandering in this darkness: yes, that's what it is. My eyes will need some time to adjust to the light of the sun after having being immured in this subterranean vault…

I stop in my tracks, faced suddenly with a fatal floor in my conjectures. This is a *subterranean* vault; ergo, I'm underground. So how can I be approaching an exit to the outside world? How can this light I am fast approaching be the light of day?

But it *has* to be; I can hear the birds, I can smell the trees and flowers, I can feel the warm air… I start walking again. I increase my speed… However seemingly impossible it may be, I feel sure that my escape from this pit of darkness lies ahead of me…

The light, it is all around me now; objects begin to solidify and take form, swimming into focus…

Apple trees… I can smell apple trees…

…I'm standing in a garden, amongst apple trees. It is a big garden, and beyond this small orchard, neglected and overgrown, a jungle of weeds and long grass and thickets of brambles. The sky above me is blue and cloudless, and the air is warm, but not oppressively so. I turn around and now I see a house, rising above a tall hedgerow; it is an old and rambling house with gables and tall chimneys; a house that I know very well. It is my parents' house; the house in which I grew up…

How have I come to be here…? I haven't seen this house for years…

I was underground… There was a doorway… Where's the doorway…?

Wait a minute. How is this house even standing? It was demolished; knocked down to make way for a new bypass... Yes, it happened more than ten years ago, just after I had left to attend university; that was when it happened... This house doesn't exist anymore...

Then am I dreaming...?

I start to walk towards the house. I pass through a trellised arch in the hedgerow and before me now is the cultivated part of the garden, with its neatly-trimmed lawn, its flower borders; the bird table, the greenhouse... The back garden being so extensive in length, my horticulturist father had elected to only cultivate the portion of it immediately adjacent to the house, allowing the remainder of it, the area beyond the orchard, to become an overgrown wilderness, concealed from sight by the tall hedgerow—an acknowledged continuation of the property, but not part of the 'garden' as such.

A pathway of irregular slabs extends from one end of the neatly-trimmed lawn to the other, from the patio at the back of the house, up to the archway in the hedgerow where I now stand. I recall that when traversing this path as a lad I would like to jump from stone to stone, deeming it a fatal error to land on the turf between the stones...

Obeying a sudden impulse, I jump now, landing adroitly on the next slab. This garden, especially the overgrown portion at the rear, was my playground back in those days; my solitary playground for the most part, as my mother would rarely allow me to entertain schoolfriends... That was the main drawback of living here in this isolated dwelling in the countryside: my town-dwelling schoolfriends all lived within easy walking distance of one another; on weekends and during school holidays, it was a simple matter for them to just call on each other whenever they wished to; to play in each other's houses, to go exploring together...

I remember how envious of them I was...

Another leap and I alight with both feet on the next stone. I suddenly feel so nimble; as light as the air...! I jump from slab to slab, just like I did back then. Have to be careful: land between the stones and the crocodiles will get you!

I espy a cat; a black and white cat sitting on the patio close to the kitchen door... A cat... Yes; yes, we did used to have a cat...! A black and white cat...! Yes, I remember it now... Her name was... Her name was... Tufty! Yes: Tufty!

'Tufty!'

Forgetting my jumping game, I advance towards the cat, calling out her name, holding out my hand. The cat sits there, looking at me. Does she recognise me? It's hard to tell. She looks neither happy nor alarmed at my approach—just disinterested.

I draw closer, my hand extended, making clicking noises with my tongue...

And then; and then when my hand is all but in touching distance of her whiskers—the cat springs away from me!

Don't do that! You always run away from me! I only want to stroke you, you stupid cat!

She has come to a halt on another part of the lawn. I walk towards her again, calling her name coaxingly... Now she's done it again! She shoots through the archway into the orchard. Running away from me when I was almost there! You *always* run away from me! When we're in the house and I want to stroke you, you'll always run into mum's parlour or dad's study, where you know I'm not allowed! And if it's upstairs you'll go into mum and dad's bedroom because I'm not allowed in there either! You never go in *my* room! Kevin says his cat sleeps on the bed with him! Why can't you do that for me? Why can't you sleep with me on *my* bed?

She's running into the jungle part of the garden now—but I'll catch her! I'll catch her this time! 'Come here! Don't run away from me! It's not fair! You're not allowed to run away from me!'

I see her! She's jumped behind that long grass, under the bramble bush! She always goes into places where I can't come after her!

I pick up a stone and throw it at where she's hiding.

'Come out!' I cry, tears streaming down my eyes. 'Stop running away from me all the time!'

She doesn't come out so I throw some more stones. One of them must have hit her because she comes rocketing out of the bushes and runs towards the end of the garden.

'Come back!' I wail, running after her again. 'Stop running away from me!'

I see her at the end of the garden, run straight into the old tumbledown shed. Ha! I've got her now! There's no other way out of that shed! She'll have to stop and let me play with her now!

I make a beeline for the shed, as fast as my little legs can take me, and I run straight in through the open doorway…

…and I collide with one of the legs of an occasional table. The table wobbles and the vase of flowers are upset and they fall off and land with a thump on the carpet, spilling all the flowers and water!

'RANDAL CEDRIC FORTESCUE!'

I know where I am! This is upstairs in the house on one of the landings. I remember this! I knocked over the flowers and Mum found out about it! She's *going* to find out about it! She *has* found out about it!

'Randal Cedric Fortescue! Just what is all that noise about? If you've broken anything—!'

No! I don't want Mum to find me! I'll be in trouble if Mum finds me! I've got to hide! I've got to hide somewhere clever where she won't find me!

But I can't move! There's a big white light shining down on me and I'm stuck in it; I can't move!

'Randal Cedric Fortescue!'

It's too late! She's coming up the stairs! I can see her head now; her blue-rinsed curly hair, her flabby jowls, the eyes with the heavy underlids… She can see me now and she can see the spilt flowers, and I'm stuck under the white light that won't let me move. She's on the landing now; I can see her shape and she's really big, like a hippopotamus Kenny said, and she's getting bigger and bigger! She's wearing one of those flower-print dresses that look really old like the house, and she looks really angry!

'WHAT have you done, young man?'

Her voice is like thunder, like a lion roaring. I don't want to look at her angry face so I look down at the floor and the spilled flowers.

'What… is… this?' she demands. 'Look what you've done, you bad little boy! I've told you about running inside the house! Haven't I? Haven't I? And now look what you've done!'

'It wasn't me!' I wail. 'It was Tufty! She jumped up on the table and knocked the flowers over!'

'Don't tell fibs to me, Randal Fortescue! Tufty is outside! *You* knocked the vase over, didn't you? You knocked it over because you were disobeying my orders and running around in the house! Weren't you? Weren't you? Look at me, child!'

I look at her. There's a green light and it's making her face all green and her eyebrows are down and her mouth is like a line and she's staring at me with her eyes all angry and scary.

'It was you, wasn't it? I've told you time and again not to run around in the house, and I've told you time and again never to tell fibs! But here you are, running around and breaking things and then telling fibs about it! You bad, disobedient child!' She turns to Dad. 'Husband; what did we do to be burdened with such a wilful, disobedient child?'

Dad's just over there. He's sitting in a chair and he's made of wood like one of those art class dolls but person-sized, and his face is a black and white photo stuck to the head of the doll.

'I wash my hands of the boy,' says Dad. He always says that.

'He needs to be taught a lesson,' says Mum. 'He needs to be taught to obey his parents and do everything they tell him! Listen to me, young man: you need to remember that you cannot just do what you want and get your own way all the time! People who think that are the worst people in the world! Undisciplined people! People with no morals! Do you want to grow up like that! Do you want to grow up to be like one of those wretched people? Well, you are not going to! And I am going to make sure that you don't! Go to your room! Go to your room at once! There will be no television and no playing in the garden for the rest of today! And no pudding after dinner, either! To your room at once, young man!'

Banished, I turn and I go towards my room. It's a door at the end of a corridor with no walls or ceiling, just a door. I suppose I could get into my room without even going through the door, seeing as there aren't any walls or anything, but I suppose that would be breaking the rules, and then I'd just get in trouble again. If there's a door there, then I suppose you have to go through the door, because someone put it there and that's what is meant for... Otherwise there wouldn't be any point in having the door there in the first place...

'Creeping... crawling... crawling like insects...'

It's a voice with no-one attached to it; a voice in the air all around me. It's not Mum because it's a male voice and it's not Dad because it's a scary voice; it's a voice that's not angry yet but it will be angry if you don't do what it says...

And then I'm standing at the door opens and standing in the doorway is Mr Hardcastle the headmaster, and the room isn't my room it's his room, his headmaster's room. Mr Hardcastle is scary, like Mum's scary. He's big just like mum, and he's wearing a cap and gown and he's looking at me with angry eyes, and over his angry eyes are these big, tufty eyebrows. I remember those tufty eyebrows. They almost look like they've been stuck on…

'So it's you, Fortescue, is it?' he says. 'Making all that noise? Running in the hallways and breaking things? No running in the hallways, boy! No running in the hallways! How many times do I have to tell you?'

'I'm sorry, sir…' I blubber.

'"Sorry"? "Sorry," you say? If you just did what you were told, you wouldn't have to be sorry, would you? And stop blubbering, boy!'

'Sorry…' I blubber. I turn to walk away.

'And where do you think you're going?'

'Back to class…'

'Never mind "back to class," boy; I want a word with you. In here.'

He opens the door for me and I walk in. The room has walls on the inside and it looks just how I remember it with the green carpet and the grey walls and the desk and bookshelves and the sun shining in through the windows. Mr Hardcastle goes and sits in his chair and I stand on the carpet in the middle of the room because I know that's what I'm supposed to do.

'Now, boy…' he says, and he looks at me with his strict eyes and his tufty eyebrows coming down and making a knot at the top of his nose. 'You told Mrs Peters that it was David Chivers who broke the window of the greenhouse, didn't you?'

'Yes, sir.'

'And *why* did you tell her that, boy?'

'Because it's true, sir.'

'"Because it's true"?'

'Yes, sir; I saw it happen.'

'I'm not asking you if it's true that David Chivers broke the window; what I'm asking you is *why* you told this to your teacher?'

This makes me confused. 'Because she wanted to know who did it,' I say. 'She asked us who it was who broke the greenhouse window because she wanted to know, and I told her it was David Chivers because that's the truth and it's bad to tell fibs.'

'It's bad to tell *tales*, boy,' says Mr Hardcastle.

I'm still confused. 'It wasn't a tale; a tale's a story that's made up and it wasn't made up; it was the truth and you should always tell the truth.'

'Yes, but Mrs Peters didn't ask *you* who broke the window, did she? She asked the whole class, didn't she? And the reason she asked the whole class was because she wanted the person who broke the window to come forward and admit that they did it—but you, who *didn't* do it, told her who *did*, and *that* is called telling tales, boy! Do you see?'

'No, sir.'

'You don't see?'

'No, sir.'

'You don't think it's a bad thing to tell tales on your friends?'

'David's not my friend, sir. He picks on me.'

'He picks on you?'

'Yes. Him and his friends. They call me names and sing nasty songs about me in the playground.'

'And don't you think that perhaps the reason they call you names and sing nasty songs about you is because you're always telling tales on them? Because this is not the first time, is it? It's not the first time you've told tales on your classmates. Don't you think that people might be nicer to you if you didn't tell tales on them?'

'No, sir.'

'"No, sir"? What do you mean "no, sir"?'

'They started it, sir. They called me names and sang nasty songs before I ever told on any of them. So they started it.'

'And do you think that tale-bearing is the best way to get them to stop doing those things? Listen, boy: whether they are your friends or not your friends, you do not tell tales on your classmates. It's one of the golden rules.'

'Is it a school rule, sir?'

'Yes, it's a school rule!'

'And it's in the school rules book, sir?'

'No, boy. It's not in the school rules book: it's an *unwritten* rule.'

'Then if it's not in the school rules book, then it's not a proper rule, is it, sir? So it's not fair that I should get in trouble for breaking it if it's not a proper rule; is it, sir?'

Mr Hardcastle rubs his brows. One of his tufty eyebrows comes off and he sticks it back on again.

'Look, Fortescue,' he says. 'In a place like this we all have to get along with one another. You children work together, you play together, and so you have to get along together. You have to think about what is good for the whole class, and not just about what is good for yourself. And this means you have to follow the rules—and not just the school rules; not just the rules that say you shouldn't run in the corridors and that you shouldn't answer back to your teachers. There are also the unwritten rules, the golden rules which you children have amongst yourselves and which help you to get along with each other. You are not obeying these golden rules and so you are disturbing the equilibrium and at the same time making yourself very unpopular. Therefore, you must do something to correct this. You must learn to make concessions, to fit in, and then you will be accepted. Do you understand?'

'No, sir.'

'"No, sir"?'

'No, sir. I don't see why I should be nice to people who call me names and sing mean songs about me in the playground. They don't deserve for me to be nice to them and it's not fair if I can't be just as mean to them as they are to me, just because of some rules that aren't even proper written down rules.'

Mr Hardcastle looks at me. 'In that case, Randal Fortescue, I can confidently predict that you are going to grow up to become a most obnoxious, objectionable and very lonely human being. You may return to your classroom.'

He turns his back on me. I am dismissed.

Hanging my head, I exit the room and step out into the sunshine of the back garden...

The back garden... *My* back garden... Am I supposed to be here...? Yes... Yes, I was here before... Just a while ago... I was here before and there was something I was doing... something I had to do... What was it...?

Of course! The cat! I haven't finished chasing the cat! I'd just cornered the beast in that old shed at the end of the garden when I went and got sidetracked. Well, now to finish the job. Down the garden path I march, past the orchard, through the wilderness and towards the rear fence.

Stupid, ignorant cat. Running straight into the shed, its simple feline brain doubtless thinking: 'If I can't see you, you can't see me!' Ha! Well, I'm afraid I am about to disabuse you of that notion, Mrs Fancy Paws!

I march into the shed. I am pulled up short. There's a girl. A girl sitting there on the bench in the gloomy, dusty interior. A girl wearing a summer frock and sandals on her feet. Her hair is long, dark and wavy.

It's Daisy Miller. Daisy Miller from my class at school...

She's sitting there and she's looking at me and she's smiling at me. It's a big smile, with the large, strong teeth of a country girl, and it's such a warm smile and it's directed at me, and it stirs up feelings I had almost forgotten I ever possessed...

'Well sit down, then!' she says, tapping the bench beside her. 'I'm not gunna bite you, am I?'

I do as I am bid and sit down next to her. She looks at me and her brown sparkle in the hazy light filtering into the shed through its one dust-begrimed window. Her cheeks are freckled and her lips are moist and rosy; and I can smell her perfume; that scent: I remember it...

I remember it all... That day, back when I was fourteen (or was it fifteen?)—she suddenly appeared before me at the end of the garden. I'd been leaning on the fence, looking out across the cornfields, daydreaming... And there she suddenly was... She'd walked all the way across the fields from her family's farm... Daisy Miller... I wasn't expecting her at all. A girl I'd never even really thought about—because in my self-absorption I never really thought about anyone other than myself... But she had been thinking about me... That day, when she came all the way out here, she came just to see me... just to see me... It was a hot day, so we came in here into the old shed, to be in the shade...

'So, d'you come here often?' she says.

'Well, not so much recently,' I reply. 'I used to play in here when I was a child...'

She laughs, hits me playfully. 'That was a joke, silly! You're a right one, aren't you? Talk like you swallowed a dictionary for breakfast, but you're still a bit slow on the uptake!'

'Well, I don't know about being slow... I believe my acumen is commensurate—'

'Now there you go again!' says Daisy. 'Using all those big words: antisocial, that's what it is. Do that and people think you're just showin' off, else you're trying to confuse 'em. Just talk like everyone else talks!'

'But, I... I just use the words I know...'

'Well, don't use so many of them! That's what comes of having your nose stuck in a book all the time!'

'Well, I believe reading is a creditable pastime... You read books yourself, don't you? At least, you do well in English...'

'Yeah, I like reading books—but I don't do it all the time; not like you! I like going out and hanging out with my mates as well. And that's what you should be doing! You should come into town and have some fun now and then; instead of moping around in that gloomy old house of yours in the backside of nowhere. Why don't you do that, eh? Come into town!'

'Well, I... I don't really know anyone...'

'That's cuz you don't try to get to know people, do you?' says Daisy, sighing. 'You keep 'em at a distance. You're like that at school when *I* try to talk to you, aren't you? You don't smile, you give me short answers... Why'd you do that? Not very nice is it, when someone's trying to be friendly with you? Why're you like that?'

'I don't know... I suppose I thought you were... you were just talking to me out of pity... and not because you really wanted to...'

'Well, that's nice, isn't it? Always thinking the worst of people... Well, you're wrong; when I talk to you at school it's cuz I *like* you, not cuz I feel sorry for you! Mind you, I *do* feel sorry for you as well, cuz you're such a misery-guts!' She playfully rubs my belly. 'Misery-guts! Come on: smile, why don't you? Go on: it won't kill you!'

I remember this now... I did as she said, I smiled; I'm sure it was a very sheepish affair, but she seemed to be happy with it—*seems* to be happy with it...

'There, you see! Wasn't so bad, was it?' She ruffles my hair. 'Yeah... You can be nice when you want to... I'll look after you...'

This is it. It's happening now. She's putting her arms around my shoulders, drawing her face close to mine... I see clearly her epicanthic eyes, her painted-on freckles...

'I'll look after you...'

This is it... This is the moment... My first kiss... My only kiss...

Now I am clumsily returning her embrace, and, even more ineptly returning her kiss... I can feel her lips around mine... I can taste her lips, her mouth; hear the wet sound they make as we continue to kiss...

'How was that, then?' she breathes. 'Better than some old book, eh?'

'Yes…'

Oh no; it's happening now… This bad part; the worst part… She's taking my hand, drawing it towards her chest.

'Go on,' she whispers, kissing me again. 'Touch 'em. It's alright; go on.' She places my hand on her chest, and I can feel its soft warmth, feel the motion of her breathing… And now, she loosens, unbuttons, and she is guiding my hand in further, deeper…

'That's it…' she breathes. 'Keep going…'

'*WHAT* IS GOING ON HERE?'

My mother stands framed in the doorway, arms akimbo. She looks angry but it's a new species of angry; one that I've never seen on her face before; a shocked angry, an appalled, incredulous angry. I have gone beyond the pale; I have been caught in the commission of an offence so far above and beyond any I was ever thought to have been capable of perpetrating that it defies belief.

My hand flies from Daisy's dress as though it has just received an electric shock. And I push her away from me; in my fear and my surprise, I push her away from me.

My mother fixes her enraged and flabbergasted eyes on me. 'So, *this* is what you get up to the moment my back is turned!' she thunders. 'This is what they teach you at that school of yours! Wretched boy! Wretched, wretched boy!'

'It wasn't me!' I cry. 'It was her! *She* started it! She made me do it!'

That's what I say, coward that I am. And my words have the desired result: the accusing eyes of my mother are diverted from myself and onto Daisy.

'So, it's *you*, is it?' her lip curling with disdain. 'Leading my son astray! Yes… I see it now… I know your sort, girl! Look at you: an ill-mannered farm girl with the morals of the barnyard!'

'Oh, shut-up you old fart-bottle!' snaps Daisy, rising to her feet and confronting my mother. 'He's not a baby anymore, so why don't you stop bloody treating him like one! So what if we were kissing?'

'Impudent wench!' rages my mother. 'How dare you talk back to me and tell me how to raise my own child! Get out of here, you dressed up milkmaid! Get out of here at once!'

She points imperiously to the doorway.

'Don't worry! I'm going!' snaps Daisy. And then, turning to me: 'Come on, Randal. Come with me. I know she'll give you an earful when you get back, but so what? Come on; come with me. I told you I'd look after you, didn't I? Come on...'

And as she makes this appeal, holding her hand out to me, her voice is so warm, so encouraging. It is salvation she is offering me; it is life—and I look away from her. Craven wretch that I am, I turn my head and look away; I spurn that extended hand, that compassionate voice, that offer of freedom.

'He is not going anywhere with you, girl!' grates my mother. 'Stay where you are, Randal. Your mother is ordering you to stay where you are.'

And I do just that.

'Randal...?'

And then it is over. That last plea, that last utterance of my name, and it is over. Wounded (and I'll never truly know how much) by my cold, silent rejection of her, Daisy Miller walks out of the shed and out of my life...

After this day she will avoid me at school. Or perhaps it is me who avoids her... Either way, the fleeting connection we formed is severed, the moment forever lost...

If only I had gone with her, if only I had taken that proffered hand... My whole life would have been different. I know it would have, and knowing it is what kills me...

'Now come back to the house, Randal Fortescue,' comes my mother's voice, calmer now. 'And I don't want you associating with brazen hussies like that girl ever again. Nasty, common creature. I knew this would come of not sending you to the public school. Let me tell you, girls like that are only ever after you for your money!'

'I haven't got any money...' I say dully.

'Then *my* money! That's all she's after! Do you really think a girl like that could have any sympathy for a boy like you? Of course not! *I'm* the only one who understands you! *I'm* the only one who knows what's best for you! And you would do well to remember that, Randal Fortescue!'

'I'm going to university!' I exclaim, having risen to my feet to deliver this bombshell. The past is the past. I can still effect my own escape from this prison.

My mother's face is a picture of blank incredulity. 'University? What's he saying? *Going* to university? Going *away* to university?'

'Yes, mother. Away to London. It's all arranged. I have applied and have been accepted.'

'Going away to London? *Staying* in London? For how long, may I ask?'

'Three years, mother. That is the usual duration of these courses. Four, if I elect to have a gap year.'

'Ridiculous! He doesn't know what he's talking about? Who's going to feed you? Who's going to wash your clothes and tidy your room?'

'I believe I will have to learn to perform those offices for myself, mother. I am going to London, and moreover when I have completed my studies, I shall *stay* in London. In other words, this is goodbye, mother. I will not be returning to the parental abode from hence forth. I may visit you and I may not. That is all that I can say at the moment. I will be you adieu.'

And taking up my umbrella and placing my bowler hat on my head, I turn on my heel and head for the door, this being the only physical object present at the moment.

However, upon opening the door, I find myself confronting a man in a turban and with a long beard who is seated behind a desk—to wit, the section chief at the Unemployment Centre.

'Please to be coming in, Mr Fortescue,' he says. He's expecting me. Good. Then I haven't walked through the wrong door, after all.

'Please to be seating yourself.'

I seat myself in the chair facing the section chief. I notice how spartan his office is. In fact, aside from the desk and chairs, there is nothing—not even walls or a ceiling. This is doubtless the result of allocation cuts.

'I will be getting straight to the point, Mr Fortescue, and sparing us both as much grief as possible,' commences the section chief. 'So, as much as it saddens me to say, we are having to be letting you go.'

'Letting me go?' I echo. 'You mean you're firing me?'

'Regrettably, yes.'

I frown. Something is distinctly wrong here. 'But didn't I already hand in my resignation?'

'No, Mr Fortescue,' says the section chief, sadly shaking his head. 'It is far too late for the handing in of resignations. It is most regrettable, but you have been dismissed; you no longer work for this organisation.'

I hold up my hand. 'I have question: You are the section chief, correct?'

'Correct, Mr Fortescue.'

'At the Unemployment Centre?'

'Correct, Mr Fortescue.'

'Just as I thought. Then why are you talking like my erstwhile campaign manager, Mr Dhawan? I know you're not him because he didn't have a beard, just a moustache.'

'Oh, Mr Fortescue; this is hardly the time to be concerning yourself with beards and moustaches. The fact of the matter is, having assessed your case, we have reached the decision that you are not only unemployed, but are in fact completely unemployable.'

'Unemployable?' I cry. 'How dare you, sir?'

'It is not a matter of how I dare, Mr Fortescue. These facts have to be faced. You have been classified as unemployable; therefore you are being left with no choice than to be moving back in with your mother. This is the decision that has been made.'

'What?' I roar. 'You can't just tell me where I have to take up residence! I happen to have a bedsitting room—'

'—from which you have been evicted, Mr Fortescue. It has all been taken care of. Your possessions have already been returned to your mother's house; now all you are needing to do is join them there.'

'But I don't want to move back in with mother!' I protest. 'And if you think it's such a marvellous idea, then why don't *you* move back in with her! Yes! See how *you* like it!'

'Mr Fortescue, it is not for me to be moving back in with other people's mothers. This is being entirely your affair. Now please, let us be ending this conversation. I will be bidding you good-day.'

The fellow then picks up some papers and starts shuffling them and I see that I am dismissed.

I walk back out through the door. In front of me is another door. I pass through this. And through the next door. And the next. And the next.

Just as I am starting to think I have been doomed to spend the rest of my life walking through doors, I find myself face to face with my mother.

She regards me with a look of grim triumph, arms folded. 'So, you've finally come back, have you?'

'It feels like I only left two minutes ago.'

'Well, and I hope you've learned your lesson, young man!'

'And what lesson would that be?'

'I'm talking about you, of course! Everything started to go wrong for you the moment you decided to leave your mother, didn't it? When you went off to that dreadful university! Didn't it?'

'Did it?'

'Yes! Look what happened! Your back started troubling you, didn't it? You never had back troubles when you were living at home, did you? No. Psychosomatic, that's what it was!'

'Psychosomatic?'

'Yes! It was your back telling you to come back home to your mother! That's what it was! And if that wasn't enough, that Gillian Draper creature waded into your life in her size twelve boots and started you off watching that ridiculous television series, didn't she? And what came of that, I might ask? If it wasn't for her, you wouldn't have ended up living in the same house with her and then you wouldn't have been accused of killing her when the silly woman went and got herself murdered!'

'She didn't do it on purpose, mother.'

'Of course she did! And just proves that I can't let you out of my sight for five minutes!' She moderates her tone. 'But you're back now, so that's all water under the bridge. Your mother's going to look after you from now on and she's never going to let you out of her sight. Come! Come, Randal, and let me take you in my arms!'

She opens her arms to receive me.

'Come! Come into your mother's arms!'

And then she starts to change. Before my very eyes, her clothes and her skin start to drain of all colour, fading to a uniform white; simultaneously, her body starts to lose its shape, ballooning outwards; arms, legs and head all melting into the expanding torso, coalescing into an angry, quivering white mass.

I retreat from this horror, but I'm brought up by the door behind me and now there's nowhere for me to run.

With a dreadful roar the white ball lunges forward and pounces on me; and now it's all around me, pressing against me, pinning me to the door folding itself around me, smothering me, overwhelming me. I struggle against it, but to repel it is impossible; it's like being trapped inside a huge plastic bag.

I'm trapped. It's sticking fast to my face, blocking my air passages! I'm stifling; I can't breathe—

Chapter Fourteen
How I Found Myself Living in Amity

Things are mighty peaceful here in the town of Amity. We like to take things easy round these parts. Ain't no point in stirrin' up trouble for no dang reason when it's easy enough for folks to jest get along with each other and mind their own business. 'Course, this neighbourly spirit means that as town sheriff I ain't got a whole heap to do in the way of business; things jest sorta take care of themselves. But it's kind of nice this way, cuz it means that I can jest sit here in my sheriff's office, with my boots up on my desk, all cosy like, and catch up on my reading. Sure, there's a degree o' noise out there in the street: gunfire an' hollerin' an' the like; but that's jest usual here in amity, so I don't really pay it any mind.

So, like I say, I'm catchin' up on my readin', which is what I do most've the time on account o' things bein' so peaceful like. Right now I'm improvin' my mind with one of them there English 'silver spoon' novels; they're the ones with all those fancy folks with handles to their names, an' who all live in them great big mansion places, an' where the ladies are always frettin' about who they're gunna get hitched to, an' what fancy dress they're gunna doll themselves up in fer the next ball; while the fellers, them

English Gentlemen, they like to pass most o' their time shootin' up jest about everythin' that's got feathers on it—which seems like a mighty big waste of ammunition to me.

Most of the readin'-matter we get around here comes from ole England, cuz we don't write a whole lot out here in the States. I guess folks here are jest too plain busy; they ain't got the time to be sittin' around writin' books. 'Course we got some writers like ole Nate Hawthorne; but they like to keep things on the short side, y'know? Whereas them English writers sure do like to pile on the words. Don't get me wrong: I ain't complainin' about that—the more words they cram in there, the more value yer gettin' for yer money, right? Them fancy triple-deckers, they tides you over for longer, y'see?

As you can see, I got me a nice little nest here. Front part o' the room is the waitin' area for any of our good citizens who wanna report a crime—but what with things been so peaceful, I'm proud to say I ain't hardly ever troubled with any callers. And then just here's my desk an' my chair; then behind me we got the stove for cookin' and heatin' purposes, an' them cupboards in the corner is where we store the vittles; and over in the other corner is my cot, which is real comfy like. Hanging from a nail on the wall there is my tin bath-tub, which I can jest fill from the pump out back whenever I wanna perform my ablutions; and as for interior decoration, all along that wall we got a gallery of pictures o' some o' Amity's most famous citizens—and underneath it says how much they're worth. That ladder you see there goes up to the lumber room which is full o' junk left behind by previous sheriffs; my marshal, Darren Nesbit beds himself down up there.

An' if you're wonderin' where the jailhouse is; why it's right next door—but I am truly proud to tell yer that we ain't ever had to lock nobody up in it in all the time I been sheriff here. Not bad, huh?

So here I am quietly readin' my book when, speak o' the devil, the door bursts open an' in comes my marshal, faster 'an a weasel bein' chased by a bobcat, and right behind him a heavy shower of lead.

'Sheriff Fort! Sheriff Fort!' he hollers, all wide-eyed an' out o' breath.

'Shut the door, dang it! Your lettin' the bullets in!'

Nesbit shuts the door an' then scoots up to my desk. He's a little dude is Marshal Nesbit; works to his advantage, bein' little does: makes him a smaller target for folks to shoot at. Now me, I'm kinda on the stocky side, so I have to be more careful when I'm out an' about; in fact, it's on account o' this I prefer *not* to be out an' about, more'n I can help it. An' Marshal Nesbit, 'though he ain't got much in the thinkin' department, he's useful for runnin' errands and the like.

'What's all the commotion?' I ask him.

'Judge Tombs wants to see you right away, sheriff!' says Nesbit.

'Does he now?' says I, not much impressed. 'Well, he knows where to find me, don't he?'

'No, sheriff! He wants *you* to go and *see* him! He's waitin' for you over in the saloon.'

Heavin' a weary sigh, I fold back the corner o' the page I'm on, put my book down and swing my legs off of the desk.

'Well, that's jest great, ain't it?' I says. 'Judge wants to see me again—and it'll be about the same dang thing he always wants to see me about.'

''Bout you not carryin' no shootin' iron,' says Nesbit, nodding his stupid head up and down.

'Why in tarnation can't that old coot leave well alone? If I've told him once, I've told him a hundred times!' I reach for my Stetson.

'Well, won't don't you just do what he says an' put on the gunbelt?' says Nesbit.

'*Because*, I don't choose to. *Because*, as I've likewise told *you* a hundred times, it's against my principles to carry a shootin' iron. I prefer to use my wits an' ingenuity ter git things done—an' no judge or any other critter is gunna make me do any diff'rent! An' *that* is all there is to it!'

'Well, that's mighty fine, Sheriff Fort,' says Nesbit. 'But I don't see why *I* gotta go 'round with no shootin' iron—it ain't against *my* principles!'

'*This* is what I reckon about your principles,' I tell him, swattin' him round his stupid head. 'As long as I'm sheriff here an' you're just the marshal, you'll dang well do what I dang well tell you to! It's called "chain of command," sonny. You got that?'

'Yeah, I got it,' says the guy, all surly.

'Good. Now you hold down the fort while I go'n have my usual conversation with Judge Tombs. An' don't you go getting' your grubby paws all over my book, y'hear me? It ain't got no pictures anyhow, so there ain't nothin' in it ter interest you.'

I step outside. Town of Amity looks pretty much the same as any Western town you'll find on any motion picture lot the world over—they build 'em all pretty much from the same set o' blueprints. You got your storefronts, you got your hitchin' posts, your water troughs, your covered sidewalks. Saloon's right across the way, an' you cain't really mistake it cuz it's got this big sign over the roof that says 'saloon.' Plus, you got your swing doors an' the sounds of piano-playin' an' fist-fightin' comin' outta them.

I pause on the edge o' the sidewalk, cuz in Amity you really gotta look both ways before ya cross the street; but I figure that's jest common sense, an' that folks oughtta do that whoever they happen ter be.

Right now couple of cowboys ride past, whoopin' an' yellin', an' draggin' a feller along on the end of a rope; after that along comes a runnin' gunfight, with this one feller (I don't recognise him, so I guess he's a stranger jest payin' Amity a friendly visit) runnin' from cover to cover, takin' out all the snipers shootin' at him from the winders—and the guy's a dang good shot cuz he makes it outta sight without gettin' ventilated; next, comes a stampede o' longhorns, kickin' up the dust, shakin' the foundations an' makin' a lotta racket... After that there's a lull in the traffic, so this is where I make a beeline for the saloon. A few bullets kick up the dirt around me but they might jest be strays, not especially intended fer yours truly—it's best not to take these things too personal.

There's the usual brawl goin' on in the saloon: all the extras sluggin' left an' right, an' samshin' them straight-backed chairs over each other's noggins. (Seems to me them chairs ain't fit for sittin' on, the way they come apart so easy when you clobber a guy with 'em.) Anyway, I shoulder my way through the *meelay* an' mosey on up to the bar where Charlie the barkeep's dishin' out the drinks as usual.

'Glass o' cow-juice, Charlie.'

'Comin' right up, Sheriff!'

I never touch the rotgut—plumb rots your guts, that stuff. Me, I like to keep things healthy; and there ain't nothin' better than a tall glass o' cow juice, fresh from the udder. Charlie fills me a glass from the milk pail he's kind enough to keep handy in case I happen to drop by (there ain't much demand fer it from the other customers), and he puts it down on the counter in front of me—but afore I can pick the dang thing up the glass jest explodes inter tiny pieces and there's cow juice all over the counter. Now, you may be thinkin' that glasses don't jest up an' fall ter pieces like that all of their own volition; and you'd be right; but same time may glass went up in splinters I couldn't help but hear the sound o' a gunshot comin' from someplace close by—an' I can put two and two together.

Without even lookin' round to see who the wiseacre is, I jest say: 'Another one, Charlie.'

'Another one it is, Sheriff.'

So, Charlie fills me another glass o' cow-juice from the pail, puts it down in front of me—an' then *blam!* the glass goes up like a firecracker an' more good cow-juice goes to waste.

'Hit me again, Charlie.'

'Right away, Sheriff.'

So, Charlie hits me again. And again. And again. Five minutes later an' there's a sizable pile o' broken glass on the bar-top an' a whole lotta cow juice soakin' inter the sawdust on the floor—an' not one single drop of the stuff havin' seen the inside o' my mouth.

'Another one, Charlie.'

'No can do, Sheriff; I'm clean outta cow-juice!' An' he shows me the empty pail in a confirmation of this depressin' statement.

Noddin' my head, I stroll on over to the other end of the bar, where Spike, one o' Judge Tombs' goons is standin', top-hat on his head, smokin' gun in his hand an' smug grin on his face. Spike's a young'un and a skinny runt; an' he's got no sense o' style, neither: jest straps on his pants over his long-johns. Ain't the guy never heard of shirts?

'Thanks for the drinks, Spike,' I says, tappin' him all friendly-like on the shoulder. 'Mighty friendly of you. Put 'em on Spike's tab, Charlie!'

An' havin' successfully wiped the grin off of Spike's stupid face, I stroll on over to the back of the saloon where you'll always find Judge Tombs sittin' in state, in a manner o' speakin'; that's ter say, sittin' at his usual table playin' solitaire, an' a bunch of his cowboys with him for company. I don't rightly know why it is he's always in the saloon like this, seein' as he's got himself a perfectly nice ranch house jest outside o' town… Well, I guess it cuts down on the number o' sets, don't it?

Judge Tombs is a big, ugly-lookin' guy; flabby face an' about a half-dozen chins. Always dresses real fancy he does, which ain't surprisin' sein' as how he's the richest guy in Amity—swanky suit, swanky weskit, swanky string bowtie, swanky ten-gallon hat… You get the picture.

'Howdy, Judge,' I says, to let him know that I'm here.

'Howdy, Sheriff,' says the Judge, eyes on his cards. 'Nice o' you ter drop by. Take a seat. Why don't you fix the Sheriff a brandy, Tiger Lily? I reckon he must be thirsty.'

Tiger Lily's an injun squaw; one o' the gals that works this place. Tombs likes to have her in particular waitin' on him whenever he's here—which as I already said, is pretty near all the time. Tiger Lily ain't dressed like the other saloon gals; she's dolled up in her injun squaw's dress with all them tassels an' which is a touch too short in the skirt to be what I'd call decent. She's got her hair in pigtails an' one o' them headbands on, with the zigzag pattern, an' a couple o' feathers stickin' out back. She's a purdy-looking gal alright, but I gotta say her complexion does kinda look more on the yeller side than you'd be expectin' from a redskin.

'Thanks,' I says; 'but your feller Spike's jest been treatin' me to drinks. 'Sides, I ain't a brandy-drinkin' man.'

Judge looks up from his cards, fixes me with his beady eyes. 'I couldn't help noticin' that you still ain't carryin' your six-shooter, Sheriff. How's a lawman supposed ter keep the peace if he ain't got his six-shooter?'

'I reckon I don't need no six-shooter,' says I. 'I prefer ter use my head.'

Judge Tombs shakes his head sadly. 'Your head ain't gunna be a whole heap o' use to you if some feller goes an' blows it off the top o' your shoulders.' He sits back in his chair, swallers some brandy. 'Sheriff, I jest cain't figure out a guy who doesn't like guns. It jest don't fit right; it don't seem natural. Downright unconstitutional; that's what it is! An' I'll tell you somethin' else: you're settin' a bad example ter others—encouragin' conscription-dodgers, an' the like.' He thumps his glass down. 'Gimme a refill.'

Tiger Lily picks up the bottle and pours. 'Now, look at her, Sheriff,' says Tombs, meaning Tiger Lily.

'I'm lookin',' I says. She looks at me, too; jest for a second. I catch this kind o' implorin' look in her eyes.

'Don't she jest look plumb miserable? D'you figure it'd kill her to jest smile once in a while?'

'Maybe she ain't got much to be smilin' about,' says I.

'Nuthin' to smile about? This here squaw ought to be eternally grateful to me! Why, I saved her dang life, I did—last survivin' member of her tribe.'

'Well, I don't reckon as she owes you much in the way o' gratitude on that score, seein' as how it was you an' your cowboys that wiped out the rest o' her tribe in the first place.'

'Dang it, they were takin' up valuable grazin' land!' says Tombs, wearin' a look like he's the injured party. 'What's a feller supposed to do?'

'Seems to me you could o' jest moved 'em on.'

'Well, I *did* move 'em on—ter the next world!' He raises his glass. 'So, what do you say, Sheriff?'

'What do I say 'bout what?'

'About forgettin' them pesky scruples or whatever you call 'em o' yours, an' wearin' your shootin' irons like a sheriff's supposed ter. Bein' sheriff ain't jest about wearin' the tin star, y'know? You gotta carry the guns as well. I mean ter say, how're you gunna protect Tiger Lily here? Cuz y'know, I'm real concerned about this squaw.'

'Why? Ain't she okay?'

Tombs leans forward, all confidential like. 'Well, I'll tell you, Sheriff; an' this is jest between you an' me; but truth is, Spike, he's been growin' real fond o' Tiger Lily of late.'

'Has he, now?'

'He has. An' well, Spike, he can be a touch *over*-affectionate, if you catch my drift. An' Tiger Lily, well she's a delicate gal; so, yeah, I am kind o' worried she might git herself hurt, y'know?'

I shrug. 'Well, Spike's your goon; jest knock him back into line.'

'Well, it ain't always that easy,' says Tombs. 'An' anyhow, I reckon when it comes to protectin' the innocent, that's *your* job, sheriff. *I* cain't be responsible for every feller that jest happens to work fer me. I reckon you need to start doin' your dooties, Sheriff Fort.'

Now, that is jest uncalled for. That is jest hittin' a guy below the belt. Here I am, Randy Fort, been sheriff o' Amity for I-don't-know-how-long, an' every day I sits at my desk where all the folks in town knows they can find me if an' they needs me—an' if they *don't* need me then that ain't my fault, that jest means things are tickin' along real pleasant like—and *now* here's Mr high-n-Mighty Judge Tombs tellin' me about "dooty" an' about "protectin' the innocent"!

Now, that is jest plumb mean.

'Sheriff Fort? Sheriff Fort?'

Someone callin' my name. Someone shakin' me by the shoulder. Probably the same person doin' both. I wish they'd quit.

Dang it, I've fallen asleep at my desk! I hate it when I fall asleep at my desk. Sittin' slumped all over yer desk ain't the right posture for sleepin'; an happens that my back's a touch on the delicate side.

'Sheriff Fort! Wake up!'

'Dang it, Nesbit! Will you pipe down? I *am* awake!'

I sit up. It's late. The oil-lamp's burnin'. I allus have the oil lamp hangin' over my desk so's I can read after dark. I rub my eyes an' I lookit Nesbit and it ain't Nesbit at all it's that Tiger Lily squaw. She's standin' there an' lookin' all anxious an' fretful.

'What is it?' I ask her. 'Don't tell me the Judge wants to see me again—'

'Judge Tombs doesn't know that I'm here,' replies Tiger Lily. 'I've come to ask for your help, Sheriff Fort.'

Now that's a nice thing to wake a feller out of his sleep for! 'Well, I hate to disappoint a lady an' all that,' I says; 'but this happens ter be outside o' office hours. So you jest mosey on outta here an' come back tomorrow mornin' at nine, an' we can have us a nice little chat.'

Now you'd think she'd jest take the hint and skedaddle—but you'd be wrong. Instead she starts wringin' her hands an' lookin' all teary-eyed. 'Oh, please! I need your help right now, Sheriff Fort! You are the only one I can turn to!'

'Well, that's real nice an' everythin' an' there's nothin' I'd like more'n to be helpin' ya'll, but I jest cain't do nothin' outside o' office hours. Them's the rules, y'see?'

Seems to me I stated my case right lucidly jest there—but does she get it? No, she does not!—cuz instead o' rain-dancin' right on out through the front door like a good little injun squaw, she's goes an' throws her arms around me!

'But I'm scared, Randy!' she wails, cryin' all over my shirt. (An' what's with the "Randy"? Since when were me an' her on first name terms?) 'It's Spike: wherever I turn, he is there! Like a second shadow he follows me, and he stares at me with eyes full of hunger; the eyes of the wolf as it prepares to pounce upon its prey!' She looks up at me. 'I fear for my very life!'

'Well, that's... that's too bad...' I says. I'll admit to feelin' a touch discombobulated right now. I ain't accustomed to havin' a lady's arm around me, an' seein' her face this close up to my own. To ease the situation I take a hold of her arms, remove 'em from my neck an' sort o' push her away. 'Tell you what I'll do: you just come back here at nine o'clock sharp tomorrer mornin' an' you can fill out a claim for sexual harassment. How's that sound?'

'No, no!' she cries (dang her!) 'You must help me now, Randy! It must be now!'

'It *cain't* be now!' I tells her. 'I need ter dig up the requisite paperwork, an' that'll take a bit o' time! I got this real complicated filin' system, y'see?'

'You must help me now, Randy!' (I don't think she took a dang bit o' notice o' that last line of dialogue!) 'Spike will see that I have fled the saloon as soon as he returns from the outhouse! And the first place he will come to seek me will be here!'

'An' how the heck would he figure out that you'd be here of all places!'

'Because, he *knows*, Randy! He knows! He knows that you have feelings for me!'

This one brings me up to the vertical so fast I forget about the danged oil-lamp and crack my noggin against it.

'Ouch! Dang it, woman! What in tarnation are you pow-wowin' on about? Knows I've got feelin's for you, does he? Then he knows more'n I do; cuz this is the first I ever heard about it! Heck, I ain't never even spoken to you afore jest now!'

'Oh, Randy! You must not speak these words of denial! You know that your heart yearns for me, just as my heart yearns for you!'

'Lady, you sure you ain't confusin' me with some other feller?'

An' now, all of a sudden she goes from lookin' tearful to lookin' severely ticked off, an' she grabs me by the collar an' she growls between her teeth: 'We are supposed to be lovers, asswipe. Read the fucking script, you stupid sack of shit.'

Ouch! Dang it! I'm so plum astonished I hit the danged oil lamp again!

'No, you jest hold on there, missy,' I says, all serious now. 'We jest don't use language like that around these parts. Why, I never even heard the like! Sure, we all feels the needs to cuss every now an' then; but there's rules, y'see? You can say "dang it!" as much as you please; you can even say "damn it!" as long as you don't say it too often; but words like them that you jest said: no, sir. No, not ever, no how. In fact, I think you oughta apologise.'

'Forgive me, Randy!' she cries, falling back inter character—and then she goes and drops down on her knees right in front of me and throws her arms around my midsection!

'Tarnation, woman! What you doin' now?' says I, cuz this don't feel right; it don't feel right at all, her with her arms around me an' her head down there where it oughtn't ter be at all. 'Look missy, you are violatin' my personal space! That's what it is! Violatin' my personal space! So, will you jest geddup, for land's sakes!'

'Oh, Randy!' she wails, and not takin' a blind bit o' notice o' my expostulations.

She ain't about to move, so I grab a hold of her pigtails an' I'm like tryin' to pull her back up to the vertical, but dang it, she's stickin' on to me like a barnacle! So here I am pullin' on Tiger Lily's plaits, gruntin' an' gnashin' m' teeth; an' she's down on her knees in front o' me, sobbin' an' moanin' like—an' that's how things are when Judge Tombs an' his posse walks in through the front door.

'Well, I do beg your pardon,' says the Judge, takin' off his hat all solemn like. 'Appears we're interruptin' somethin'.'

This sets off a lot o' chucklin' from the posse—exceptin' in the case o' Spike; yep, he's there an' he ain't chucklin'; in point o' fact, he don't look too amused at all. Now I know that appearances are all aginst me here, but why in Sam Hill do people jest have ter go jumpin' ter conclusions the second they walk inter the room like that?

Hearin' the Judge's voice sets Tiger Lily jumpin' up on her feet—jest when it's too late to do any good. An' she don't help matters any by lookin' all guilty like an' clampin' her hand over her mouth.

'We were all wonderin' where you'd skedaddled to, Tiger Lily,' Judge Tombs tells her. 'Had us all worried, you did. Now Spike here, for reasons best known t'himself, was plumb certain we'd find you right here, at the Sheriff's office. Me, I figured the contrary, an' so me an' some o' the boys, we laid odds on it—an' now, thanks to you bein' caught red-handed like this, I'm fifty dollars out o' pocket!'

'You got it all wrong there, Judge,' says I. 'We weren't doin' nothin' unseemly. See, this here squaw jest came bustin' in here, an' me, I jest told her ter hightail it back to the saloon, an' come back tomorrer durin' regular office hours, if'n she's got any business to conduct.'

'That so?' says the Judge. 'Kinda looked to me like you was both conductin' business together jest fine. Still, now that you got yer both got it out o' your systems, we'll jest be takin' Tiger Lily back to the saloon with us. And we're mighty obliged ter you, Sheriff for takin' sich good care o' her.' He clicks his fingers. 'Escort the lady, fellers.'

Two of the Judge's goons slither across the room, grab Tiger Lily, start draggin' her towards the door.

'Help me, Randy! Help me! They'll kill me!'

Dang it! Why does she have ter cry out like that? Here am I, not inteferin'; actin' all nonchalant an' like I couldn't care less about the squaw (which I don't), an' she has ter holler out like that, callin' me by my first name, an' generally makin' it look like we're plighted lovers! And does she stop to think what a whole heap o' trouble that is gunna land yours truly int? No, she dang well don't!

Now this here is the whole reason why I make it my policy to steer clear o' the fair sex as much as I can: there jest ain't no reasonin' with 'em! Accidents waitin' ter happen, that's what they are!

Sure enough, after the rest o' the posse have escorted Tiger Lily from the premises, Spike comes struttin' up to me, his brows knitted up, his eyes all starin' an' his mouth tighter than a congressman's wallet. An' his hands are hoverin' over the butts of his six-shooters, like his itchin' to pull 'em outta their holsters. An' he comes right up to me an' he's starin' me right in the eyes. He don't say nothin' cuz he never does, but he don't need to cuz a picture tells a thousand words.

'Now, now, Spike,' comes the Judge's voice. 'You cain't be drawin' on an unarmed man like that. Leastways, not when it's outside o' office hours. Why don't we just head on back to the saloon, where you can let Tiger Lily know how much you bin missin' her. If you got any business with our good Sheriff here, I reckon it can wait till tomorrer.'

Now Judge Tombs is the only guy who's got any control over Spike, so Spike, he does what he's told an' backs off, but you can see he don't want ter. Spike he thinks I've been grazin' on his pasture-land, an' he ain't gunna forgive somethin' like that cuz he's a mean critter.

Spike walks out through the door, and the Judge, he turns to foller him, an' he looks back at me. 'You might wanna think about dustin' off your shootin'-irons, Sheriff. I reckon yer gunna be needin' 'em real soon.'

An' we these words o' comfort an' consolation he walks on out, leavin' the door open to accommodate the moths.

Morning.

I crack open my peacemaker an' slip six slugs into the cylinder. Then I slide it inter the holster an' I strap on my gunbelt, an' tie the cord around my thigh. Straightenin' my Stetson, I have a gander at myself in the shavin' mirror. Face that looks back ain't seen a razor this mornin,' but it's a face that says that I'm ready, that I'm gunna do whatever it takes, an' ain't nobody gunna git in my way.

'Never thought I'd live ter see the day,' says Marshal Nesbit, an' he's got a look o' awe and admiration on his homely mug. 'That overnight you'd jest throw out them principles o' yours, an' strap on yer six-shooter.'

'Well, these are kinda exceptional circumstances, ain't they?' I says. 'An' sometimes a feller's jest gotta do what a feller's gotta do.'

Nesbit shakes his head with a dumbshow o' respect. 'An' you're really gunna take on Judge Tombs, an' Spike an' the rest o' his posse an' rescue Tiger Lily...?'

Now, where the heck did that come from?

'No, I *ain't* gunna do a stupid thing like that,' I tells him.

'Then what *are* you gunna do, Sheriff Fort?' asks Nesbit, lookin' confused.

'I'll tell you what I'm gunna do: I'm gunna get the hell out of town, is what I'm gunna do! Think I'd be fool enough to stick around when I know that crazy varmint Spike is gunnin' for me? Sure, he may be a non-speakin' part, but let me tell you: it's them quiet ones you gotta watch out for. *That's* the only reason I've put on my gunbelt: so's no-one tries to git in my way while I'm hightailin' it outta here!'

'Now, jest hold on there a second, Sheriff!' blurts out Nesbit. 'You cain't jest up an' skip town! You're a goldarned sheriff, Sheriff! You cain't have a town without a sheriff!'

Dang the feller and his nit-pickin'. I tear the tin star off o' my shirt and slap it inter his hand. 'Fine! Then *you* can be the goldarned sheriff! I'm promotin' you! Congratulations!'

An' with that, an' while Nesbit's still comin' to grips with his accession ter glory, I walks outta the sheriff's house fer the last time. I walk out inter the street, an' suddenly it hits me that's quiet—too quiet. Now it ain't never this quiet in Amity, 'ceptin' maybe in the small hours when everybody's passed out drunk: but right now, it's liked a dang ghost town. Ain't a soul in sight. Nothin' movin'; not even a tumbleweed.

An' then I turn round an' I see why it's so quiet. Spike, he's standin' there in the middle o' the street about fifty paces off, standin' there with his legs apart, arms out at his sides, an' all keyed up, an' starin' right at me.

Dagnabbit! I've jest gone an' walked out inter the middle of a showdown! The very self-same showdown I'd been aimin' ter avoid by skippin' town! Now, that jest ain't fair! An' I cain't even cry off this time cuz I'm wearin' my goldarned gunbelt!

An' the whole town's lookin' on. I cain't see nobody, but I knows they're all there: watchin'. You can feel it in the air.

Then I ain't got no choice. My time has come. I turns to face the guy, adoptin' the stance; an' I'm kind o' shakin' a tad, cuz Spike, he's well-known for being fast on the draw; an' me, well, I don't rightly know how fast on the draw I am, on account of never havin' drawn before.

So, here's hopin' fer beginner's luck.

There's a close-up o' Spike's beady eyes. Then there's a close-up o' *my* beady eyes. I see his hand movin' closer to his gun-butt, so I do the same...

Now, the way I figure it, you gotta be ahead o' the game in these showdowns. If you both draw at the same time then you jest shoot each other an' nobody's the winner; and what the heck's the point in duellin' if *that*'s the outcome? You jest both look stupid lyin' there dead. You might as well have stayed home. No, you gotta draw first, while the other guy's still *thinkin'* about drawin'. You gotta draw so sudden like that you take *yourself* by surprise, never mind the other guy—if you can surprise yourself, stands to reason the other feller ain't got a chance.

I draw. I draw so sudden that I ain't even ready for it m'self, an' the danged shootin' iron slips from my hand— an' that's when everthin' goes inter slow motion.

I'm watchin' the gun spinnin' through the air, real graceful like; an' jest as it's about to hit the dirt, the business-end comes up pointed right up at me; an' then I don't rightly know how it happens, but the gun hits the ground an' *blam!* the dang thing goes off!

I've jest gone an' killed myself.

'Cut!' cries out a voice. 'Cut, cut, cut!'

The guy who hollered out is sittin' in a chair an' he looks real annoyed; there's a lotta other folks around him; some o' 'em I recognise as Amity folk, but the rest o' them are a set o' complete strangers, an' they must be from back east cuz they're wearin' real funny-lookin' threads; an' they got somethin' that looks like a fancy canon pointed right at me—

An' I'm as sure as I am o' anythin' that they weren't there a minute ago. Where the heck did they come from?

An' what's more, why am I still even in the land o' the livin'? Didn't I jest blow my own head off…?

The anoyed guy strolls on up to me; he's a blond-haired feller with a moustache. 'What was all that about, Howard?' he asks. 'I thought you'd been taking quick-draw lessons from Steve McQueen and Sammy Davis Jr?'

'Well, I…'

'So tell me: which one of them was it that taught you how to drop your gun and shoot yourself in the face with it? Was it McQueen or Davis Jr?'

'Well, I…'

'This is meant to be a serious Western, Howard. We're not doing *Blazing Saddles* here.'

'Why do we have to do a crummy Western episode, anyway?' It's Tiger Lily says this. She's smokin' a cigarette an' lookin' cheesed off.

'Because *every* show does a Western episode,' says the director, turning to her. 'Conventions of the genre: we *have* to do a Western episode! Especially when we're getting near the end of the season and the scriptwriters are running out of ideas.'

So I'm… This is a…

'Pretty cheap lousy Western we're doing,' says Tiger Lily, contemptuously. 'Look at it: just three sets for the whole segment: the saloon, the Sheriff's house and this street.'

A set…? Yeah, that ain't the sky up there, it's a ceiling with a lotta of lights…

'That's because we ran over-budget with the last two episodes,' says the director. 'We don't want to wind up having to shoot the season finale on a shoe-string, do we? Hey! Don't wander off, Howard! We're setting up for the retake.'

Who's Howard...? Don't know no Howard... These horses... They ain't real horses at all! Look at 'em: they're jest, just, cardboard cut-outs...

An' over there, there's a doorway, smack in the middle of the backdrop... like a doorway standin' in thin air...

A hand clamps down on my shoulder. I spin round. It's Judge Tombs... Tombs... Two... 'Whatchya doin', Howard?' he asks, grinning at me real mean like. 'You weren't figgerin' on runnin' out on us, was you?'

Running out. That sounds like a very good idea. I hightail it for the door and suddenly the studio is in an uproar, everyone shouting at me to come back, calling me Howard, which isn't even my dang name...

'After him!' yells Judge Tombs. 'Git the varmint!'

I look back, and it's like a lynching mob: they're all after me! Judge Tombs leading the pack, Tiger Lily and the director guy right behind him; and then there's the rest of the cast, the film crew, the extras; all of them shouting and yelling, waving pitchforks in the air—they're after my hide!

Now I'm running down the corridors, taking every turning I come to, trying to lose my pursuers. They're right behind me, all riled up, sticking to my tail like glue. I've gotta keep running; can't let them catch me and drag me back to Amity, or they're gunna be fittin' me with a hemp collar...

I turn another corner and suddenly there's two nurses standing there with a bathchair, calm as you please. One of them looks the living spit of Tiger Lily, the other's a negress.

'Come along, Howard,' says the nurse that looks like Tiger Lily. (She's wearin' glasses.) 'We've got to get you to makeup, stat.'

Her and the other nurse come up either side of me, take an arm each and sit me down in the bathchair. And then we're barrelling down the corridors at a rate that has me gripping the armrests for dear life, the black nurse pushing and Tiger Lily running alongside. We soon leave the lynching mob far behind and then we're through a door and into a room full of clothes on racks and they wheel my chair up to a big mirror with lights all around it. Tiger Lily takes of my Stetson and tosses it, while the black nurse starts lathering up my jaw.

'What's going on here?' I demand.

'Costume change,' says Nurse Stella. 'We've got to smarten you up for the next episode, Howard.'

'Next episode?'

'Correct. Here you go.'

She hands me a script. I take a look at the cover. It says:

```
         AGENT: SECRET DANGER MAN

         Shooting Script, Episode 015

            "Learning the A, B & C"

                  written by
                 John Croxley
```

Chapter Fifteen
How I Learned My A, B & C

Being a man of mystery, a lone wolf secret agent, I don't really have much of a backstory, and what little backstory I do have is always subject to change at the whim of the script-writers. My boss at headquarters, for one thing: I never know who I'm going to be working for from one assignment to the next; I just never know who's going to be sitting behind the executive desk when I open the big door. I open the door now, and I discover that today it's Colonel Sinden. Good old Colonel Sinden. Salt of the earth. Always know where you are with Colonel Sinden. True, you don't always know what he's saying: tends to 'nyah-nyah' a lot when he's talking; but still, a stalwart chap.

'Morning, Colonel.'

'Nyah, Danger Man!' he says, rising from his chair, extending his hand. 'Afternoon, old chap. Take a seat, take a seat, nyah nyah!'

Having shaken hands, I slip into my usual chair.

'You have an assignment for me, Colonel?'

'Nyah, of course! A devilishly ticklish case, and one which can only be handled by Danger Man, the celibate secret agent who never carries a gun, preferring to rely on his wits and ingenuity to get the job done. Can always count on you when the chips are down, nyah nyah!'

'You flatter me, Colonel. Tell me more about this "ticklish" case.'

'Nyah, fact is, Danger Man, we've stumbled onto something; and it's something big; very big... We've been hearing rumours for some time now; at first we thought they were just fairy stories, but now it's starting to look like there might be something to them after all... As you well know, in our line of work people disappear; it happens all the time and we accept it as one of the risks attached to the profession; people disappear, and sometimes they come back again and sometimes they don't.'

'I'd say on balance that they *don't* come back more often than they *do*.'

'Quite right, quite right. Well, if there's any truth to these rumours we've been hearing, then there may be a pattern to some of these disappearances; it might even be all of them. In other words, we are looking at the possibility that these people are all being taken away by the same people and taken away to the same place. Ever heard of the Village, Danger Man?'

'*The* Village? Definite article?'

'Nyah nyah, nothing's definite yet. That's the whole problem. It might be a place; it might be an organisation; it might be both. But the gist of the rumours is that there's a very powerful organisation out there who are quietly taking people out of circulation, and spiriting them away to some unknown location.'

'For interrogation?'

'Nyah, that we don't know. Interrogation is the obvious reason to suspect. People in our line of work always have a lot of valuable knowledge tucked away in their heads—but there may be other reasons. That's just what we need to find out; what I want *you* to find out.'

'I take it you've got a lead for me to follow up?'

'I've got three,' says the Colonel. 'Three people; three possible leads. And it just so happens that all three of these people are going to be gathered in the same location two days from today.'

'I get the picture. You want me to be there as well. What is this location?'

'Paris. Or, to be more exact, at the Chateau Grenadine. One of Madam Grenadine's celebrated parties is being held there two days from now; our three subjects have all received invitations.'

I allow myself a brief smile. 'And it just so happens that I have also received an invitation to that party myself.'

'Really, Danger Man? Splendid! Wonderful how these things work out, isn't it?'

'Truly marvellous. And just who are these three people?'

'Nyah-nyah, nyah-nyah, nyah-nyah-nyah.'

'Sorry Colonel, but I didn't catch a single word of that.'

'Beg your pardon, old chap. I said that two of them are old friends of yours.'

'Would these two friends be "friends" in inverted commas?'

'Well, depends how you categorise your friends, old chap,' says the Colonel, his eyes twinkling with mischief. 'I'm talking about A and B.'

'A and B? Well, if I were to categorise my friends in terms of how often they've tried to kill me, then A and B certainly rank amongst my very best friends. Who's the third person? I'll be in serious trouble if they happen to be an enemy of mine.'

'The third one's something of a mystery, old chap; an enigma. We know next to nothing about them except for their name: C.'

'Right,' I say. 'Better get my tuxedo ready.'

'Your flight to Paris has already been booked. You can pick up the ticket on your way out. Best of luck, DM.'

'Please don't call me DM, Colonel,' I say.

'Sorry, old fellow; slip of the tongue.'

Outside the window of the office Big Ben is chiming the hour. As I rise from my chair, I check my wristwatch. Funny; Big Ben seems to be an hour slow.

I pass through the gates of Chateau Grenadine, and the set swims into focus. The gardens are strung with lanterns. Groups of people are seated at the tables, and couples stroll along the gravelled pathways. The light from a dozen chandeliers blazes from the windows of the chateau. I turn my steps towards the main entrance. I step through the portals, and there is Madam Grenadine, effusively greeting each of her guests as they arrive. Madam Grenadine is a redhead, charming and vivacious. Tonight she wears a white silk gown with a pink wrap, and diamonds around her neck, on her fingers, and hanging pendant from her ears. She and I are friends of long standing, and her face lights up with a warm smile when she catches sight of me.

'Ah, *Destinay-shon*!' (My name around here.) 'So wonderful to see you! And you are looking as 'andsome as ever!'

'And you as beautiful as ever,' I gallantly reply, bowing to kiss her hand.

'Ah!' she sighs. 'It is such a tragedy that you are *célibataire!*'

'Your husband didn't think so,' I remind her.

'Oh, 'im.' She waves a dismissive hand. 'Jealous 'usbands are such a bore.' She studies my face. 'So, what brings you to Paris, *mon cher ami?* Not just to see me, I think.'

'Always to see you,' I say. 'But yes, I do have some "business" on hand: one or two acquaintances I'm hoping to discuss matters with tonight.'

'Mixing business with pleasure, eh? It is always the way with you men. My 'usband; 'e was just the same. Well! Just as long as you remember to enjoy yourself while you are 'ere!'

'I will most certainly endeavour to do that,' I assure her.

Leaving my hostess to greet her next set of arrivals, I stroll into the main salon. As is always the case at the Grenadine parties, the front salon is for music and conversation, while the gaming tables have been set out in the rear salon; the folding door which separates the two has been opened to its fullest extent.

I spot A almost immediately. He's standing alone by the fireplace and looking directly at me. He nods a greeting, white teeth smiling beneath the elegantly-twirled moustache on his copper-hued face. I return the greeting, and stroll unhurriedly over to him.

'Waiting for someone?' I ask.

'For you, of course,' is the smooth reply. 'It's been a long time.'

'Not long enough.'

'People change.'

'Some people.'

'We're not so different, you and I.'

'I beg to differ.'

'Have you tried the wine?'

A stops a passing waiter, takes two champagne glasses, passing one to me.

'Care to guess the vintage?'

I sample the bouquet. '*Chateau de Foie Gras* '59.'

'Our hostess has impeccable taste. *Salut.*'
'*Salut.*'
'Ah!' A smacks his lips. 'Chilled to perfection.'
'Naturally. Drinking a *Chateau de Foie Gras* at anything above the temperature of thirty-eight degrees Fahrenheit would be as bad as listening to the Beatles with earmuffs.'
'Ah, yes,' sighs A. '"All You Need is Love." Words like that are to be savoured, just as this exquisite '59 should be savoured.'
I take another sip. Pretty strong stuff. Full-bodied.
'Ever heard of the Village?' I inquire.
'Country life bores me,' replies A.
'Never wanted to get away from it all?'
'Never. Why? Do you?'
'Perhaps. Care to recommend somewhere?'
'I might know of a place… But if you went there, you'd never want to leave.'
'Sounds too good to be true.'
'Oh, it is.'
'Been there yourself?'
'My dear fellow: if I had, I'd still be there.'
'Wouldn't be able to tear yourself away?'
'Quite impossible.'
'Pleasant scenery?'
'Perfect.'
'Fresh air?'
'In abundance.'
'Climate?'
'Exquisite.'
'Many people go there?'
'Yes. You'd meet a lot of old friends.'
'People I haven't seen for years?'
'People you'd given up for dead.'
'How does one go about making a reservation?'
'You have to know the right people.'
'You, for example?'

'Perhaps.'

'You're in the tourist trade?'

'I can cut you a deal.'

I drain my glass. 'I'll give it some thought.'

'I'll be here when you've made up your mind.'

I take my leave of A, and walk further into the gilt and crystal salon. A soft adagio permeates the air. I straighten my cuffs and bowtie, accept another glass of the '59. Heady stuff.

It's a trap, of course. They've laid out the bait, and I'm the catch they want to reel in.

We'll see about that.

I find B in the gaming room, sitting at the roulette table. She's dressed in a sleeveless, high-collared Chinese silk dress, her raven hair cut in bob, the ends curled upwards. Mascara accentuates the upward slant of her jetty eyes. Between her glossy lips rests the stem of a long cigarette-holder.

I stroll up to her.

'Fancy meeting you here.'

She removes the cigarette holder from her mouth, blows out pungent smoke in a thin stream. She regards me slyly through her long-lashed eyes, a smile curling her lips.

'It's been too long, darling.'

'This seat taken?'

'I reserved it for you.'

I sit down beside B. She casually passes me some of her chips.

'Care to try your luck?'

'My thanks. I am feeling lucky tonight.'

'Then you can't lose.'

I place my chips on black. A waiter places a glass of champagne in front of me.

'What do you know about the Village? Is it a place or an organisation?'

'It's both, darling; it's everything: a place, an organisation, a state of mind.'

'I'm intrigued. Tell me more.'

'The Village is getting bigger all the time. It's been around for a long time.'

'Since the war?'

'Before the war.'

'Which war?'

'A long time. Its beginnings were humble. Imagine you have some people who have a bit too much information in their heads; more than is good for them, or perhaps for you. So, what do you do?'

'Make them disappear.'

'Yes, but how?'

'Liquidation has always been the preferred method.'

'Yes, but these people are valuable; they're not your enemies and you don't want to harm them; you just want to put them out of the way for a while; somewhere safe.'

'Build a prison for them.'

'Yes, but you don't want these people to feel they are prisoners and you don't want to treat them like felons.'

'So the cage has to be a gilded one.'

'Quite. So you find yourself an out-of-the-way location, somewhere off the map, and there you build a Village; a beautiful, idyllic Village. And you put those people, the people you need to take out of circulation, into this Village, and you assure them that you're doing this entirely for their own good.'

'And do they accept that?'

'Yes, they do. They find their home from home to be a charming one, and they are grateful for all the care and attention being paid to them. And there you are; you have your desired result: the people you want to put on ice have been securely relocated , and what's more they are perfectly happy in their new surroundings. You have created the Village.'

'So you have your gilded cage and your contented prisoners. What's the catch?'

'The catch is, that it doesn't stop there. Obviously your prisoners can't be left entirely to their own devices; you have created a small community, and your community needs to be administered and maintained. And so you must perforce create an administration for the Village, a small body of custodians to watch over the prisoners. And this administration, they start to get ideas. They see potential in what has been created here, they see scope for enlargement. If the Village exists as a place in which to *protect* information, then equally it could exist as a place in which to *extract* information.'

'In other words, the Village becomes an interrogation centre?'

'Yes, but of a very different kind. Your cage is still a gilded one. You want your new prisoners, the ones from whom you want to extract information, to be just as happy in the Village as the ones you merely want to keep on ice. But inevitably, these people won't have been brought to the Village by choice, and at first they will be rebellious. Methods have to be developed by which these people can be not only pacified, but be made to love their prison. And so you to turn to science for assistance. You add a scientific staff to your administration, scientists who will develop techniques for both subduing the rebels and extracting the required information from their heads.'

'Science is never infallible.'

'No, it isn't. And therefore, to protect your precious community and prevent escape, you must now introduce security measures; but you don't want to turn the Village into a concentration camp, with armed guards patrolling the streets—therefore you introduce a surveillance system, invisible but comprehensive; personal privacy has to be abolished. And again, you have to increase the number of your staff to operate this blanket surveillance.'

I sip my champagne. 'Big Brother is watching you.'

'Exactly. But not all acts of rebellion can be nipped in the bud, even with the most thorough surveillance, so you will still need your police force—but you want a police force that can remain invisible until the moment it is needed; and you want your police force to be infallible, which a police force composed of human beings can never be. So, you turn to your scientists and technicians again, and they create for you an infallible security system; inhuman and unstoppable.'

'It sounds incredible.'

'It's out of this world.'

'And what name do you give to this infallible security system?'

'You call it Rover. And now you have your Village operating to its fullest potential. A peaceful, contented community, watched over and protected from harm. And you're pleased; in fact, you think that what you have created is so good that really it ought to be a template for the rest of the world to follow; that the Village should become the entire world, and the entire world the Village.'

'And that's what they want to do?'

'They're doing it as we speak.'

'So that they can bring about world peace?'

'Yes, but at a cost. They use the numbers system in the Village.'

'Numbers system?'

'Yes, darling. Everyone has one. They take away your name and give you a number in its place.'

'For administrative purposes?'

'And for other reasons. Names encourage self-identity, which encourage individualism and free-will—and individualism and free-will encourage dissatisfaction and dissent. Therefore, they have to abolish individualism, and they have to abolish free-will; such concepts as these can only undermine the community.'

'And that's the kind of world they want to create?'

'Exactly. And they're making great strides in achieving their goal. And it goes without saying that people like you and I darling, wouldn't last long in their kind of world. They would soon haul us in for some major adjustment.'

'Adjustment? What kind of adjustment?'

'The lasting kind. They call it Instant Social Conversion. We would never be the same again.'

'You say they're making great strides and yet you don't sound very worried. Do you have some plan up your sleeve?'

'Darling, I'm not wearing any sleeves,' extending a shapely arm; 'and no; I don't have any plan. I'm just making the most of things while they still last.'

'They call that fiddling while Rome burns.'

'And why not, if you like the music? Listen: they're playing our tune.'

I listen. The hitherto unobtrusive background music has suddenly given way to something much more brazen. I recognise the piece: *Bienvenue Mister Jones,* by Jack Arel. The green baize layout of the roulette table starts to swim before my eyes. My head is buzzing, vibrating to the rhythm of the music. I hold my empty champagne glass, and I slowly turn it in my hand, watching as its surfaces reflect the light of the chandeliers.

'Anything the matter, darling?' comes B's voice, echoing as though from a great distance.

'I'm not feeling myself…'

'That's because you've forgotten yourself, darling.'

'Forgotten myself?'

'Forgotten who you are. You never drink alcohol, but since you got here you've had three glasses of champagne. It's gone to your head, darling.'

'You're right. Perhaps I'd better step outside…'

'Perhaps you should. Have a nice trip, darling…'

I rise to my feet. I start to make my way across the salon. The music, the accelerant to the intoxicant circulating in my system, has permeated the air of the room, altering the atmosphere to conform with itself; and the partygoers have become intoxicated by it, laughing uproariously, their eyes alight with sensuality. All restraints and inhibitions are being cast aside.

Madam Grenadine is suddenly at my side.

'It is so wild, darling!' she tells me, smiling with guilty pleasure. 'It will all end in tears!'

'All the best parties do!' I say.

'Oh, darling: you're so caribou!'

Admonishing me thus, she departs, her laughter echoing across the room.

'Caribou? It's dreamy!' I cry out in sheer bliss. This is a dreamy party!'

The room sways around me, a giddy landscape of glittering jewels, gowns of every colour of the rainbow, it slews back and forth like the deck of a ship in a turbid sea. The air is thick with laughter and tobacco smoke. A mirror, elaborately-framed, catches my eye. The salon has listed to one side, and the mirror is the only thing besides myself that has remained perpendicular.

I stagger across the canted floor and reaching the mirror, I grab hold of the frame as a drowning man would a piece of driftwood.

Perhaps… perhaps if I can just turn this mirror, then I can straighten out the room… I tighten my grip on the frame and begin to turn the mirror… It's stiff, like a rusty wheel… But I persevere, and slowly the mirror moves, and I can feel the floor beneath my feet slowly return to the horizontal…

Now that equilibrium has been restored, my head feels somewhat clearer. I cross to the French windows, and out on the terrace I pause to breathe in the fresh night air. I see a maid crossing the gardens. She's carrying an envelope and looks to be in a hurry. She skips up the terrace stairs and presents the envelope to me.

'For you, *Monsieur Destinay-shon*,' she says. 'A lady asked me to give this to you.'

'Thank you, Bettine.'

The maid curtsies and departs. I tear open the envelope. Inside is a folded sheet of paper bearing this brief message:

Meet me in the arbour.
C.

I set off across the gardens. So, I am about to meet C; the last piece of the puzzle. The arbour is at the far end of the garden, away from the chateau and the noise of the party. There are few lamps this far back. A perfect place for an assignation—or an ambush.

The trellised arbour, standing with its back to a tall, neatly-clipped hedge, comes into view. As I draw nearer, I can descry a figure seated at the table, but whose upper body is involved in shadow. Curious, but whoever C is, they don't exactly look like they're dressed for a party. I see a pair of heavy boots, jeans, the pattern of a lumberjack shirt...

It's strangely familiar...

'Well, don't we look dapper, all spiffed up in our tuxedo?' comes a female voice, a mocking yet friendly voice which I think I know... I think I used to know very well...

I find myself slowing as I come closer to the arbour, my steps becoming hesitant...

Thoughts intrude themselves, forgotten memories...

The shadows lift and the seated woman now becomes visible to me. A tall, robust woman with glasses and untidy hair. She's smiling at me...

Gillian...! Good lord, it's Gillian...!

Chapter Seventeen
How Events Came to Fall Out

'Well, come on then,' says Gillian. 'Don't just stand there gawping at me. Take a pew, Randal Fortescue. Ha! That's good: it rhymes!'

'Who's Randal Fortescue?' I demand weakly.

'You are, stupid.'

'No, I'm not.' I straighten my bowtie. 'I'm Danger Man.'

A splutter of laughter. 'Yeah: you're not in any Danger of ever being much of a Man. Just sit down, will you?'

Impudent baggage! First time we've met for months and already she's making digs at me...!

Haven't met for months... We haven't met... The last time I saw her... The last time I saw her was... it was... No... No, it can't have been...

'You... You're dead...' I say, staring at her smiling face. 'I saw you... I found you... How can you be...?'

'How can I be here talking to you now if I'm dead?' she says, completing my sentence. 'Well, if you'll just plant your arse on that chair, I'll tell you.'

Vulgar as always. It's Gillian, all right. I do as I am bid and take the seat across from her. I see that there's a can of lager on the table in front of her. Drinking beer from a can at the Chateau Grenadine...! Still as uncouth as ever. She has to be a gate-crasher; there's no way she could ever have received an invitation card...

'You know why you're here, don't you?' says Gillian. 'You're starting to remember now, yeah?'

'I... I'm here to try and find out about the Village...'

'You already know about the Village, Randal,' says Gillian. 'Think about it. You're Randal Fortescue and you're a fan of the television series *The Prisoner*. The Village has another name and it's Portmeirion. You went there, remember? That's how this all started. That's how you ended up here.'

'Here?'

'Yes. You're right in the middle of it; you're playing the starring role; that's what you've always wanted to do, isn't it? Deep down, that's what you wanted; to be like him, the original Number Six, Patrick McGoohan. Probably some homoerotic thing you've got going on there.'

'I beg your pardon?' say I, my tone chilly. 'I am *not* homoerotic; I am heterosexual. And why do you always have to bring sex into everything?'

'It's you who always likes to keep sex *out* of everything,' returns Gillian. 'Another thing you've got in common with McGoohan, isn't it? Anyway, that's what you're doing now: living the life. And I'm supposed to be C, who's got something to tell you about the Village. And yeah, I have got something to say on the subject.'

'And what would you know?' I inquire.

'More than you, chum,' says the insolent one. 'Have you ever asked yourself what the Village was there for? I mean in the TV series: what was the Village there for? What was its purpose?'

'Well, if that's all you've got to say... I know very well what the Village was there for: it was a place to keep people who knew too much, or who wouldn't reveal what they did know... a place for information to be protected or extracted...'

'Yeah, that was what they *said* the Village was there for... And it was supposed to have been around for a long time, hadn't it? Since before the war, which war, right?'

'Yes...'

'Yeah. But in pretty much every episode of *The Prisoner*, what were they actually doing in the Village? What was the Number Two of the week always trying to do?'

'He was always trying to get information out of the Prisoner, of course,' I reply. 'They wanted to find out why he resigned from his job.'

'Yeah, and don't you think that was a bit funny? How it was that just about everything that happened in the Village revolved around the Prisoner? It was like the whole place, the entire apparatus of the Village, had been created just to hold and interrogate *him*. It was all about *him*. Well, what about the other prisoners, the other Villagers? They were all supposed to be people like him, spies and whatnot with information in their heads, right?'

'Well, not entirely all of them,' I demur. 'Some of them were actually spies, working for the Village authorities.'

'Well, yeah: "Who are the prisoners and who are the warders" and all that. Fair enough. And once or twice he met people he's known in the outside world; and in that crappy episode there was that subversive group, the Jammers—but then, how do you explain the fact a lot of the time the Villagers, the entire population, were just this great big mass, this gestalt; they were like puppets the authorities could control, the same way they could control Rover. On demand they could be made to be a cheering crowd, or a bloodthirsty mob, or they could just become completely inert. In one episode they even made the entire Village population disappear into thin air, and then reappear again right out of nowhere. And the only one who was never affected by this crowd manipulation was the Prisoner himself. He was the only one who was different. So, what do you make of that?'

'Well, what am I *supposed* to make of it?' I inquire.

Gillian sighs. 'A great response. And from the man who was supposed to be writing the definitive book about the series... Look, I'm just saying it was always all about *him*, wasn't it? All the way up to the last episode and his meeting with Number One; it was all about *him*. Yeah, I know you could say that in *The Prisoner* it was all allegorical, it was all metaphor and symbolism, and that nothing you saw should be taken literally—but then there's one interpretation that says the whole thing was an hallucination of the Prisoner's; that the Village was a mental landscape conjured up by the mind of a delusional egotist. And that would be where you come in, Randal.'

'Are you implying that *I* am a delusional egotist?' I inquire haughtily.

'Well, duh. Of course I am! I mean, who are you? You're nobody! But the Prisoner, he was like this larger-than-life character, wasn't he? A paradigm figure. The ultimate rebel. Fearless and resolute. But what about you, Randal? You're nobody. You never were a spy; you haven't got any important information locked away in your head. The only reason you're a rebel is because you were born one: a Rebel Without a Choice; the Eternal Prisoner: that's what you are.'

'Well, perhaps I am more important than you give me credit for being,' is my frowning response. 'You may consider me to be a "nobody," but perhaps others have a truer estimation of my value.'

'Yeah, that'll just be your ego speaking; and here you are, right in the middle of your own delusional, egotistical odyssey. But it can't be real, can it? For one thing, you're talking to me—and I'm dead, aren't I?'

'Yes...' I look at her. She looks very unconcerned for someone who has just confirmed the fact of their own demise. 'You're dead... I found you... Or was that an illusion as well...?'

'Oh no, that was real enough,' says Gillian cheerfully. 'I'm dead alright. Killed in my own bed.'

'Then it happened... You were murdered... And it was my double...'

Gillian bursts into laughter. 'Your double? You're not still going on about tha—'

She breaks off midsentence. There's a look of surprise fixed on her face; like she's suddenly remembered something important...

'Yes?' I say eagerly. 'What is it? What is it?'

And then Gillian slumps forward onto the table and I see that the reason she was so surprised is because someone has just stuck a knife into her back.

I hear the sound of chuckling from the shadows.

I leap from the arbour. A figure stands in the shadows of the hedgerow, a stocky figure. I see him. A blazer with white piping; beige trousers; canvas shoes. It's him! It's my double! My doppelgänger!

'You!' I cry. 'You've killed Gillian! You've killed her again!'

The fiend chuckles again and then disappears through a gap in the hedge.

'Oh no you don't!' I yell, and I take off in pursuit.

Through the hedge and I am in a deserted, lamplit street. There is no traffic, not a pedestrian in sight; the street is like an abandoned filmset. My double flees along the centre of the road. I give chase. At last! At last, my double has shown himself to me. Well, he's not going to get away from me now. There will be a reckoning!

'Why don't you face me, you fiend?' I yell. 'Face me instead of running away like a coward!'

His only response is another taunting peel of laughter. Curse the fellow!

I continue the pursuit. He turns a corner and I follow him. Yes! Yes, the distance between us is most certainly closing. I'm catching up with the fellow. Well, of course I am! I mean, he's me, isn't he? Ergo, he can't run any faster than I can, can he? Yes! All I have to do is put just that little more effort into my running and will be able to overtake myself!

Distance still closing… I can clearly see the back of his head now. Something's not right about the hair… I'm reminded of one of those location shots you see in which you know it's just a stand-in you're looking at, and not the actual actor…

And now I reach out… and I grab the fellow by the shoulder.

'Got you!'

I throw myself on him and I spin him round and we stand face to face. I see now what was wrong with the hair: it's a wig, a Patrick McGoohan wig. It hasn't even been fitted correctly; it's all askew and you can see the fellow's grey-steaked hair around the hairline…

Grey-streaked hair… It's not me at all! A jowly face with heavy lower eyelids and a self-satisfied smile… It's that wretch Number Two!

'You!' I cry out, enraged.

'Well, of course it's me, Number Six,' he replies. 'Who were you expecting?'

'My double, of course!' I fume. 'Where's he got to? Why are you pretending to be him?'

'My dear fellow, you really are slow on the uptake, aren't you?' says the wretch. 'I thought you would have worked it out by now.'

'Worked what out?' I demand.

'That *I* am your double,' replies he. 'Or rather I am the person who you, in your delusional state of mind, believed to be your double.'

'What do you mean? What are you talking about?'

'Good lord, do I have to spell it out to you? I mean that you never *had* a double; you never had a duplicate. It was just me; it was always just me; and we're not exactly identical twins, are we? Roughly the same height and build, yes; but that's as far as it goes. Do you get it now, or would you like me to repeat it?'

The hand that was grasping his shoulder I let fall to my side. 'You…? It was just you…?'

'At last! He's got it. Yes, it was just me; you never had a duplicate. Of course, we did do one or two things to help plant the idea in your mind; dropped a few red herrings here and there—but the rest was just you and your delusions, old chap.'

'It was you...?'

'Well, I told you, didn't I? Remember: back at the hospital? I told you repeatedly that the doppelgänger was just a delusion of yours. But you weren't having any of it, were you? Convinced you knew better than me; that you were right and I was wrong, weren't you? Perhaps in future you'll pay more attention to your doctor's advice.'

'It was you...? Lying on my bed...? Standing across the road...?'

'Guilty.'

'Yes, I remember now... The first time I saw you... as Dr Tombs at the hospital... There was something familiar about you...' Now I remember something else. My bowels tighten. 'Then it was you... it was you who murdered Gillian...'

'*Of course* it was me,' is the smooth reply. 'I've killed her twice, now.'

I am horror-stricken, incensed. 'Then, that time... in your office...when you were telling me about how Gillian died... Were you... were actually describing to me the things that you... that *you* actually did to her...?'

His smile widens, the smile of a depraved epicure. 'Oh, yes; that was no third-person account. I was actually reliving that night; reliving every exquisite moment, step by step, of that unforgettable time I spent with your friend Gillian; our moment of supreme intimacy... Yes, I think I can truly say that in those final moments that I really got to know your friend more thoroughly than you'd ever known her yourself...'

He sighs.

Blind rage floods over me.

'You monster!' I roar, and I pounce upon him, my hands clamping themselves around his blubbery throat. 'You fiend! You wretch!'

And I can feel the windpipe under the fat, and I tighten my grip on it, squeezing and squeezing, and I am bellowing like a beast, foaming at the mouth like a madman... A dark haze appears before my eyes, a buzzing rings in my ears, growing louder and louder... Everything dissolves to black...

And then, when my vision returns, Number Two no longer stands before, and my hands hang limply at my sides. I feel drained, inert. I look down and I see Number Two's body lying prone on the cobbled surface of the road.

'Congratulations.' It is Number Twelve. He has appeared beside me. 'We won't be needing the body for evidence.'

'What happens now?' I ask him.

'Your inauguration.'

'My inauguration?'

'Yes. You've won. Everybody's waiting.'

Number Twelve beckons with his finger, and leads me across the street to a pair of metal doors.

'We thought you'd feel more comfortable as yourself,' he says, and I realise that I'm no longer dressed in a tuxedo; I'm back in my Prisoner clothes.

The doors slide open spilling out bright light. A rough-hewn passageway lined with vintage jukeboxes stretches out before me. A band strikes up and I recognise the opening strains of 'All You Need is Love.' They're playing my song. This is it. My moment of glory. I straighten my back, square my shoulders and I set forth, advancing impressively along the corridor, Number Twelve following respectfully in my wake, the music all around me, booming from the speakers of the jukeboxes.

At the end of the corridor there is another metal door, this one bearing an illuminated sign, saying: 'Well Come.'

The door, as I reach it, swings open, and now the sound of thunderous applause is added to the strains of the song. The room before me is a vast natural cavern, a leftover set from *Battle Beneath the Earth*. Two rows of people, energetically clapping, their smiling faces directed upon me, form a corridor between the doorway and a dais, upon which stands a throne—that is to say, a toilet. A blue carpet extends between this human concourse, and climbs the steps of the dais to the foot of the throne.

I now pass between the two rows of clapping people, casting the occasional brief smile or inclination of the head to the left or the right. Number Twelve joins the column to the left, taking his place beside the section chief from the Unemployment Centre, Mr Dhawan, Malcolm the orderly, and A. On my right stands first Number 16, and then Dr Wakabayashi, Takaco with one K, Nurse Stella, Daisy Miller, Tiger Lily, and B. Also present are Ralph and Russ, Nurse Patricia, and two Spikes, mental patient Spike and gunslinger Spike… As for the rest of the crowd, this is composed of anonymous figures dressed in white hooded robes, their faces concealed behind half black, half white comedy/tragedy theatre masks.

I reach the foot of the dais, and the chorus of the song now comes crashing in. The applause continues unabated as I ascend to my throne. The tank of the toilet is emblazoned with the Village penny-farthing logo and within the big wheel the numeral '6.' The seat of the toilet (down) is adorned with a blue velvet cover of the same shade as the carpet.

I turn and with grace and dignity take my seat upon the throne. The onlookers, all smiling up at me, continue their tireless applause with renewed vigour.

Yes. I am Number Six. I have persevered, maintained, held fast, won through, resisted coercion, and attained the same lofty heights of my illustrious predecessor. I have indeed earned myself the right to be called and to call myself Number Six.

I wave to the crowd.

Yes: I am Number Six!

Number Six!

Wait a moment. I think I might be overlooking something here; something important; something about being not a number, but a free man…?

Oh well, that can wait for another time.

I pull the chain on the toilet.

Be seeing you!

* * *

I awake to find myself lying on my own bed and in my own room. My body feels leaden, as if I have been sleeping like the proverbial log. I feel as if I have just awoken from a very long and very vivid dream; an epic of the subconscious. I lie still for some time, gathering and sifting my thoughts, endeavouring to separate dream from reality.

I am at home. I am no longer in the mental hospital. I am back in Morsham; therefore, the mental hospital must have been located in Morsham after all—which is to say that I am back in Morsham because I never left Morsham.

I must have been discharged.

I can return to my old life.

My old life, and perhaps a new start… Yes, I can make a new start! I can… I can… What *can* I do…? Wait a minute. I know: the book; my definitive guide to *The Prisoner*. Yes! Now is the time to really get to work on it! Time to knuckle down and actually start writing the thing! I've been planning the thing for way too long. As Gillian was always telling me, the way I was going before, I could've spent the rest of my life just 'planning' the book and never actually getting round to writing it. Planning is preparation; and to be perpetually 'preparing' for a task that needs to be performed is actually nothing more than a way of delaying the performance of said task. Well, no more of that! No more dithering; no more avoidance! It is time to roll up my sleeves and put my nose to the grindstone!

And I shall start it now! Immediately! This instant!

As soon as I've had some breakfast.

Dance of the Dead.

That's funny. A thought has just popped into my head: the episode of *The Prisoner* entitled 'Dance of the Dead.' Gillian and I, we'd always wondered why that episode was actually called 'Dance of the Dead.' Episode four in production order, Episode Eight in transmission order, at one point mooted to be aired as Episode Two (which most fans think it should have been,) it is regarded by many as being the definitive episode of the series. But why was it called 'Dance of the Dead'? We could never understand that, Gillian and I. True, the episode did culminate with a fancy-dress ball, but still there seemed no especial reason why this function should have been referred to as a 'Dance of the Dead'...

But now, suddenly I know the answer to the enigma.

It was to have been the final scene of the episode. After the teleprinter (or whatever the thing was) the Prisoner had ripped the guts out of started working again, Number Two's triumphant laughter would have been abruptly terminated when the Prisoner proceeded to kick the machine over, thus disabling it a second time. He then would have exited the room, stepping out into the corridor where the costumed party-goers were still milling around, he then would have taken the nearest woman in his arms and waltzed off with her down the corridor. And *this* would have been the 'Dance of the Dead'; Number Six having been officially declared dead to the outside world in this episode.

Patrick McGoohan hated this ending; and on account of it he had the episode shelved and it was very nearly not transmitted at all. But one of the film editors took the episode off the shelf and he reedited the conclusion, removing those final moments, so that the episode ended at the point at which the teleprinter burst back into life and Number Two laughed at the Prisoner's discomfiture. So now the episode, instead of concluding with the Prisoner's gesture of defiance, concluded instead with his abject defeat. McGoohan was satisfied with this adjustment and the episode was reinstated—but nevertheless, in this final version of the episode, its title had been rendered obscure.

I know this; I didn't know it before but now I do. I know and yet I haven't the foggiest idea *how* I know. How and when did this information find its way into my head? Did I discover it online? Did someone tell me? I cannot remember either of these things happening... Good heavens! Did I dream it? Is this just something that was mixed in with that chaotic *Prisoner* dream I experienced last night? And if I dreamt this explanation, how do I know that it's even true? I mean yes, it fits; in fact it fits perfectly. I'd always known McGoohan had had the episode shelved and that someone had subsequently taken it off the shelf and reedited it. I'd always known that much: I just hadn't known what precisely was changed; what it was about the original version that McGoohan had hated so much... And yes, I had always thought that that final shot of Mary Morris laughing cuts off rather abruptly... But then, maybe my dream has just manufactured this explanation, conjured it up from my subconscious mind based on the little information I *did* possess...

I'll need to look into this. I cannot put this into my book unless I can confirm its authenticity... Mind you... if I can't find any source that confirms all this, I could still perhaps include it in my book in the form of some very shrewd and informed speculation on the part of the author—to wit, me.

Galvanised, I throw back the bedclothes and dress myself. My Prisoner clothes, of course. I cannot think of wearing anything else today, as I settle down to writing my book about the series. That's strange... There's a Number Six badge on my blazer... I never wear a Number Six badge with these clothes, just as the Prisoner never wore his badge, refusing to accept his status as a number... Oh, I know! It's just the badge I wore at the mental hospital!

No, that's not right. My hospital badge just had my first name on it.

But then there was... I see it now... Peeling off the top layer... Number Six badge underneath... No! No, that was just part of my dream. Wasn't it...? Must have been...

And then something catches my eye: standing on the table near the window: a lava lamp! I have never owned a lava lamp; it just shouldn't be here in my room...

A sudden horrible thought occurs to me. I rush over to the window and pull back the curtains—and instead of seeing a treelined street, parked cars and a row of terrace houses, I see a lawn, a bandstand, a square with a fountain, a church tower; I see uniform architecture, neatness and order...

The Village. I am in the Village.

An urgent beeping now sounds from the adjacent hallway—and I recognise it as the telephone ringtone peculiar to the Village. I walk through into the hallway. The front door is now of different design, and the hallway abruptly terminates where before there was a staircase. The telephone on the hallway table has become an old-fashioned device with a number '6' in the centre of the rotary dial. I pick up the receiver.

'Hello? Is that Number Six?' asks the voice of Fenella Fielding.

'Yes...'

'I have a message from Number Two: will you please report to the Green Dome immediately? Be seeing you!'

'What does he—?'

I break off. The line has already gone dead.

I go to the front door, open it. My last hope that it might still actually be Gissing Street outside is crushed. I am standing at the door of Number Six's residence in the Village. Not the Prisoner souvenir shop, Portmeirion, but the much more commodious dwelling in the Village. A fingerpost sign adjacent to the door bears the legends '6' and 'private.' The sky is a dull grey, and it is very quiet. At first there doesn't seem to be a soul around, but then, looking down the road towards the beach I espy the workmen Ralph and Russ! Yes; there they are standing in the very same hole in which they stood on the occasion of our first meeting! I hurry over to them, observing that they are today dressed in beige overalls and without their usual reflective orange vests.

Should I code-change? No; I remember now: my Fred Blogs persona has already been exposed as a fraud; in fact, these gentlemen and I did not part on very good terms on the occasion of our last meeting…

'Good morning, Ralph and Russ!' I greet them, affecting a tone of breezy cheerfulness.

Ralph looks at me, horrified. 'Keep it down, will you?' he protests, casting fearful looks up and down the street. 'You trying to get us all in trouble? We don't use names around here, do we? I'm One Hundred and Twenty-Five and he's One Hundred and Twenty-Five B. Says so right here on badges, see?'

And I do see: both men are wearing penny-farthing badges.

'My apologies,' I say.

'Alright, then,' says Ralph, mollified. 'Just remember it in future, right? Don't go rocking the boat.'

'Of course not,' I assure him. 'Erm… I've been summoned to see Number Two…'

'Well then, you're going the wrong way, aren't you? The Green Dome's back that way; that's where you want to be going, isn't it?'

'Quite so. I am cognisant with the location of Number Two's residence… It's just that I wanted, prior to answering the summons, to ask you two gentlemen… who *is* Number Two?'

'Who is Number Two? What sort of daft-bugger silly question's that? Number Two's Number Two! Who else would they be?'

'Well, yes... But what I am anxious to know is, who precisely is the present incumbent?' I lean forward, lowering my voice, and say, with some trepidation: 'Is it still... Morris Tombs?'

'And there you bloody go again!' explodes Ralph. 'What the bloody hell's wrong with you? I just got over telling you not to use any bloody names and then you bloody go and do it again! No names! No bloody names!'

'Yes, but I—'

'Look, mate: if Number Two wants to see you, then you'd better get your bloody arse over there, hadn't you? Instead of bloody bothering people while their trying to do their bloody jobs!'

Interpreting this as a dismissal, I bend my steps towards the Green Dome.

'Oh!' calls out Ralph.

I turn around.

'And have a lovely day, and all that.'

'My thanks. The same to you.'

I proceed up the hill. Will it be him? Will that monster Dr Tombs still be Number Two? I mean, yes: I did strangle the fellow to death, but attached to that memory is the fact that I'm just not sure if the event even really occurred...

I am disoriented; I just do not know anymore which of my recent experiences are reality and which are just illusions...

I reach the foot of the stairs. I look upwards and the Green Dome looms above me, sharply defined against the grey backdrop of the sky... I start to climb. I really don't want to do this... But I have to find out... I have to know whether that fiend is still my tormentor...

When I reach the porch, I espy a black feline perched on the balustrade, and I pause to stroke the creature, as it seems like the thing to do. The beast seems well-disposed towards me and starts to purr. I now turn to the door, which swings open automatically. I step into the hallway. There's a table with some flowers on it and a pair of doors facing me. No midget butler. No public conveniences. I cross the room and open the doors. Behind them, the polished surfaces of a pair of metal doors. These now slide apart and before me, as expected, is the futuristic chamber that is Number Two's office. A globe chair, its back to me, begins to rise from the floor.

And now it slowly begins to turn towards me.

This is it. I am about to know the worst... Is it...? Is it going to be...?

Relief and surprise assail me in tandem. The chair's occupant is an Asian woman in whom I immediately recognise Number Sixteen. Dressed as when I first saw her, in her striped jumper, blue slacks, white hat and dark glasses; but now with the addition of a college scarf wrapped loosely around her neck and a shooting stick umbrella cradled in her lap. Number Sixteen... And I had always believed she was on my side...

But then she removes her glasses and her impassive expression seems to be shed along with them, for suddenly her face is glowing and wreathed with smiles. 'Hey there, Number Six! Hope you slept well! Come on in!'

That smile, that effusive greeting—it's not Number Sixteen at all; it's Takaco!

Bewildered, I slowly approach her.

'What's wrong, Number Six?' she asks me. 'You look confused about something.'

'I confused about *you*,' I confess, coming to a stop before her chair. 'Are you Takaco with one K, or are you Number Sixteen?'

'Silly! I'm not Takaco anymore, and I'm not Number Sixteen, either!' she says, tapping her badge. 'I'm Number Two now! I'm the new Number Two!'

'I see...' I say, not really seeing. 'Then what happened to...?'

'The old Number Two? He's dead!'

'He is?'

'Sure he is! You killed him, remember?'

'I did? You mean… that really happened…?'

'Sure it did!'

'And am I… am I going to be in… trouble for doing that…?'

Number Two waves a dismissive hand. ''Course not, silly! You only did what we wanted you to do! Don't worry about it; everything's okay now!'

'You say you… wanted me to kill Number Two…?' I ask, struggling to comprehend.

'Yeah… He was way overdue for replacement.'

'Then did he… You actually mean *he*… wanted me to kill him…?'

This sends Number Two into gales of laughter. She falls back into her chair, kicking her legs in the air with childlike glee. With an effort she at last recovers her composure, wiping the tears from her eyes with the back of her hand.

'Sorry, Number Six! That was just so…! Wanted you to… No, the old Number Two didn't know you were going to be killing him; we kind of wrote that into the script without telling him. You see, it was Degree Absolute: the final test. The old Number Two: he thought he was the hammer and you were the anvil—but you turned the tables on him! And you got your revenge for your friend Gillian, as well!'

'So, it was him who killed her…?'

'Yep! It was him.'

'And I never had a double…?'

'Nope.'

'I see…' I say. 'And… what happens now?'

'What do you mean what happens now?' asks Number Two, confused.

'I mean, what happens to *me?*'

'To you? Nothing! Everything's back to normal now! You can just go back to your ordinary day-to-day life.'

'My ordinary day-to-day life...? You mean, here in the Village?'

She looks confused by this question. 'Yeah, here in the Village. Where else? This is where we all live, right? And I'm Number Two and you're Number Six.'

'Yes... But then, who is... Number One...?'

'Hmm... That's kind of complicated. You could say that Number One is an abstract concept; different things to different people. For me, Number One's just a voice that hoots at me down the phone.'

'Hoots at you...?'

'Hoots at me,' she confirms, nodding. 'Well, that's about it really. I just wanted to say hi! Yeah... we're going to get along just fine, you and me!' and she winks at me, smiling contentedly.

I turn to take my leave.

'Oh! There is one more thing, though,' says Number Two. 'You'll find your friend waiting for you outside.'

'My friend? What friend?'

'It's a surprise! Just go outside and you'll see!'

I walk back to the sliding doors. They part and the black cat from the porch darts into the room, tail aloft. It makes a beeline for Number Two and jumps straight into her lap. I should have guessed, really... These female Number Twos always have their familiars...

She looks up from caressing the cat. 'Be seeing you!'

And she favours me with the village salute, thumb and index finger forming a circle, remaining fingers extended.

'Be seeing you,' I say, returning the salute.

I step out onto the porch and pause to survey what will from now on be my home...

Anyone who thinks that the Prisoner escaped from the Village at the end of the last episode is someone who doesn't understand the last episode. You can never escape from the Village, once it has you in its toils; it just follows you wherever you go. One much-debated point regarding that final episode is whether or not we were meant to understand that the Village was destroyed when the rocket whose countdown the Prisoner set in motion, blasted off. This rocket was housed in a silo beneath the Village, and there is reason to believe that, although it was not explicitly shown, that when the rocket took off, the blast from its exhaust reduced the Village to ashes—otherwise, why was it so necessary to evacuate the Village when the countdown commenced? This theory could also serve as an explanation for the episode's title, 'Fall Out.' And perhaps the on-screen destruction of Rover, which we see reduced to slag, was designed to be symbolic of the destruction of the Village in its entirety. Nevertheless, regardless of the destruction he unleashed, the Prisoner's efforts were ultimately fruitless; for, upon his return to London, the front door of his abode was seen to open automatically, just as the door of his residence in the Village had opened.

And my own 'escape' from the Village, on the very first day of my arrival here: it had been nothing more than a carefully-orchestrated farce; the opening act of the comedy. That day had been the first day of my imprisonment, not of my escape from imprisonment.

I descend the steps from the Green Dome, and discover the 'friend' Number Two appraised me of, sitting at the foot of them. It is Darren Nesbit, in his bumble-bee striped village attire; Number Forty-Two badge pinned to the chest. When I appear before him, he reacts but slowly, raising his head, which gently rocks from side to side. There is no recognition in the eyes that meet my own; and no words, only a thread of drool, issues from that vacantly smiling mouth.

I smile at him and extend my hand. He looks at it, raises questioning eyes. I nod my head, smile encouragingly, and he slowly raises his own hand and takes hold of mine. His grip is limp. Responding to the firmer grip of my own hand, he cautiously rises to his feet.

Together, we set off along the street.

Printed in Dunstable, United Kingdom